BRIDGE ACROSS THE OCEAN

BRIDGE ACROSS THE OCEAN

The Story of Three American Cyclists,
Two Japanese Espionage Agents,
A Taiwanese Businesswoman and
The World's Most Revolutionary Bicycle

A Novel
By
Jack B. Rochester

brilliant light publishing
BRILLIANT LIGHT PUBLISHING/MEDIA, L3C
NORWICH, VERMONT

Bridge Across the Ocean is a work of fiction. Although the author describes some actual people, places, things, events and locales with faithful, reportorial accuracy, they are used fictionally and the story is the product of his imagination. Any resemblance to current events or known individuals are simply reference points for scene-setting and should not be construed as anything else.

Cover design by Melanie Marston
Interior design by Sophie Hanks

Published by Brilliant Light Publishing/Media, L3C,
Norwich, Vermont 05055

Printed in the United States of America by Books International, Herndon, Virginia

This book is available in bulk quantities for groups. Please contact Books International for pricing and shipping at:
https://booksintl.presswarehouse.com/

All profits from sales of *Bridge Across the Ocean* are donated to bicycling safety. For more information, please contact the author.
BridgeAcrossTheOcean.com

ISBN: 978-0-980369-6-7

Library of Congress Control Number: 2021906161

This book is dedicated to Asian-American unity and to everyone who loves riding a bicycle.

Foreword
By
Jon Meyer, Publisher
Brilliant Light Publishing/Media

Bridge Across the Ocean is a vibrantly creative book, a metaphoric crescendo of intertwining insights into New England and Taiwanese cultures. The bridge of the title, pictured on the cover, is not only a metaphor, but real. Nearly three kilometers in length, it connects Taiwan's Penghu Islands of Xiyu and Baisha, and does in fact cross a stretch of roaring ocean. The main characters, Jed and Jung-Shan, pedal their bikes across it, fighting strong crosswinds. This is a metaphor within a metaphor about cultural differences, east vs. west philosophies, and the challenges of forging a cross-cultural relationship.

They find themselves working together on a complex business deal to create a revolutionary new cycling device, the Spinner, which stores pedaling energy without a battery. Their efforts are fraught with business espionage; meanwhile, each of them is discovering a new love when they thought one would never be again.

On one level, this novel delights the reader as an insightful description and analysis of what makes American culture contrast with that of the Taiwanese, in language, cuisine, customs, and relationship protocols. This comparison serves as a basis for the ensuing action, adventure, and love to build upon.

On another level, the mouth-watering descriptions of Taiwanese culinary experiences invite us to join the characters at the dining table, and on their island excursions on high-tech bicycles, too. This while intrigue keeps building as the business intelligence thieves make repeated attempts to steal the Americans' valuable prototype and intellectual property.

Throughout, descriptions of urban Taipei's street scenes and architecture are juxtaposed with more rural environments. We are taken there as if we were the sweep rider on one of their beautiful bikes. For example,

> They walked the narrow footpaths past row upon row of rather nondescript bunker-like houses. Chunks of coral, far from the pretty pinks and reds common to jewelry, were visible in places where the plaster had broken. "Coral beds under the sea are now protected as our national treasure," said Jung-Shan. "It is forbidden for harvest coral unless you possess government permits." Tourists milled about, taking pictures for which villagers posed and smiled and were tipped. Life-sized concrete statues of abstract cows dominated one villager's yard; beadwork and figures carved from wood and stone abounded in the few tiny shops.

On a deeper level, *Bridge Across the Ocean* is a love story between two people who have many obstacles to overcome. At an intimate dinner, Jung-Shan and Jed share their sorrow and heartaches with one another, hers while at the London School of Economics, his as an Army intelligence officer in Afghanistan. The author brings their stories together with the beauty and sensitivity of their growing romance.

Unexpectedly, Jed and Jung-Shan find themselves sequestered at a remote Confucian temple, thinking deeply about Lao-Tzu and the *Tao Te Ching*:

> "Master Lao-Tzu says awareness is what man seeks," she said. "It is attained by the man who has humility, understanding, and patience. These are the three treasures. They bring man into agreement with nature. That is awareness. That is the highest goal."

They both take the time to reach inward, which helps them understand themselves and their love for each other.

An excellent novel entices the mind's eye and draws the reader heuristically. *Bridge Across the Ocean* achieves this as a superbly written, vivid journey containing illuminating detail based on the author's personal experience and assiduous observations, blending extraordinary reporting accuracy with writing quality.

Jon Meyer's book *Love Poems From Vermont* won multiple national and international awards, including best poetry book of 2020. He has written for many publications including *The Village Voice, Arts, ARTnews, Q, Dialogue,* and *Fictional Café*. He currently serves as Vice President of Independent Publishers of New England.

In Memory of
Alexander Motsenigos, 1971-2012

I've been a serious cyclist since 1988. I've been run off the road my share of times. I won't soon forget the teenaged girls in a convertible who intentionally tried to run me into a ditch with their blood-curdling screams. More than a few drivers have tried to squeeze by me without crossing the center line.

Yeah, it can be scary and dangerous out there on a bike. But it's also hard to beat the exhilaration and feeling of freedom that come from pedaling yourself to peak physical and emotional experiences. It took me five tries to summit the Kancamagus Pass, but I'll never forget that endorphin-high when I finally made it.

So as a cyclist, I was inspired to write this book because on August 24, 2012, Dana McCoomb, driving of an 18-wheel truck, ran over and killed Alexander Motsenigos, who was riding his bicycle on Weston Road in Wellesley, Massachusetts. At the time, Mr. Motsenigos was a 41-year-old husband and father of a six-year-old son. McCoomb drove off, but was caught on surveillance cameras. The police stopped him later. He claimed he didn't recall hitting anyone.

A grand jury failed to charge him with a single infraction.

Bridge Across the Ocean is for Alexander Motsenigos and the hundreds of the cyclists who are struck and killed by cars every year in this country, some by hit-and-run—which ought to be a crime—others by simple accident. In 2015, the *Boston Globe* stated:

"At least 13 people have been killed while bicycling on (Boston) streets in the last five years, ranging in age from 8 to 74. They have been hit by buses, struck down by cars, fallen into traffic, and — most frequently and recently — swallowed under massive trucks."*

In 2019, as I was completing this latest version of my novel, A 71-year-old man named Cary G. Coovert was killed when he collided with another cyclist—who to this day remains unidentified and uncharged with any crime—on the Minuteman Bikeway, just a block from my home. It is this inability of the law to take these crimes against cyclists seriously that troubles me so much. As my fictitious police chief says in *Bridge*, it was just an accident.

There are among us those who commemorate these "accidents" by installing a *ghost bike,*** a bicycle painted completely white, where a cycling fatality has occurred. The ghost bike, also called the white bike, is a worldwide phenomenon. The story of Greater New York's ghost bike activities, in words and photos, are at the Mashable site ** below.

You can also learn more about ghost/white bikes at Wikipedia ***.

In 2016, a 59-year-old man was run down and killed by a vehicle in Lincoln, Massachusetts. A white bike was chained to a stop sign, but two days later was taken down by the police, who remarked that Lincoln residents didn't like to be reminded of such things. It is one of the most egregious acts against cycling safety I've ever encountered.

Although we need to remember and honor cyclists in traffic accidents ****, I feel it's most important for all of us to actively help lower the number of cycling casualties. To that end, I'm donating 100% of my royalties from *Bridge Across the Ocean* to organizations or causes involved in improving cycling safety in the United States. There are many worthy recipients for such donations, and the gift will likely be awarded to different organizations over time. You can follow my donations and activities and read much more about these issues at the book's website, www.bridgeacrosstheocean.com.

References

* "Death toll mounts for bicyclists on Boston's streets."
https://www.bostonglobe.com/metro/2015/08/11/boston-accidents-have-claimed-cyclists-years/7obC56A1OfleGcp2z21PTM/story.html

** https://mashable.com/2015/04/20/ghost-bikes/
Not to be confused with Ghost, the German bicycle.

*** https://en.wikipedia.org/wiki/Ghost_bike.

**** The US Department of Transportation states the number of cycling fatalities is just under 900 per year. Compare that number to the Netherlands, one of the most bicycle-intensive countries in the world, with annual cycling deaths around 200 per year.
https://www-fars.nhtsa.dot.gov/Main/index.aspx

Contents

"Above all else, I want you to think for yourself,
to decide
1) What you want,
2) What is true and
3) What to do about it."
– Ray Dalio, author of *Principles*

Car Back
July, 2011

"Car back!" Jed Smith heard Rick Saundersson call out to the three cyclists in front of him at the same moment he heard the truck's engine clanking away. *Diesel*, Jed thought, then it was past him, a massive white Chevrolet dually pickup with the New England Energy Cooperative logo painted on its door, a New Hampshire "Live Free or Die" license plate on its bumper. The big exhaust pipe growled as it spewed diesel smoke in his face. He held his breath. He watched the truck begin drifting to the right as it passed him, then David Bondsman, drifting, drifting toward Shieh-Seng "Luke" Lin. *He's gonna hit Luke!* Jed thought, the words sticking in his throat as the truck's big right-side mirror caught Luke behind the head, pushing him and his bicycle sideways, Luke struggling even as his wheels began to disappear beneath the truck. Its massive rear tandem tires spewed blood and made a sickening sound as they rolled over Luke and his bike, kicking a tangled mass of man and machine out in their wake. Jed swerved to the right, just barely avoiding his fallen friend. "STOP!" he cried, his voice that of a wounded animal, Rick and David bellowing at the top of their lungs. A whiff of diesel exhaust was the only reply as the truck picked up speed. "Nine-one-one!" Jed called over his shoulder. He took off after the truck, standing up to pedal as hard as he could, gulping air, feeling the lactic acid burn in his thighs. Jed could feel the wild pounding of his heart, the veins bulging out at his temples. His mouth twisted in pain as a keening cry left his lips: "Luke! Luke! Luke!"

It was early afternoon, a beautiful July day in the White Mountains. At least it had been. The Tour de France had just concluded, an event Jed and his buddies had followed closely as they did every year, even though Lance Armstrong's triumphal reign had ended six years earlier. The four cyclists had set out on a favorite century ride that would take them from the town of Franconia over Kinsman Notch, down through Woodstock to Lincoln, up the Kancamagus Pass to Bear Notch Road, across Crawford Notch and back to Franconia. They'd completed the precipitous Highway 112 descent from Kinsman, dropped into Woodstock, and had ridden underneath Interstate 93 on their way into Lincoln, heading for the steep fourteen-mile climb up to the Kancamagus summit.

The white truck was heading into Lincoln as well, in heavy traffic. Jed slammed down on the pedals in a wild frenzy, his knees splaying side to side with each powerful stroke, the bike careening up to thirty,

thirty-five miles an hour as he tore after the truck. In less than a quarter mile he crossed the railroad tracks that served as the entrance to Lincoln's commercial strip, but now cars were turning in and out of traffic and the truck was disappearing from Jed's view. *Shit! Shit!* He thought. *This was hit and run! It was almost like he planned to hit Luke!*

John Jedediah Smith felt his life spinning out of control. One of his best friends in the whole world, probably dead. The four of them—Lin Shieh-Seng, whom they all called Luke, Rick Saundersson, David Bondsman and Jed—were college mates at MIT. They had shared nearly twenty years of life together, through their college years, then on to Smithworks, Jed's bicycle company. *Their* bicycle company. And now this, when they were out on the final test ride for the drive system they had invented. The drive system that would change cycling forever. The drive system worth at least ten, twenty, maybe fifty million dollars. *Shit!* he cried again through clenched teeth, but the wet tears streaking away from his eyes were closer to what he was really feeling. They'd had plenty of cycling accidents—bad bruises, road rash, sprains, a broken clavicle or two—but replaying in his mind the big tandem tires, the bike breaking apart . . . well, Jed didn't think Luke would recover from this one.

I haven't felt this awful since . . . since . . .

Blinking away the tears, Jed saw the white pickup's cab roof a dozen cars ahead, its colored running lights splintering rays of afternoon sun. They served as a beacon for Jed as he zigzagged through the slow, heavy summer traffic. Lincoln was in full tourist groove. Most of the cars bore Massachusetts license plates; New Hampshire locals called them "Massholes" under their breath, but smiled and took their money for food and lodging, camping, hiking and skiing gear, whitewater kayaking tours, bungee jumping, ziplining, water slides, trained bear shows and just about any kind of designer outlet shopping experience one could ask for. The vacationers loved New Hampshire, but they created massive gridlock on these old two-lane roads.

Jed was raised in a land-trust family on a two thousand, five hundred-acre farm in Holderness, New Hampshire, a quiet little town on the edge of the Squam Lakes. Holderness had steadfastly resisted the commercialization of the outlet-mall towns of Lincoln, North Conway, Tilton, Merrimack; its main attractions remained boating, camping, hiking and a nature science center. Growing up here, he'd learned to respect the thickly forested mountains, the unpolluted lakes and streams, the abundant wildlife. He'd ridden a bicycle since he was nine, bumping along over two-lane country roads around Squam Lake, out to Robert Frost's farm near Franconia, down to Weirs Beach and the amusement parks, up the Kancamagus Highway and over the summit into the Mt. Washington Valley. He'd ridden anywhere and everywhere he could on his heavy old bike because it was freedom. Pure, joyous freedom. One of his dad's favorite sayings was, "Son, if a man has his freedom, he has everything."

Jed attended Holderness School, where he learned table manners and ways of smart young men and women. Thus prepared, he was accepted at the Massachusetts Institute of Technology and experienced five years of the eclectic stimulation which was life in Cambridge. Forsaking a car for his bicycle, he'd become a bike messenger to earn spending money while an undergrad. After college and a stint in the Army, starting his own bike company was the coolest thing in the world. To do so with his three talented best friends was a dream come true.

Now that dream had been dashed to death beneath the wheels of a monstrous pickup truck.

He saw the sunlight glint from the running lights again as the truck turned off Main Street. A long, two-story clapboard building next to a New Hampshire style mini-mall stood a hundred yards further on; the truck disappeared behind it. Jed cut between two cars to get to the right side and burned down the short street, swooping after the truck. The rear of the building bore doors with shop names. A corporate sign over one read NEEC. *New England Energy Cooperative*, he thought. *Boy, does that ever make a lousy acronym.* Five identical white pickups were parked in a neat row outside the NEEC steel door.

Jed slowed, taking a close look at each. Chevy Silverado diesels. Crew cabs. Dually rear wheels. 4X4 logos. The only distinction was each had a different serial number painted on its rear flank. The last in line was L-213. He could see scrapes and streaks of red paint from Luke's bike on the right-side mirror, doors, and the huge bulging rear fender. Jed thought about Luke, felt his stomach lurch, and for a moment thought he was going to upchuck. He gritted his teeth, circling round and round until the feeling passed. Then he clicked his cycling shoes out of his clipless pedals and glided to a stop. Pulling his iPhone from his jersey's rear pocket, he punched the camera icon and snapped photos of L-213's scarred flank.

Jed walked his bike to the NEEC door, leaned it against the wall, grasped the doorknob and pulled. A cloud of cigarette smoke hit him in the face. In the cloudy beyond he could see several cafeteria tables and chairs, a Coke machine, a counter with a coffee urn and stacks of Styrofoam cups. The low-pitched sound of men talking and guffawing rose out of the smoke. Jed entered, cleats clicking. Half a dozen men were sprawled around the tables, dressed in Carhartt overalls, T-shirts and heavy boots.

"Who drives L-213?" Jed snapped.

The men swiveled to look at him, standing there in his black spandex shorts and red Smithworks jersey, his helmet tucked under one arm. "Who wants to know, cutie?" said one of them, and they all began laughing.

"I do. My name is Jedediah Smith."

"As if that's s'posed to mean somethin' to us," said another. Jed slowly scrutinized face after face, the faces of rough-hewn country men, the kind he'd seen working on his father's property all his life. Big men. Little boys. He wished he'd gotten a good look at the driver. All he could look for were signs. Signs of concern or fear. "You!" he said, pointing a finger from his fingerless glove at a burly one with shoulder-length black hair and a heavy black beard concealing his face. "L-213 your truck?"

"We drive diff'rent trucks ever day," said a lanky one. "Nobody's belongin' to any pahticalah truck."

"I'll bet that's not true," said Jed, "and I'll bet I can prove it. But then again, why should I have to? I'll just get the police to take a look at L-213, which a few minutes ago caused a hit-and-run accident, and we'll let them figure out who ran over and *murdered* my best friend!" He turned to leave.

"Hey, pal, waitta minnit," said the lanky one, standing now. Jed turned back. Several others stood up now, their fists hanging loosely at their sides. "I'm not your pal, *pal*," said Jed.

"Whata ya doin', bargin' in heah on private proppity and, uh, sayin' we runned over some bicycle?"

Jed silently glared at the man. "Who said anything about running over a *bicycle*?" said Jed. He turned again and exited, strapping his helmet on as he pushed through the door. He swung a leg over his bike, popped a cleat into a pedal and pushed off. The men were coming out the door behind him.

By the time Jed and Lincoln Chief of Police Bertrand Lemieux returned, all five of the big white trucks were gone. Lemieux tried the door, but now it was locked. He walked to his Ford Edge AWD police interceptor and reached through the window for the radio handset and clicked the transmit button.

"A-1 to A-2," he said, then waited. The speaker squawked and a female voice said, "A-2. We're 10-57, Chief."

"10-4, Madigan," Lemieux said. "Report." He turned to Jed. "You sure you want to hear this?"

Jed, too stunned to think it through, said nothing.

"A-1, he's a male, looks Oriental, in his 20s or 30s, run over," said Officer Michelle Madigan. "Must have been a tandem pickup. I can see two tire tracks on his body, right across his chest and head. It sure isn't pretty. He's all mangled up with his bike."

"You touch anything?" said Chief Lemieux.

"No sir, we're just protecting the scene."

"Those other two bikers there?"

Jed cringed when he heard the word biker. He wanted to tell the Chief they were cyclists, not bikers, but decided it wasn't that big a deal under the circumstances.

"Yessir. They're standing off the road. The ME is coming, right?"

"*C'est vrai*. From Littleton. It will be half an hour or so. You just sit tight, honey. We have to bring those boys to the station for statements. Is Buxton–ah, A-3, with you?"

"Of course, Chief," said Madigan. "You wanna talk to him?"

"Negative. Just relay what I told you."

"He heard it, sir. He's standing right here beside me."

"Buxton is?" said the Chief.

"Yes, sir," Madigan said.

"Hand him the mike, Madigan!"

"Buxton here, sir," said Patrolman Elmer Buxton.

"Eddie, I do not want you two standing *tous ensemble!* Next to each other! Git your ass and your vehicle behind the *assay-dent* scene and stay there!" said the Chief. "Light bar on full. Divert the traffic. Keep the cars moving. Madigan stays at the site. Michelle, *ma chérie*, put up the yellow tape."

"Yessir," Madigan and Buxton said together. They had already encircled the scene with the POLICE LINE DO NOT CROSS streamer; Buxton walked back down the highway to stand behind his car, its light bar flashing red and blue.

"A-1 out," said the Chief. He turned to Jed. "We have only two officers and I need to check on them all the time. Buxton in par-tic-u-leer. He is waiting for promotion. To detective."

"Who's your detective now?"

"We have none. No budget for one. Not much need for one either, yet I have promised I will promote him. *Alors*, I am sorry about this friend of yours. We will do what we can to find out what happened. But these things happen all the time. *C'est un assay-dent*. Happens all the time."

Jed noted Lemieux's French. *Probably Quebecois.* "That pickup from the energy Co-op ran him down. Number L-213."

"Now, *mon ami*, you cannot prove that."

"Sure can. Just find the truck and you'll find the scratches and dents and paint and . . ."

"No, those boys over to the Co-op, they are good boys. They wouldn't do nothing like that on purpose."

"That's what you might think, but Chief, I saw it. I was there. I was maybe twenty feet behind Luke. The four of us were riding a tight formation. That truck passed three of us, then intentionally veered into Luke. Plain as the nose on your face." Jed looked at the Chief's nose. It was bulbous and red and riddled with bright red veins. "And the one guy, the tall one, maybe the supervisor, he practically admitted it."

"Still and all, it was just an assay-dent, I am sure."

Jed, Rick and David stood with the medical examiner, watching as the paramedics carefully separated Luke as best they could from his bicycle. Bits of flesh, hair, bone, plastic, rubber, clothing, littered the pool of blood on the pavement. Luke was gently placed in a body bag and moved into the waiting ambulance, to be taken to the trauma center at Pillsbury Hospital in Concord to await the outcome of an autopsy. Under the flashing lights, Jed walked over to the bicycle; he squatted and examined the mangled mess of titanium tubing, cables, handlebars, twisted wheels violently stripped of their tires. He started to feel sick, very sick, and closed his eyes. He opened them to look carefully at the rear wheel; the drive was smashed, little pieces of black ceramic and a printed circuit board obliterated. He got up and went back to Rick and Jed. "The drive is toast," he said.

"So is my best friend," said Rick. David looked down.

Chief Lemieux arranged for the three to park their bicycles inside the White Mountains Visitor Center, just a few hundred yards from where the accident occurred. They spent hours at the police station giving Lemieux their statements and answering questions, but mostly waiting. Afterwards, Buxton and Madigan drove the three in their Ford Police Special patrol car to get their van. Rick, the tallest, sat in the middle of the rear seat, flanked by Jed and David. Madigan drove and Buxton rode shotgun; the boy was so fat his shoulder touched hers across the console. *Why are country people so fat?* Jed wondered for the millionth time. He knew cycling had kept him slim and fit, and it made him sad to see so many North Country people unhealthy.

It was twilight when they arrived in Franconia, where they had parked their Dodge Ram Grand Caravan. By the time they had followed the police car back to Lincoln, the Visitor Center was closed. "Well, this sucks," said Rick. "Now we have to drive back here tomorrow to pick up our bikes."

"This is the last place I want to see again tomorrow," said David.

"No worries," said Madigan. "We have keys. We'll get your bikes all right."

The black Grand Caravan, Smithworks painted on its flanks, was fitted with four Thule Low Rider fork mounts in the rear. The three men locked in their bikes and stood staring at the empty fourth, then at the empty seat Luke had always occupied.

David genuflected and said quietly, "A moment of silence for Luke."

They stood shoulder to shoulder, hand in hand, each in his own way giving himself over to Luke's spirit, for a lot longer than a moment.

Cherry Hill Farm

"Guys, it's nearly dark and I'm not really up for a two-hour-long drive back to Nashua tonight," said Jed, breaking the silence. He was at the wheel as they left Franconia; David rode shotgun, and Rick sat behind Jed, his long legs splayed out. The seat beside him, once Luke's, remained stubbornly unoccupied. The sun rode the mountain saddlebacks off to the west. "Why don't we stay at my folks' house tonight?"

"OK by me," said Rick. David nodded. They passed through the hushed gloaming of the White Mountains, each silently consumed with his memories of their fallen friend, fellow cyclist and business partner. Rick twisted in his seat, muffled sobs emanating from tight lips. Silent miles on, they came to the Ashland exit off I-93 and headed east to Holderness, passing Little Squam Lake on the right, turning onto Route 113 at Big Squam, heading into the mountain darkness. Jed turned uphill at an unmarked dirt road; they bounced along for nearly a mile until summiting at a white board fence enclosing a horse paddock, a lighted post lamp at its corner. A large oval hand-carved sign hung below the light, the words CHERRY HILL FARM arcing over a garland of red cherries. They continued along the fence and turned into the horseshoe driveway between the paddock and the two-story Colonial farmhouse above.

Cherry Hill Farm was Jed's ancestral home; it was built by his great-great-great grandfather in 1860, just before he went off to fight in the Civil War. Every Smith male fought in a war thereafter: Jed's great-great grandfather in the Spanish-American War, his great-grandfather in World War I, his grandfather in World War II, his father in the Korean War, and Jed in Afghanistan. Inside the house were six bedrooms upstairs, always for guests and their children; downstairs was the master bedroom with an adjacent bath (added once there was indoor plumbing) for the parents. Jed pulled up in front and switched off. Looking up at the house, he could see figures standing inside the screened-in porch. The three of them climbed out.

"Jed?" His father's strong voice rose in the night air filled with the sound of crickets.

"Hi Dad. Hi Mom."

The screen door creaked and his mother stepped out. "Well, come on in," said Helen Smith. "You boys been out ridin' your bikes?"

The three gingerly made their way up the granite steps in their cycling shoes and stopped on the porch.

"You boys hungry?" she asked, at the same time Jed's father, John

Jedediah Smith III, said, "You boys want a beer?"

"No, thanks," they muttered.

"Where's Luke?" John said. Three grown men fell apart, weeping, howling, barking out hoarse sobs. Helen rushed to them, wrapping her arms around them as best she could.

"What's happened? What's happened?" Jed's father's voice boomed in deep modulation to disguise his emotions. They blurted it out in bits and pieces, their voices breaking as they crashed through sobs. "That was you boys? Up to Lincoln? I heard about an accident on the police scanner. God almighty, this is the most awful thing I ever heard of! Now, sit down and tell us all about it." He pulled the big rattan deck chairs into a circle. Helen went into the house and re-emerged with a fifth of Jack Daniel's and glasses. The guys shook their heads, but John insisted: "Now, just have a slurp or two. It'll calm your nerves."

Jed began; David and Rick filled in with details. When they'd finished, John shook his head. "An *assay-dent*, huh? That what the Canuck says? He's gonna hear from me in the morning. Accident my ass!"

"You boys look terrible, just terrible," said Helen. "You need some sleep. Are you hungry? I'll fix you some dinner."

"Thanks, Mom," said Jed. "Actually, I guess I am hungry." Jed looked at David and Rick; they nodded. "Why don't we wash up and change clothes?"

When they entered the dining room, bike kits replaced by T-shirts, shorts and sneakers, dinner was waiting: piles of sliced pork roast, garlic mashed potatoes, string beans from the garden, longneck bottles of Rolling Rock. Sated, they adjourned to the front porch again, fresh beers in hand, to watch the moths bang away at the screening.

"Well, son, accidents do happen," said John Smith, now more circumspect. He took a deep draught from his tumbler of bourbon. "You know this is true. You've had enough of 'em on that danged bicycle. Remember that one time? You came home, what were you, 'bout ten or eleven? Bleedin' from the wrists to the elbows, up and down your legs—"

"But Dad, that was a *real* accident. I think this was some kind of . . . premeditation. It looked intentional to me. I *know* it was. I just don't know *why." But I think they were after the drive*, Jed thought.

"I agree," said Rick. "I was behind Jed. I saw it all. David was even closer."

"I gotta say, that truck was on top of me before I could get out of his way," said David. "He could've hit me first. Maybe even Rick. He was in a steady drift to the right and could have knocked into all of us. We're lucky we got out of his way in time."

"Still, he could have been talking on one of those damned cellphones. Or changing radio stations, not really paying attention," said John.

"Yeah, yeah, I get all that," said Jed. "But why didn't he stop?"

"That's the question, all right," said his father. "You think it was a Co-op truck?"

"I *know* it was," said Jed. Rick and David nodded. "And I followed it to the Co-op building in Lincoln. It was parked there and I saw the scrape marks from Luke's bike."

Helen was shaking her head. "I'm so sorry, so sorry to hear about all this. Poor Luke."

"Poor Luke is right," said Jed, "and I got the feeling Chief Lemieux would be mighty happy to write the whole thing off as an accident and forget all about it."

John reached out and patted his son's knee. "Of course he would. There's the paperwork and the investigation. The autopsy. Now, son, don't fret no more tonight about this. I still got some pull around the North Country. I'll speak to Bernie . . . ah, the Chief."

Later, upstairs, Jed paced the floor in his bedroom while Rick and David sat on his bed. The walls were covered with cycling posters: Le Tour de France, Eddie Merckx, Lance Armstrong, Greg Lemond, Miguel Induráin, a poster-sized photo of Jed, Rick, Luke and David standing with their bikes under the Smithworks sign at their Nashua factory. On his desk was a photo of his childhood horse and another of him in a pale-blue tuxedo with his girlfriend, Betsy Hobbs, at the Holderness School senior prom.

Jed saw none of this, his vision blinded by tears that would not stop. Rick sat glumly, his head down, fidgeting with his fingers. David held the cross hanging from his neck, genuflecting every so often.

"A lot's gonna change now," said Jed.

"A lot," said Rick.

"You're talking about the drive, right?" said David.

"Well, yeah. We've lost our electronics genius," said Jed. "Our circuit design is working, but what if we have to update the software?"

"I think we're all right on that," said David, "I can handle it, at least for now. Luke and I debugged the crap out of the drive."

"I'm more worried about the trip to Taiwan," said Rick. "I mean, Luke was the guy who set it all up. He speaks—spoke—the language, he knew the companies. Should we go forward?"

"Absolutely," said Jed.

"Without Luke?" said Rick.

"We have no choice," said Jed. He stopped pacing in front of the corner window overlooking the forest and the paddock below. He stuck his hands in his pockets and hunched his shoulders. "Suzie," he said. "She's from Taiwan, too. We can take her with us."

Rick fidgeted and said, "We gotta tell Sun Xiaohui . . . Suzie . . . what happened to her . . . fiancé. Like right away tomorrow. And we need to call a meeting with Gregg."

David nodded and said, "We need to call an *all-company* meeting."

"Oh, man," Rick said, pacing again, faster, holding his head in his hands. Then he cried out, "Oh, man, oh man," and broke into sobs. A moment later, all three of them were crying again.

In the morning, They ate a hasty breakfast and headed over to Rhino Bike Works in Plymouth. Slade and Mike, co-owners and long-time friends, were in the shop, working on bikes. Jed explained what had happened. Mike stood, dumfounded, while Slade pounded his fists on the workbench. When everyone had calmed down, Jed explained what they needed.

An hour later, they headed north on I-93 again, stopping at the site of Luke's hit-and-run. They parked and pulled the old beater bike, now painted pure white, from the back of the Grand Caravan and chained it to the Route 112 road sign post near where Luke had fallen. Rick picked some wildflowers from the nearby field and stuck them in the white spokes. They gripped hands tightly and silently wept once again for Shieh-Seng.

Smithworks

Gregory Colarusso sat on his stool in his design studio at Smithworks, paintbrush in hand, contemplating how he was going to execute the artistic idea floating around in his head. Instead of an easel, the bike frame he was about to paint was mounted on a stand he had designed himself.

Gregg's office-studio belied the fact it was in a four-story brick building once a 19th-century textile mill in Nashua, New Hampshire. Standing at a lazy crook in the Nashua River, it was a winsome place, now home to Smithworks. This topmost floor was divided into five executive suites, one of which was Gregg's, and a large conference room overlooking the river. Gregg's and David's offices were next to each other; they'd lived two houses from one another growing up in

Bedford, Massachusetts, and so in a way they still did.

Gregg had earned his BFA at the Massachusetts College of Art and became a popular, well-known artist. Galleries from Boston to San Francisco showed his work, but often kept fifty percent of the selling price as their commission—a rude confirmation of why most artists starve. When David offered to make Gregg Smithworks's artist-in-residence, it suited him just fine.

Slender, dark-haired David Bondsman was the quiet, methodical one of the original three COOs—now just two, Rick and him. He'd earned his undergrad degree in mechanical engineering at MIT, then continued his studies for an MBA/MS in manufacturing engineering/operations management at the Sloan School. That was where he'd met Jed, who majored in materials science and engineering but subsequently earned his own MBA in entrepreneurship and innovation. The two discovered their mutual interest in cycling and ended up moving out of Ashdown House, the graduate student dorm, to share an off-campus apartment near Central Square. Now David was in charge of Smithworks manufacturing.

At six-two, Minnesotan Rick Saundersson was the tallest of the four, and Taiwan-born Luke Lin the shortest at five feet six and a half. Their height difference might have made their friendship seem a Mutt-and-Jeff, but it was far from true. They had bonded through math and cycling, and Rick was forever cracking dumb jokes which had Luke in stitches. One that recurred often went, "What do you call an elephant that doesn't matter? irrelephant."

Jed, Luke and Rick had met in Calculus with Applications their freshman year. It was a required course for math majors, as well as for Jed's materials science program. Luke's fascination with high-tech drove him to earn an MS in electrical engineering, while Jed's focus turned to alloys that would make bicycle frames stronger, lighter, and more responsive.

Rick had chosen a more eclectic course of study. To look at him, one would never guess he was Smithworks' COO/CFO: long, soft, curly brown hair; hazel eyes behind big glasses; just another MIT techno-geek in jeans and an Aerosmith T-shirt. Computer science was his minor which, combined with his lightning-quick understanding of business assets, drove his inquisitive mind toward a finance-track MBA. Rick and Luke were the first to join the weekly rides with the MIT Cycling Club, which drew David and Jed in.

Over the course of their studies, the six degrees of separation between the four young men narrowed considerably. It was Rick who first got to know David from Sloan classes, but it wasn't until the Pan-Mass Challenge cycling event that they all met for the first time.

The PMC is the premiere cycling event in Massachusetts, a two-day, two hundred-mile ride from Sturbridge to Provincetown at the tip of the Cape Cod peninsula. As a fundraiser for cancer, it drew thousands of riders each year from every level of proficiency, on bikes ranging from racing to cross to mountain. A few kids on BMX bikes. A guy on a unicycle.

It was on their PMC ride, noting how many of the bikes were in poor condition (not to mention vast numbers of their riders) that the four quickly became fast friends. They chatted about cycling problems they observed, in particular riders whose constant gripe was that the route wasn't flat as a pancake. It soon turned into a grad-school case study, each applying their individual perspectives and expertise to inputting comments and complaints as variables into the greatest of all problem-solving tools, the what-if analysis.

As the miles rolled by, a solution gradually emerged: replace the conventional multiple-speed gear train with an energy-storing drive. There would be no shifting; the drive would have a logic circuit that released the stored energy to make it easier to pedal when climbing hills or to gain more speed on straight, level stretches. Jed realized they possessed the collaborative skillsets to devise such a gizmo, and that an untapped market—the emerging urban bicycle rental innovation launching in major cities, such as Boston—was theirs for the taking.

They were able to envision the drive as a viable business, to be sure, but they needed R&D funding. Venture cap was quickly dismissed; none of them wanted to be beholden to a shark. Banks would need more collateral than just a good idea, and none of them wanted to ask their parents for seed money. Jed suggested they meet with some of their Sloan professors for advice.

One asked, "Where's your business plan?"

Another commented, "It's a brilliant idea. I recall reading that Thomas J. Watson, Jr., said he saw the market for computers as water, and IBM was the sponge. Your drive could be the sponge for the growing commuter bike market."

Another said, "If you boys love bicycles and cycling so much, why don't you open a bike shop and fund your idea with its profits?"

Rick's investment management prof agreed, but she thought they might also try crowdsourcing. "It's the guild idea for the Internet age," she said. "Back in the 1800s, guilds were formed by tradesmen and carpenters to pitch in and build a man's house. Then he and the guild helped the next fellow and so on. Crowdsourcing is the same idea. You get peer investors, not sharks, and you can get funded pretty quick. You can invite the investors to evaluate the merits of your business plan, even make recommendations. It's creating a community. A guild. You give back to it with your product."

They raised nearly a hundred and fifty thousand dollars in a month to launch Jet Cycling and an instant market for the custom bicycles they wanted to build. Now they had enough capital to open the shop and build the bikes, but to fund the drive development, too.

Jet Cycling wasn't the typical family-centric bike shop, inflating tires and adjusting brakes, but rather a high-margin, high-end racing bike enterprise building custom bikes for customers with expensive, discriminating tastes. It was just the kind of bike, and bike shop, the young, affluent denizens of Cambridge and Boston sought.

They found a cheap rental location in an abandoned warehouse across the street from their old dorm on Albany Street. Jet's first customer was one of their riding buddies from the MIT Cycling Club. Their own bikes were their advertising, and word of mouth and crowdfunding did the rest as member after member bought their custom rides. Jet favored the frames of Colnago and Cervelo, components like Campagnolo Record and Shimano Dura-Ace, wheels by Mavic and Hed—the latter because Steve Hed, a cycling guru, was a friend of Rick's growing up in Minneapolis.

Rick managed the shop and Jet's ROI. It was his idea to innovate repairs and upgrades by instituting prepaid service contracts. Meanwhile, Jed, David and Luke were building the bikes and working on the drive whenever possible. Jed first suggested using ABS plastic for the housing, but Luke's interest shifted to hafnium ceramic compounds.

They had electrical conductivity properties, which made it possible to store energy in an embedded web of wires and transistors which he likened to the brain's neural network. The stored energy was controlled through integration of the ceramic storage network and a controller embedded in a removable SanDisk microSD card. The guys couldn't stop telling Luke how brilliant he was, to which he modestly replied, "It's just an iteration of the von Neumann computer architecture of 1945. Nothing new."

Meanwhile, Jet had amassed a six-month backorder list for custom bikes. Within a year, they had pulled in enough to lease the ground floor of an abandoned mill just across the state line in Nashua, New Hampshire. No more buying frames from others; they bought their own tube stock, hired top-drawer machine shop men and women, and began manufacturing their own branded specialty racing bikes from Reynolds steel and aluminum tube stock, eventually graduating to the more exotic, expensive and desirable titanium. A year after the relocation they added a mountain bike; two years after that they bought the entire building. This was Smithworks, and although they all shared in its ownership, no one ever quibbled with naming it after Jed. After all, it had been his idea. And besides, the name rolled nicely off the tongue.

Every Smithworks cycle was a special order, designed and built to the customer's specifications, as were Gregg's paint jobs.

Over the music, Gregg felt more than heard the sound of multiple feet treading in. He lifted his headphones and heard voices; it was The Magnificent Four, as he called them, an oblique reference to the horsemen in the movie, "The Magnificent Seven," returning from their hundred-miler in the North Country. Something Gregg would never be inclined to do. His thing was what he termed "extreme urban" mountain biking: he rode to work "365," regardless of the season or the weather. Gregg stood and opened his door as Jed, Dave and Rick walked in. "Morning, boys," he said, "How were the White Mountains?"

"Meet in five," said a grim-faced Jed.

Gregg noted it was just three of the magnificent ones. Where was Luke? He raised his eyebrows, stuck his paintbrushes in a jar of dirty-gray water, and shuffled into the hall to join the others.

Gregg, Jed, Rick and David piled into the conference room. Morning sunshine poured in. The entire wall of ancient, drawn-glass window panes, glazed into a metal matrix resting atop the brick wall, had been torn out, replaced with floor-to-ceiling thermopanes. At the corner were twin atrium doors opening onto a small deck, its railing trellised with clematis. The same bright sun shone into Gregg's studio next door, natural light for his painting.

Rick manned the Nespresso Lattissima, passing out coffees while Gregg activated the Voice Tracker they used to record meetings. The conference table, a two-inch thick slab of white pine sawn from a 150-year-old tree felled by Jed's father, was surrounded by sleek black Aeron chairs. They took their seats, Jed at the head, the others on each side.

"Where's Lukie?" asked Gregg. The explanation left him dumbfounded. Dead? He'd never known anyone who died, had no frame of reference to comprehend death other than as a conceptual abstraction. He just couldn't imagine Luke not walking into the room, sitting down and joining the conversation. Gregg found he had no words to speak that made any sense. They all sat in silence for a long while, their partner's death sinking in once more, now in an entirely new way for involving Gregg's shock. David sniffed and wiped at his eyes with the heels of his hands. Rick just sat looking into his lap. Jed tried to answer Gregg's questions factually, but his suspicions about the cause rose up again and as he shared them, his voice grew angry. He suddenly realized Gregg was undeservedly taking the brunt of that anger and quieted. "Sorry, Gregg," he said.

"Yeah, it's OK," said Gregg. "I get what you're feeling."

"No, you probably don't. Unfortunately, nothing can change the fact that Luke's gone and we're all trying to figure out why. Wondering how we're going to move ahead without him."

"Geez, Jed, maybe we ought to rethink this. I mean, if somebody's after the drive, we could all be in big-time danger," Gregg said, imagining being run over on his daily commute.

"No," said Jed, calming down, "I don't think we should change our plans at all. Not one bit. For one thing, I could be completely wrong. It really could have been an accident. That's what my dad thinks. It might just be my anger at losing our friend and partner getting the best of me. Or a way of trying to understand it rationally. But then again," he lifted both hands in the air, "say it really is a plot. Say somebody really is trying to get the drive away from us. A hit-and-run attack? If that was the plan, they are really D-U-M-B."

"Yeah, it was one really clumsy, stupid stunt," said Rick, anger brimming in his words, too. "And why Luke?" Rick clenched his fists and slammed them down on the table. "Why my best friend, dammit!" He pounded the table again.

Jed reached out, rubbing Rick's shoulder and extended his other hand to David. They all clasped hands, mourning their fallen mate, until they had regained their composure.

"The worst thing we could do right now is give up," Jed continued. "We've worked so hard on this drive over the past couple of years and had so many doors slammed in our faces. Now, thanks to Luke, we have real interest from Joyful Bike. The meeting's set. I say we stick to the plan."

"And we've already bought expensive, nonrefundable plane tickets to Taiwan," said CFO Rick. "I have no idea how much it would cost the company to cancel or rebook. I don't even want to know. We *gotta* go."

"And now we gotta go for Luke, too," said Jed. "That reminds me of something else: I need to call his folks. I think they'll want us to bring . . . him . . . home to Taipei for a proper funeral. I need to ask them about doing this. See if they want him in a casket or cremated . . . aw, geez," his voice broke and he fell silent, twisting in agony at the thought.

"What about Suzie?" said Gregg.

"Oh, man, yeah, Suzie," said Jed. "We talked about her last night and now we've forgotten about her." He glanced at his iPhone. "Where is she? What time does she come in?" He paused. "Oh, man, this is terrible! How could I forget about her?"

"Don't be so hard on yourself," said David. "This has been tough. On all of us. And besides, she works on the third floor."

"Well, somebody's gotta go tell her," said Rick. "Luke was my best friend, so Suzie . . . well, I'll do it."

"Thanks, man," said Jed. "Really."

Everyone murmured assent.

"What about the drive?" said Rick. "Luke was riding it and now that one's destroyed."

"Jed's is identical," David said. "Does everybody agree it's ready? Are *we* ready?"

Jed thought for a minute. "Sure, it would've been great to test the drive for the whole century ride yesterday, but we've ridden both of them hundreds and hundreds of miles before. We know it works. Yeah, I wish we could have pushed it going up the Kanc, but I can't think of a single technical reason we can't demo it, as is, for Joyful Bike." He looked at the others. "So yeah, I think it is. Ready. As for us, we *gotta* be. " They nodded assent.

"Too bad the 3D printer is so damned slow, said Gregg. "It would take two weeks to make another ceramic cone."

"Do we have another controller?" said David.

"That's a no-brainer," said Rick.

"Look, guys, forget it! We have what we need right now," said Jed. "We'll take mine off my bike. I'd just as soon take one we've road-tested anyway."

"Makes sense," said David.

"Dave, is your PowerPoint done?" said Jed.

"Just about. I need a few more graphics and photos. Gregg, can you help me with that today?"

"Sure, once I finish Diego Henderson's bike. The California hippie's. Tomorrow at the latest."

Jed leaned across the table. "Gregg, can you set Henderson's bike aside for a day or two? We leave for Taiwan in one week. The presentation needs to be our top priority."

Gregg nodded.

"Rick, you and I need to get those performance charts finished for the presentation," said Jed.

"I can have them in a few hours, no problem."

"If we all do our stuff, I think we can have the presentation wrapped up by the end of the day," said Gregg.

"Good," said Jed. "First, I think I need to make that phone call to Luke's folks in Taipei. And Rick, call Suzie. Let's see, the Lins are . . ." he thumbed his iPhone " . . . twelve hours ahead of us, so it's ten at night there. Maybe I ought to wait until morning. But I'd sure like to get it done and over with."

"Guess there isn't really a right time for delivering this message, is there?" said Rick. "But I'd like to tell Suzie in person."

Jed nodded, drank some coffee, then set his cup down. He stood and said, "No, I guess there really isn't." He turned and left the conference room, closing his office door behind him.

Half an hour later, Jed returned to the conference room, where David and Gregg stood in front of the Smart Board 800 interactive whiteboard, working on the PowerPoint presentation. David added a bullet point and said to Gregg, "Agreed?"

Gregg nodded. He touched the board with his finger and drew a circle, then touched the menu to open a preloaded Web page displaying cycling statistics. He dragged the stats into the circle, which became an Excel pie chart and was inserted into a PowerPoint slide. "Agreed," he said.

"Guys," said Jed, "I just got off the phone with Luke's family. I talked to Luke's younger sister—I think she said her name is Bao—but it was kind of hard to understand her. Anyway, the parents don't speak any English, but I told her what happened and she translated for them. I could hear Luke's mother wailing and wailing, then Bao started crying, too." He wiped the back of a hand across his eye. "It sure wasn't easy."

Rick had entered while Jed spoke. He stepped over and gave Jed a big hug, and was joined by Dave and Gregg. They stood together in a long, four-way huddle-hug until Jed pulled back, wiping his eyes again.

"Anyway," he said, his voice cracking, "They want us to bring him home in a casket. The family doesn't cremate, so that's out of the question. Smithworks will buy him the best. Bao said something about a funeral, so we ought to be prepared to attend. Probably means bringing a suit and tie. Everybody still got one?"

Wry smiles broke the tension.

Dave said, "But this also means we need to get somebody to be making the arrangements for Luke's . . . uh, body . . . and a funeral parlor, somebody who knows what-all paperwork and stuff needs to get done if we're going to get him on the plane. The four of us have too much to deal with."

"Suzie," said Rick. "She's from Taiwan, too. I saw her. Told her. She kinda scrunched up in a ball like she was holding everything inside, trying not to start crying and falling apart."

"Is she OK?" Jed asked.

"About as OK as we are," said Rick. "I told her to take some time off if she wanted to, but she said no. I told her we were phoning Luke's parents and how we have to do a bunch of things to fly him back to Taiwan. She said whatever we need for Luke, all we gotta do is ask her. That's what she said."

Several minutes passed as everyone digested this news.

"Another thing's come up, Bossman," he continued, looking at Jed, David, pausing on Gregg.

"Yeah? What?" said Jed.

"Well," said Gregg, "While we were working on the PowerPoint, we realized we've never given the drive a name."

"Didn't we name it in the patent filing?" said Jed, turning to David.

"I just checked that recently," he replied. "They didn't ask and we didn't specify. It's just called a 'stored-energy drive,'" David said, wiggling his fingers. "Our attorney filed the simple provisional patent and all it asked for was a description, how it works, and who invented it. We have permission to say, 'Patent Pending.' That's all we needed to do at the time, right? We just flat-out forgot to give it a name."

"Geez," said Jed, "I've had the name in my head for a long time. Did we never discuss this?"

They shook their heads.

"We're all ears," said Gregg.

"'The Spinner,'" said Jed.

Jed looked at Gregg, then Dave, then Rick. They were nodding. Jed grinned, nodded and said, "Make it so." He loved to use that phrase from Captain Jean-Luc Picard of *Star Trek* fame. "Now, let's get back to work on the presentation."

Information Worms

"Hey, man, this presentation is awesome!" said Jed. "Gregg and Suzie did a great job on it, didn't they?"

"With my help, of course," said Rick. Jed was looking over Rick's shoulder at the PowerPoint slides scrolling across the screen on Rick's MacBook, resting on the tray table of the Japan Airlines Boeing 787 Dreamliner. Rick stopped on a slide.

"Hey!" said Jed. "When did you put *that* in?" It was the napkin drawing of the Spinner, Jed's very first sketch. Rick and David laughed.

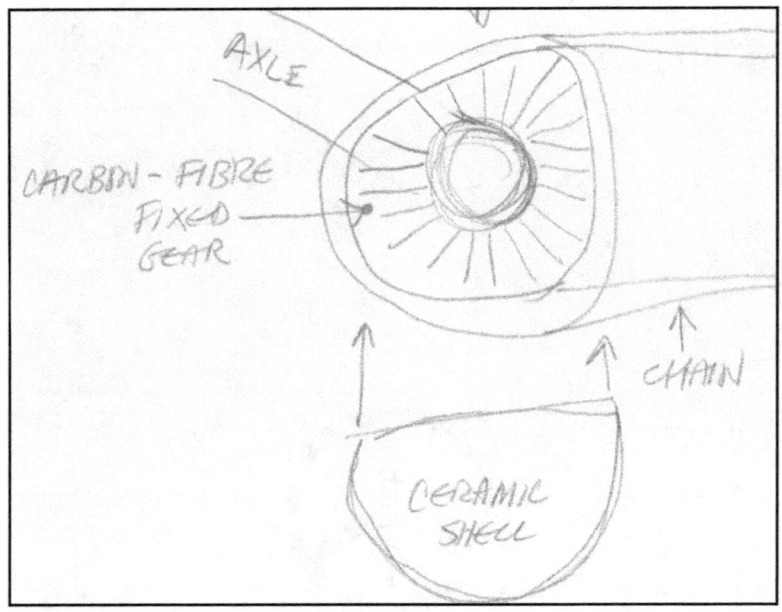

David watched from the pod-like seat next to Rick. Jed's pod was across the aisle, adjoining Suzie Sun's. He looked at Suzie—Sun Xiaohui—asleep in the nearly silent aircraft, its shimmering blue LED lighting turning the cabin into a TRON-like electronic game environment. Jed was glad they'd brought her along. The funeral arrangements aside, she was from Taipei and spoke Mandarin; she would be their guide and interpreter and seemed happy to be going home. Still, Jed felt concern for her emotional condition so soon after her fiancé's murder.

"All the research is accurate and up to date?" asked Jed.

"Absolutely," said David and Rick in one voice.

They were forty-two thousand feet over the Great Lakes, flying at nearly nearly six hundred miles per hour, about two hours into the thirteen and a half-hour nonstop flight to Tokyo's Narita International

Airport. A petite Japanese flight attendant approached, bowed, and asked if they would like something to drink. "Water for all of us, please," said Jed. The pretty young woman bowed and retreated, returning shortly with three square bottles of Fiji, crystal glasses filled with ice, on a black lacquered tray with sushi and sashimi.

They fell silent as they drank. "Think we should wake up Suzie?" said Rick.

"Nah, let her snooze," said Jed. "Poor kid, she's been working her tail off getting us ready for this trip. Quite honestly, I don't know how she stood up, losing Luke and all."

"Yeah, I agree," said David. "So, we're meeting her friend at the Tokyo airport?"

"Yep, Angela Xiao," said Rick. Pretty name, huh? She's one of Suzie's high school friends from Taipei. I understand she's a hot-shot lawyer in Tokyo now. I wonder if she's as pretty as her name. Can't wait to meet her!" They all grinned.

The Pacific crossing took them across the International Date Line to land in Tokyo mid-afternoon of the next day. Narita was vast, immaculate, complex, sophisticated. PA systems made polite announcements in Japanese, Chinese, English. Every premium watch, perfume, and handbag had a duty-free storefront in which beautifully garbed women bought things from attentive Japanese clerks while their suit-and-tied husbands stood outside jabbering into their smartphones.

Suzie led the way to the Japan Airlines Sakura Club, which she remembered from previous journeys across the Pacific. They showed the hostess their boarding passes and were welcomed in. "You will like it," she said, leading them down the wide marble hallway.

"How come we get in here?" asked Rick. "I mean, I thought you had to pay to belong to these airline clubs."

"We are business class travelers, so it is included at no charge," said Suzie. "There is a three-hour layover here before flying to Taipei, and I always come here for refreshments and relaxing."

The Sakura Club looked like nothing so much as a high-end cocktail lounge on multiple levels: a curving staircase, stone wall, food buffet islands, a shimmering bar set against a vast window wall. Japanese hostesses wearing the JAL uniform—a gray business skirt and vest, white blouse and British-style cravat—bowed in welcome.

"You see over there?" Suzie pointed to the rear of the dining area. "That is where you will find drinks and foods. Sushi, miso soup, very fine Japanese rice. On the Chinese buffet is usually a very delicious beef curry. Also lots of American foods. If you wish, you can even have a shower on the lower level."

Rick looked around. "I don't see a checkout cash register."

"No charge," said Suzie. "All the food and drink is free."

"I'll be," said Rick. They found a table near the stone wall. Outside the window, huge Boeing 747s and 767s waited for flight. A moment later, a hostess welcomed them and took their drink orders. They were about to head for the food islands when Suzie's phone rang.

"*Wei*," she said. Hello, the typical Chinese greeting. She continued speaking in Mandarin, so the guys had no idea what she was saying. She clicked off and said in English, "Angela will be here within a few moments. She is looking forward to meeting you."

Drinks came, and shortly thereafter so did Angela. She was handsome in a business-professional way: willowy, dressed in a pantsuit that fit her figure quite charmingly. Her coal-black hair, drawn tightly into a pony tail, shimmered. She wore only a dab of lipstick and eyeliner. She needed nothing else.

Suzie and Angela exchanged a few words in Mandarin. Rick thought he heard "Shih-Seng" spoken several times, then the women hugged. Rick glanced knowingly at the other guys. Then Suzie switched to English and introduced Angela, who gave each of the guys a firm handshake. Everyone sat down.

"Can I get you something to eat or drink, Angie?" said Rick, smiling.

"Yes, I would like a Johnny Walker Black on the rocks, thank you, and it's Angela."

"My apologies," said Rick. "Awful American custom, always turning a nice name into slang. In your case, a lovely name."

"It's all right," she said, perhaps brusquely. "Don't give it another thought."

The hostess arrived with bottles of Kirin beer for the guys and a cup of hot water with lemon for Suzie. Rick ordered Angela's drink and they talked as they awaited it.

"So, you're a lawyer?" said David.

Angela smiled at him. "I have a degree from New York University called an LL.M. It is not the same as being a lawyer with a J.D. My degree is specialized. It is in global business law. I studied at NYU in Singapore, then in Shanghai and New York City. My undergraduate degree was in economics and finance from Hong Kong University. I practice business law for clients of my firm who are engaged in international trade and finance."

"Is that why you have a bit of a British accent?" said David.

Angela smiled. "Perhaps," she said, nodding in acknowledgement. "I am so very sorry to hear of the passing of your friend and my countryman, Lin Shieh-Seng." She looked down, then cast her eyes from one face to the next.

Her drink arrived and Rick called for a toast: "Here's to the memory of Luke." They clinked glasses and bottles.

"And may I add on a happier note, to the success of your business venture in Taiwan," said Angela.

"Woo-Hoo!" said Rick, startling everyone as he raised his bottle for another toast.

"Please, do not speak so loudly," said Angela. Her eyes darted around the lounge, her head unmoving.

"Sorry," said Rick. "But this beer tastes awful good after nothing but water all the way over here."

She smiled a forgiving smile at Rick. "You were very wise to drink only water, not alcohol."

"That's what we were told," said David, "by Suzie, of course."

"Of course by Suzie," said Suzie, and they smiled. "It is so good to see you again, Angela. By the way, do you know those men at that table behind you? They are staring at us."

Now Angela turned her head slightly. Several tables away, two hard-looking Japanese men had just sat down. They wore expensive suits of the type tailored in Hong Kong. Their French-cuffed dress shirts were open at the collar; cuff links fitted with large chunks of gold extended from their coat sleeves. "Oh, I do not know *who* these are, but I know *what* they are. In my law firm we call them *Xìnxī rú chóng*. Information worms. Their type follow me all the time."

"Why?" said David, suddenly alert.

"They are business intelligence thieves. Agents of industrial espionage. Corporate spies. They are—what is your American word?—low lifes."

Angela became very agitated. "They are very worst kind of business spies, like assassins for hire if the price is right. Digital espionage pirates. They steal anything. Everything. Eww, they make me sick even to talk about."

"You're kidding," said David. "I thought that stuff only happened in, like, James Bond movies."

"Ha!" said Angela. "If only that were so. Unfortunately, what happens in spy novels and movies is very often based on true to life events." She tilted her head ever so slightly toward the two well-dressed Japanese men. "Those two are freelance information worms. They are sometimes called private collectors because they do not work for any agency or corporation. They are professional thieves of business, or economic, espionage. They steal anything of value from anyone and sell to the highest bidder. They make a lot of money. They know I am a corporate lawyer, so they follow me everywhere. They try to find out what companies I visit that might have valuable new technology—*for them to steal.*" Angela hissed the last words as she looked slowly, thoughtfully, at David, Rick, Jed. "They are very clever in the ways they try to steal business information."

Jed listened without speaking, recalling how information was classified and protected when he was in the Army. It was often his responsibility to safeguard military technologies. He remembered one instance when his troops were given a new kind of night-vision binoculars; he was sternly warned not to let them fall into enemy hands, no matter what.

"No shhhhh . . . kidding," said Rick. "The world has become *so* Machiavellian. But isn't stealing business information illegal?"

"Yes and no," said Angela. "It is how the world operates these days. No information is safe, whether it is military or government or business.

In our law circles, we refer to information as intellectual property. My specialty is helping my clients protect their IP. No theft is legal, but it can be difficult to prosecute, especially across international borders."

Jed was about to tell Angela they were carrying the Spinner technology to their meetings in Taiwan. He wanted to ask her how best to safeguard it when he looked over at the other table. The two Japanese had pointed a small tubular electronic device toward them and were fiddling with it. One kept touching his ear. "What are they doing with that thing?" he asked Angela.

"I do not want to turn to look because they will think we are persons of interest, but it is probably a laser microphone attached to a digital audio recorder. They will listen to our conversation to see if we have IP they can steal. We should now change the subject of our conversation."

"This makes me very unhappy," said Rick. David and Jed looked at Angela. Rick gave the other table a sidelong glance. "Very, *very* unhappy," he said. He got up and went to the drinks bar. A few minutes later he started back carrying four to-go cups of coffee on a tray, taking a rather circuitous route through the tables. As he approached the two information worms, he pretended to stumble. The tray flew forward, followed by the cups. Coffee splashed on the men's suits, table, gadgets. They jumped to their feet, screaming in Japanese. The one wearing heavy black-framed glasses glanced at Angela, then flashed furiously back at Rick. The other began spewing a string of loud, guttural, unintelligible sounds, sounding very much like Toshiro Mifune in a samurai movie. The first man barked at his partner, who began stuffing the recording gear into a briefcase. The two hurried away.

A hostess rushed over. The lounge had fallen silent but was easing back into relieved conversation. Rick stood by the now-abandoned table, coffee running off its edges in rivulets, grinning at his mates, who grinned back. Suzie raised her hands and silently applauded. Angela looked very worried.

As Rick rejoined the table she said, "You are traveling on a business trip, is that not so?"

Jed and David began speaking at the same time, just above a whisper, only to be interrupted by Rick's loud voice.

"Here, let me show you our presentation," said Rick, opening his messenger bag to pull out his MacBook.

"No, no, please," said Angela, touching his arm. "Do not. Do not let anyone see your computer. And do not use public wi-fi networks. You can be very easily hacked." Each time one of them spoke, she shushed them. "Tell me nothing. The business you are conducting is privileged information. To tell me would imply we have a lawyer-client relationship, which we do not, and I do not want to be responsible for knowing your IP. Or for anyone else learning it." She glanced surreptitiously around the lounge again.

"Gee, maybe we oughta hire you to watch out for us in Taiwan," said Rick, a charming smile crossing his face.

"Maybe you should, but as of right now we do not have that relationship." She looked him in the face. "Or any other kind of relationship." They held each other's gaze for several moments.

"However," she continued, "I now must tell you two things. One, because of what you did, those information worms will be after me with fierce interest now. And two, they will now be interested in you as well." Angela shifted her eyes from Rick to Jed to David and back to Rick. "You may have enjoyed your coffee spillage joke on them, Rick, but you also signaled that you have something to hide."

Rick visibly cringed.

"I am contaminated for you now. We should not consider a business relationship, and you should not stay in the Taipei hotel I recommended. Information worms are dangerous. They will steal for any master. They will bribe a taxicab driver, a bar hostess, a hotel concierge. They tried to bribe me once. It does not matter to them. Whatever they can steal is for sale to whomever wishes to buy it. Once they start, they will stop at nothing to get what they are after." Angela leaned forward. "*Nothing.* Now we must be very careful. All of us."

The Assault

E VA Air flight BR2197 was a wide-body DC-10 with rows of seats split into three sections separated by two aisles, both of which were in chaos. People streamed on board, talking loudly, bumping into those who were trying to get seated or busy stowing their bags in the overheads. Virtually everyone except Jed and Rick had black hair, leading to the conclusion they were Asian and that differences in manners and patience were in play.

"Hey, man, take it easy!" Rick said to a small, burly man butting into him with suitcases in both hands. "Nobody gets your seat except you!" The man blinked, then wedged his way between Rick and the aisle seats. Turning to Suzie, Rick said, "And I thought Americans were obnoxious." She grinned but said nothing.

Jed, Rick, David and Suzie allowed themselves to be jostled along until they reached their row. Jed's and David's briefcases, Rick's backpack and Suzie's carry-on went into the overhead. Jed took the starboard aisle seat, next to David; Suzie sat between David and Rick, where she felt safe.

Soon the plane was nearly filled and the flight attendants had begun their pre-flight announcements when two Japanese men, trying awfully hard to look like American grunge-band rockers, came down Jed's aisle, preceded by a flight attendant. Their smooth faces and neat haircuts belied the black jeans and epithet-riddled T-shirts they wore. The trim, uniformed young woman turned, bowed and spread her hands toward two empty seats, a middle one in front of Jed and the other across the aisle from him. The Japanese man wearing glasses quickly threw himself into the aisle seat; the other looked at him and let loose a string of Japanese at high volume and maximum anger. His seated partner, pointing to the seat in front of Jed, replied with equal verbal force. An exchange ensued until the smiling flight attendant encouraged the other man to sit down. The rocker seated across from Jed took a book bag from his shoulder and tossed it at his partner with a gruff command. The other turned, glared over his shoulder, stood, opened the overhead in which Jed and his people had stowed their bags, and shoved it in. Jed and David exchanged looks. Weren't they the same two from Narita?

The inevitable safety video started up in both Chinese and English as the plane began to taxi. In moments they were airborne. Jed opened his Jack Reacher paperback novel, but he wasn't reading. He was thinking about the bizarre chain of events over the past ten days: the accident, the last-minute trip changes like getting Suzie booked in place of Luke, fighting with the Chief Medical Examiner to avoid an autopsy, having Luke embalmed and his casket prepared for the flight, other endless last-minute details. And now this . . .

Was Luke's death an accident or intentional sabotage? Why Luke? If it were accidental, the truck wouldn't have angled directly at him. It might have struck any one of them, even several, like a bowling ball knocking down pins. His dad had contacted Police Chief Bertrand Lemieux and Albert Goncourt, the general manager at NEEC. But John hadn't been able to get anything out of any of them, nor had his long-time friend Colonel Sam Hooper at the New Hampshire State Police. *Maybe it was just what it was, an accident, and NEEC was simply trying to avoid a lawsuit. Like his dad said, it could have just been a moment of distracted driving.* But if so, why did it feel like there was a cover-up?

Or could it really have been an attempt to get the Spinner? *If so, it was a total fiasco,* thought Jed, since the truck had run over Luke, and the bike, and completely destroyed the Spinner. To the unsuspecting eye, Luke's bike looked like any other road bike. If it wasn't a plain and simple accident, someone had to know about the Spinner. Jed's refusal to sell their technology to any of the big-box American bike makers could have triggered an attempt at business espionage, to use Angela's term. Now it appeared these two Japanese information worms, as Angela called them, were attempting to do the same.

That at least made sense. The Spinner would compete directly with Japan's Shigerumaki, the world's largest maker of cycling components. But, Jed wondered, why wouldn't Shigerumaki just approach Smithworks in a normal businesslike manner to discuss acquiring the Spinner technology? And what was to be made of the event in the Sakura Lounge today? Did Angela's presence unintentionally turn them into a target? Then these two faux-rockstars just barely making it on board their flight; it had to be the same two guys. Did any of this make sense? Jed shook the speculations from his head and, with one eye on the overhead compartment, turned his attention back to Lee Child's novel.

It was growing dark as the aircraft began its three-hour flight from the island of Japan southward across the Pacific to the island of Taiwan. Passengers dozed or watched the seatback video entertainment. A tasty dinner was served, a choice of Chinese or American cuisine; they all chose Chinese. Jed opened his novel again, but soon tilted his seat back, laid the open book across his chest and closed his eyes. He felt, rather than heard, the taller rocker seated in front of him stand, turn, and open the overhead. He rustled around, glancing down at Jed and the others, then slammed the compartment lid closed and returned to his seat. Still pretending to be asleep, Jed was certain nonverbal communication passed between the two Japanese.

Ten minutes passed, then ten more. Jed sensed the man's presence and opened an eye a bit to see a belt buckle. The rocker was very quietly opening the compartment once again. He looked up and saw the Japanese with both hands in the overhead. Jed shifted in his seat, swung his arms up as if to stretch, and bumped an elbow into the guy's thigh. The rocker instantly closed the compartment door with a sharp snap and sat down. Jed followed his movement, then looked across the aisle. His partner was glaring at Jed, who gave him a big grin before returning his attention to Jack Reacher's quest to figure out which town was worse, Hope or Despair.

Arriving at Taipei's Taoyuan International Airport after nine PM, the four were exhausted. They dragged themselves through immigration, had to wait far too long at baggage claim, breezed through customs, and passed along an opaque glass wall into a spacious lounge area filled with plants, trees, and art exhibits. Bubble-gum pop music played over the PA system. The multitude of people seemed to be in good spirits, calling out to arriving friends and family.

"Man, am I thirsty," said Rick, looking for a snack bar or vending machine. He looked around and pointed, "Over there!"

"Forget it," said Suzie. "It needs NT—New Taiwan dollars. We have to convert our US dollars."

"Oh, yeah, forgot about that," said Rick. "Maybe I can find a water cooler."

"No, Rick. It is not good to drink street water here," said Suzie. "Only drink bottled water."

"Hey, look," said Jed, pointing into the crowd. An attractive young woman was holding a sign that read BIKE. "Do you think she could be here to meet us? Someone from Joyful Bike?"

"I will see," said Suzie and approached the woman. They spoke briefly, then Suzie turned and brought her back. "This is Lai Jung-Shan," said Suzie. Suzie introduced Jed, David, and Rick. Jung-Shan bowed to each of them in turn, then said, "I cannot express the sorrow I feel for your loss of Lin Shieh-Seng." Her eyes filled with tears. Rick sniffled; they stood in silence until Jung-Shan presented her business card to Jed with both hands.

> Lai Jung-Shan
> Director of Business Development
> Joyful Bicycle
> Taipei, Taiwan R.O.C.

Her loveliness was not lost on any of them. She wore a sleekly-tailored black pantsuit and a pale-yellow chemise with ruffles down the front, a black string tie at her throat. Her thick, glossy black hair was tied into a knot, not a loose strand anywhere. No makeup. Her eyebrows arched over intelligent, liquid-brown, almond-shaped eyes. Her slender nose gently tapered toward full, naturally pink lips. Jed was instantly smitten, yet for some reason had trouble getting her face into focus. She was like a bike passing too quickly to see if the rider was male or female, or if the bike was a Trek or a Cannondale. It was almost as if she vibrated ever so slightly, preventing him from sharply focusing on her; in his mind heard Bono singing, "she moves in mysterious ways."

"Can we get something to drink?" Rick said again. "I'm dyin' of thirst."

"Of course," said Jung-Shan. They followed her to the selfsame vending machine Rick had spotted, where she bought square plastic bottles of Fiji water all around. "Please enjoy, and always while you are in Taiwan drink only bottled water purchased from a machine or a store. Do not buy from a street cart, please." She tapped the flower on the Fiji bottle label. "This is always reliable quality."

As they drank, Suzie told Jung-Shan about Luke's casket stowed in the plane's cargo hold. Jung-Shan nodded, dialed her iPhone, and spoke in Chinese for a minute. "All taken care of," she said. "It will be delivered to the family. I am so sorry for your fallen partner. From great sadness I hope you will find great joy from this journey." She bowed. "Now, if you will please accompany me, our car is waiting."

Glass doors slid aside into the underground car park and the Americans were struck by a wave of Taiwan summer air, heavy with humidity and the smell of car exhaust. A gleaming black Cadillac Escalade SUV limousine waited at the curb. The driver bowed, opened the doors for them, stowed their luggage in the wayback. The five climbed inside, Jung-Shan and Suzie seating themselves on the soft leather bench seat on one side, the guys facing them on the other. Inside it was cool again; soft music was the only sound.

"Are you tired?" said Jung-Shan as they drove past the high-speed rail station.

"Well, yeah, a little, I guess," said Rick. "I mean, we've been traveling for about twenty-five, twenty-six hours now—"

"Is that the bullet train?" said David, pointing at a train running on an elevated track.

"Yes. We call it THSR," she said, "Taiwan High Speed Rail. You will have a ride on it when we travel to the Joyful bicycle factory in Kaohsiung."

"Nice," said David. "What's its top speed?"

"I believe it is three hundred kilometers per hour. You will see the precise speed displayed at all times on information screens in the train."

"Wow, I'm impressed," said David. "In miles per hour, that's—"

"About a hundred seventy-five," Rick said. "Beats the wheels off the Acela, doesn't it?"

"Without a doubt," said David.

They grew quiet as the big limo entered an expressway. Far ahead, Jed watched Taipei shimmer in the darkness, a penumbra of golden light. David and Rick quickly fell asleep. Suzie and Jung-Shan spoke quietly to one another in Mandarin; Jed, lulled by the SUV's steady speed, watched them, trying to clearly see Jung-Shan's face in the softly-lit interior. Every so often she would look up; Jed hoped she was looking at him, but it was difficult to tell.

They had traveled for fifteen or twenty minutes when the driver turned to speak to Jung-Shan. There was a brief exchange; the driver made a call from his cellphone, then she turned back and reached a hand toward Jed. "We are being followed," she said. "Do you know why someone would be following us?"

Jed sat bolt upright. A wave of cold perspiration dampened his face. He leaned toward her, and she and Suzie did the same so they could speak without awakening Rick and David. "Yes. Possibly. I think so," he said. "Two Japanese men, apparently. Information thieves. Business espionage agents. They saw us in the Tokyo airport, then boarded our plane."

"How did you know who they are? How do you know they are interested in you?" Jung-Shan said. Suzie told her about Angela and how she was frequently shadowed by agents on the lookout for valuable business intelligence. Jed started to mention the hit-and-run in New Hampshire, but thought better of it. "I see," she said. "So we already have large problems. They know you are in this limousine. They will follow us to your hotel and enter your room when you are not present. We have these problems from time to time with these *Xìnxī rú chóng*. Excuse me, please." She turned and spoke to the driver again, who kept saying "*Hǎo! Hǎo!*" to her, intermittently speaking rapidly into his phone.

She turned back to Jed and said, 'They are everywhere, always to steal our information and sell to our competitors. They are thieves, but there is nothing the authorities can do about them. It is very hard to maintain our business and economic growth in Taiwan when these agents are working against us. They come from China. They come from Japan. Other countries as well. Russia. India. America. It seems all countries engage in economic espionage."

Jed said, "I remember my dad talking about the Japanese tourists back in the 1950s. He said they weren't really tourists. They would visit the United States and take pictures of everything. They would buy transistor radios and take them back home to reverse-engineer them and make cheap knockoffs. Eventually, the Japanese dominated the consumer electronics market."

"It is the same now. Only more of the same. Often it is software they seek because it is so simple to steal, but also business plans and schematics. Just about any information property they can put hands on." She leaned forward intently and said, "Jed, do you have the drive with you?"

"Each of us brought part of it. Rick has the fixed gear hub we made and the belt drive. David has the carbon-fiber sprocket. They're in checked luggage. I have the ceramic cone in my messenger bag." He patted the beat-up US Army canvas camo bag he held. "Suzie has the microSD card. We bought a disposable phone and replaced the SIM card with it, to keep it hidden. We have our presentation for you on Rick's MacBook in his backpack, here," Jed said, pointing between Rick's feet.

"This is very good," Jung-Shan said. "The MacBook is secure?"

Jed nodded. "Password-protected, and all the files are encrypted." He was close enough to see the curve of her cheek, the way her lips moved as she spoke, but in the darkness he could not see all of her face. He badly wanted to, but she seemed to fade in and out of his vision, as if looking at her for too long was forbidden. As if his gaze would turn her into a pillar of salt.

"You have been reasonably careful."

"Well, thanks. We didn't know a thing about these information worms, but it just made sense after . . . well, it just made business sense to take precautions." He paused, then said, "We've also filed for patents, and they're pending approval."

Jung-Shan said, "I regret, your US patent means nothing to information worms. They work completely outside laws. If they copy your drive and put it on the market, you would have to spend millions to defend in lawyer and court fees. A foreign court might not rule in your favor."

"What about Taiwan?"

Jung-Shan pursed her lips in a most alluring way. "That is complicated. Very complicated. We are not close to America any longer. Your leaders are not favoring Taiwan as sovereign. We are separate from the People's Republic of China, and yet your government expects Taiwan to honor your copyright laws and trademark laws and trade agreements, but always in the US favor. Politics are always changing and make everything complicated. Very complicated."

"So, it boils down to the strength of the relationship between us as business partners."

"Yes, I believe that is true. Always, each of us must protect our own business interests. Excuse me." The SUV had reached a stretch of elevated roadway and was mounting a graceful arc. She looked out the windshield and spoke to the driver again. Jed watched them converse in rapid-fire staccato Mandarin, which he could not possibly understand. It reminded him of his early days in Afghanistan, not understanding a word of Dari or Pashto. Back in the moment, Jed looked through the windshield and saw, up high and ahead, a tall, beautiful Chinese building painted red with twin golden roofs, one atop the other, their corner gables upturned in the classical Chinese style.

The roadway curved into a rotary. The Cadillac banked to the high right side of the overpass, near the outside railing, then accelerated. As it entered the rotary, the driver cut to the left across three lanes of swiftly moving traffic, eliciting numerous horn blasts. On the inside now, they accelerated. Ahead was a traffic signal—a red light—but he blew through it and merged with the traffic entering the rotary from the right. He accelerated hard and cut all the way back to the far right and up a steep incline. Jed watched, fascinated and a little nervous. David and Rick had been awakened and were asking what was going on.

Ahead was a massive Chinese portal poised on four tall red pillars where several men in uniforms stood at attention. The driver rolled down his window and barked something at the guards, who quickly raised the barrier. The driver hit the gas up a wide drive around a terraced garden, coming to a stop in front of the great red Chinese building Jed had seen from the overpass. Porters rushed out to open the SUV's doors.

"This is the Grand Hotel Taipei," said Jung-Shan. "Come with me, please. Quickly." They all jumped out and followed her up the broad steps into the hotel's elegant lobby. It was hard not to pause to take it all in. "Come with me, please," Jung-Shan repeated, and they followed her to the right side of the grand staircase. Another porter awaited them, holding open a door disguised in the wall paneling. They entered, the door was closed, and they descended a stone stairway, down, down, to a small anteroom. Lights glowed dimly on the stone walls. Jung-Shan stopped.

"We are within the Grand Hotel," she began, knitting her fingers together in a prayer-like manner. "We wanted very much for you to stay here for your visit, had it not been for this information worms problem. I regret that. Please accept my apologies for Joyful Bike."

"We actually had our own reservations," said David, "at another hotel."

Jung-Shan bowed slightly toward the visitors. "Yes, I know. At the Jianguo Hotel. We will allow those reservations to remain for two days."

"Wait," said David, "how did you know that?"

"Very simple," said Suzie. "I told her in the limousine." She giggled and they all laughed in relief.

"Your luggage will be taken into the Grand Hotel to your reserved rooms. The agents will be led to think you are guests here," Jung-Shan continued, "so they will try to obtain lodging but they will be delayed by the hotel staff because they do not have reservations. They will be confused by the staff telling them different stories: Perhaps you are here, perhaps not. They will think maybe you are at the Jianguo Hotel, but you are not. If they try to break into your rooms at either hotel, they will be arrested.

"While they are, um, confused by this, we will take all measures possible to protect you and our common business interest. We are going to escape through this famous secret tunnel used in World War II to evacuate hotel guests during air raids.

"There are two such tunnels. Very few people know of these today. Many think it is no longer possible to go into the tunnels. Now you know that is not so." Jung-Shan laughed, a muted, throaty laugh. "Now we will pass through this tunnel and exit into Jiantan Park and cross the street to the Taipei Metro Jiantan Station. I will escort you to other lodging where, with certainty, you will be safe and undetected."

Jed noticed slight differences in her English pronunciations, which he found charming. "What about the SUV?" said Jed. "Can't they find out that it's registered to Joyful Bike and still find us?"

"They cannot," said Jung-Shan. "It is a leased vehicle, registered to the Cadillac dealer who will never release information about us."

Jung-Shan took her iPhone from her purse, opened the flashlight app, and said, "So, is everyone ready? It is not far to go through the tunnel. Soon you will be safe. Let us go."

Escape

The stone tunnel was about two hundred yards long, its walls slightly cool and damp, the ceiling low enough that Jed and Rick had to crouch slightly as they walked. The five emerged from it into a small, unlighted stone bunker with a heavy steel door. Jung-Shan found the spring lock, turned the knob and pushed the door open. "Please follow me," she said. Rick closed the door behind them as they went out into a warm, humid night and an equally dark, dense forest: Jiantan Park. They made their way down the secluded hillside until they came to a stone pathway. Soon they saw lights in the near distance, heard peoples' voices, tinkling music, cars and trucks and motor scooters. Scooters whizzing past, scooters parked in the hundreds on the sidewalks.

"Wow, so many scooters!" said Rick.

"Scooters are truly the primary means of travel in Taipei," said Suzie.

"The scooter is much easier to park," said Jung-Shan, "and uses much less petrol than the automobile. Just wait until you see how many there are in the daytime. They are like bumblebees!"

Across the busy street was the Jiantan Station subway station and nearby some kind of fair or celebration. Dozens of food stands were clustered on the sidewalk near the subway entrance, filling the air with delicious smells. Even at this late hour people were everywhere, hundreds and hundreds of people. Rows of tents receded into the distance.

Traffic was heavy. Jung-Shan stopped them to wait. "This," she said, pointing at the tents and people across the street, "is the Shilin night market. It is only open at night, but it stays open very late. People shop here for everything. Clothing, shoes, food, things for the household. As you see, there are many places to eat. Taiwanese love to eat fresh foods at the night market from these carts and also at food tents. All these foods are very *very* fresh. All very delicious foods, like dumplings, pork sausage, noodles, chicken feet, stinky tofu, oyster pancake, Taiwan hot dog—"

"*Chicken feet? Stinky tofu?*" said Rick. "You must be kidding."

"All these foods are very good," she said, smiling as she rubbed her tummy. Everyone laughed. "We will walk to the signal light so we can safely cross." They still had to dodge cars and scooters, but once across the street Jung-Shan stopped at a cart where a man was baking small pastries. "Please try these. They are *hóng dòu bing*, little pancakes with red bean and custard. You will enjoy." Inside the thin delicate shell was a sweet filling. People were buying them as fast as the man could pop them from the cast-iron muffin pans.

"Ummm," said Rick, "these are wicked tasty, aren't they? Can I have another?" They munched seconds as they walked around, checking out the different tent merchants selling shawls, Yankees baseball caps, flip-flops, spices, jewelry, and anything branded "Hello Kitty."

"Follow me to Jiantan Metro station," said Jung-Shan, turning and pointing. "This is perhaps the most special station design, made to look like the ancient Chinese dragon boat. Maybe hard to see the dragon so well in the night." They walked down the stairs into the station; it was spotless and the train gleamed under the brilliant illumination. Jung-Shan made a call from her iPhone.

"Look at this place," said David. "Brilliant design. Colorful, happy. A wall of safety glass to keep passengers from falling onto the tracks. Digital signs with train numbers and arrival time countdown. Everything is so clean and orderly. Look, a cellphone quick-charge station! I'm just really impressed. They really thought this through. The Boston MBTA is a dinosaur by comparison."

"Ha, ha, ha, ha, said Rick. "From the dinosaur to the dragon!"

Jung-Shan bought passcards and they boarded the Red Line, changing to the Green Line. Twenty-eight minutes later they arrived at Dapinglin Station. It was nearly midnight. "We have just a short walk," Jung-Shan said, which made the others all the more aware just how tired they were. They crossed Beixin Road, busy even at this late hour, and followed Jung-Shan down the uneven sidewalks past steel accordion garage doors marked with signs in Chinese for the businesses within, except for a Subway. Outside one, "Hello Kitty" posters covered the wall.

Few people were out walking. Jung-Shan led them across Bao'an Street and turned onto Lane 11. Just before it dead-ended, she turned left and they followed her down a wide stone drive to a gated entry. She pulled out her iPhone and made a call; the gate opened onto a terrace and a lighted area beyond. Ahead, lights lined the walkways radiating out from the terraced center garden. Ahead was a glass-walled entrance that bore no identification. Jung-Shan touched buttons on a keypad and twin glass doors slid apart. Inside was a reception area with leather sofas and chairs. Chinese tapestries covered the walls. To the left, a very pretty young woman wearing a dark skirt and vest, a white dress blouse and a lavender scarf at her neck, sat behind a rosewood desk. Her black hair, tinted with reddish-brown streaks, was pulled back into a multi-hued pony tail. Coal-black bangs fell like a delicate curtain over her forehead, hiding her eyebrows. Her eyes danced as she smiled at the guests.

"Where are we?" said Jed.

"*Ni hǎo*, Lai Jung-Shan," the girl said. Hello. Then in English: "Welcome to Serenity Garden Executive Inn."

"*Xiè xiè*, Lucy," said Jung-Shan. Turning back to Jed, she said, "We are in the Xindian District, New Taipei."

Jed turned, wiggled his eyebrows at the others, and said, "So glad I asked. Hey, isn't that our luggage over there?" He pointed toward the wall behind Lucy's desk. "How did you get our bags here before us?" Jed asked Jung-Shan.

"They were sent from the Grand Hotel by taxi," she said. The elevator doors opened and their limo driver stepped out. "In the company of Derek Hurst."

"*Ni hǎo*," Derek said. "Now for a more respectable welcome to

Taipei." He bowed slightly and shook hands with each of them.

"So you left the limo at the Grand Hotel and hopped a taxi over here with our stuff," said David, ever the engineer.

"He is not really a driver," said Jung-Shan. "Derek is the Joyful Bike head of security."

"Well, I'll be," said Rick.

Jung-Shan said something to Derek in Chinese. He nodded. She turned to the guys and said, "Derek was born and raised in Hong Kong. He is half Chinese, half English. He is fluent in Cantonese, Mandarin and English."

"Quite so," Derek said with deference. Turning to Jed, "Please feel free to converse with me in the King's English. Or your American adaptation," he said, grinning. "And please excuse me while I assure your rooms are secure."

"Thanks," said Jed and the others chimed in. Turning back to Jung-Shan he said, "So, I'll ask again: Where are we?"

The receptionist named Lucy said, "Serenity Garden is private retreat lodging for foreign business travelers. Very private. Not open to the public. People think this is Christian meeting center because sometimes church leaders stay here. All others are traveling business executives. Very nice executive suites." She smiled, obviously pleased to answer the question in English.

"But it is far away from downtown, and our offices," said Jung-Shan. "Our first preference was for you to stay at the Grand Hotel, but due to circumstances this must be our second best choice."

"Your management skills are most impressive, Ms. Lai," said David.

She gave him a slight bow and said, "*Xiè xiè*. Please call me Jung-Shan."

"She-she? Which means?" Rick said.

"It is 'thank you' in Chinese," said Jung-Shan. "You say it like this: *syeh-syeh.*"

"Oh, yeah, now I remember Luke saying it once in a while," said Rick. "Shew-shew, Jung-Shan!"

Jung-Shan laughed and bowed slightly toward Rick. "Although I am sure you are tired and wish to sleep, we must discuss several matters before you go to your rooms. Please come with me to this coffee shop." She pointed and led them out to a stone-paved sidewalk; ahead was another glass door and beside it a green sign bearing the word DANTE in gold. They passed the two counter girls, who nodded and smiled, and entered a small private room in the rear. Jung-Shan handed Suzie some money and spoke to her in Chinese.

"I've been in a lot of coffee shops back home, but I don't think I've ever seen one with private rooms," said Jed.

"We are a private people. Many times, important business must be discussed in private," said Jung-Shan, glancing around the walls and ceiling.

"What are you looking for, surveillance devices?" said David.

"Yes, but I am sure we have privacy. Dante would suffer much loss of face if these private rooms were not secure. That is also true for Serenity Garden Inn guest rooms. I do not think Derek will find surveillance equipment."

"Dante is an interesting choice of names," said Jed.

"Yes," said Jung-Shan. "Coffee is a newer taste for our culture. We are more used to enjoying tea, as you might think. But Dante coffee is a very, um, sophisticated drink. Very fine preparation. Each cup is made just for you. And this is a peaceful atmosphere, with relaxing music."

Suzie returned with a teapot and cups. "This is Chinese herbal tea. It will not keep us awake. The Chinese believe warming is good for the stomach," she said with a smile.

"Xiè xiè, Sun Xiaohui," said Jung-Shan. She poured tea and they all touched their tiny teacups. "Now, to business. Tomorrow is introductions for all. We will host the meeting at our offices at ten o'clock. You will first meet our president and I will be in attendance. Jed, you will please attend this meeting."

Jed looked at her, hesitating before he answered. "You mean by myself?"

Jung-Shan nodded. "It is customary for first business meeting to be presidents only."

Jed looked at the others, then said, "No. The three of us are all owners. Not exactly equal owners, but pretty close. We all started this company together and decided to call it Smithworks just because it sounded good. All-American. But when we meet Mr. Zheng, it should be all . . . three of us. That is customary for Americans."

Jung-Shan nodded. "Very well. Then Joyful will have in attendance the same chief executives as Rick and David. Then the meeting will be in harmony." Jung-Shan nodded and raised her tea cup again. They all sipped.

"Make it so," said Jed, which made Rick and Dave grin. "I'll introduce the company, then David will make the presentation." He looked at Jung-Shan. "You said you will be there?"

"Yes, I will attend. I have been assigned to work with you and your company." Jung-Shan smiled at Jed. He wished with all his might that he could see her face clearly. There was plenty of light here in Dante, but she remained adamantly out of focus. She raised her teacup to him.

He returned the gesture.

"You have a MBA?" Jed asked.

"Yes," Jung-Shan replied, from "From LSE. London School of Economics."

"Boy, you Chinese," said Rick, "you sure don't mess around when it comes to your education. We met Suzie's Taiwanese friend Angela in Tokyo and she's got degrees comin' out her ears."

Suzie said, "Our parents love their children very much, want all the very best life has to offer them. We are brought up to become very well educated, to have very good careers, to become very great successes. That is why I came to the United States. And to be with Luke, of course." She smiled a bittersweet smile. "I was in love with Lin Shieh-Seng in second grade."

Jed reached out and took her hand. "Suzie and Luke were engaged. She's been working part-time at Smithworks since she graduated," he said to Jung-Shan. "She has a very good education, too."

"Rhode Island School of Design," Suzie said.

"She's our executive planner and webmaster and graphic designer for anything and everything," Jed continued. "She also works with Gregg Colarusso, the artist who does the custom paint-jobs on our bikes. He has a MFA from—"

"*Hai,*" said Jung-Shan. Yes. "I understand. Sun Xiaohui and I discussed some of these subjects in the limousine ride. I will help her make arrangements for the funeral.

"It is getting very late and we should all get some rest," she said. There were murmurs of assent. "But before we part, I want to give you some important information." She picked up her phone and tapped a text message. She got an instant ping back. "Derek is coming. He was an IP lawyer in Hong Kong. Before worked for many years as a business traveler security agent. We think maybe he worked for MI6, too," she said with a wry smile.

Derek entered the room and bowed. Jung-Shan gestured toward a chair and he sat down. She poured him tea. "He will explain to you about your business information in this hotel."

"Taiwan," he began, "is a very safe country, but do not assume you will always be safe. That is because there are business intelligence pirates everywhere and Taiwan is no exception. Wherever business people travel, they follow. That is why this hotel is a total secret. At least we hope it is!" He smiled around the table.

"Please assume nothing is secure. There could be hidden microphones or cameras in your rooms, although my scan didn't find any. Regardless, do not say or do anything you would not want others to know about. Best not to talk at all in your room. Do not open your door to the unknown stranger. I recommend you do not use either your mobile phone or the room phone to make calls. Texts are safe. Do not use the wi-fi. And do not leave anything unsecured in your room. When you leave, take everything—your papers, your phones, your computers, with you. Do not allow *anyone* the opportunity to see or touch your information or your tech devices. OK?"

Everyone nodded. "Geez, I hope we can have some *fun* while we're here," said Rick. "You make it almost sound like we're prisoners."

Derek frowned a bit.

"Yes, it may sound that way, but it is not all so serious," said Jung-Shan. She smiled at Derek and around the table, saving her last and brightest smile for Jed. "I have made plans for your enjoyment after the meeting tomorrow. I will introduce you to many wonderful pleasures of my island country. If you will be careful now and keep security in your mind, we will have great fun together. And so I say again welcome to Taiwan. We are very happy you have come, and we have only the highest expectations for our business success.

"Before I leave," said Jung-Shan, "please allow Derek to gather your Spinner IP and other personal technologies. I will keep them locked inside my office safe until they are needed."

Jed looked at David and Rick and said, "Make it so." They grinned and reached into their bags, passing everything to Derek.

"Very good, then," she said, "I wish you a good night of sleep."

Jed had kept his eyes glued on her during the entire briefing, trying to memorize her face, but once he got up and began walking toward the elevator, try as he might he could not bring her to mind. *What is it that's so mysterious, so . . .* inscrutable *. . . about this woman?* he asked himself.

Meanwhile – Outside the Grand Hotel

After creating a scene for being denied accommodations, the two Japanese information worms were escorted to a waiting taxi by Grand Hotel security men, who slammed both rear doors shut almost simultaneously. The driver said, "Where to?" in Chinese, but the passengers didn't reply. He repeated it in English, then Japanese. Still no reply. The men lit cigarettes and the driver said, "No smoking! No smoking!" but they ignored this, too. "Out! Get out of my car!" said the driver.

"Jianguo Hotel," said the shorter man wearing glasses.

The driver put the Toyota in gear and began to pull away, lowering the electric rear windows to expel the smoke, but all it did was let hot, humid air flood the car. The taller Japanese reached for his window switch, but the driver pressed the lock button. And grinned. The men tossed their cigarettes out the windows. The driver unlocked and closed the windows, and drove down the hotel promenade through the arches and into the night traffic.

The foot traffic on Nanjing Road and Jilin Street, in front of the Jianguo Hotel, was as heavy as the auto and scooter traffic. Tourists and families clogged the hotel entrance and thronged the sidewalks with apparent disregard for keeping right—or left. Lovely young women, their long black hair flying, strode by purposefully on tall spike-heeled shoes. A boy wearing a chef's hat and apron stood outside the corner pizza-pasta restaurant, handing out menus. The occasional scooter dodged pedestrians on the sidewalks, seeking a place to park. The two Japanese, now free to smoke their cigarettes, found it impossible to stand outside without being jostled, so they entered the hotel lobby.

"You think they will be here?" said the tall Japanese.

"*Hai.*" Yes.

"*Why you think they will be here?*"

The shorter man scowled at his partner. "Because I like it here."

They sat in the waiting area, sullenly facing a group of college students who were talking and laughing at the tops of their voices. They observed every person who entered or left through the swinging glass doors for two hours. No sign of the Americans.

The smaller man stood, pushing his glasses up on his nose. "Come," he said to his partner. They hailed a cab and returned to the Grand Hotel. The smaller man studied the hotel valets; they were not the same, so apparently there had been a midnight shift change. "Wait," he told the taxi driver. He crossed to the steps and spoke to the head doorman. "I was leaving the hotel earlier tonight and set my luggage in the rear of a minivan taxi. Then three men and two women jumped in and the taxi took off."

"Do you remember the name of the taxi company?" the doorman said.

"No, but it was green and yellow."

"Shi de! That is not much helpful. *Did you see the license plate?*"

"*No.*"

"*Then I am sorry, but I cannot help you.*"

"*Are you sure you cannot?*" said the Japanese man as he slipped a NT500 banknote into the doorman's hand.

Nodding, smiling, the doorman said, "Perhaps I can . . . do you remember the time?"

"Yes. It was exactly 10:32. You can identify the destination?"

"That may be possible. Please excuse me while I phone the dispatcher."

Welcome to Taiwan

J ed woke up to a roomful of sunlight and disorientation. He couldn't figure out where he was or remember how he had got here. Wherever here was. He was hot, sweaty. He threw off the heavy comforter, untangled himself from the sheets and crawled out of bed. Tugging at his underpants, he walked toward the daylight. There was a sliding glass door and beyond it a narrow balcony; he unlocked the door, slid it open and peered out. The strange scents of a foreign country rose in his nostrils. Sounds of traffic filled his ears. Below, he saw odd-looking trucks, small unfamiliar cars, motor scooters and an occasional bicycle moved at a steady pace up and down the wide, divided road. Mostly it was scooters, which appeared to share a separate lane with bicycles, but they rarely stayed within its lines. Large yellow Chinese symbols were painted on the traffic lanes.

Ah, right. I'm in Taiwan. Luke's Taiwan. He felt an uncomfortably large chunk of emotion rise from his chest into his throat.

As far as he could see, hundreds, perhaps thousands, of scooters were parked on the wide stone sidewalks in a more or less orderly fashion, perpendicular to the street. Handsome stone planters filled with shrubbery and trees lined the streets. The median between traffic lanes was a deep green lawn with trees, plants and flowers growing riot.

Across the boulevard, two-story buildings formed a single continuous facade from one to the next. On street level were small shops, each uniformly about twelve feet wide. Those which were still closed had the same steel roll-up shutter doors he'd noticed last night. Above the doors were signs identifying a Family Mart drugstore, scooter repair shop, household goods, hardware, a fruits and vegetables stall, a golf shop, some businesses he did not recognize and, of all things, a 7-Eleven. Air conditioners hummed in every window above the shops. *Probably apartments.*

He leaned on the concrete balcony and watched the scene below. People walked by, often with cloth shopping bags, popping in and out of the markets. Scooters whizzed by—*bumblebees*, just as Jung-Shan had described. Jed's attention drifted to her. He reviewed what he knew about her—not much—which intensified his desire to know more, to know everything about her. Most of all he wanted to freeze-frame her face so he could *see* her, really see her clearly, capture her image in his mind's camera to recall whenever he wanted. He was certain she was beautiful, but he wanted a perfect photographic image. It was strange; he hadn't felt such a powerful tug toward a woman since . . . well, since he'd met Martina. How long ago was that? *I'm thirty-five. So that was, what, almost ten years ago. How old is Jung-Shan? Is she single? Married? No way to know. Why even think about it? Am I thinking of her as a possible love interest? Come on. No way. She must have a boyfriend. Husband. No way a beautiful woman like her wouldn't be all married up, no way. Besides, I don't want to get involved with a woman again, ever.*

Jung-Shan. The ten o'clock meeting! What time was it? Jed freaked and dashed back into the room. His iPhone rested on the bedside table. He grabbed it up: *Whew, only 7:30.* Then he thought, *is this the right time?* He thumbed his way through Settings to Date and Time: it showed Taiwan. Jed breathed out. Had they discussed breakfast last night? Not that he remembered. They should all have breakfast together to discuss the plans for the day. Maybe Suzie knew . . . His phone dinged with a new text message:

Jed, Please enjoy a complimentary breakfast in the Serenity Garden restaurant. I will come for you at 9AM. Regards, Jung-Shan.

He smiled. Boy, she was a pro.

As he showered, Jed reviewed the events of the previous evening. The Japanese agents. Rick's stunt with the coffee cups. Them trying to paw through their carry-on bags on the plane. *I wish I'd elbowed the guy in the balls instead of just bumping his thigh.* Tailing them from the airport, wrecking their stay at the Grand Hotel. *That place was so beautiful. I wish we could have stayed there and had a normal couple of days of business and sightseeing.*

Still, it was hard to believe this was happening; it was a dark side of business Jed had never encountered. By comparison, warfare in the Army was simple, straightforward. *This kind of thing didn't happen in the States . . . or did it? Well, it probably did. If I gotta play hardball with the Big Guys, so be it. If I gotta fight off information worms to protect the Spinner, damn sure I will.*

He toweled off, shaved, brushed his teeth, and dressed in dark maroon slacks, cordovan loafers, a blue Oxford cloth button-down collar dress shirt and his favorite old MIT necktie. Business casual. It was 8:15. He texted the others:

Heading for breakfast. I'll grab a table for us.

Except Suzie, Rick and David were already waiting for him. The restaurant hostess smiled, bowed, checked his name off her guest list, and led him to their table, one of many fanning around a pentangle of serving tables. Each bore a different kind of food: one just for fruits; a chef making omelets at another; Chinese dim sum, American and European breakfast cereals, breads and pastries, a coffee, tea and juice bar.

"So, you beat me down here, huh?" said Jed, then excused himself to fuel up. He was surprised to see fresh-squeezed orange juice and a European bistro machine for making individual cups of espresso, cappuccino, and *cafe au lait.*

"I don't know about you guys," Jed said to Rick and David, sitting down with his orange juice, cafe au lait and *congee*, a Chinese rice porridge, "but I could sure use a spin. My legs are cramped up like crazy from sittin' on airplanes."

"Yeah, for sure," said Rick.

David nodded, said, "Maybe Jung-Shan can loan us some bikes."

"Duh, why I didn't think of that," said Jed, spooning porridge into his mouth. "How're you doing, Suzie?"

"Very well, thank you," she said, smiling sweetly. "If you do not mind, I will go to see Luke's family today to discuss his funeral."

"We'll come, too, as soon as the meeting is over," said Jed. I'll text you."

"I will let you know if that is their desire," she said, "but do not be disappointed if they wish to remain private in their grieving."

Jung-Shan was waiting in the hotel turnaround, standing with Derek beside a white Cadillac stretch limousine. She wore a black skirt and matador's waistcoat over a crinkly pink silk blouse. A small piece of pale green jade clung to a silver chain at her throat. Her hair was pulled back and gathered at the nape of her neck. She looked beautiful and businesslike all at once. She pressed her hands together and dipped her head ever so slightly. "Good morning," she said. "Did you rest well? We have not detected any cars following us today, so that is good."

"Sure is!" said Rick. "Boy, that was enough intrigue yesterday to last me a lifetime! You have a nice ride today, Derek," patting the Cadillac's fender. Derek smiled and nodded.

"Gentlemen," said Jung-Shan, "you will be wearing American business clothing, yes?"

Jed looked at Rick and David; both wore slacks and open-collared shirts, the same as he but sans ties. "Uh, yeah, we are," he said, touching his hands to his shirt. "We call it business casual. It's pretty typical in America."

"Here it is customary to wear a suit and a tie to business meetings," said Jung-Shan. "Do you have?"

"Um, no," said Jed, realizing he had forgotten to bring a suit for

Luke's funeral. He tried to remember the last time he'd worn one. Graduation? "Dave? Rick?" They shook their heads.

Jung-Shan tried not to seem disappointed. "I see. All right, today you must go to the meeting this way. Do you have gifts?"

"Gifts? For who?" said Jed.

"With Chinese, It is our custom to exchange gifts when meeting. President Zheng will have gifts for you, and you must have gifts for him. David, Rick, this is also etiquette for you when meeting Joyful vice-presidents. It is our way to show respect." She looked at Derek and said, "We will make a shopping stop."

"What about the other heads? From Taiwan Integrated Industry and Taiwan Micronics? Don't we need gifts for them, too?" asked Jed.

"We do not meet with them today," she said. "Only President Zheng and two vice-presidents of Joyful Bike."

"I don't understand," said Jed. "I thought we were meeting everybody today so we could work out the partnership. I thought that was what Luke set up . . ." He dug into his camo messenger bag for his MacBook, as if he needed to review email messages.

"I am sorry. It is my mistake, not Luke's. I did not express our agenda with clarity last night. I apologize for not giving you detailed briefings." Jung-Shan looked down, then back at Jed. "Here, business moves more slowly than in the United States. Today is for Joyful Bike to get to know Smithworks. This is customary for the first meeting. Then in two days or so we will meet again with the other companies and more of Joyful people. Then everyone will get to know one another. The Chinese custom is to learn first about the people they wish to do business with and make sure there are good feelings about each other. Today you should not expect to discuss business or Spinner technology. Maybe not even at the next meeting. Maybe in a few meetings. Maybe Lin Shieh-Seng did not tell you about this custom?"

The guys looked at each other. Jed looked at Suzie. She shrugged her shoulders and said, "I am sorry, Jed. I should have known about gifts and business suits, but I was not so very familiar with this custom. I have only worked in America."

Jed thought, then said, "So we get to know each other, develop trust between us. OK, that makes a lot of sense. Now we *do* know what to expect. See, the thing is, we have reservations to fly back to the States on Friday. I thought three days would be enough. Probably not. We'll just have to change our reservations, I guess." He looked at Rick, whose face registered a CFO's disappointment.

"Good idea," said Jung-Shan. "We will need more time. I am sorry we did not have this conversation sooner."

"Yeah, me too," said Jed. "I thought we were emailing with the head of business development before, but—"

"It was my assistant."

"Right. Your assistant."

"So sorry," said Jung-Shan. "May be a language problem. She might have made assumptions that you knew these customary things. She and I will provide very clear information for all customs and events in the future."

"I can help," said Suzie.

"*Hǎo*," said Jung-Shan. She paused, thought for a moment. "Not your mistake, Jed. My mistake. I am sorry." She looked at him. "I will have my assistant make new reservations at the expense of Joyful for ten days hence."

"Xiè xiè," said Jed, nodding, hoping it came out of his mouth properly. Suzie, David and Rick followed suit, then Rick said, "Jung-Shan, what does 'hǎo' mean?"

Suzie, grinning, said, "Okay. Good. Great. Super. Excellent. *Awesome!*" Everyone laughed and relaxed.

Jung-Shan spoke rapidly to Derek in Mandarin as they drove away. He stopped at a street market, parked, went into a store, and then another. He got back in the Cadillac with three fifths of Johnnie Walker Blue Label Scotch, each in a silk-lined box, and two neckties.

"Wow," said Rick, "I'm mostly a beer drinker, but even so, I don't think I've ever seen Blue Label."

"Much less tasted it," said David. "Very special." He and Rick began tying their new ties.

"Very expensive," said Jed.

"Yes, a most special gift of respect," said Jung-Shan. "My bosses will be very flattered." She smiled.

"You're always paying for us," said Jed. "We need to exchange our money and pay you back."

"I will go to a bank while you are in the meeting, Jed," said Suzie.

"That would be great, Suzie." He dug into his messenger bag and handed her an envelope full of American dollars.

The Joyful Bike building was a formal contemporary stone structure ten stories high at Linsen and Zhongxiao Roads, Zhongzheng District, New Taipei City. Set at a 45-degree angle to the corner, its architecture was three rectangular towers: a large central edifice flanked by two which were slightly smaller. Its façade was gray marble with contrasting black cornerstones, low-E gray-tinted window glass, and stainless steel trim. Each tower was topped with a traditional Chinese *paifang* arch, those on the left and right complementing the larger center arch crowning the tripartite design. Each paifang was supported by nonstructural pillars of pale white marble integrated into the building's façade. There was no sign or logo to indicate who occupied the building. As they entered, they passed through a semicircular two-story glass atrium lobby. Full-size statues of Fú, Lù and Shòu, the Chinese gods of prosperity, status and longevity respectively, stood to one side of the information desk that dominated the center of the lobby; on the other side was another Dante coffee shop.

After obtaining their visitor passes from the lobby security officer, Jung-Shan escorted them into the executives-only elevator and pressed the eighth-floor button. They stepped out. The central arch, now clearly visible, began at this floor and could be seen in its rise over the top of the building through the floor-to-ceiling windows that swept all the way around. Every office had a stunning view except for the conference room, which was walled in for privacy. The executive lounge area was, in essence, an open living room with several leather sofas, Eames chairs, a magnificent rosewood-and-glass coffee table and high-intensity floor lamps, all resting upon an expansive carpet bearing a Buddhist mandala design woven in blue, yellow and deep purple.

Jung-Shan seated the guys, then spoke quietly: "Please present mmm—Mr. Zheng—his bottle of Scotch gift first, Jed." She gave him a quick, sweet smile. She showed the guys the two-handed business card offering ritual and had them practice it, then said, "Excuse me," and left the reception area, returning with Joyful Bike's president, Zheng Ming-Chiang. Seconds later, Mr. Wen, the vice president of operations and Mr. Tan, vice president of manufacturing, appeared from the elevator. Jung-Shan made the introductions, hands were shaken, and business cards were properly exchanged.

Zheng was an older man, perhaps in his mid-fifties but it was a little hard to tell. He looked to be in good shape; his hair was coal-black; his face was unwrinkled, yet it revealed a world of experience. Jed gave Zheng his bottle of Scotch, followed by David and Rick doing the same with their Joyful counterparts. Everyone nodded to one other, exchanged xiè-xiès, and took seats on the sofas. Zheng and Jung-Shan sat in the black leather Eames chairs. Tea and petit fours appeared and pleasantries ensued.

"You are president of a very successful bicycle company, Mr. Smith," said Zheng Ming-Chiang to Jed.

"Thank you, sir," he said. "And so are you! We're very proud of our bicycles, as I'm sure you are as well."

"It would seem we are in different markets, but yes, I am very proud of the quality and respect our bikes are given worldwide. It is my understanding each Smithworks bicycle is built for the customer, is that so?"

"Yes, it is," said Jed. "Our philosophy is to build a bike of such high quality that the customer will never find another one that compares. First we learn what kind of bike he, or she, wants—racing, cross-country, mountain bike. We take the customer's measurements, then put him on a fixed dimensional bike and analyze his fit on a computer. The customer can choose between titanium or aluminum or steel for the frame. Not too many ask for steel any more. Most opt for the most expensive and lighter titanium. We buy our tube stock from Reynolds. It really is the best."

"Ah, we agree," said Zheng, looking at Mr. Wen, who nodded his head. Apparently everyone spoke, or at least understood, English.

"So, next we help him select his gruppo, headset, handlebars, seat and post, paint job. Some of our customers want a custom design and we have our own artist, Gregg Colarusso, to paint it. So yes, every Smithworks bike is a totally one-of-a-kind custom."

"This is very impressive. How long does it take to make a customer bike?"

"Two to three weeks from approving the package and getting measurements. We only make thirty to forty bikes a month. Unless we get backed up with orders, of course."

"How many bikes do you make a month?" David asked the vice-president of manufacturing.

Mr. Wen looked at Mr. Zheng for approval. "In this year of 2011, we will make over five million bicycles," he said. "70 percent Joyful bicycle, and 30 percent OEM."

"Your OEM customers are US companies?"

"Some are," said Mr. Tan, "about 25 percent of our OEM. China is 40 percent. Rest is Japan, Europe, India, other countries. Your bicycle is only for US customers?"

"No, some go to other countries," said Rick. "Professional cyclists, mostly from Europe. Serious American cyclists, often doctors, lawyers, business leaders. Some musicians and artists. Wealthy people. One-of-a-kind collectors."

"Your bicycles are very expensive," said Mr. Zheng.

"From about ten to twenty thousand," said Jed. "Dollars. That would be . . ." he glanced at Jung-Shan and she performed the dollars to NT currency exchange in Mandarin.

"*Zěnme yàng*," Tan said, clearly impressed. You are doing well. "Your company is privately held, yes?"

Jed nodded. "There are . . . four owners. I own the controlling stake."

"You manufacture each bike frame in your place of business?" Mr. Wen, the vice president of manufacturing asked.

David nodded and said, "Yes. We cut the tubing to size for each customer's bike, braze it, grind and polish the welds, prepare it for painting. I assume just like you do in your factory." Wen turned toward Zheng and said something in Chinese.

I wonder why they're asking these questions, Jed thought. *They could get all of this information and more on our website.* "I'm looking forward to seeing your manufacturing facility," he said.

"And I am looking forward to showing it to you," said Zheng, glancing toward his veeps. "It is in the countryside, near the south tip of our island. You have been in business for ten years, is that not so?"

"Almost. Ten years on November eighth," said Jed. He was beginning to see how each question, each verbal interaction, was turned back to Smithworks.

"Eight is a lucky number in Chinese culture," said Zheng, smiling. "And you," he said, waving his hand at the three guys, "were students together at the Massachusetts Institute of Technology?"

"Yes," said Jed. "And with Lin Shieh-Seng. We all studied different subjects—"

"Yes, I know of the great loss you have," he said, his face suddenly quite sad. There was a long pause, then Zheng continued, "MIT brought all the business expertise together, yes?" Zheng put his palms together. "Turn Smithworks into gold! *Ha!* Now you want to build this new bicycling drive to become world famous another time."

Jed leaned forward, resting his elbows on his knees. "Yes, sir. Not because we want to be world famous, but for two reasons. The first is that we are innovators. We love bicycles and can't stop playing with bicycle technology. The second is we want to see more people riding bikes. Some would call this doing good, or having a social conscience. For us, it's both. But now there is a third reason, and that is to honor the man who made the drive a reality: Lin Shieh-Seng."

"This is indeed honorable," said Zheng. "I would like to know more about how you plan to do this."

"We've only begun thinking about it," said Jed. "Luke's only been .. . gone . . . eleven days."

"He was our most highly valued business asset," said David.

"And my best friend," said Rick, nodding solemnly.

"It is indeed a great loss, for all of us," said Mr. Zheng." His eyes revealed heartfelt sympathy. And you were an Army officer, Mr. Smith?"

"I was, for not quite two years," said Jed. "I was injured by shrapnel from an IED—that's a—"

"Yes, I know, roadside bomb," said Zheng. "Very sorry to hear of this misfortune for you. But you are healed?" Zheng lifted his heavy eyebrows and smiled. Jed nodded. "Then you are very lucky you still can ride bicycles!" He laughed, and everyone laughed with him.

"I've been crazy about bicycles since I was a little kid," said Jed. "The injury made me want to keep riding more than anything in my life. The Army gave me a good rehabilitation program and I worked it hard."

"Yeah," said Rick, "if you saw him ride, you'd never know he'd had a chunk of steel embedded in his thigh. Speaking of riding—" Rick caught Jung-Shan's look and stopped talking.

Zheng smiled at Rick. "Yes, I thought you would want some bicycling," he said. "We will arrange this for you." He looked over his shoulder at Jung-Shan. "They will need a guide, will they not?"

"Yes, sir," she said.

"Then please give them a tour of our beautiful island country."

Jung-Shan smiled and nodded.

"Fine. Will you gentlemen have more tea?" said Zheng. As if he had pulled a bell rope, the young woman who had brought the tea reappeared with a fresh pot and refilled their cups.

Zheng Ming-Chiang raised his cup and everyone followed. "To our businesses, Mr. Smith. To Smithworks and Joyful Bike. I hope we can achieve objectives that are mutually beneficial with new ventures." They clinked cups. "And mutually profitable," he added, chuckling.

Everyone chuckled.

Zheng rose, and so did his vice presidents and director of business development, followed by Jed, David and Rick. "I regret that I must attend to some other business matters, but I hope you will share the midday meal with me in a short time. Until then, perhaps you would like to tour our bicycle museum?" He gestured to Jung-Shan, who bowed and escorted the guys out.

As they walked away, Mr. Zheng called out, "Mr. Smith?"

They all stopped. Jed turned. "Sir?"

"You have brought the Spinner with you, is this not so?"

Jed looked at Jung-Shan. "Yes, sir, we did."

"And of course you will permit my people to examine and test it?"

"Of course," he said, both he and Jung-Shan nodding.

As they rode the elevator, Jed looked at Jung-Shan and said, "Not at all what I expected, but it seemed to go well."

She glanced at him; her face was once more out of focus. "It was an excellent meeting. A perfect meeting. They were very impressed with you and your company." She spoke slowly, carefully gathering her thoughts into words. "The *chi* is flowing very nicely among all. It was a great privilege for you to be asked to share *wǔcān*—the midday meal—with Mr. Zheng. Now we wait for the next meeting."

"You were, like, kind of ignored," Rick said to her.

"Yes, as I explained to you, this was a meeting for Joyful executives to meet Smithworks executives. Presidents and vice-presidents meet to get to know each other. No Smithworks director of business development to meet with me." She made a mock pout.

"But even though he seemed to ignore you while we were meeting, I felt like Mr. Zheng has a lot of confidence and respect for you," said Jed.

For the first time, Jung-Shan looked directly into his eyes, and for the first time she was not a blur; she seemed willing to let him really see her. The contours of her face, the way she pressed her lips together, the lilt of her eyebrows, her eyes, all were instantly revealed. "Yes," she said, "what you say is true. After all, he is my father."

Joyful Bike

"**A**nd so you see Joyful has a history of diversifying, first by making bikes for other known brands and growing from 1953 until today when Joyful is a known brand name bike itself," Jung-Shan was saying as they emerged from the Joyful Bike museum on the third floor. "The high regard for Joyful is key part of NewBike strategy to make the most successful commuter bike for the all cities of the world." She smiled and pressed the elevator Up button.

"NewBike? That's name you've chosen for the city bike?" said Jed.

Jung-Shan blushed and looked down. "Yes," she said. "I thought you knew. My father chose this name."

They elevator door opened. They stepped on and she pressed the tenth-floor button.

"I think it's a good name," said Jed.

"Xie xie," said Jung-Shan

"Almost sixty years. I had no idea anybody was making bikes in Taiwan so long ago," said David. "The first bicycle was made in the 1890s. Somewhere in Europe, wasn't it?"

"David, the bicycle has been the primary transportation in China for much longer, since the 1860s," said Jung-Shan.

"So, you made the famous racing bike, the Yoshigawa, for Japan," said Rick.

"And Joyful invented the folding bike?" asked David.

"Hai, also for the Japanese," said Jung-Shan.

"And more recently the sloping top tube racing bike."

"And today you make the Simmons replicas, the oldest American name in bikes," said Jed.

"Yes, yes, yes, yes," said Jung-Shan, a proud smile on her lips. Then she burst into laughter, a deep, throaty yet quite feminine laugh.

They all laughed. "Gentlemen," she said, "we have been a very long time in the museum, and now it is time to again join Mr. Zheng," she said. "Um . . . you know how to use chopsticks?"

Rick laughed and said, "Yes, we do. There's a great little Chinese restaurant just down the street from our offices."

"We eat there all the time," David said, wiggling his imaginary chopsticks.

The elevator stopped at the tenth floor and the doors opened on a formal Chinese restaurant. Tables covered with starched white tablecloths were surrounded by black-lacquered tallback chairs. An enormous and very active fish tank dominated the room. Jade trees grew from colorful porcelain pots. Golden dragons snarled from red-flocked wallpaper.

"I hope you will enjoy your *wǔcān*," she said, extending her hand in welcome.

"Wait," said Rick, "Didn't your father invite you to our . . . wǔcān?"

"Yes, of course he did, Rick. Please remember, it is very important to respect my father by not bringing attention to our family relations," she said. "Please show Mr. Zheng proper respect for the oldest man and host of the luncheon. He will speak first. No talk of business, OK?"

"No business talk?" said Jed. "But I have a lot of questions—"

Jung-Shan touched her lips with her fingertip. "Not during the meal. Food is for enjoyment."

A waiter appeared and bowed. The guys exchanged exasperated, impatient looks, then crossed the room to a table near the window, Jung-Shan at the rear, where the owner of the world's largest bicycle manufacturing company awaited them.

Zheng Min-Chiang stood, shook hands with Jed, David and Rick, and beckoned them to preassigned seats on the left and right. Jung-Shan sat opposite her father. A waiter set teapots on the revolving glass *lǎnduò de sū shān*, or lazy Susan. Mr. Zheng and Jung-Shan began pouring for the guys. Mr. Zheng raised his teacup in a toast, then invited his guests to drink Taiwan Beer with him. Jung-Shan looked around at the guys with her index finger touching her cheek: *just one*. Bottles and glasses arrived instantly, and Mr. Zheng toasted his guests again. Within minutes, waiters began rushing to the table with dishes of food: a cold cucumber and parsley dish, scallion pancakes and fried dumplings for appetizers, followed by the main courses: pork, chicken and beef dishes with mushrooms, green beans, carrots, red peppers, peanuts, each in delicate sauces; eggplant, ma po tofu, steaming bowls of rice.

The lazy Susan went round and round as chopsticks made the entrees disappear. Soon everyone was so full they couldn't eat another bite, then a fish stew was served. "Soup to warm the tummy, make it happy," said Jung-Shan. Amazingly, the guys found room for it. *Fen yuan*, a delicious dessert pastry, concluded.

The plates and dishes were collected and replaced by tea and toothpicks. David noticed that Mr. Zheng and his daughter covered their mouths as they used the wooden picks with their delicately carved crowns. Mr. Zheng turned to Jed and said, "What is your philosophy of bicycling?"

Jed was caught off guard and wondered how he was supposed to respond to such a question. "Well, Smithworks, even before when it was Jet Cycling, was started on the premise that only the highest quality materials and workmanship mattered, and—"

"I will tell you my philosophy, learned from Confucius," Zheng interrupted. "Confucius say, whatever path you take in life, go with all of your heart. This is a good philosophy. I always feel in my heart that the bicycle is my destiny, even when I was a young boy growing up in China. With my heart I followed this path all my life. I give this path to my daughter and to every people who make Joyful bikes, and those people who ride them. I am sixty-seven years old and I still ride my bicycle. I ride my bicycle to live for a very long time." He smiled around the table. "Each year I take my best of Joyful employees on a ride all around the island of Taiwan. I tell them another Confucius philosophy: It does not matter how slow you go, but do not stop. *Ha!*" Everyone laughed with him.

"Around the whole island?" said Rick. "How far is that?"

"I do not know how many kilometers. Each year we change routes. Like Tour de France! *Ha*! In days, it is eight."

"You ride in this race, too?" Jed asked Jung-Shan.

"Yes, of course, but it is not a race. It is a tour. Joyful Bike has words for this in our advertising: 'Love the ride, love life.'"

Jed fell silent, remembering Luke who probably loved the ride more than all three of his mates put together. He looked at the guys and saw that the comment had stirred them similarly as well. "All right, then, to answer your question, Mr. Zheng, my *philosophy* of bicycling is to ride stronger and farther every time I ride."

Three waiters came out with gift-wrapped boxes and set them before each of the guys. "Mr. Zheng asks that you please accept these gifts," said Jung-Shan. They pulled at the ribbons and lifted the lids. Inside were Spandex cycling kits: white bib shorts with red and blue bands around the thighs, jerseys, sweatbands, fingerless gloves. Jed pulled his bright red jersey from the box and held it up: a red Chinese dragon was emblazoned the chest. Rick's and Dave's kits were the same but in different colors, and each bore their names on the left breast. Jung-Shan said, "To celebrate your visit. You will soon see why the dragon was chosen." On the jersey back, in both Mandarin and English, were the logos and names of Joyful Bike and Smithworks, overlaid on background images of Taiwan and the United States.

"Mr. Zheng," said Jed, "we are very honored to receive these gifts." He stood, and so did Rick and David. "Xiè xiè, xiè xiè, xiè xiè," they intoned together and bowed.

Mr. Zheng, smiling, stood and bowed back. He looked at Jung-Shan and said, "Perhaps we take them outside now?"

Jung-Shan nodded with obvious pleasure. "Yes, sir." Turning to the guys, she said, "Please accompany me." They all rode the elevator down and passed out the glass atrium doors. Parked at the curb was a silver GMC Yukon SUV. "This is, I believe you say in America, your ride?" she said.

"You are sh . . . kidding!" said Rick. "It's frickin' gorgeous!"

The driver's door opened and a small man jumped down from the big Jimmy Yukon, grinning. "This is Wei-Ting," said Jung-Shan. "It is possibly dangerous for you to drive in Taipei, and you may not have the International Driver's License." Jed shook his head. "So we have provided you with our expert driver to take you wherever you wish to go." Wei-Ting had walked to the rear of the SUV and pressed the clicker button; the motorized tailgate rose. "Come," she said to the guys, a grin on her face. "Here is the rest of your gift, so you have reasons to wear your new cycling clothes."

Inside were four Joyful racing bicycles. Wei-Ting carefully rolled one to each of the guys: a high-gloss *rosso corsa* for Jed, coal black for David, electric blue for Rick. The colors matched their jerseys.

David stood quietly for a moment, then pointed at the words and Chinese characters on the down tube and said, "Do you get it?" Jed and Rick looked puzzled. "The dragon on our jerseys! Our bikes are branded Dragon Fire CF! Carbon fiber!" Everyone started talking and laughing at once. The guys repeated xie-xie over and over again to Mr. Zheng.

Zheng stood on the sidewalk, arms crossed, smiling, and said, "This is our own carbon-fiber formula. We give it the name Dragon Fire CF. Tubing is especially made in Japan, only for Joyful. Very light, very strong. Very fast! Hahaha!"

"Oh, man," said Jed, looking at his, then Dave's and Rick's. Their names were painted on the top tube. Jed swung his leg over and mounted the saddle; he fit perfectly. Rick and David were similarly engaging with their bikes. Each bike was equipped with the rider's personal preferences in components, headset, handlebars, saddle. "How did you do this?" Jed asked Jung-Shan. "How did you get our fit and gruppos and everything?"

"Me," said Suzié, who had walked up behind them. "I gave them to Jung-Shan."

"You're amazing, Suzie," said Jed, and gave her a hug.

She grinned proudly.

"By the way, where did you disappear to?" said Rick.

"After breakfast, I went to the bank to exchange dollars," she said, handing Jed an envelope of Taiwanese NT currency. "Then I visited my parents. This afternoon I will visit Luke's family, then I will stay with my parents until we leave. I think you will be riding bikes this afternoon?" She grinned at the guys. "It is fine. Lin Bao asks that only I visit today. You may be invited to visit later. Of course, I am available to you at all times."

"I do not think we will ride today, Sun Xiaohui, but please do not let this change your plans," said Jung-Shan.

Suzie made a small bow toward her.

"Your cycling shoes and helmets are in the truck," said Jung-Shan, turning back to the guys. "If you need adjustment, we can provide services at the bicycle shop in the rear of our building."

Rick said, "I can't wait to see how this carbon fiber rides." He ran his fingers over its elegant curves. "What a beautiful bike!"

"We haven't built with carbon fiber," said Jed. "Yet. Perhaps you will tell us more about this process, Mr. Zheng?"

"Perhaps," he replied, sanguine.

Wei-Ting bowed to the guys and made gestures indicating he wanted to put the bikes back into the SUV. Rick raised his and passed it in; Wei-Ting locked it into the fork mount. There was a fourth bike still inside. It was identical, painted an elegant pearlescent white. "Is that . . ." Rick said, choking up, remembering the ghost bike they had placed as Luke's memorial.

"It is mine," said Jung-Shan.

A kind of relief flooded Rick's countenance.

"Thank you again, sir," said Jed.

"You are most welcome," said Mr. Zheng.

Jung-Shan said, "The Dragon Fire CF is the same bicycle Mr. Zheng rides. And as you see, me as well. Now we will drive to the inn so that you may rest for a while. Would you care to have a massage this afternoon? One Path is most outstanding in New Taipei City. Tomorrow we have no meetings, so I will take you bike touring."

"That would be great!" said David.

"Woo-Hoo!" said Rick. "Can't wait!"

"We would love it," said Jed. "The massage *and* the ride tomorrow. We're pretty cramped up from the long plane ride."

"Of course. I shall arrange for massage and return shortly."

As they waited in the atrium for Jung-Shan to return, Suzie said, "I have news about Luke's funeral. Lin family are of the wealthy class. Came to Taiwan from Fujian Province of China during the Yuan Dynasty in the 1300s. Long, long time."

"Like the Pilgrims came from England to America, huh?" said Rick.

"My family is from Fujian also," said Jung-Shan, rejoining them. "Fujian is the closest mainland China province to Taiwan."

"How close?" said Rick.

"Less than one hour by airplane," said Jung-Shan.

"Whoa," said Rick, "Didn't know China was *that* close."

"Soon we will have a high-speed ferry to cross the Strait of Taiwan to Fujian," said Jung-Shan. "It will take only three hours. It is a sign of growing peace between China and Taiwan. Perhaps."

"So, back to Luke's funeral. When?" said Jed.

Suzie said, "That I do not know. Lin Shieh-Seng was family's only son. You have spoken with his younger sister, Lin Bao. I have known her for a long, long time. Lin Bao and Lin Shieh-Seng and I went to grade school together. Family is so sad now because they have no boy to carry on the family name. They wish for a most honorable funeral and so will consult a *zi wei dou shu* master to choose the most auspicious date."

"We know what feng shui is," said David, "but what's the zhway . . . ah . . ."

"It means a astrology reader," said Jung-Shan. "It is from Taoism. Very, very old practice."

"I see. So, like Jed said, when is Luke's funeral?" said David.

"Maybe in one day or two, but probably not. Maybe a month," said Suzie. "Maybe longer. There are not many auspicious dates. It takes the master a great amount of time and concentration on details to choose the right date."

"Sun Xiaohui is right," said Jung-Shan. "Such matters cannot be rushed. Families sometimes wait months for a lucky or auspicious date for a wedding or funeral or important celebration. All depends on the almanac."

"The almanac?" said David.

"The Chinese almanac, every year. Just like a calendar with dates for important celebrations or historic events. For auspicious and, um . . . not auspicious dates."

"Well, sounds like you Chinese have been at this for a while," said Rick, "so I guess you know what you're doin.'"

Suzie and Jung-Shan laughed, and the guys joined in.

"I'd kind of expected we'd attend Luke's funeral while we were here for our meetings," said Jed, "and now we know our business visit has to be extended. And we know nothing about the funeral date. So, maybe we ought to move our return flights out two weeks instead of ten days like we discussed. What do you think, Jung-Shan?"

"Marco Polo said these famous words, 'business done quickly is business done badly.' Yes, two weeks sounds like a better idea. I will call the office and have your flights changed."

"I'll need to speak with my office, too," said Jed.

"I should go back," said David.

"Me, too," said Suzie.

"No, David, I need you here. But Suzie, I agree, you can go back whenever you're ready. We have no idea when Luke's funeral will take place, and I think Gregg could use your help running the shop."

"OK," she said. "I will stay one week, if that is OK with you."

Jed nodded.

Jung-Shan placed a call to Joyful. "I have communicated this decision to my assistant. She will take care of your new reservations."

"I hope she'll take care of communications better this time," said

Jed, grinning.

Jung-Shan's cheeks colored; she leaned toward Jed and said, "You just wait. I will take care of *you*," she said, a smile playing on her lips as she opened the Yukon's passenger door and climbed inside.

Night was falling, but Taipei was still an oven. They sat in a small café, enjoying a light meal of dumplings, potstickers and wontons after their massage.

"That was the best massage I have *ever* had," said David.

"Awesome, that's what it was," said Rick. "Getting a massage through a dry sheet was different at first, but definitely better."

"Why did the masseuse check my pulse?" said Jed.

David and Rick said, "Yeah, what was that about?"

"It is about chi," said Jung-Shan. "Oriental massage practice is to learn your chi from testing your pulse, then working on pressure points to bring your body and spirit into harmony. What we have—had—at One Path is Tui Na massage, acupressure points to, um, bring life to meridians. You know the meridians, yes? They guide the way chi flows through and through. Chinese Tui Na ways are very respected medical techniques, passed down for thousands of years."

"One Path is a classy place," said Jed, picking up the last dumpling with his chopsticks. Jung-Shan raised an eyebrow. "Classy meaning sophisticated. Elegant. It was like a spiritual garden. The waterfall. The Chinese music. The gentle people who work there. But there is one thing I wanted to mention—"

"*Shénme?* I mean, what is it?" said Jung-Shan.

"I'm not positive, but I think the two Japanese information worms came in while we were in the waiting room having tea."

"Before or after massage?"

"Before. Remember, I was sitting next to the tea and water table? I looked up as they walked past on their way upstairs. Short guy with big black glasses and a taller guy. It was just a second, but I'm pretty sure they saw me."

"Oh, sh . . . sugar," said Rick.

"They probably are staying at the Jianguo Hotel, across the street," said Jung-Shan. "It is popular with Japanese tourists. Did you see them leave One Path?"

"No. But remember, we had long massages, an hour and a half. They might have only had theirs for an hour."

"I wonder if they're out there right now, watching us," said David. Everyone cast an eye out to the street.

"I'm tired," said Rick. "Let's get out of here."

Jung-Shan texted Wei-Ting, who was parked somewhere discreet in the SUV. When he pulled up, they ran out, jumped in and sped down Nanjing Road.

MEANWHILE – ROKUYO (LUCK)

"What luck!" said the tall Japanese information worm.

"Fool!" the man wearing black glasses snapped.

"What? Master, this is a lucky day, to find the Americans right across the street from our hotel. This is rokuyo!"

"No, fool, this is tradecraft. I have thought logically about our target and employed my knowledge to determine all possible outcomes. My intelligence-gathering experience made it clear we would cross paths with the target. All that remains now is to act on what we have learned."

"What is it we know, Master?"

"We know there are three American men and two Asian women. One of the women is a leader of some sort. From the taxi dispatcher information last night, we can assume there is another possibly Asian man helping them. We also know from the dispatcher that they are lodging at the business inn in the Xindian District. We know their vehicle is the large American truck. We know there is the truck driver, who we may be able to exploit for our purposes. This big truck is a great mistake for them."

"Because it is so easy to see and follow?"

"Hai, desu." Yes, exactly. "If—when—we go to their place of lodging, we are likely to find this big truck parked there. This would confirm our assumption."

"They must have the big truck for a reason, Master."

"Fool! I just told you the reason. I am certain that within the big truck there is business intelligence. They likely think their assets are safe and secure in it. They may act as if there is nothing of value inside of it. They are foolish to think I do not know they have prized assets in their big

truck that will soon be mine!"

"Hai, Master. Yes. How do we find out exactly what is inside?"

"I am forming a plan. It is actually two plans that are flowing together in my mighty brain. Plan One: We must spread a web of constant surveillance of the big truck until we find the driver alone. Plan Two: We need to compromise the driver in some way into letting us see inside. For that, I am thinking we need a woman. Therefore, put Akiko on the next airplane from Tokyo. I want her here right away."

"Akiko? Why do we need her?" said the tall man. "It would be very costly to buy another airline ticket, and we do not have a sponsor as of yet."

"Idiot! You are demonstrating how pitifully poor is your knowledge of tradecraft. Or of the nature of men. What is a man's greatest weakness? Women! Any man can be manipulated by a beautiful young woman, and I do not need to tell you that Akiko is both young and beautiful. I will bribe the inn manager to give her a housekeeping job. Then she will be able to give us entry to their rooms when they are away. Under my teaching, she can lure the driver into opening the truck. Hai! Get Akiko here at once, then we shall deploy our plan."

"Ah so, that is a very clever strategy, Master. I am certain your plan assures our success. Soon we will know precisely what assets the Americans possess. We will be able to determine their value and then we can offer them to the highest bidder. I think we will soon be very rich!"

"Hai. And so now you see that luck has nothing to do with intelligence work."

The Ride

After breakfast, the four went back to their rooms to change into their cycling clothes. Jed, entering the hotel lobby, found Jung-Shan in Team Joyful pink-trimmed black cycling shorts and a pink-and-mauve jersey. She looked at him over her shoulder, then turned to face him and smiled. She was breathtaking to behold, her feminine curves gracefully pronounced by skin-tight spandex.

"Not polite to stare, Jed," said Jung-Shan, giving him a coquettish smile. "Where is yours?"

"My . . . mine? My what?" he spluttered.

"Your helmet. Your gloves." She pointed at a table. "Oh, look! They are right here. You see, I am taking care you." She gave him a mischievous grin.

"Ah, yeah," he stammered. "Thanks."

Holding the door open, she said, "The others are waiting for their captain outside," delighting in the effect she had on him. Jed grabbed his helmet and gloves and hurried past her.

Wei-Ting drove them from the Serenity Garden inn to Longshan Riverside Park to begin their day's ride. The early August morning was already hot and quite muggy, but once the bikes were rolling the riders cooled right down. Following Jung-Shan's lead, they pedaled the wide paved bikeway north alongside the Tamsui River, warming up, getting a few muscle kinks stretched out. All around them people walked, pushed strollers, sat on benches smoking, gazed at river boats, practiced the ancient Chinese movements known as Taijiquan on the lawns. Cyclists of every ilk rode bikes of every ilk: kids on BMXs, women on rusty clunkers with wire baskets filled with fruits and vegetables, young men on racing bikes streaking along, teenaged girls pedaling in twos and threes, three-wheeled bike-carts transporting cartons of commerce and who knows what else, all cruising along with utter disregard for a left-right traffic flow.

They rode northwards, following the river, feeling the travel tension diminish. The bikes were performing flawlessly. David said, "Hey guys, what do you think of the carbon fiber?" Jed and Rick raised their fists in approbation. "I think we ought to look into this when we get back home."

Jed said, "I keep saying this! I don't know why we haven't already."

"But I told you, a CF fab shop is gonna cost a lot of money," said Rick. "It's a whole different process. Lots of handwork."

David said, "That's true, Rick, but the cycling world is moving toward CF and we ought to, too, before we become heavy-metal dinosaurs. I remember seeing the first CF bike back in the mid-eighties. A Kestrel, I think. A few guys in the MIT Cycling Club had 'em. In fact, I rode a guy's once, a Specialized. I wasn't overly impressed at the time, but this Joyful bike is turning my head."

Jed smirked to himself, *Yeah, like Jung-Shan is turning mine.*

She rode breakaway, five to ten meters in front of the guys, but always close. Her long hair, pulled into a ponytail, fanned in the breeze at her back. Jed had no trouble keeping his eyes on her.

They drew deep breaths to oxygenate their blood, all the while laughing, swilling water, grabbing the lead from one another while taunting the others to catch up, but never once getting ahead of Jung-Shan. They rode through Yanping Riverside Park, where fully clothed people lay sunbathing on the manicured lawns. A young guy with long hair flew a radio-controlled helicopter with great skill, making it dive and swoop and climb, flipping it to hover upside down. A photographer with several cameras slung around her neck shot pictures of three college-age kids, two girls and a guy, wearing matching team kits as they stood astride their bikes. They rolled on, crossing the Tamsui on a bridge ramp designated for bicycles. Rick called out, pointing ahead, "Hey, Jung-Shan, isn't that the Grand Hotel?" She raised two fingers in a V and wagged them. *Yes.*

They rode kilometer after kilometer along the Tamsui until they reached the bright red double-arched Guandu Bridge. Traffic was heavy. "Please be careful and stay in one line behind me," Jung-Shan called out. They crossed to the east side of the river and turned north on Longmi Road, stopping at a rest area on the Gold Coast Bicycle Path where food stands congregated in a grove of banyan trees. Outdoor toilets designed for a person *and* their bicycle stood nearby. Rick said, "I gotta take a picture of this!"

They continued riding through the Mangrove Preserve, crossing over little wooden bridges, the swamps below filled with birds, sharing the trail with scooters, dog-walkers, jitneys and bikes. Boats of all types navigated the river, shimmering in the bright sunlight. Cruising around the BaLi District, Jung-Shan pointed out the beautiful Hanmin Shrine, where they turned and rode back to the BaLi Pier and took the ferry across the river to the Tamsui District, New Taipei City.

The town was filled with interesting shops but the streets grew increasingly narrow, shared equally by cars, scooters, bikes, and jaywalkers. Jung-Shan popped out of her clipless pedals and stopped. "I suggest we walk our bikes." Even that was difficult: the sidewalks were overrun with tourists, shoppers, scooters. They ate some street food for lunch, little *gua bao* sandwiches with a slice of pork and a sprig of greens inside, and refilled their water bottles at the 7-Eleven across Zhongyang Road.

Jung-Shan said, "If anyone is tired, the Danshui MRT station is near. We can ride the train back to Taipei. Bikes are allowed." The guys cried "NOT!" in unison. They remounted and eventually were riding north again, heading toward where the Tamsui flows into the Strait of Taiwan. The river was enormously wide here; they stopped to caffeinate at a Starbucks where they could gaze upon its mighty effluence.

Jung-Shan, "Come. I will show you something special." They swung back on their bikes, still heading north, pedaling along a narrow spit of land with the Tamsui on their left. A beautiful bridge came into view on the right. "This is called Damsui Lover's Bridge," she said. It was pure white, suspended by cables from a single gracefully curved wishbone-shaped tower. "Ready to go across?" she said, smiling. "We must walk our bikes."

"Why do they call it a lover's bridge?" asked Rick.

"The bridge construction started on a Valentine's Day," she said.

"I thought I heard you call it Dam-shoey," said David.

"Yes. Often there are many ways to spell in English," she said. "Danshui, Damsui, all means the same thing as Tamsui. They can sound the same when you speak."

"We have some names like that, too," said David. "Like, the English spell the name of Köln, Germany, differently than the Germans do. They—we—write it like the perfume, Cologne. I know there are lots of other examples."

"Peking," said David. "Beijing."

"Tao, Dao," said Jed.

Crossing the bridge, they turned south and rode back to the Tamsui District. Jung-Shan stopped them at the MRT station plaza and said, "OK, if you are warmed up, want to have some fun?" Straddling her bike she tilted her head, grinned, and shook her handlebars back and forth.

That got a laugh. "Sure!" said Rick. "What have you got in mind?"

"Follow me and you will see!" she said as she clicked back into a pedal and pushed off.

They rode a few blocks south, then Jung-Shan signaled for a left turn. There was a fair amount of traffic, discouraging much sightseeing. Soon they were moving away from city congestion on Denggong Road, which became increasingly rural. The road went up and down—more up than down—tracing a route through hills and valleys as it turned south. Then it became steeper, narrower and more twisty. They took a sharp right turn onto Fuxing Road and began climbing in earnest. Homes and Buddhist shrines sprouted out of the thick semi-tropical forest on the mountain slope; no guardrails prevented a sheer drop on the opposite side. Jung-Shan was still leading, constantly downshifting and standing to pedal the more strenuous climbs. Although it was enticing to watch her lithe body in motion—the smooth rise and fall of her pumping leg muscles, the gentle sway of her hips, her beautiful shimmering pony tail dancing behind her—but the guys instinctively knew everyone had to take their turn pacing the ride. They rounded a nearly 180-degree turn and began another steep climb that slowed all four of them. David called out, "I got it," and jumped into the lead.

Jung-Shan got right on David's rear wheel and began drafting him. "Thank you," she puffed. They formed a single line and took turns in the lead, one after another, sustaining the wind pocket to help each conserve energy. One rider pumped away for a minute or two, then dropped back for the next rider to lead the paceline. Not only did everyone begin to feel better, but the klicks went by much faster. At last they crested the final mountaintop where they stopped to rest, hydrate and take in the view of the rivers and the vast valley below.

"There is Taipei, of course," said Jung-Shan, pointing. "The small river flowing east to west is the Keelung. We will ride to it. The larger one to the right is our old friend the Tamsui."

"Awesome," said Rick.

"Far away you see the mountains?" she said, pointing east "There is Yangmingshan National Park. I love to go there. Once it was a place of living volcanoes!" She swung her arms into the air. "Many rare flowers grow there. Nice place to stay longer." She stretched her arms up again, then out, up, and rotated her shoulders. "OK, all ready for the gift of the mountain?"

"Gift? What gift?" said Jed.

"Every mountain that goes up also comes down. We have now earned our ride down. Please be careful for cars on our narrow road. It is just like the road up. When we reach the bottom, we will arrive in Beitou. It is a nice town with the culture of mineral hot springs for enjoyable health bathing."

"Hey, crazy," said Rick. "I would love to do that! All us would, right, guys?"

"Rick, you are probably only crazy one," said Jung-Shan, laughing, and they all joined in.

The ride down was exhilarating, scary, fun, both hands on the brake levers all the way. They cruised into busy Beitou, its streets clogged with the usual mix of auto, scooter, bicycle and pedestrian traffic. The guys wanted to linger, just to pedal alongside the hot springs stream and the boardwalk beside it where pretty Taiwanese girls strolled with their colorful parasols, but it was late in the afternoon and Jung-Shan said they should keep going.

They followed Daya Road south out of Beitou, eventually crossing a bridge over the Keelung River. They rode a short distance to the Dajia Riverside Park, filled their water bottles and sat on the lawn to rest. Jung-Shan pointed back across the river. "What do you see, Rick?"

"Oh, wow, there's the Grand Hotel again! What a great day! Awesomely great riding and scenery and, wow, just fun!" said Rick. "It's different here, but it's not. I don't know . . . you know?" He looked helplessly at David and Jed.

"I think I speak for all three of us," said Jed, looking at David and Rick, "but Jung-Shan, this Dragon Fire carbon fiber is just, well, I can't say it in a single word. Your frame design engineering is exceptional. The CF ride's smooth, really absorbs the road. It handles beautifully; no work. It's fast, and it responds instantly. I thought our Smithworks bikes were about the hottest bikes on the market, but this Dragon Fire beauty . . . and yeah, it's beautiful, too. It might be as good as our titanium bike with the same gruppo."

"Maybe better," said David.

"Yep, I would agree," said Rick, "Maybe. Even. Better."

"So I guess that means we're in agreement," said Jed, "we look into carbon fiber when we get home?" They nodded.

Turning toward Jung-Shan, Jed said, "What are we doing tonight?"

"We are having dinner," said Jung-Shan.

"Sounds good!" said Rick. "I could eat a horse."

"Oh, Rick! You eat horse?" said Jung-Shan, her eyes widening in mock surprise. More laughter. "At dinner we will be joined by Derek."

"To discuss security, I imagine," said Jed.

"No, Jed. I told you before, no business talk while sharing a meal. But I am concerned about what happened at One Path," she said. "What if we were discovered?"

"I'm a little worried about that, too," said David, "but I have no idea what we can do about it."

"Except wait and see if it happens again, I suppose," said Jed.

"This is not the first time we have had problems with information worms. I have told you this before, too. You will be surprised when you learn how well prepared we are to protect you," said Jung-Shan, getting to her feet. She brushed grass off her shorts and headed toward the bikes. Jed watched her walk away. Every step. Rick gave him a poke and a wink, and Jed got up.

"How long will it take us to ride back to the inn?" David asked as they put on their helmets.

"Oh, one hour, perhaps," said Jung-Shan. "Can you make it?" She smiled, not serious.

"Of course we can," said David. "We're used to four- and five-hour rides. In fact, we were out on a hundred-miler with major mountain-goat climbs just before we left . . ."

The silence that followed spoke for itself. Thoughts of Luke drifted back. Jed replayed the crash scene in his head, a bad, bad movie. He shook it from his thoughts.

Wei-Ting was waiting for them at the Longshan Riverside Park, squatting with two other men, all of them smoking and talking and laughing. He jumped to his feet as they rode up and quickly walked to Jung-Shan. She spoke to him briefly; he nodded, ran to open the Jimmy's rear hatch and began stowing their bikes.

Jung-Shan drew the guys together and said, "Wei-Ting informs me he is confident he has not been followed today. This is a good sign. Perhaps the information worms have not been able to find us after leaving One Path."

"You can just say we shook them off our tails, like American cowboys would say," said Rick, grinning.

"I thank you for teaching that to me, Rick. I'm sure it is simple to translate into Chinese," she said with a withering smile. "Shook them off our tails."

But they had not.

MEANWHILE – A MEETING AT DANTE

"This is all you have for me?" The man with black glasses was staring through the thick lenses at Akiko. They were having tea at Dante, in the same private room the guys and Jung-Shan had occupied two days earlier.

"I cannot find things that are not there!" Akiko said in a huff. *"I tell you again, nothing but suitcases in the Americans' rooms. No papers, no computers, just a few clothes in suitcases."*

"Did you look in the suitcases for secret storage compartments?"

"Of course I did!" said Akiko. *"You told me to look, so I looked. I know how to do this from the times before. All I could find was the little folding phone in the pants pocket."*

"Ah so desu ne, but that did not take any intelligence," said the man with black glasses. *"So what? Any fool could find that."*

"Thank you for the compliment," she snapped back. *"So, I can go back to Tokyo now?"*

The two men chuckled lightly. *"Master,"* said the tall one, *"the mobile did help us. We captured all of its data with the MantaRay machine."*

The man in black glasses, lighting a cigarette, sneered. *"What little was there,"* he said. *"Some phone numbers, some text messages. No email messages, no smartphone information. I am surprised the American uses such an outdated cellular phone. But we will, of course, examine what is in the MantaRay again to see if there is anything useful."*

"We can call the phone numbers and see who answers," said the tall man.

"Hai. Akiko will call the phone numbers," said the man in black glasses. *"Perhaps we can find out who we are dealing with."*

"Ah so, Master," said the other man. "Very clever."

"She will hide surveillance devices in the inn rooms and the truck. She will seduce the driver and learn all the secrets of their business intel. She will be our Kawashima."

Yoshiko Kawashima, the greatest female Japanese spy of World War II. Akiko smiled.

Compromised

It was late afternoon as the four entered the Serenity Garden Inn lobby. They paused to discuss dinner plans. The guys, still doing a bit of jet lag, wanted a shower and a short nap. Jung-Shan wanted to shower, change clothes, and return briefly to her office.

In the elevator they agreed to meet at seven, exited and walked the hallway to their rooms. Jung-Shan opened her door first and waved to the others as they walked past. Jed was about to slide his card key into the door lock when David called out, "Hey! Hey, Jed! My door is open!"

Jed and Rick ran over to him. "My door!" he said. "It's not closed. I just touched the handle and it opened. It wasn't closed all the way. Do you think somebody's been in there?"

"I doubt it," said Jed. "Are you sure it was locked when we left?"

"Yes. Totally certain. I double-checked."

"Could have been housekeeping," said Rick.

"That's true," said David. "Sometimes the housekeepers leave room doors ajar for the supervisor to check."

"Except there isn't a housekeeper or a cart or a supervisor or another soul in this hallway," said Jed. "I think we should open it, but just a little and with extreme caution."

"Spoken like a true US Army intelligence officer," said Rick.

"Knock it off, you idiot," said Jed.

"Yessir, Bossman," said Rick, giving him a left-handed salute.

"Maybe we should get hotel security?" said David.

"We could, we could," said Jed, "but let's take a peek first."

Jed touched the door with a knuckle. It opened halfway to reveal an empty room. "Dave, can you tell if anything's been touched?"

David peered through the open door. His street clothes were lying on the bed. He took a step inside.

"Don't . . . touch . . . anything," said Jed.

David stopped. "My clothes. I left my pants folded and the shirt spread out on top to air out." His pants now lay with splayed legs on top of the shirt.

"OK, come on out in the hall," said Jed. "None of us goes into our rooms. Dave, you stay here and watch so nobody goes in. Rick, go get the house detective to check things out. On second thought, let's go see the manager first."

At the reception desk sat a small Asian man with a wisp of a mustache wearing a short-sleeved dress shirt two or three collar sizes too large. In nervous, broken English, he said the manager had left for the day. Jed asked after Lucy, recalling she spoke English. With some difficulty, the man conveyed that she came on duty at six o'clock—not for two hours. Jed and Rick moved back to the lobby. He said softly, "Let's call Jung-Shan."

"We shoulda done that first," said Rick.

Jed punched in her number on his iPhone.

"Did you tell the front desk clerk what happened?" she said after Jed explained.

"No. He barely speaks English. I just asked for the manager."

"That simple inquiry is likely to attract attention. Do nothing more. Wait in the lobby. I will call Derek, then soon I will come down. We will have an investigation of our own."

Jung-Shan arrived ten minutes later, her hair still wet from showering. As she entered the lobby, she raised her phone to her ear; Derek had just arrived. He beckoned to the guys to follow him outside. "Into the limo," he said, "so we cannot be overheard."

Derek listened carefully as David explained, then said, "I have my doubts this was a housekeeping mistake."

Jed thought about the nervous little man at reception.

Derek's Hong Kong British accent was crisp and confident as he continued, "It's possible the staff were bribed by the information worms to gain entry. Otherwise, who would think this place a hotel? How would anyone get past its well-protected entry? Whomever entered your room was a bit of a tyke for leaving the door off-latch. Yes, we must surmise these same agents have once again found you."

"But how?" said Jed. "We were so sure we ditched those guys at the Grand Hotel."

"Jed, you thought you saw the same two Japanese last night at One Path," said David.

"You're right, you're right," said Jed. "They could have staked us out."

"And then followed the SUV back here," said Rick.

"Either way, they found us. And somehow, they got into this supposedly private inn," said Jed.

"There are several scenarios we might paint," said Derek. "These espionage worms may have bribed a doorman at the Grand Hotel for the taxicab's number, the driver's name. They may have learned where your luggage was taken. They could have bribed the front desk staff here."

"I do not believe that would be possible," said Jung-Shan.

"They could have bribed a housekeeper to let them into your room," Derek continued. "That is quite possible."

"OK, OK, we get it," said David. "Anybody can be bribed."

Derek nodded. "Now let us see if your rooms have been, as we say, bugged." He rose and crossed to the elevator, then stopped. "As I mentioned earlier, the best rule is to say nothing nor to do anything in your room which you do not wish others to know about. This is not merely a suggestion, gentlemen. For protecting your business relationship with Joyful, it is de rigueur."

They stood in the hallway, now speaking in whispers as Derek examined the door handles.

David described for Derek how he had left his clothes; the security expert said, "Again, they are not very professional or they would have put them back exactly as they had found them. Either that was the case or they wanted you to know they can compromise you. But that is less likely. Did you have anything of a personal nature in your pockets? Your passport?"

"I left their passports at the front desk, as was requested, of course," said Jung-Shan, keeping her voice low as well.

"I didn't know you did that," said Jed. "I thought you were keeping them."

"Commonly, foreign travelers are required to surrender passports upon hotel registration for legal purposes," she said. "This is lodging for international executives, so they always collect guest passports. Also for security. Also why they ask for your room key when you leave the inn."

"It's commonly done 'round the world," said Derek, "but rarely in the United States. It is for your protection, so your papers or room key are not lost or stolen. But also to guard against espionage. The government can demand a guest's papers from a hotelier. It is as concerned about spies and criminals as we are. You see, it can cut both ways."

Jed's stomach flopped. He turned to Jung-Shan. "Did you have us checked out before we came here?"

"Of course," she said, "to make sure you were the, um, the correct persons. Who you said you were. There is much information about your company and your photos on the Internet. It was not difficult to verify you."

"You didn't hire private investigators to check us out?"

"No. There was no need. Besides, it would show lack of respect. Joyful would lose face. No. As you see, we have always helped to protect you."

"That's true," said David. "She's mentioned several important things we never would've known."

"Or even thought of," said Rick. "For example, here we are in a hotel hallway while our door locks are being dusted for fingerprints." Derek had finished, but found nothing but smears. "It doesn't appear they entered Miss Lai's room, but they wore cloth or latex gloves when they went in David's. Or yours," he whispered to Jed and Rick. "All fingerprints are obliterated."

"They were in all our rooms," whispered Jed. Derek nodded. "Are there surveillance cameras looking at us?"

"It is unlikely," said Derek. "Not commonly in hotel hallways. Guests would complain. But I want to check your rooms to see if there are any video or audio surveillance devices."

"Wait!" said Rick.

"Quietly, please," said Jung-Shan, holding her fingertip to her lips.

"Sorry. But wouldn't people complain if their room had hidden cameras or mikes?"

"Of course," said Derek, "but how would they know? Surveillance depends upon the art of concealment. Besides, all rooms aren't bugged. Screening is commonly determined prior to making room assignments. If you are, or appear to be, a person of interest, you're assigned a room with surveillance equipment already installed."

"Oh, geez, now we're persons of interest?" said Jed. "So, how do they decide that? I guess I already know the answer."

"From your experience at Narita, I assume," said Derek. "You are also likely to be screened by the taxi driver asking you seemingly innocent questions about your visit whilst driving you to your hotel. You, proudly and rather foolishly, tell him all about your business trip. He makes a phone call or tells the hotel's concierge you may be a person of interest. The surveillance plan is thus set into motion."

"Oh, man, how did we get into this mess? Next thing you know, we'll be suspects in some international spy ring," said Jed.

"No. Please do not have that fear," said Jung-Shan, touching his arm. "It is bad luck."

"That would only happen if you were actually involved in something suspect. Or downright wrongful," said Derek. "You are here on a legitimate business mission with Joyful Bike. Miss Lai told me you might have picked up a tail in Japan. This is not uncommon. Business information pirates will follow you until they are certain about you, one way or the other.

"IMO," said Derek, touching his chest, "you may have communicated that you are not a person of interest because there were no mobile phones or computers or briefcases chockablock with business plans in your rooms. Is this not correct?"

"Yes, I suppose it is," said Jed.

"It's possible the only message you have communicated to them is annoyance and your wish to be let alone. Finding nothing of value, their espionage efforts may end here."

"Ah, there is one thing," said Rick. He glanced at Jed. "I didn't take my phone on the bike ride this afternoon. I forgot and left it in my pants pocket."

"Oh, no!" said Jed. "Did they take it?"

"Nope. Besides, nobody could get into it because I password-protect it," said Rick.

"Oh, well, thank goodness for that," said Jed.

"Unfortunately, a password is not much protection," said Derek. "These people carry laptop computers they can connect to your phone. They can download all its information—email, address book, caller lists, and so forth—without your password. You'd never know they'd hacked into it."

"Well, I still don't think it's a problem," said Rick. "It's not a smartphone and I only use it for voice calls and text messages with Jed and a couple of friends."

"Then it's possible you have not put your mission in terribly serious jeopardy. Please go to your room and get this phone. We'll remove its battery pack and destroy the SIM chip. Henceforth we all will use burners. Disposable phones."

The guys stood silently in the hall, assimilating what Derek had told them.

"Let's check all our rooms," said Rick. "Let's see if there are surveillance devices. If I find one, I'm gonna smash it to bits!"

"No, you are not," said Derek. "The last thing you want to do is communicate to the agents that you are aware of them. We will do nothing tonight. Tomorrow we will depart but will not return. You will go about your business with Joyful as if nothing had happened. This is the safest thing you can do."

"He is right," said Jung-Shan. "Derek is very wise. You should trust him."

"I will check your rooms tonight, though," he said. "In the darkness. I can use a scanner to see if I pick up a surveillance bug. But regardless we do or we don't, I advise against making any business calls or using the Internet from your room. Just don't."

"They can use Joyful phones and Internet," said Jung-Shan. "We know they are secure. As to sweeping rooms, that may not be important. They will keep these rooms, but I will move them to the Crystal Palace Taipei hotel, closer to Joyful offices."

"Indeed," said Derek, "it is certainly more secure at the Crystal Palace. I know the security team there. They would lose much face if agents penetrated their environs. There is no security here at Serenity Garden Inn because they do not believe there are ever security problems. Now we know that to be naive. I would hope today's breach was nothing more than a one-off and does not impugn this fine establishment, but nevertheless I will speak to management about what has happened."

"OK, well, thanks for all this," said Jed to Derek. "It's extremely upsetting, as I'm sure you can guess." Derek nodded. "You know what's really weird? I was an intel officer, responsible for protecting classified information, but we never had to deal with spies like these guys."

Derek gave Jed a lachrymose smile and said, "Sun-Tzu, one of China's greatest generals, said, "One good spy is worth ten thousand soldiers.""

MEANWHILE – ROOM 602, JIANGUO HOTEL

Akiko is pouting, lying face down on one of the beds in the Jianguo Hotel room in which the two agents of espionage are staying. "I want my own room!" she snarls. "I am not going to sleep on the floor like you made me last night, and I'm not going to sleep with you, so get me my own room or I'm on the next plane back to Tokyo!"

The Japanese man wearing black glasses sinks his hand into her soft, thick hair, takes her by the neck and pulls her face to his. It is a beautiful face, with perfect Asian porcelain complexion, but right now it's twisted in pain. "You do not give the orders here, little one!" He thrusts her face down into the pillow until she cannot breathe. She flails until he relents. She lies very still.

"My own room or I will not help you, even if you kill me," says Akiko.

"You will help us, then I might kill you anyway," says the short man. The tall man, smoking a cigarette, smirks. "Now listen to me, Akiko," the man in glasses continues. "These men work for a private security consulting firm in the New Hampshire States. They are in Taiwan on top-secret business for the Federal Bureau of Investigation. We know this, Akiko, because they met with Angela, the Taiwanese lawyer at Narita, and you know what that means. We have followed them and they are covering up everything they do and hiding their computers and acting very suspicious. You know what that desk clerk at the Serenity Garden told you: they are traveling in the disguise of bicycle sports men. You know he said they had secret meetings in Tamsui yesterday. The reason we know they were in secret meetings is because the Americans were in the disguise of riding bicycles, as was the Taiwanese woman. That old fool clerk let us in while they were away. It cost me a very large bribe and

all we got was the name of the false front company in New Hampshire States from the Nokia mobile the idiot left in his room. Now he is afraid to do so again. We may not be able to plant surveillance devices if they find out we were in their rooms. But we know they are staying there, Akiko, and now you have the job of a housekeeper."

Yes, she thought, they know, because I purposely left one of their doors off-latch.

You will make yourself very useful. You will tell us everything they do. You will help us fool their fat little driver so we can put a tracking device on their big truck."

He paused, lit a cigarette, then said, "I always know when there is some intel of value, and these men have just such intel. I know it is intel of great value because it is my business to know these things. We will get their intel, and you, my darling Akiko, will be rewarded with great fortune for your usefulness—"

"If you get me my own room!" Akiko squirmed on the bed and kicked her feet at the man with the heavy black glasses.

"Ii toshi shite, nani yattennda! Gaki ja arumaishi!" Act like a grownup, not like a little brat! "Now get ready to go to work!"

Cognac and Conversation

T he guys had gone to their rooms and showered; Derek had driven
Jung-Shan back to the office. Jed lay on his bed, thinking about
her, about everything, but did not sleep. He didn't believe in worrying,
because his Army experience had taught him worry never solved a
problem. Yet the lesson stuck; every time a troop said, "No worries,"
he silently said, "Right on." Shit happens; you roll with it. You get hit
with an IED, you die or you don't. No point in worrying about that. No
point at all.

His thoughts drifted to his son, how he had worried when he was a
baby and a toddler, worried he might have an accident. Be hurt or die.
Nope, worry didn't change anything.

Jung-Shan and Derek returned to join Jed, David and Rick for dinner. Befitting an inn catering to executives, the restaurant on the third floor was an elegant, labyrinthine series of private seating areas behind hand-painted Chinese panels depicting egrets in flight. Against one wall in each room was a sideboard upon which rested a five-foot tall braided lucky bamboo plant, surrounded by tea, coffee, and an array of wine and liquor bottles. Before it, waiters stood ready to leap into service at a diner's gesture.

The five were escorted to their table and tea served. "May I have a glass of ice water?" said David; Rick and Jed asked for the same. Moments later, a waiter brought three small glasses. Rick lifted his, took a sip, and said "Hey! This is *warm* water!"

Jung-Shan laughed. "Rick, you already know it is customary for Chinese to warm the stomach. It is believed to help digestion. The Chinese believe cold water is not good for internal organs." She signaled to the waiter, who returned. She gave him stern instructions and he returned with tall glasses of water with a few small chunks of ice floating at the top. "You will have to make do this way," she said. "You have a remark in Western culture, when in Roma, do as the Romans, yes?"

Jed laughed. "Yes, we do. It *is* Taipei, not Boston, and I think we can manage so long as it isn't warm water. Right, guys?"

Dinner was *haute cuisine*, Taiwanese dishes served in the French style: delicately braised leg of lamb, grilled green beans, oysters, truffles and whole garlic cooked into a thin crêpe, pan-fried Sichuan-spicy bean curd, sliced sweet potato drizzled with a buttery sauce, and thin slices of tender abalone *en croute*. The head waiter asked for drink orders. Jung-Shan explained all drinks were included in the *prix fixe* dinner, and encouraged the guys to order whatever they liked. They chose wine, careful to resist having more than one glass.

The final course was a large ceramic tureen. "This is delicious sweet potato and lotus seed soup," said Jung-Shan, "to help clear toxins from the body."

Dessert was a Taiwan specialty, *fengli su*, or pineapple cake, served with espressos and cappuccinos. Jung-Shan raised her coffee cup and said, "Pineapple cake comes with a wish for wealthy happiness. To our success!"

"This was a rare dining experience for me," said David, "a delicious dinner but no feeling of having eaten too much."

"Taiwanese cooking is very simple," said Jung-Shang. "We do not eat more than the eye of the stomach says."

"Ha ha ha ha, I like that saying," said Rick. "We Americans could probably learn a lot from you."

"We probably already have and just don't know it," said David. "Jung-Shan, I was wondering how the Spinner tests are going. I sort of wanted to, you know, be there to point out some stuff—"

Jung-Shan touched a finger to her lips and said, "David, you already know it is impolite to discuss business at dinner." David flushed. Jung-Shan smiled. "But the testing is going very, very well. I will make inquiries to see if our engineers will invite you into their laboratory."

The table was cleared. Jung-Shan invited the guys to have an after-dinner Courvoisier; she, Derek, David and Jed sipped theirs politely while watching Rick chug his down in two gulps, then order another. Ten minutes later, Rick declared it was time for bed. David said he, too, wanted to hit the sack. Derek followed, having decided to stay at the inn in case of trouble. After they had left, Jung-Shan signaled the waiter for a second cognac for herself and Jed. They sat across the table from one another, the only thing between them a tiny candle floating on oil in a crystal dish.

"Are you fatigued?" she asked him.

"I'm wired and tired."

"What does that mean?"

"It means I'm–um, full of energy but also exhausted. Both at the same time. It's how we feel after a big bike ride, like today. The adrenaline is flowing, the endorphins are popping, but you've run out of fuel so you want to rest and recharge. That's pretty much it. How about you? Big ride; six hours. Was it a big ride for you?"

"Yes, big, if you mean long, but not hard. Quite invigorating. I know this feeling of the endorphins, too. I like it. Unfortunately, I do not often have the time for riding all morning and afternoon."

Jed leaned forward, his arms on the table. "I wanted to ask you, now that I've had a little time to think about something you said. About how this business espionage, as Angela called it, might affect our business relationship—"

Jung-Shan smiled and reached across the table, surprising Jed by touching his lips with her fingertip. "No talk of business while dining, remember?" Jed smiled. Jung-Shan smiled back. They sat quietly, just smiling at one another.

Jed gazed into her eyes, barely visible in the dim restaurant. "Jung-Shan. I love saying your name. What does it mean? Translated into English, I mean, what is it?"

"Jung means to embrace the whole world. Shan is Chinese for coral.

My parents gave me this name because coral is for happiness, good luck, and strength of character."

"That's very interesting," said Jed. "Um . . . can I add something?" Before she could respond he said, "You have the most beautiful eyes."

Jung-Shan cast her gaze downwards, shielding her eyes with her hand. "Jed, I already told you it is not polite to stare."

"I'm sorry," he said, paused, thought, then decided to blurt it out: "It's just that you're so beautiful. Not just your eyes, but, um, all over. It's hard not to want to look at you. All the time."

"Thank you, Jed," she said, continuing to avert her gaze. "But please remember always, we have a business relationship."

"I know, I know. But I have to tell you, I know your eyes are brown but a few times it seemed like they were green."

"Yes, it is true," she said. "I am surprised you have seen this about me. Chinese guard the eyes because they are for looking into the soul. Maybe that is why Chinese eyes are dark brown. We wish to pull the curtain down!" They both laughed. "An old story is told that Roman soldiers came to conquer China. Soldiers, of course, who took Chinese women to wife. Some had children with blond hair and blue eyes or green eyes." She held her thumb and forefinger slightly apart and smiled. "Most of it was all bred out after two thousand years, but my family line is so very long I think I still have a little bit of the oldest genes.

"I will tell you a secret," she said. "I think green comes to my eyes when I have strong feelings." She quickly glanced up at him, then looked down again. "I cannot let you see if the eyes are green or not tonight," she said, laughing her throaty laugh. It was utterly alluring. She raised her snifter in both hands, sipping cognac. Jed noticed for the first time that her nails were polished but not painted. Her hair fell softly upon her shoulders and down her breast. *She wears no makeup, no nail polish. All natural.*

Jed seized the moment to let his gaze capture her face. Finally she looked up at him, but it was too dark to see if her eyes had turned green. "Are you married?" he blurted out.

"No," she said. "Are you?"

"No. I was once. For five years. Five years ago. We're divorced."

"I was married for one year," she said, looking away. "In England. To an Englishman. We were students together at LSE. He was, to use the British word, insufferable. I divorced him as soon as possible and came home to Taiwan."

"That's funny," said Jed, tasting his cognac. "How was he insufferable?"

"He was a prude. He thought he was an aristocrat because of his family. He treated me like I was something he had purchased, like a beautiful car. He took me to fine restaurants, formal balls, the symphony, the opera. Many high society events. He bought me lots of clothes and jewelry. He told me if I would behave like a good girl, he would introduce me to the Queen."

"Weren't you a good girl? You seem like a very good girl to me."

"Of course I was the good girl, but there was no girl good enough for him. He tried to make me drop out of LSE because business was not what the aristocratic lady should study. I was on the equestrian team, but he said riding a horse was not ladylike and made me stop. All because he was forming me into his perfect wife. Actually, it was his mother telling him to do these things. She opposed our marriage because I am Asian." She raised herself up straight in her seat.

"Sounds like no woman was good enough for her little boy," said Jed.

"She think Asians an inferior race. But more it was about him. He was a control freak."

Jed, silently wondering if Martina ever felt the same about him.

"But you got married anyway?"

"Yes. Once our families began making wedding arrangements, it was very hard to back away. I thought I could make the best of it. No marriages are perfect, after all. But I soon realized how big a mistake this was."

Again, Jed reflected on his own marriage, how it had been hard to reconcile two people with deep-seated athletic prowess and competitive egos. "A . . . *big* . . . mistake?"

Jung-Shan lifted her brandy snifter and took a rather long draught, set the glass down and looked across the dining room, out the French doors, into the night. She was still for a long time. Her fingers remained wrapped around the stem of her glass. Jed reached across the table and touched her hand. He moved his other hand and enclosed both of hers in his. He slid his fingers between hers. He looked at her determined face, staring into the dark night, and saw tears on her cheeks. Tears of sadness? Shame? Clearly, she'd been made to feel she wasn't good enough for the Englishman. Jed wished his heart could leap from his chest and comfort hers. All he could think to say was, "Jung-Shan."

She pulled away from his hands, took her napkin from her lap and dabbed at her cheeks and eyes. "I am sorry," she said. "I should be good Taiwanese girl. Not drink so much cognac. Keep such things to myself."

"I'm glad you could . . . share . . ."

"You were married five years?" she asked, intent on drawing attention away from herself. Jed knew it was his turn to tell his story.

"I joined the Army after I graduated from college," he began. "Like every Smith man before me, I felt I owed my country an obligation to serve. I'd finished my master's degree. Was commissioned an officer. Trained in intelligence work. Sent to Afghanistan. You know I was injured by an IED." She nodded. "Well, they sent me to Brooke Army Hospital in San Antonio, Texas, for surgery and physical rehab. I was there seven months. So long, in fact, that I got promoted to captain while I lay in a hospital bed." Jed laughed a little.

"So, once I was restored to good enough health, I asked if I could get a bike for my leg rehab, and of course they said yes. I got out of that place every day and rode like hell—um, sorry, excuse my French—" Jung-Shan gave him a quizzical look.

"So, I was training like I was Lance Armstrong on the old flat two-lane roads outside San Antone. I was doing twenty-some miles an hour, and here comes this rider pouring it on past me. Not a guy. A she. Had to be going thirty, maybe more. I had to find out who she was. She gave me a heck of a run, trying to catch up with her."

"And that was how you met . . . ?"

"Martina. Marty. Yeah." She was practicing for a triathlon, doing the bike ride segment. I did catch up with her and we started talking. We pretty much hit it off like jocks do—"

"Jocks?"

"Athletes. It's a slang word for athletes. So, I was getting stronger and figured I could do the triathlon, too, and we started training together almost every day. And I did compete in it. I finished about in the middle of the pack, but Marty took second place in the women's group.

"We had a funny kind of relationship. It was all based on physical toughness. We were pretty much always competing with each other, even if it was just in little day-to-day things. Like who could climb the stairs to our apartment faster. Carry the most grocery bags at once. Or clean up the kitchen better. There was always that competitive edge to things. At first I didn't care, but the more we were together the more competitive we got. *I got.*"

Jed leaned forward. "Marty came from a poor family. Her dad was a roughneck. That's a guy who works on the oil rigs. Her mom was a stay-at-home mother of six kids. Marty was next-to-last. She was small and wiry and didn't have an ounce of fat on her body. Lean and mean. And I guess insecure. She took all her insecurity out on the world. Including me.

"But working out with her helped me get rehabbed faster, and for some reason I thought that meant we loved each other. I really wanted her to feel loved too, so I asked her to marry me. We ran away. Eloped. Got married by a justice of the peace in Hondo, Texas, about an hour from San Antone." He stopped speaking and grinned as he recalled, "They had this funny sign at the town limits that said something like, 'This is God's country, so don't drive through here like a bat out of hell.'" Jung-Shan laughed a little. "We spent our wedding night at the Hotel Armstrong. The name was just a coincidence, but it reminded me of Lance Armstrong."

Jed laughed too, and stopped to drink some water. A waiter rushed over with the Courvoisier. They waved him away.

"So I got discharged from the hospital, then from the Army, and Marty and I moved back to New England. She didn't give two hoots about staying close to her family, but I said I did and she was fine with that—at first. We rented an apartment on Marlborough Street in Boston, two hours from my parents up in New Hampshire, and I started looking for a job. Marty got pregnant—well, she was already pregnant before we actually got married—so you know what happened after nine months. John Jedediah Smith the fifth was born."

Jed leaned back in his chair; it was his turn to gaze out into the night.

"Would you like to walk outside?" said Jung-Shan.

"Yeah," he said. They rose; Jung-Shan made a gesture to the head waiter and he bowed. Exiting through the French doors, they found themselves on a stone veranda with steps down to ground level, spreading out into a wide stone walkway that led through a verdant garden and back to the terrace in front of the inn. Jung-Shan put her arm through his and hugged. They came to a park bench surrounding a grand old banyan tree and sat down.

"So, did you find a good job?" she asked, pressing close to him.

"Yes, I did," said Jed, "working in mechanical engineering. It wasn't the most interesting work for someone with a materials science degree from MIT, but it was designing structural components for aerospace, so it was kind of an introduction to bicycle design, at least for me.

"It turned out Martina didn't much like Boston. It was too big, too noisy, too gentrified for a girl from Texas. She didn't like motherhood very much, either. Interfered with her exercise, she said, but also with her ego. But she was good to baby Jed, and he grew and gradually got easier for her to handle. Then—"

Jed's throat caught.

Jung-Shan waited, silent until he was ready to speak again.

"Marty was pushing little Jed in his carriage at a busy intersection. Clarendon and Boylston." Jed paused and exhaled. "In Boston, the law says no right turn on a red light, but a young guy in a BMW came tearing down Clarendon, ran the red light as he whipped around the corner and slammed into the carriage. He missed Marty, but the carriage went flying into the air. I think the cops said fifty-eight feet. Bounced off another car coming down Boylston and threw my son into the side of a parked car. By the time Marty got to him, he was gone."

It was Jung-Shan's turn to take Jed's hand. "I am so very sorry for your loss. I cannot imagine losing a child."

Jed snuffled. "Thank you. It's been a long time. No good to think about the past. Good things will happen in the future. They're happening right now." He poked his finger twice into his palm, as if to assure himself.

He fell silent, then said, "The driver was cited for reckless endangerment. He got a year's probation and lost his driver's license for three years."

"That was all of his punishment?"

"Yep. Rich kid. For a long time I wanted to make him hurt like I did, but eventually I found a way to forgive him. Martina, though, was inconsolable. She blamed everything on herself, but it wasn't the accident she blamed herself for, actually. It was for not loving her son like she thought she should. We stumbled along for another year or two, but as time passed neither one of us—*neither* one of us—could stand the sight of the other. All it made us think about was our lost, dead son. We talked about this openly. Martina was working out harder and harder, spending days and nights at the gym. I hardly saw her. Then one morning over coffee we called it quits. Just like that."

"You became divorced?"

"Yes. And walked out of each other's life."

"Where is she now?" said Jung-Shan.

"I don't know. I found out later she'd been accepted on the US triathlon team. She travels around the world to international competitions. I never hear from her."

They stood up, still holding hands. The garden night was thick with humid air and the sound of cicadas scratching out their love songs and the blinking pinpoints of light from fireflies. Jed lifted Jung-Shan's small hand and kissed her palm. "Thanks for listening. It eases the pain a little more." She took his arm again, squeezing it tightly, as they began walking back toward the inn.

"How long have you been divorced?" Jed asked.

"Long time."

"Do you mind if I ask if you're seeing anyone?"

"No."

"No, you aren't seeing anyone, or no, you don't mind if I ask?"

Jung-Shan burst into laughter, pressing her hand to her lips.

"OK, how's this. Are you seeing anyone?"

"No."

"Good. Next question: How old are you?"

"How old do you think I am?"

Jed stopped and turned toward her. "To be honest, I can't tell. You look so young that you could be twenty. I'm not sure. If I had to guess . . . twenty-five?"

Jung-Shan smiled at him, her dark eyes as bright as her smile. "In *Shēngxiào*—that is the Chinese zodiac—I am a sheep. Now you figure it out."

Kaohsiung

"Hello, Gregg? Hey, it's Jed. How are you? Yeah, I'm great. Everybody's great." The guys were sitting in the white Cadillac limo outside the Serenity Garden Executive Inn. Jed was using the disposable CelloMobile phone Derek had bought each of them to talk to Gregg at the Smithworks office. He had it on speakerphone so Rick and David could join in. "No, no funeral yet. Luke's parents are consulting a feng-shui master to schedule the service. No, Buddhist. What's going on back on the farm?"

"Not much," said Gregg. "Hey, I miss you guys!"

"Yeah, well, we don't miss you," said Rick.

Gregg disregarded the comment and said, "You've had some no-message calls, Jed. I answer and a voice, speaking very softly, asks for you. I say you're not available and she—pretty sure it's a she—hangs up."

"What's the caller ID?"

"Out of Area."

"OK, no worries," said Jed. "Hey, we gotta get going. We're taking the Taiwan High-Speed Rail today to the Joyful factory." Jed paused. "Gregg, don't answer any of our phones. I'll always call you on your cell, like I did tonight."

Jed disconnected the call, switched off the phone, popped the SIM card out and snapped it into pieces.

"What was that about the out-of-area phone calls?" said David. "Who is it?"

"Boys," Jed said, looking back and forth at his partners, "I think our espionage agents are checking up on me—on us—to see if we're here or back home."

"How did they find us?" said Rick. "I mean, your phone number, your name, what—"

"Just a wild guess here, Rick," said David, "but maybe from your cellphone? From my voicemail ID?"

"Aw, man, just because you're paranoid . . . ," said Rick.

Jed said, "But it does make sense to be a little paranoid right now. I've been thinking about this. A lot. I don't think these spies have a clue about what we're actually doing here. I think they just want to find out if we have something valuable they can steal."

David said, "Why would she be whispering, not leaving her name? Maybe we should mention the calls to Jung-Shan. She's been all over this from the start. Or Derek."

"I agree," said Jed. "We'll tell her on the train tomorrow."

The next morning, Derek dropped Jung-Shan, Jed, David and Rick off in front of the Shin Kong Mitsukoshi Department Store on Nanjing Road West. It was nearing ten o'clock, the store's opening time, and at least a hundred people were congregated out front. When the doors opened they merged into the crowd, entered, went separate ways, browsed for ten or fifteen minutes, then took different elevators and escalators to the underground level where they walked through crowded tunnels to the Zhongshan MRT station. Each took a different train several stops, then a taxi to the Taipei Main railway station. Surely if any worms were following, they would have lost their trails by now.

Half an hour later they were reunited, but persisted in tactics to shake off anyone tailing them. Jung-Shan led them through the railway station's complex of passageways, tunnels and escalators, past streams and clots of commuters, to a gated waiting area. An extraordinarily tall young woman in a crisp THSR uniform checked their tickets, boarding passes and passports, and thanked them in English.

"It is about ninety minutes' travel to Kaohsiung City," said Jung-Shan. "We go almost all the length of Taiwan, three hundred sixty kilometers."

"That's . . . about two hundred and twenty-four miles," said David. "In an hour and a half."

"Yes, the high-speed rail is very efficient," Jung-Shan said, "and although it stops at each city on its route, it is only for one minute," raising her index finger, "then off we go again. So please do not get off for any sightseeing!"

At the precise boarding time, a pleasant female voice announced in Mandarin, Taiwanese and English that passengers could now board. They descended an escalator to the train platform.

The HSR train was a sleek silver bullet with an orange racing stripe. A female attendant stood at each entry door, bowing, checking passports and boarding passes once again. Right on time, the train began to move. Their business-class seats were wide and comfortable; within minutes, a smiling hostess pushing a cart with free drinks, snacks and newspapers came through the car.

"What a smooth ride," said David, holding a cup of coffee without concern for its spilling.

"Yes," said Jung-Shan. "Most of the train tracks run on raised viaducts built of concrete."

The guys looked out the windows; the train was picking up speed. Although it was somewhat deceptive, they soon realized they were really flying across the countryside. The train made a brief stop at Taichung, which Jung-Shan said was the third largest city in Taiwan after Taipei and Kaohsiung, and the home of Taichung Bike Week, then continued south.

"Look," said David, pointing at the LED sign above the compartment door. It displayed their speed: 310KM/h. "That's about . . . 190 miles per hour. Did you guys know there are sections of track between Boston and New York that are so old the Amtrak trains have to slow down to, like, thirty miles an hour? That makes the Acela Express trains not much faster than a regular train."

"Huh!" said Rick. "So, big surprise? Most of the world has faster trains than the US. But we have cars, man!"

"Yeah, the great American symbol of independence," said David.

They talked about nothing in particular for most of the short trip to the handsome Zuoyong Station in Kaohsiung. Outside the station, a driver waited beside a boxy black Mercedes G550 SUV sporting Yakima bike racks—one attached to its trailer hitch, the other mounted on the front. "We sometimes take groups of visitors to our factory," said Jung-Shan. "Sometimes more than can fit into this big truck!" she laughed.

"So what do you do then?" said Rick.

"We have three of these trucks," she said.

The driver sped down city streets, passing cars, scooters and bikes, to an expressway, the Mercedes G-wagen sloshing a bit around curves. Traffic was surprisingly light. In twenty minutes they were west of Kaohsiung City in an industrial district. Trucks and smokestacks spewed foul, dark smoke into the air. Vast spaces were filled with ship's containers, stacked six and eight high, with cranes like praying mantises swinging them through the air. They came to an exit, then drove for miles on a frontage road past more of the same until they reached a high brick wall running alongside the road for at least a mile. Finally, they arrived at a guarded gate; beside it, a bronze plaque read "Joyful Bicycle" in Chinese and English. The guards waved them through.

Behind the walls, the Joyful factory was a small city. A three-story-tall fountain stood in the center of a circular lawn as large as a soccer field. Buildings arced around the park-like area, where people relaxed on benches, ate lunch, smoked cigarettes, did t'ai chi exercises. Directly behind the fountain was a Gothic 1930s-style stone edifice. Above it rose a four-story tall tapering tower, a clock at the top. Spanning out to either side were handsome one-story buildings clad in stone and steel, each with a sign bearing a Roman numeral and Chinese characters. Beyond them were massive corrugated steel buildings the size of aircraft hangars with corresponding numbers—the manufacturing facilities.

The G-wagen chugged up the circular drive around the fountain and stopped in front of the old stone building. Jung-Shan jumped down from the passenger seat and the guys began piling out of the back. She turned to them, bowed, and said, "Welcome to Joyful Bike. We are honored you are visiting us and hope you will have your eyes and ears pleasantly satisfied with your visit."

A man came out of the building and approached, bowed and said, "Miss Lai, it is good to see you again." Jung-Shan bowed back. He tipped his head and shoulders toward the guys: "Welcome, Smithworks executives."

"Xiè xiè," she said. "This is our factory manager, Mr. Gau Tai-Ping. He will give us the tour of the factory. His English is excellent. Better than mine, you will see!" She glanced at Rick, then introduced the guys. Everyone began shaking hands.

"Hey, good to meet you," Gau said. "Please call me Ping. Ah, first, may I say how sad all of us at Joyful Bike are for the great loss of your partner, Lin Shieh-Seng. I had the honor and the pleasure of speaking with him on the telephone many times. He was brilliant. We will miss him very much." Everyone nodded in a moment of silence. "I'll give you an overview orientation first. You probably guessed this is our headquarters building. It's a Taiwanese historical site, because it was actually a train station. The tracks are still here so the train can pull up behind the manufacturing buildings and take our bicycles to market."

"The clock tower reminds me of a New England church steeple," said Jed.

"Hǎo, Hǎo," said Ping. Yes. "So travelers could locate the station— or the church from a distance, and also see the time." He pointed up at the clock. "The clock face is on all four sides." He turned and swept his arm. "Here we have eight factories, four on each side. We make three different types of Joyful bikes in metals: road bikes, mountain bikes, cross bikes. The fab for carbon fiber is the smaller building over there. We make OEM bikes for five brands, all sold outside Taiwan in China, United States, Canada, Europe. We have the highest respect for privacy of the intellectual property of our OEM business customers."

"Hey, your English is really good," said Rick. "How did you learn to speak so well?"

"I lived in America for eight years," Ping said. "I went to college at Carnegie Mellon University."

"Wow, man, I'm impressed," said Rick.

"You guys are all graduates of MIT, right?" said Ping.

"Yep, that's right, all of us SBs, Jed and me MBAs and David a combined MBA and Master of Science," said Rick, trying not to think about Luke. "What about you?"

"Undergrad and Masters in mechanical engineering. I took a Ph.D. at Wharton in strategy and technology innovation management and analysis and logistics. Then I worked. I learned steel in Pittsburgh, learned bicycles at Trek in Milwaukee, Wisconsin. Then I came home to work at Joyful. I speak five languages.'"

"Whoa! You are the man!" said Rick.

Ping bowed and smiled. "Today, I will only take you only to Joyful facilities. No mixed OEM manufacturing lines. As I said, we honor our customers' intellectual property privacy rights. OK?"

"Sure, it's totally OK," said David. "If we partner with you, we'll expect the same. But," he said and paused, "I would like to visit your CF fab."

"We all would," said Jed. He hooked his thumb at David and said to

Ping, "Dave's the manufacturing guy at Smithworks. He wants us to get into carbon fiber."

Gau Tai-Ping looked at Jung-Shan, who nodded, then he looked back at the guys. "Of course. We will have much to discuss," he said. "Let's go. Lots to see."

As they entered the first building, marked 1, an electronic display board lit up reading

Welcome

Jedediah Smith, David Bondsman, Rick Saundersson

Smithworks Bicycle USA

"We have been in business since the year 1953," he continued, leading them through a Romanesque portal to an indoor/outdoor patio. The Dragon Fire CF was on display. "Our first bikes were for Taiwan and China, but soon we were making bikes for Japan. Then a Japanese bikemaker asked us to design and make a racing bike to export to the US, because there were no American racing bikes, only English or Italian or French."

"The Yoshigawa," said Rick.

"Yes! So you already know that Joyful is good at this bike stuff. We are a Taiwan Tiger!" Ping was grinning.

"They have learned much already from Mr. Zheng and a visit to our history museum," said Jung-Shan.

"Of course," said Ping. "We also manufacture in China. We own two leading brands in the US but—" he said, "I cannot tell you their names because then I would have to—"

"Kill us," Rick chuckled.

"Ha-ha-ha!" Ping laughed out loud.

"But we can make an educated guess," said David. "What is a Taiwan Tiger?"

"See the counter there?" Ping was moving on. He pointed to an LED display; numbers clicked up every several seconds. "This is our daily production counter. This counter clock is displayed everywhere in the factory. Just seeing the production counter is a reminder for workers to stay on schedule. Building 1 manufactures between five hundred and six hundred bikes a day. That's a lot."

"Yeah, sure is," said David. "We make two a day."

"What's behind that door?" said Rick, pointing to a steel door with a sign that read NO ENTRY.

Ping smiled and said, "That is the testing laboratory. I understand your Spinner has become the focus of the engineers behind those doors. Now please follow me." He led them outdoors. Small electric pickup trucks moved quickly between buildings, replenishing cranksets, headsets, handlebars, components, tires and tubes. He pointed east at a large tract of land where construction was underway. "The building under construction is for the NewBike." He looked introspectively at the foursome. "It's my understanding we are going to have this brilliant new technology of yours to make it possible to produce more profitable bikes for us. We are certain the NewBike will be very popular for citizens to ride in the USA and other countries."

"And in Taiwan, too?" said Rick.

"Of course in Taiwan, too," said Ping.

Rick exchanged smiles with the guys, Jung-Shan and Gau Tai-Ping.

Ping took them on a walking tour that ended at the cafeteria. "I will drop you at the CF fab after lunch, but now, please excuse me to attend to business while you dine." The food was delicious. As they sat sipping tea, Jed told Jung-Shan about the anonymous phone calls to Smithworks and what he surmised.

"I think they got into Rick's cellphone, one way or another, and saw all the text messages and phone calls to me at Smithworks."

"Or maybe saw nothing," Rick added.

Jung-Shan frowned at Rick. "That is unlikely. Rick, they are not stupid. After they exploited your phone contents, they probably used the Internet to learn what a Smithworks is. All they need is one little clue. One clue on the internet leads to another and another." Jed could sense her suppressed anger. "This must stop. We must talk to Derek when we return to Taipei. We must put a stop to this. At once."

The FUD Factor

The late afternoon sun hung low and hot outside Jed's window as the THSR train sped north. Jung-Shan sat curled up on the seat beside him, her head resting on his shoulder, fingers entwined in his. It felt good to be here, in this country. Even better to be with her in this moment. Yet troubling thoughts kept trampling his good feelings: thoughts about the information thieves. Had it started in Lincoln with the truck driver killing Luke? Were Luke's hit-and-run and the day-in, day-out surveillance that began with Angela two completely separate and coincidental events? Did the agents learn anything about the Spinner from reading Rick's text messages or phone numbers on his cell? Were their rooms in the executive inn compromised—as Derek said, bugged? Maybe, but they hadn't discussed business there. Regardless, not Jed, nor any of them, knew to what lengths these information worms would go to steal their IP. Was this the cost of doing business in the highly competitive, fast-paced, big-bucks circles of international business? If so, Jed wondered if it was worth it.

He turned his head, resting it on top of Jung-Shan's, and closed his eyes. It was tiring to have this dread running through his mind and heart all the time. It reminded him of the constant, sometimes panicky dread that gripped him when he had been an Army second looey, taking his squad out on recon missions in Afghan'. The inescapable fear of being injured or killed. The queasy feeling when they were out on routine patrols in the Humvee, wondering if the next pothole hid an IED. Which, of course, was basically what happened to him and the two new hump-a-lots. Not in the Humvee, but when the patrol dropped them off to set up night-vision surveillance. Digging a foxhole in the side of a sand dune where they would be hidden from view, partially sheltered from the wind and cold. Perhaps comfortable enough to get through the night. Except they didn't. Who would have thought one of them would strike an unexploded IED with his entrenching tool? Why was the damned thing buried in a sand dune, sixty feet from the road?

Ah, thought Jed, *the same questions, just different circumstances. Why ask why? There was no "because" answer; it just was what it was.* He survived the explosion, as did the two grunts, probably because the sand absorbed a lot of its impact, but there was enough damage to send them all home on medical. He was the only one with a shrapnel wound, but he survived it.

He would survive this business espionage terrorism, too. He was a soldier; an intelligence officer. He had been trained in humint. He'd executed black bag ops. *So why am I cowering and cringing at this business espionage?*

Time to cut the crap. I've had enough. I'm not gonna take any more. Jung-Shan and Derek and I can handle this problem. Jed began digging back into his intelligence training, thinking about how to apply it in the present situation. He dissected the problem over and over, viewing it from different perspectives, assessing what he knew to be true as opposed to conjecture. He began to see the problem more clearly. Not only the problem, but possible solutions. These agents were clever— perhaps cleverer than even they realized—because they had introduced a huge FUD Factor into the game.

Fear, Uncertainty, Doubt. The FUD Factor created a totally defensive mentality. The more he thought about it, the more Jed realized his intelligence training could help him devise an offensive strategy that wouldn't antagonize the agents or make them more curious or aggressive, but would instead lead them to conclude there was nothing of interest here. The first step was to think like one of them. Take their espionage operation apart, piece by piece. Then he could analyze it like the counterespionage intelligence officer the Army trained him to be.

Oh, it had been a while, for sure, but a soldier never forgets his or her training. He just had to bring it back up to the surface of his consciousness. Make it operational again. Jed realized he'd actually lost a lot of that power over the years as he turned his attention to cycling and running a business. Well, now the business needed him to lead with his counterespionage experience. Besides, he'd forgotten his family heritage, one of strong-willed men who forged a way of life out of the New Hampshire wilderness. All he had to do was look at his father and his achievements. Now it was Jed's turn. His will was his Way. He could do it. *I'm gonna do it. By god, I have to do it.*

Darkness had fallen, obliterating the horizon between earth and sky. The train sped almost soundlessly north into the night. Jed lifted his head slightly and looked at Rick and David across the aisle, sound asleep. *I love these guys. I need to take care of them, like I took care of my troops. Well, better than that, I guess. Careful now, don't take all that on your shoulders again. Worked that all out with the Army psychiatrist. It wasn't even* your *shovel that hit the IED.* Nevertheless, he'd brought his best friends from college into this business, and they were his troops, his responsibility. And now, so was this beautiful woman sleeping on his shoulder. Here he was, already thinking of her as his to protect, his to care for. He'd brought her—in fact, her entire company—into the business espionage danger zone. *Shit, I've done it again. Maybe not my fault this time either but it's still my job to do whatever it takes to bring them back to safety.*

Jed recalled how much fun they'd had that afternoon in Kaohsiung, following the Joyful factory visit. They'd been driven back into town where they happily got out of the boxy, uncomfortable G-class Mercedes beside Lotus Lake and climbed into a pair of Joyful three-wheeled jitneys awaiting them. A strong man, handsome save for the hairy mole on his chin, pedaled Jed and Jung-Shan around the area adjoining the lake for a while, but before long they all wanted to be walking.

They bought bottles of water and set out. "What's that?" said David, pointing toward a massive tiled-roof building near the lake. Jung-Shan said it was a Confucius temple. "A Confucius temple? There's more than one? Are those temples too, further down the shore?"

"Yes, a Confucius temple," she replied, "No, not the others. They are called pavilions, where different Chinese ancestries are celebrated. You will see. There are many Confucius temples in Taiwan. Also in China. In Qufu, Shandong Province, is the original Temple of Confucius. Here you see the Kaohsiung Confucius temple. Most Chinese cities have one because almost all Chinese respect his wisdom. He guided Chinese culture, just the same as your Socrates or Plato."

They walked to the temple. Hundreds of small red wooden plaques were tied with ribbons to a nearby tree. "These are wishing plaques, to honor the great Confucius," said Jung-Shan. "People buy one, write on the plaque a thanks, a wish, a prayer, their love for Confucius, and tie it in this apricot tree. You can put your plaque just about any place, really." Nearby on the stone plaza, a woman at a cart sold them each a plaque. They returned to tie them in the tree's branches. "Under the apricot tree is where Confucius taught his students. The fruit is very delicious, like his teaching!" She smiled.

A young Asian woman wearing a plaid mini-skirt over black leggings, a snug-fitting Bad Company T-shirt and flip-flops, her black hair cascading to her waist, walked up. She tied her plaque in the tree, then stood for a long time with her hands together in a prayerful pose before leaving. Rick stared after her, then turned to the others and said, "Did you see her? Man, she's the most beautiful girl I've ever seen! Ah, present company excepted, of course."

They walked around the temple, which reached to the lake edge. "You see all these lotus plants in the water?" said Jung-Shan. Indeed, there were thousands upon thousands of them, their broad leaves floating on the surface, their flowers in bloom everywhere. "The lotus is just like people. All of life loves to be close to Confucius."

They walked back to the foot of the broad steps leading inside the

151

temple. A number of people stood around an elegant incense brazier burning joss sticks. The guys joined the crowd and lit a few, then put them in the brazier. The air grew thick with smoke. A Chinese man standing next to Rick spit on the ground near him. Rick looked at him as the man continued to feed incense to the brazier. A minute later he spat again.

Rick turned to Jung-Shan and said, "Is this guy spitting at me because I'm American?"

"No, Rick, he is not. It is very common for Chinese to spit. Probably because of breathing the bad air."

"Well, that's good to know, because I was about to punch his lights out."

"To punch his lights out?" said Jung-Shan. "I don't—"

"Never mind," said an embarrassed Rick.

Leaving the Confucius temple plaza, they walked along the shore, stopping at a street cart to eat *hóng dòu bing*, then turned onto the joyously decorated promenade to the Pei Chi Pavilion upon which sat the enormous figure of Xuantian Shan Di, the Taoist god of war. They walked past the octagonal Spring and Autumn Pavilions which David had asked about earlier. A huge dragon, some kind of god astride it, stretched in front of the towers, reflected perfectly on the surface of Lotus Lake.

Further along stood the Dragon and Tiger Pagodas, elegant twin seven-story hexagonal buildings of Chinese gingerbread. They were brightly painted in red and yellow with delicately carved tiled roofs tapering to golden spires. Docks connected each to shore; People entered the mouth of the tiger on the right and exited the dragon's maw on the left. The heads were enormous. The tiger bore its native stripes, while the dragon was painted in a riot of primary colors.

"Are these religious creatures or temples or what?" said David.

"No, not really," said Jung-Shan. "They are called Dragon and Tiger Pagodas. Kaohsiung City built them for tourists to enjoy."

"Oh, like Disneyland?" said Rick.

"Nooo," said Jung-Shan, looking like she didn't want to say more. "They are to remind people of the older culture, but they are not religious temples either. Follow me." They began walking toward the Tiger Pagoda.

"Then why do they look like religious temples?" asked Rick, falling into step.

They passed through the tiger's mouth and stopped before entering the pagoda. "It is simply traditional historic design," she said. "In ancient days, all buildings looked similar like these. We discussed this once before. The dragon MRT station." She paused. "To your eyes, yes, the pagoda probably looks like a temple. Very similar, yes, especially because they look like bright and colorful Taoist temples, which are more colorful than Buddhist temples."

"What's the difference between Buddhist and Taoist?" said Rick. "What are you?"

Jung-Shan paused, then said, "For visitors, it is good luck to go into the tiger mouth first, walk to the top of pagoda, go back down, go into the Dragon Pagoda, go up and go down, then out the dragon mouth." Needing no further encouragement, David and Rick moved more quickly than Jed and Jung-Shan, who shortly found themselves alone at the top of the Dragon Pagoda.

They stood looking out at the other pavilions along the shore, the Confucius temple on the nearby peninsula, the tall buildings of downtown Kaohsiung on the other side of the lake. A light breeze blew off the water, a sign the day was cooling. Jung-Shan lifted a hand to brush her long hair out of her face and turned to look up at Jed. He bent toward her. They kissed. It was a gentle kiss, full on the lips but not long, yet it lingered in their smiles as they walked down, holding hands, out the dragon's mouth and across the street to the row of tiny stalls, each one selling the same exact kitschy souvenirs and trinkets.

Danger on the Streets of Taipei

Now, later on the train, Jed was still feeling their first tender kiss again and again. He finally joined his friends in sleep, waking as they arrived at the Taipei Main Railway Station. Following Jung-Shan, they made their way through the crowds. "Please be alert for pickpockets," she said.

Rick said, "I never saw so many rude people, always banging into you and crowding you out. They can't all be pickpockets!"

"You're just tired, Rick," said David. "Chill."

"Follow me," said Jung-Shan, "Wei-Ting is waiting for us." They reached the street and headed for the small car park. "There he is," she said, pointing into the darkness, and sure enough, there was their silver Tahoe. As they approached, they saw Wei-Ting standing near the driver's door with someone, moving his arms and torso in animated fashion. Closer now, they heard him speaking loudly, excitedly; he was chatting up an Asian woman in a skintight sheath dress. She was about as tall as little Wei-Ting himself.

Jung-Shan spoke sharply to him in Chinese. He and the woman looked at her. Wei-Ting stopped speaking; Jed could see the open hatch door. Apparently Wei-Ting had been showing their bicycles to the woman. There was movement at the rear, and Jed stepped smartly toward it, Rick right on his heels.

Two Asian men were peering in through the hatch. One wore glasses and held something in his hand; by the dim light from the overhead, Jed recognized a smartphone with a photo of the bikes on its screen. "What are you doing?" he said in a loud, authoritative voice. The men jumped back; the taller one cracked his head on the overhead hatch door. They said nothing. Jed said, "You want to see our bikes? OK, take a look." He reached in, unlatched one, and lifted it out.

By now, everyone had congregated at the rear. Wei-Ting was speaking in a rapid jumble to Jung-Shan, but she was ignoring him. The woman stood between the two men, who were examining the bike. Jed was saying, "You see? Just a plain bike." He threw a leg over the top tube and wiggled the handlebars. "See? Hold the handlebars. Feet on the pedals. Ride the bike." The woman began translating what Jed said to the men. Jung-Shan looked at her, then the other two. *Wasn't she speaking Chinese?* thought Jed. *Perhaps not; was she translating his English into . . . Japanese?* He got off and pointed to the front brakes, squeezing the lever. "Brakes." He pointed to the derailleur and said, "Shift." He picked the bike up and let it drop a few inches back to the pavement. "Tires." He stared at each of the three faces, which were staring at him like he was nuts. "See? Look? Touch? OK?" Jed grabbed the woman's hand and made her grasp the top tube, then paused to stare at her impassive face. "OK? OK?"

The three looked at him, but apparently understood "OK." Each nodded.

"Now GO! GO!" said Jed.

The woman translated. The threesome turned and walked away.

"Leave us alone!" Rick called after them.

The woman translated again. When they were out of sight, Jed looked at the others and laughed. Everyone joined in. Wei-Ting scurried to Jed's Dragon Fire CF and said, "Excuse me, Mr. Jed, I will put back." He turned to Jung-Shan and bowed. "So sorry, Miss. So sorry. Very pretty Japanese lady—"

Jung-Shan spoke rapidly and sharply to him. He shut up and got to work.

Jed led the others a few meters away from the Jimmy. "Don't say anything about this in the truck," he said in a low voice. "Derek said they might have planted a bug in it. Talk about being hungry, getting dinner, bike-riding, something like that."

"Didn't Wei-Ting just say the girl was Japanese?" said David. "I thought she was speaking Chinese."

Jung-Shan said, "I think she speaks Japanese *and* Chinese. It may be difficult for you to tell the difference. Many people speak more than one language, of course. We will go to dinner now and discuss this."

They got in the Jimmy and drove away. Jung-Shan sat shotgun, firing directions at Wei-Ting to turn this way and that. They stopped near the end of a tiny narrow street and parked, waiting to see headlights appear behind them, but none came. Finally, Jung-Shan said, "I think I remember the way. Follow me." They climbed out. Wei-Ting drove away and she walked them halfway back down the street, took a few steps into an alleyway and entered a nondescript restaurant.

"We cannot know if we are in danger now," she said as tea was served. They were in a tiny cafe with only eight tables; it would be impossible to enter without being seen. "Jed, you were very convincing to say we have nothing they want. I do not know what Wei-Ting said to them. He told me they had only just arrived. The men got him to open the Jimmy somehow, but he talked to the girl only. All romantic talk, he said. I hope he is telling the truth, but we cannot be sure. He has a good heart, but he is Chinese and will always try to save face."

"Thanks," he said, "and of course you're right. By now, they might have several pieces of useful information about us. We can't know for sure. One thing they know is that Wei-Ting is a weak link."

"What do you mean by weak link?"

"He has several," Jed explained to her. "One, they obviously saw how easy it was to distract him with a pretty woman. Two, those men—I'm convinced it's the same two as before—had time to install a GPS tracker or a listening device in the truck. Three, they know it's our car, and four, if Wei-Ting hasn't already told them where we're staying, it's now likely they can surveil or track us and find out anyway. Which leaves us with this question: Do you think it's safe for us to continue staying at the executive inn?"

"I am sorry. It has been such a busy day that I have forgotten to share this important message. You are now staying at the Crystal Palace Taipei, as we had discussed. It is near the Joyful building. All has been arranged. We will leave your luggage as if you were still in residence, but you will not return to the executive inn. We will buy you new clothes—and suits," she added with a wry smile. "All your business documents and Spinner parts and Rick's computer remain in my office safe. They are, ah, as safe as possible. Only two people have my office and my safe codes, Derek and myself. They are in our memory, not written down. Not even my assistant has this access. The hardest thing to know is if these information worms will still always follow us. Trying, always trying, to learn something." She fell into thought.

Jed said, "I think our showing them the bikes, that we have nothing to hide, was good tonight. We're just Americans here to ride bikes. But we need to keep this up if they have a tracker on the Jimmy. We can keep trying to elude them, but I'll tell you, as a way of doing business, it stinks."

"I think the more we try to shake them, the harder they'll try to get to us," said David. "Yes, we're here to ride bikes. Yes, we own a bicycle company. Yes, we are visiting Joyful. So what? We just keep on doing our thing."

"You're right, Dave," said Jed. Everyone nodded. The door opened; Jed looked up to see a couple enter the restaurant and take a table across the room. "Oh, man," he said. He looked at Jung-Shan. "Don't look up, anybody, but the Japanese woman just came in. The guy with her is one of the worms."

"So, it seems possible they did plant a GPS device on the Jimmy." said David.

Rick said, "Well, I don't know about you guys, but I've had enough. I'm gonna put an end to this right now!" He smacked his left fist into his right palm and started to get up.

"No, no, no, you're not," said Jed, pulling Rick down. "Cool it, will you? You want to start a fight and get us all arrested? We're in a foreign country, Rick! Geez, man, you can be so hotheaded!"

"Sorry," said Rick, "but I can't help it. I really hate feeling like this and I really, really hate those ffff . . . worms for putting us in this spot."

An unease settled over the table. "We should leave," said Jung-Shan.

"No, wait a minute," said Jed in a low voice. Then: "I thought about this a lot on the train. I didn't think we'd be implementing my plan tonight, but OK, here we go. We'll stay right here, have our dinner and ignore them. Now is the time for each of us to act like counterespionage officers. Proactive, not reactive. Pretend we don't recognize those two. We're just enjoying dinner after a long train ride. Needless to say, we don't talk business." He winked at Jung-Shan.

"After dinner, we still go back to Serenity Garden. Tomorrow morning we'll go out riding. They won't be able to tail us, and poof! We just fall off their radar screen. Maybe it'll finally occur to them that we're just a bunch of guys visiting Taiwan to ride bikes and now it seems we've left. That's it. That's the plan." He looked into Jung-Shan's eyes, then David's, then Rick's. Each nodded their agreement.

Two waiters began delivering food. Jung-Shan described the dishes as they were placed on the small table, alongside bowls of steaming rice. "This is called *guancai ban*. It is a chowder in a bread bowl, therefore sometimes called coffin bread," she said with a deadpan look. They all laughed.

"Ummm, it's delicious. I've had something like this at a deli back home," said David.

"Deli? What is deli? Oh, I know. This is the beef dish," she continued. "Next is the very special Taiwanese pork sausage stuffed with rice. More dishes are coming. All good. You will see, it is the truth when my people say food is god!" She laughed again and they all joined in, surely confounding the spies across the room.

Wei-Ting was waiting in the executive inn turnaround at eight o'clock the next morning. "Please accept apologies for last night," he said to Jed as he jumped down from the Jimmy. "So sorry, Mr. Jed, sorry sorry sorry." He took Jed by the arm and led him around to the rear of the SUV. "Wei-Ting like to ask you lady question. Japanese lady come to talk to Wei-Ting. Wei-Ting think Japanese lady very pretty. You think lady is maybe interested in Wei-Ting?"

Jed stood looking at him, trying to decide whether to laugh or cry.

Wei-Ting drove Jed, David and Rick north into Taipei while Jung-Shan remained at the hotel; she would take a taxi to the MRT station and go into work later. The big Jimmy was a formidable presence in congested morning traffic of scooters, buses, autos, taxis; Jed kept thinking they ought to be in a less noticeable vehicle, but such a suggestion might offend Mr. Zheng. *Besides, I need to think of it as an offensive counterespionage tool.*

Per the plan, Wei-Ting stopped again and again: a tiny alleyway stall for a Taiwanese fast-food breakfast of *you tiao*, fried dough rolled into a stick and dunked in sweet soy milk, and fresh-brewed coffee, followed by a short visit to the Guang Hua electronics marketplace, six stories tall (not yet open); a superstore selling scooters, motorbikes, and all types of bicycles and crazy helmets (too small); a loop past the Grand Hotel and a tour of the nearby Dalongdong Baoan Temple and neighboring Taipei Confucius Temple, with its array of ceramic creatures lining the red-and-blue roof eaves. Just a bunch of Americans, sightseeing.

Wei-Ting parked at the information center at the Jiantan MRT; the guys went inside and stayed a while, watching people enter. "I really think this is a beautiful subway," said David.

"Just keep your eye peeled for those information worms," said Jed, but no one they recognized—although it was a daunting task—followed.

"OK, shall we administer the *coup de grace*?" said Rick. The others nodded. The rode the escalator back to the street, climbed into the Jimmy, and Wei-Ting expertly drove them through a convoluted network of overpasses and underpasses, stopping at the outskirts of Dajia Riverside Park near the stunning Dazhi Bridge. Still no cars or taxis on their tail. They got their Dragon Fires out, rode to the bridge and crossed over the Keelung River. The segregated bike route was as wide and well-marked as were the lanes for cars on the opposite side of the concrete barriers. They could see the Keelung flowing into the Tamsui.

"Boy, I gotta say these people build beautiful bridges," said David, "and take bike travel into full consideration when they do, too."

"This is for all two-wheeled vehicles," said Rick, pointing at a sign. "Scooters, too."

They rode the north side of the Keelung, kilometer after kilometer, crossed the river again, and rode back on the south side, eventually passing beneath the Dazhi, still on the bike route, diverting through busy streets and a congested underpass to emerge on the Tamsui Riverside Bikeway. They turned south toward their rendezvous with Wei-Ting at Longshan Riverside Park, as before.

He drove them to the unmarked Crystal Palace Taipei Hotel underground car park entrance on Zhong Xiao Road, around the corner from the hotel on Linsen. Although the Jimmy might be bugged,

Jed thought it would be difficult if not impossible to get a tracking signal in the vast underground warren. They walked through the car park and several tunnels until they reached the Crystal Palace, then continued another city block through the underground shopping mall until they reached the elevator entrance to the Joyful Bike building, an unmarked steel door with a numeric keypad next to it.

They were met in the Joyful lobby by Derek Hurst, who escorted them through security and up to the eighth floor, where they entered the executive conference room. He closed the door and leaned back against the conference table, an unhappy look on his face.

"I understand there was a security breach last night at the train station," he said. Jung-Shan had already explained, but the guys added their versions. Jung-Shan's phone pinged. "Excuse me, I have been called by Mr. Zheng," she said and left the room.

Jed said, "I don't know if they put a tracking device on the Jimmy or not, but I do know they followed us to our restaurant, which was not otherwise easy to find."

"We'll run a sweep on it," said Derek. "Where was it parked last night?"

"Outside Serenity Garden. Wei-Ting dropped us off and parked."

"If they followed us this morning, we shook them," said Rick.

"That's good, but I'm a bit more concerned about the elicitation."

"Elicitation?" said Rick and David at the same time.

"It's when the information worms trick the target into revealing information," said Derek. "Precisely what the Japanese woman did—or was attempting to do—with Wei-Ting last night. We term the subject of an elicitation a *mark*."

"Wei-Ting is still her mark," said Jed. "Just this morning he asked me if I thought she was, you know, interested in him."

"This presents a conundrum," said Derek, shaking his head. "On the one hand, he poses a serious security risk and we should relieve him of his duties immediately. On the other hand if we do so, it signals that we know he's been elicited. That increases their interest and ups the ante for their getting to our IP."

As the men pondered their options, Jung-Shan returned. "The meeting is canceled," she began. "Taiwan Micronics and TII both decline to meet today. Due, they say," she caught her breath, 'to other pressing business matters.'"

"What?" said Jed, rising to his feet. "What business matters could be more pressing? Do they know about—"

"So sorry for this," said Jung-Shan, cutting him off. David and Rick sat silently, elbows on the conference table, mouths agape. "My people always practice good manners, especially in business, and especially with foreigners. They will not say things directly like I say to you." She held Jed's eyes. "Instead, they say 'no' in the most polite way possible. In other words, we never say the word 'no.' What they are saying now is, the business climate for meeting with Joyful and Smithworks is not good today. They say the meeting must wait until the business climate is more auspicious."

"They just decided this? Today?"

"Yes, in a message to Mr. Zheng he just shared to me, but he told me what he thinks is the real reason. He thinks they suspect you are followed by information worms, as we already know."

"How would they learn something like this?" said David.

She turned to him. "Taipei is a small business world. Very few secrets, and no secrets linger for very long. Everybody knows everything from how the grape grows."

"You mean to say they heard it on the grapevine," said Rick. "Rumors. Suspicions. Gossip."

Jung-Shan pretended to glare at him.

"And probably from their own security people. If Joyful has a Derek, the other companies have 'em too," said Jed.

"Of course you are both correct," said Jung-Shan.

"Damn!" said Rick. "Now what do we do?"

"This may not be a totally bad thing," said David. "We don't want to force this. We've come too far, literally, to hurry or trash the deal in any way."

"I agree," said Jed. "Guys, what we never realized is how dangerous it is out here in the big bad world of business."

"Sadly, this is the business environment today," said Jung-Shan. "Everybody steals from everybody else to get product to market the fastest. Business espionage is everywhere. My father says competitive advantage is now only six months, and growing shorter."

Derek said, "So, if they got their hands on some plans or a prototype, other companies would be eager to buy the technology. It easily could be worth hundreds of thousands of US dollars to them."

"Huh. You have no idea, Derek," said Rick. "We were offered five million for our technology by an American bicycle maker, which we thought was too low."

Derek's eyes widened.

"Yup," said Rick, "a straight cash sale. Of course we said no, because we want to partner." He paused. "Well, as I've said before, over and over again, what do we do now?"

"I laid awake last night, thinking about what happened," said David. "I wondered what would be the, you know, business outcome if they keep chasing after us. Because I think we're all agreed this can't go on indefinitely, right?"

Heads nodded.

"The way I see it, we're kind of hemmed in," David continued. "We're damned if we do nothing and damned if we actually do *do* something."

"Do-do is right," said Rick. David grimaced and continued.

"We can't really convince them that we don't have something they want, because we do. We're Americans in Taiwan. They have to be thinking we're here on business. I think they're invested, if you get what I mean. I don't think they're going to quit until they get *something*."

"So we throw 'em a bone?" said Rick. "Give 'em a useless blueprint or something?"

"That's got its risks as well," said Derek. "If they were to find out it was a deception, they would know with certainty you have something of value you're hiding from them. They would pursue with renewed vengeance."

"Yeah, I thought about that, too," said David. "We need to de-escalate before they run us into the ground."

"David," said Jung-Shan, "From a business perspective, I agree."

"And from a counterespionage perspective, it sounds substantial to me as well," said Derek.

"My thoughts precisely, Derek," said Jed. "And this is the kind of reasoning David excels at. He can really think a problem through deeply and effectively. Like Luke used to. I was thinking about how we've become trapped by the FUD Factor."

He paused and looked at David. "We can use this extra time to get our sh . . . to get better organized against these creeps. "David's strategy may help us do that. I want to hear more, like how we actually do the diversionary stuff."

"I want to hear more, too," said Rick.

"Maybe the best thing for us to do right now is head back to New Hampshire. Just disappear, let this whole chain of events get flushed down the toilet and start over later on. Give these weasels enough time to forget all about us."

"That might be a good starting point," David began, resuming his seat, "But I think we ought to create several scenarios, play them out in simulation and see what we get for outcomes. Multiple, step-by-step outcomes. Contingency planning. Each of us has something to bring to the table, so since our other meeting is now canceled, let's make use of this room and time and get to it."

"Yes, I strongly agree," said Jung-Shan. "I have an idea. Please excuse me to discuss this idea with Mr. Zheng. I will return shortly."

MEANWHILE – DINING WITH SPIES

The tall agent of espionage picked up his tea cup and looked over the top of it at Jed, David, Rick and Jung-Shan sitting a few tables away, happily eating. "I wish we could know what they are talking about," he said to Akiko. He drained his cup and refilled it. "You are a stupid girl, Akiko. Why could you not control the driver? Why could you not give us more time to inspect the bicycles and the contents in the truck? You did nothing, nothing, that helped us. We do not even need you here if this is all you can do."

"Then buy me a plane ticket back to Tokyo," she snapped. "If I had my way I would not be here either." Her mobile beeped. She pulled it from her hip pocket and began texting at a crazy speed. "My friends are all asking for me and here I am, a prisoner in this awful country where I barely understand the language."

"Shut up, Akiko. Shut up!" said the tall man. "Be satisfied that we now have a client. We get the intel now, then we will be paid large amounts of money for this very little work. Then we can go back to Tokyo."

"So you say," said Akiko, continuing to thumb her phone as it beeped again and again.

"We are going to learn nothing here," said the tall man." Eat your meal and stop texting. We will follow them once they leave. We need to see if they return to the same hotel. I hope the little man will park where I can put the GPS tracker on the truck. That will make our work much easier."

"Big deal," she said. "They are a nothing but a bunch of rich Americans riding bicycles. Nothing more. You two are wasting a lot of time and money following them."

"You forget, little Akiko, our new client bike company thinks there is a

business reason these Smithworks people are here. If they think so, I think so, too. And besides, it is truly none of your business. You have your job. Just do what you are told and never mind the rest. Ah, here is our food."

Akiko glared at him from under her pink bangs, picked up her chopsticks and poked dan-dan noodles into her tiny, pouty mouth.

Disappearing Act

"Jung-Shan, how far is it to the Pongew Islands?" asked Rick. The transport, a Fokker 70, seemed to begin its descent almost as soon as it gained altitude.

"Approximately thirty to forty minutes," said Jung-Shan. "And it is said Pongh-Hoo. We are flying west, over the Strait of Taiwan. The Penghu Islands are very close to Taiwan. Farther across the Strait is China, maybe one more hour."

They sat in first-class leather seats, rearranged in a circle around a table, in the renovated airliner. Behind them were a few rows of seats facing one another with work tables, and further back stowage for luggage and bicycles. A cheery flight attendant served bubble tea.

It was now Monday, a week since they had arrived in Taiwan. The previous Friday, Jung-Shan had left the conference room to confer with Mr. Zheng about the threat from the information worms and the canceled meeting. "The Americans are very strong, facing into these adverse conditions," she said, speaking in Chinese with her father. She told him about Jed's suggestion that the three of them head home to let things cool down for a few months.

Mr. Zheng shook his head. "I have already consulted Master Wong. Most auspicious time is now. It is why I agreed to extend their visit as well, to capture all good days for negotiations. If they go home, we lose face with Kueh and Huang."

"Yes, sir, all these matters are true," said Jung-Shan. She fell silent, knowing she must wait for her father's recommendation.

Finally he spoke. "You take them to Penghu. Stay at Villa Italia. It is safe. Go cycling. Have a good time. No one to know except they have the need to know. Let people think they went back to US. Derek will keep eyes on situation until it is safe for them to return. I will keep eyes on a new meeting. We will make this work, daughter. I want the Spinner for NewBike. It is a most superior competitive advantage and will be so for many years. No time to let opportunity go into the wind."

"Yes, father. I will do as you say."

Jung-Shan, Derek, Jed, David and Rick created the deception that the Smithworks guys were returning to the United States. "Misdirection is the term the intelligence community uses to describe it," said Derek. Jed said he remembered the term from his Army intelligence work as well.

At Taoyuan International Airport, Jed, David and Rick passed through security and entered the gating area beyond. At 11:24 AM,

China Airlines Flight #8 took off for Los Angeles. The worms, if they were in the airport, would note the flight schedule announcement and assume the Smithworks men were aboard.

Meanwhile, at the China Airlines customer service counter, the guys were returning their tickets as their bikes and luggage were removed and routed to the freight desk. They took an airport bus to Songshan Airport in downtown Taipei, where they met Jung-Shan for their flight to Penghu.

"Pretty cool, having your own plane," said Rick.

"This is the Joyful company plane. Mostly sales and marketing people use it to go to trade shows, and visit customers," said Jung-Shan. "Mr. Zheng has his own plane, Bombarder—Bombbaodan—oh, I can never say that word!"

"Bombardier?" said David. "The Canadian personal jet?"

"Thank you, David. Yes. It once belonged to a Taiwan Air Force general, then was a Mandarin Airlines commuter airplane. Both of our airplanes were bought for a song. Mr. Zheng is quite good as a business negotiator. Our helicopter? Hmmm, maybe it was bought for quite a few songs." Jung-Shan laughed her throaty laugh. "It flies to the factory and back to Joyful offices quite often."

"Hey, how come we didn't get to take the helicopter?"

"I am sorry," she said, bowing her head. "I thought you would enjoy the scenic train ride better."

Rick grinned. "No, the train trip was great. I'd happily take either one."

"Fasten seat belts light is on, everybody," said Jed. "Here we come, Penghu Islands!"

The Fokker glided to a smooth, faultless landing, and taxied to the small terminal.

"We will wait in the terminal now," said Jung-Shan.

"For somebody to pick us up?" said Rick.

"No, I thought we would ride our bikes," she said, a big smile on her pretty face. "They will be here in a few minutes."

"Yay!" said Rick. "Colossal!"

Leaving the airport, Jung-Shan in the lead, their speed began to wick the perspiration from their bodies. They glimpsed the ocean off to the left, then pedaled through five or six klicks of mostly open countryside. She kept glancing over her shoulder, looking for Jed, so he rode up beside her. By the time they reached Magong City, the four were pedaling a tight two-by-two peloton formation, past a corner gas station with a two-story tall statue depicting three dolphins leaping toward the sky. Traffic was light and people were few, perhaps because it was a sleepy little town, or perhaps too early for the tourists to be up and about.

A kilometer or two beyond Magong City was the Villa Italia B&B, a charming three-story Florentine-style chateau perched on a stony outcrop overlooking Penghu Bay. Their luggage sat on the front porch, already delivered by taxi. To the right side of the porch stood a four-bike rack, as if just for them. The owners, a charming couple—Ashton, an Australian, and his Taiwanese wife Min—stood waiting for them. They greeted Jung-Shan like a daughter as she introduced them to the guys. "Ashton was my English tutor for many years when my family visits here," she said.

Ashton said, "Ashton still is your English tutor," smiling at her, "although I'm now retired and my lovely, charming, talented wife and I operate this bed and breakfast. As you will learn, her talent at the piano is only exceeded by her talent in the kitchen. We welcome you. Do come in, but please remove your shoes." The guys stepped into slippers embroidered with lotus blossoms and crossed the living room to gaze out a large picture window overlooking the beach just below and the Taiwan Strait beyond. The tide was apparently in; the deep blue water lapped at the beach.

"A black sand beach," said Rick. "That's definitely excellent."

"This is a palace," said David, looking around at the marble walls, polished stone floors, pillared room dividers and mahogany stairs ascending to the upper floors.

"Might be just what we need, a few days to relax," said Jed.

"And hide," Rick snarked.

Jung-Shan gurgled and covered her mouth.

"And do some more cycling!" said Jed. "Jung-Shan told me there are four islands linked by bridges. This one, Penghu, is the biggest, but they're all small, so we can ride anywhere and back in a day."

"Cool," said Rick. "Maybe we can take a spin this afternoon, see some sights. Check out the beach!"

It was a small strip of black sand. The wind blew steadily against it off the water. Here and there were small tide pools, shells, chunks of basalt. Hearty cacti and large aloe vera plants grew in the sawgrass at the beach's perimeter. The guys walked back and forth, chatting about the discoveries at their feet. Jung-Shan came out onto the rear patio and waved. They walked back to join her and she said, "This is a very special place for me and my family. Sometimes my uncle and auntie join us, too, and bring my cousins. But now we are here, like we are a new family and have the inn all to ourselves!" She spread her arms and smiled, looking at Rick and David. "Your room is on the second floor," she said, pointing up the staircase. "It has two beds, very comfortable if you do not mind to share the bathroom." They shook their heads. "We will stay on the third floor, Jed. This room always just for me and my sister." He smiled back at her as he felt a quiver run through his loins. She looked at her watch. "We have all of the afternoon. We can go for a bicycle ride, eat some bites of lunch somewhere as we ride, if you like, come back and rest and have showers. Dinner here is excellent, but our reservation must be made in advance. Would you like to enjoy Min's homemade Taiwanese cuisine?" They nodded. "OK, then, let's go!"

Jung-Shan again proved to be an excellent guide. As they rode around Magong City, she explained they were visiting the sixty-four-island Penghu archipelago, a volcanic formation. "Penghu, the largest island, was the first settled by Chinese. I already told you my family came here from Fujian," she said. "People always wish to be explorers of the world. Chinese people are no exception. So my people left Fujian hundreds of years ago, coming here first to the Penghu Islands and then later to Taiwan.

"Penghu has had many foreign occupations," she told them as they drank bottles of Coke at an outdoor snack shop. "Pirates, Japanese, Dutch. Taiwanese have had to defend these islands against the navies of China and Japan. You will see signs of this as we tour on our bikes. Today, both China and Taiwan say Penghu is their own. The happy news is, it is both!" she laughed.

"Did you say pirates?" sad Jed.

"Yes, pirates. Many pirates. Japanese. Dutch. Spanish. More I cannot remember. There is story in our family that a distant relative, also named Zheng, was a famous naval commander and explorer in the fourteenth century. His story is told in a Chinese history book called The Great Voyages of Zheng He."

"Whoa," said Rick, "I'm impressed. That is, if he wasn't a pirate." He grinned.

"No, not a pirate," she said. "He killed pirates. He was the explorer, very good at making maps of trade routes. Zheng brought treasures taken from pirates to China. Animals, too, even a giraffe! But he was not a pirate!" She grinned, so nobody believed her.

The four climbed back on their beautiful bikes, attracting looks as they rode through Magong City. Pedaling its narrow streets, they passed through the old Shuncheng Gate which had stood at the town entrance for hundreds of years. They passed by the Pescadores Hotel and Plaza, the docks, along narrow little walled streets and verdant lanes until they reached a park. Pulling up in front of a pedestrian gate, Jung-Shan made a phone call. "We are at the Taiwan Veterans Memorial," she said. "Please walk your bikes from here, then I will have a gift for you!"

The gate opened onto a stone pathway that passed through a bower of mulberry trees toward a stunning white sand beach stretching in both directions almost out of sight. Soon they reached a gourmet coffee shop called Caffé Pescadore; they locked up their bikes and entered. A tiny teenaged girl wearing an apron over a dress swept over to their table, greeting Jung-Shan by name. She smiled and spoke in Mandarin to the girl, who nodded and stepped behind the counter to the chrome

Faema espresso machine. She ground beans for fresh coffee and made perfect lattes for them. Conversation ensued and their energy revived, they headed back to the Villa Italia.

Dinner was, in a word, delicious. Ashton and Min were gourmet chefs, darting back and forth together in the kitchen. The meal was entirely local Penghu fare: peanuts spiced with red pepper and anchovies, three kinds of the day's catch, handmade angel hair pasta, fresh vegetables from the daily farmer's market, blood oranges for dessert. Jung-Shan signaled Jed to leave one last bite.

Jed had begun to notice that a certain number of dishes were always served and as they sat drinking tea, he asked Jung-Shan about it. "It is expected there are more dishes than the number of people," she said. "If we are four, the expectation is to serve at least six dishes. Eight is a special number in China, so to serve eight dishes is always best. It is the host's responsibility to make sure you do not leave his table hungry. That would mean losing face. Is also the reason we leave one bite. This tells the host we have full bellies." Smiling, she patted her own. "If you eat all bites, host will make more food for you!

"The best meal is to serve all three meats—beef, pork, chicken, then fish last, sometimes as a soup. Each type has rich meaning, for example chicken is the promise of prosperous life. Whole fish or fish stew means the promise of abundance. Like that."

Jed watched the joy in her face as she explained. Clearly, it made her happy to know they were interested in her culture. Of course, she must know that by now; didn't they already know how to use chopsticks?

After dinner, the foursome walked along the water's edge toward the distant twinkling lights of Magong. Rick took off his shoes and stepped into the water. "Hey! It's warm! Like a bathtub warm!" The others joined him, glad they were wearing shorts and could wade into the water. Breakers popped up, and in no time they were chasing waves like schoolchildren.

Jung-Shan said, "This beach feels nice to the feet, does it not?" They agreed. "It is sand, of course, but also coral and shells, made very fine by the sea. In sunlight, it is like filled with stars. Many coral reefs grow along the islands, most wonderful to see under the water. We could do scuba diving if you like."

"Oh, yes, we would like very much," said Jed.

"We will make plans for more activities at breakfast," said Jung-Shan. "Now it is growing late. A good time to rest."

They walked back to the inn; Jed's heart was pounding in anticipation of their spending the night together. When they arrived on the third floor, he noted a lavish two-person marble Jacuzzi was set atop a raised marble dais. A large picture window above it revealed a beautiful view of the beach and ocean below. *It's so elegant, so Roman,* he mused. *I wonder if she would like to hop in the Jacuzzi together. That would be very nice. More heart-pounding.*

"Excuse me," Jung-Shan said as she headed into the bathroom. when she came out, she had her hair up in a pony tail and wore an embroidered silk dressing gown that fell all the way to her feet. In her arms she carried a stack of towels. She set them on the bed and began rolling them up. She pulled back the covers and placed the rolled towels end-to-end down the middle of the bed. She sat down on one side, wriggled out of the robe and, now clad in matching silk pajamas, slipped under the covers. Jed watched all this, thinking no Jacuzzi tonight, and went into the bathroom to perform his own ablutions.

He crawled into bed, decidedly aware he was not beside her. He settled on his back, his preferred sleeping position, and turned out the light. He felt her move about, heard her body sliding this way and that between the sheets on the other side of her Cape Towel. Then there was silence.

"Jed?" she said after several minutes.

"Yes, Jung-Shan?"

"I was thinking about last night. At the train station. You were very good with the agents. You did not let them know that you thought they were doing espionage to us. You showed them the bikes, as if that was what they wanted to see. But at the same time, you showed them there was nothing to see. To see there was nothing to see." She laughed lightly, her shoulders moving in sync.

"Uh-huh," he said, smiling, now turned toward her, up on his elbow.

"I think . . . you said something . . . now I remember . . . it made me think you were thinking like the agent of espionage, except better."

"Uh-huh. Actually, I was using my Army training as a counterintelligence officer. My objective was to neutralize the event, not to escalate it with . . . emotion. You know, anger or aggression."

"That was very good. Maybe they will stop, go away now."

Silence again. Here they were, lying in bed talking, mere inches from one another. Close, but so far away.

"Jed?"

"Yes?" Jed was trying as hard as he could not to quiver with desire.

"I am happy to speak so much English. In my new position I will be traveling often to other countries where Chinese is not spoken and I will have to speak English as the common language. Perhaps I will even travel to America. I am fortunate to practice with you and David and Rick. Is my English good enough?"

"Absolutely," he said. "And it gets better every day."

"Oh, good. Xiè xiè. Wǎn'ān, Jed." Good night. A moment later, her soft breathing told him she was asleep.

The Penghu Islands

Jed and Jung-Shan sat on the warm sands of Aimen Beach watching Rick and David windsurfing. Or trying to. The two had already been out for an hour and were obviously tired from hanging onto their booms; surely they would quit soon. Jed's eyes weren't tired of gazing upon Jung-Shan sitting beside him, wearing red satin running shorts trimmed in gold and a white silk tank top bearing an image of Taiwan, a little bare tummy exposed. Jed leaned back on his elbows to stop staring; she took the opportunity to gaze at his bare chest with its dark curly hair. How thin he was, not thin in the too-skinny way, but sleek, toned. No fat, firm abs, strong arms, the heavily muscled legs of a cyclist. In the same way he found her beautiful, she thought him exceedingly handsome.

Jung-Shan slipped on a gauzy long-sleeved shirt and shifted slightly to get into the beach umbrella's shade. Jed remembered something, perhaps from a movie seen long ago, how Asian women often did not consider it fashionable to get a suntan.

"Want a bottle of water?" he asked, opening his backpack.

"Yes, please," she said.

"Why did you go to the London School of Economics?" Jed said.

"My father wanted the best education for me," she said. "He believes Taiwan has a very bright future in Asian-American relations. I have a very high education in international relations and finance and, as you know, I speak fluent English!" She smiled the prim, earnest-student smile.

"Wow, seems like it paid off."

"Not as he expected. He did not anticipate the United States shifting economic interests to China and the effect it would have on Taiwan."

"How so?"

"Jed, this is a sad, long story. Taiwan has grown as an economic leader in Asia. You know from Ping it is one of the Asian Tigers. But strife between China and Taiwan is the story of communist versus democratic government. Very sad, very long story."

"Yeah, he called Taiwan a tiger, but what are the Asian Tigers?" said Jed.

"The four highest-growing Asian economies after World War II. They are Hong Kong, Singapore, South Korea and Taiwan. Taiwan very strong trading partner with America once upon a time, but then America takes China's side. China says Taiwan is not independent. Says Taiwan is a Chinese territory. It seems America took China's side. So now once again we must deal with China in economic warfare."

She continued, "Two parties in Taiwan, Green Party and Blue Party, disagree if Taiwan should be part of China or not. Green Party favors independent Taiwan, but Blue Party wishes Taiwan and China to unify. Probably this will be a long story for another hundred years!" She laughed ruefully.

They grew silent, watching David and Rick as they negotiated the waves, clutching at their boom bars like contortionists.

"You have a sister?" he asked her.

"Hai, she is seven years younger."

"What does she do? Where is she?"

"She lives in Los Angeles with her boyfriend. We call her Nini. She is a professional wedding photographer."

"Uh-huh," said Jed. "So, how old is she?"

"Hǎo! Jed, you are trying to trick me into telling you my age! I told you I am a sheep. You must learn the Chinese zodiac to figure it out," she said with her throaty laugh, giving him a little push on his shoulder. "You are clever, but not clever by enough! Therefore, I will give you a clue. Nini is a tiger. She is very creative and loves to take pictures of happy married peoples."

Jed stood and said, "I will find out your age, Jung-Shan. Depend on it. I will."

"I will be happy when you know," she said, smiling up at him and lifting her hand to be helped up. "Is it time for cycling?"

After returning the rented windsurfers, the foursome walked north along the beach to Lin-t'ou Park where they lunched on their new favorite gua bao sandwiches and cactus fruit icees. Having walked to

Aimen Beach, they took a taxi back to the Villa Italia, changed into their cycling kits, then headed back south through town, two by two.

After a few kilometers they swung off onto a smaller road leading to Shanshui Beach. It looked like a California beach, surfers everywhere. As they stopped to watch, a kid wearing colorful surfer trunks and a backward Giants baseball cap over a long golden pony tail walked past them, his board under his arm. "Hey!" Rick said. "Where you from?"

"California," he said, stopping. "You dudes American?"

"Yep, we are," said Jed. "Boston."

"Sweet. First Americans I've seen in a loooong time. Well, surf's up. See ya." Rick grinned, his gaze panning over the bikini-clad girls sunbathing.

Back on 201, they passed a tall white building that swirled up like a soft-serve ice cream cone, surrounded by a wavy pink wall. "What in the heck is that?" said Rick. Jung-Shan said it was a homestay, a tourist B&B like their own.

The road ended abruptly in the tiny village of Fenggui. They passed through a magnificent Taoist arch; next to it was an extraordinarily ornate Taoist temple, and beyond the water's edge.

Jung-Shan said, "All Penghu islands are volcano rock, so what happens is the ocean wears these blowholes in it. Now water comes in from the underneath side and is forced up through the holes, making loud sounds." With a sound like a thunderbolt, a small geyser erupted right in front of them. "Like that!"

They laughed and listened for a few more, then retraced their route back toward Magong. "Tomorrow," Jung-Shan shouted over her shoulder, "we will go pedaling all day, crossing three bridges between islands. There will be many interesting sights."

"Woo-Hoo! Can't wait!" said Rick. The road was nearly devoid of traffic, so they raced one another hard and fast. Jung-Shan slowed them as they approached a Buddhist temple with a three-meter-tall golden Buddha seated on its steps, then to the Taoist Ziwei Temple, where the towering figure of Emperor Yu the Great, founder of the first Chinese dynasty over four millennia earlier, presided from atop its roof.

Back at the inn, they rested on the veranda overlooking the ocean, cooling down, sipping iced tea, watching the terns and gulls float just off the beach as they searched for dinner. "Which reminds me," said David, "what are we doing for dinner tonight?"

"Why don't we walk to the Magong downtown?" said Jung-Shan, stretching her legs, bending to touch her toes. "Lots of choices."

"Sounds good to me," said Jed, "But first I'm hitting the shower." A very cold shower, he muttered under his breath.

The night air was hot, heavy and humid, thick with street scents mixed with the ocean's smells. They walked from one darkened, cobblestoned street to another, past open-front cafes, a café with sliding wooden Japanese-style doors, tiny shops selling cosmetics, tea, herbs, sneakers and flip-flops, Kymko scooters, and of course the ubiquitous 7-Eleven, all still open for business. Soon the guys were hopelessly disoriented. Rick continually complained of being jostled: "Hey, watch where you're going!" he cried again and again to ears that clearly could care less what he was saying, even if they understood English. "Please be quiet, Rick," said Jung-Shan, who kept walking as if she knew exactly where she was going. Which she did.

They stopped at a nameless storefront which, on first glance, did not appear to be a restaurant. Outside stood large tanks filled with live catch. Staff and street people milled around, oblivious to getting in each other's way. Jung-Shan greeted a woman who was apparently the hostess and they entered into a back-and-forth. Jung-Shan pointed at the fish tanks and buckets of shrimp, crab and lobster on the rack.

"Man, where can I stand and not get shoved?" said Rick.

"Rick! Let it go, will ya?" barked Jed.

Rick moved to the street and stood between a parked car and two scooters.

Soon enough they were seated in the busy, noisy restaurant at a large round table they shared with a family. The mother and father were dishing out food to the two children, talking nonstop to a small boy while the adolescent girl texted away on a big HTC smartphone. The mother spewed harsh Chinese at the girl, who would dutifully pick at her food with her chopsticks, all the while looking at her phone.

"I already placed our order," Jung-Shan said, pouring tea as the peanut appetizer arrived. Soon, dishes were being set before them on the lǎnduò de sū shān, one after another. They shared a pasta with shrimp, small sandwiches with abalone, a big slice of something like grouper or perhaps sea bass, spicy string beans, a dish with small curly chunks of lobster meat, rice.

"What're these?" asked Rick, picking up a skewer of something strangely grotesque.

"Do you like this taste?" said Jung-Shan.

"Yeah, it's good, I guess. Kind of spicy."

"Maybe you do not want to know," she said, wrinkling her nose.

"No, really, tell me."

She gave him an in-your-face look and said, "Squid."

"You mean like the giant squid that tried to eat Captain Nemo's submarine?" said Rick. Everyone burst into laughter. The Chinese family looked at them, but quickly returned to their meal.

After eating their fill they headed back to the inn, Rick and David in front, Jed and Jung-Shan falling a little behind, holding hands. "Tell me about New Hamster," she said.

"New Hampshire."

"Sorry."

"It's mostly rural. Forests and farms and mountains and lakes. I grew up on a dirt country road. Anywhere I went was pretty much on my bike."

"Your family lived on a farm? Your father was a farmer?"

"Yes. He was—is—a very wise and thoughtful man, but he also learned politics. He kept New Hampshire, I don't know how better to say it, pure? Simple? So people can live close to the land, close to nature. Now he's retired, but he still has his finger in a lot of stuff."

"Um, to have finger in, that means, um, to be powerful?"

"Yeah, you could say that. He naturally took to politics. He's, um, influential, but in good ways."

Jung-Shan, frowning, nodded again.

"I love New Hampshire. We value small government and individual freedoms, things our country was founded on. Live Free or Die!"

"What? What does that mean?"

"It's the New Hampshire motto. It's on our car license plates. There was a general named Stark, way back when we fought our revolutionary war, who said, 'Live free or die: Death is not the worst of evils.'"

"Oh, Jed, it is not good to talk about death. Chinese believe in a long life. Also we know we cannot be free. Too many responsibilities to society for people to be free like you say."

"But we all have to die sometime," said Jed. "Doesn't make much sense to live a long life if you aren't free."

"Yes, but the ideal we believe says live as long as possible. Longevity is our way to live free, like you say." She stopped, turned toward Jed, took ahold of his shirt with both hands and gave him a serious look. "Chinese do not wish to talk about death."

Jed laughed. "I'll say you don't!" She relaxed and laughed back. He wrapped his arms around her and gave her a bear hug. She wrapped her arms around him, too. He kissed her forehead, her nose, her lips. He took her hand; they turned back to the road and continued walking.

"Here is the thing I mean," she said. "There are dangers that hurt or kill people. We must avoid these. Of course all people must die, but the important wisdom taught by Confucius is to live the most moral life and share this wisdom with others in all things we do. More wisdom comes better to people when they are older."

She paused and when Jed didn't say anything, continued. "All people must strive in this direction, but also must know when to let matters go on their own course. That is fate and it is always beyond our control."

"How can we tell what is to be? Our fate? What events or circumstances are within our control and which aren't?"

"Very simple," she said. "If you feel your life is always going into the strong headwind, you are fighting against fate."

"But if old General Stark didn't fight into the headwind so America could be free, we might still be a British colony."

"Who is to say which is the best Way?" said Jung-Shan. "Maybe people would have been happier as a British colony. I cannot know.

You cannot know. Only fate can know. But sometimes the will of fate is beyond our knowing. We may not know if something is right in our lifetime. It might take five hundred years, even five thousand years, to know. Who can know? We may never know."

They reached the inn front doors. David and Rick had apparently gone inside. "Well, that may be true. It's an interesting philosophy. I grew up in a family—the Smith family—of strong-willed men. We go back a few hundred years. My ancestors were some of the first settlers in New Hampshire, brave explorers who left the Massachusetts Bay Colony to build homes in the dense wilderness forests. There weren't even roads in New Hampshire back then! My grandfather was that kind of man, an explorer like your ancestor who ventured across the seas, and so was my dad. I'm like that, too, but for me it's more about being a business and innovation adventurer. My dad gave me a poem when I was a kid. Oh, yeah, your other question—I'm an only child. So, the important line is, 'I am the master of my fate, I am the captain of my soul.'"

"This is very different from our culture," Jung-Shan said. "We are a culture over five thousand years old. Maybe America is a young culture, still not as wise as ours." She gave his arm a squeeze.

"You may be right," said Jed. They walked along the porch to check the bikes; they were locked in the rack. They continued around to the veranda. Jed wanted to talk with her some more. Not go to their room yet. One of two things could happen up on the third floor: they would make love or they would sleep as they did last night, with the towel peninsula between them. For some reason, he didn't want to contemplate which would or would not occur. He was afraid that whichever happened, he would prefer it was the other. Which is my fate tonight?

A soft breeze blew from the ocean, rich with the scent of salt and seaweed, tossing Jung-Shan's hair around her face. She reached up, back, pulled it into a knot and tied it.

"Shall we sit out here for a while?" said Jed, gesturing toward the large wicker chairs.

Jung-Shan yawned politely. "It has become very late, Jed. Tomorrow we have a long cycling day. I am very tired. Shall we . . . ?" She reached out for his hand and they walked through the rear door and up the stairs to their suite.

As before, Jung-Shan was first to the bathroom. Jed stepped out on the patio. a tiny island a few hundred yards offshore was only slightly visible. Hmmm. He recalled it being much more prominent earlier today, but now it seemed it would be lost to the rising tide. It made Jed long to be immersed in the Jacuzzi with her, watching the island disappear.

Once again, Jung-Shan emerged with armfuls of rolled-up towels.

When they came downstairs for breakfast the next morning, their bikes were gone.

Dragon Beach

"Have you seen this, Jed?" yelled David, pointing out the dining room window at the empty bike rack. "Can you believe this? What in god's name have we done to deserve this?" David was angry, angrier than Jed had ever seen him. Rick stood beside him, furious but dumbfounded.

Min, the innkeeper's wife, had been preparing breakfast. She rushed into the dining room and began speaking rapidly in Chinese to Jung-Shan; what sounded like a heated exchange ensued. Jung-Shan turned toward the guys. "She is apologizing," she said. "She says this has never happened before. Magong is a very peaceful town. No crime. She is calling the police. She says the bicycles will be found quickly and returned."

Jed seethed. "We know who stole them," he said. "This is it. This is war. I've had enough of this bullying espionage bullshit." He looked at Rick, then David. "We're going after them. And when we find them, I'll pound them into the sand, once and for all."

"I wouldn't advise it," said Ashton, who had just walked in. "We'll call the blueheels. They know us well. In fact, I'm surprised anyone would even consider kipping the bikes, since there are patrol cars here frequently. They'll take this quite seriously, mark my word. After all, they have practically nothing to do because there's so little crime here. I'd bet your bicycles are back here in a day or so. No need to be a cowboy, Mr. Smith."

"No cowboys in New Hampshire," said Jed.

"You know what he means!" said Jung-Shan. "Now. Please? Guys? We sit down and have a nice breakfast. We make new plans. Let the police find bikes. If they don't find them today, I will get new bikes flown here for us. No problem."

"But I like that bike," said Rick.

Jung-Shan gave him a look.

They sat down around the table to their bowls of tongzai migao, a rice porridge, luobogao turnip cakes, mantou steamed buns and tea.

"I have an idea," said Jung-Shan after a few bites. "Today we were to go on the island-to-island bike ride. Our bikes will be found, so we will do it tomorrow. Today, let us go to sweet Jibei Island. We will ride scooters, relax on the very beautiful beach, ride the jet skis. Go for the ride in glass-bottom boats. We can snorkel, dive to the coral reefs to see beautiful colors and shapes and lots of fish. We will forget our anger and have a lovely resting day, OK?"

The guys grudgingly agreed. Jed was still furious, but held his anger in check. All he could think about was how he was going to catch those information worms and put an end to their harassment. His highly organized mind came up with scenarios:

- Catch them with the bikes and beat the living crap out of them
- Bait a trap to lure them into Riverside Park, beat the crap out of them, then tie them up and dunk them in the river until they confess
- Beat the living crap out of them, then put headphones on their ears and fry their brains with a shrieking police siren
- Catch them behind the Jimmy, beat the living crap out of them, tie them to the bumper, drag and dump them in the woods
- Lure them into an alley, beat the living crap out of them, tie them up, take all their identification and chain them to a tree in Jiantan Park.

It felt good to know he had so many options.

They took a taxi from Magong City to the Bei Hai Visitor Center docks on the adjacent island of Baisha and jumped on a ferry to Jibei Island. It took all of twenty minutes. Jung-Shan purchased an equipment rental package from the boat operator so there wouldn't be a driver's license problem renting scooters for the guys. They grabbed a bunch of water bottles, jumped on their Taiwan Golden Bee scooters and rode north along the coast to see the weirs.

"Jibeiyu has the most weirs of any Penghu Island," said Jung-Shan, pointing from the cliff down at the fishing traps, stone circles just below the water's surface. "Eighty-eight. You remember eight is the most lucky number to Chinese. This way, tides bring fish in and when the tides go out fish are left in the weirs for fisherman. Very efficient way to catch the most fresh fish, yes?"

They rode on to the northernmost tip, Jung-Shan laughingly reminding the guys how the TGBs sounded like bumblebees, until turning south along the western coastline. It didn't take long to reach the beach the islanders called "a dragon in the sea." It was a paradise: a brilliant white sandbar extending south of the island proper as far as the eye could see, surrounded on three sides by dazzling blue-green waters. "You see the sand?" said Jung-Shan to David and Rick. "I told Jed about this. Penghu Island sand is also coral and seashells, ground fine as salt but white, not black. They cause the sparkle. It is called Dragon Beach because . . . surprise! It is the shape of a dragon," the happiest of smiles sweeping across her lovely face.

Another white peninsula, thought Jed.

The snorkeling was astounding and the day a success. They had pushed the bicycle theft from their thoughts and given themselves over to the pleasures of Jibei—not the least of which, at least for Jed, was seeing Jung-Shan in a two-piece bathing suit—never once succumbing to the desire for the massive amounts of cycling they normally thought of as relaxation. They spent most of the day at Dragon Beach, then rode their scooters back to the ferry port and took a glass-bottomed tour boat from the North Sea Visitors Center to the massive coral reef that lay off Sianjiaoyu, a smaller island they had passed on their way to Jibeiyu.

But as they rode the boat back to Penghu Island, the trepidation began turning everyone introspective. They rode in near silence back to the inn, paid the taxi, and turned up the walk toward the front door. A glint of reflected sunlight caught Rick's eye just as he said, "Hey." Their bikes stood in the bike rack on the side porch, exactly where they'd been the day before. Everyone began talking at once.

Ashton and Min came out the door all smiles. "Zênme huí shì?" said Jung-Shan in Chinese—what happened—but they answered in English: "Our caretaker had put them in the garage," said Ashton. "He was doing some minor repairs to the railing and pruning beside the porch. He said the bicycles were so beautiful he was afraid he would harm them."

"Why didn't he tell you?"

"He said the house was still asleep when he came this morning," said Min. "He didn't want to wake us." She laughed a nervous laugh, hoping for forgiveness, then everyone joined in sharing the laughter of relief.

Min served a light meal of baozi, steamed buns filled with spicy pork, mushrooms and onions, and a deliriously spicy ma po tofu. After dinner and recounting the day's adventures, they adjourned to the rear veranda. The surf was up, the island was gone; waves crashed softly against the shore, chamber music to accompany their quiet nighttime mood. For a long time no one spoke, then Jed said, "What do you all think?"

"I'm having a great time," said Rick. David chimed in and said, "Me, too."

"I mean about, you know, escaping the information worms. We've been gone—well, out of Taipei—like almost three days. No sign of the scumbags. Do you think we've shaken their tail on us?"

"No way to know," said David. "If we assume they aren't the brightest light bulbs in the string, I think our plan probably worked."

"So, what's our schedule? When do we need to go back? When are we expected back in Taipei?"

"There is no expectation," said Jung-Shan, "but tomorrow is Thursday, so if we are to meet Friday with Mr. Zheng and the others, we would have to return tomorrow night or Friday in the morning."

"How long will we be out on the bikes tomorrow?"

"I do not know. I have not performed this ride all at one time. Maybe we should get early start. As much as I love it here, might be best to fly back tomorrow and get prepared to meet on Friday."

"Fine with me," said Jed; David and Rick concurred.

"I will call Mr. Zheng and inform him so," said Jung-Shan. She dialed her father as she took a few steps away, spoke briefly, then rejoined them with a smile.

"Well, if we're getting an early start, I'm going early to bed," said David. "Funny, isn't it? Out here on this island I want to go to bed when it gets dark and get up with the morning sun."

"Yeah, I've noticed that myself," said Rick. "Or is it you waking me up with your grunting while you do pushups?"

Jed and Jung-Shan remained behind. She reached over and touched his hand. "I am thinking about our talk last night. Americans seem always to be talking about freedom. I think this word freedom also means quality of life. What do you think?"

"I agree. Quality of life is difficult to sustain."

"That is because we do not control our fate," she replied. "But it is not so hard to sustain when we work with others toward a common good, which is quality of life."

"Where is your own personal freedom in this?"

"Personal freedom is not as important as working for the common good. If I must give up some personal freedom, I know it is for the best. For my good and the good of all my people and my country. As I just said, that is the most quality of life."

"Yes, of course," Jed said. He was silent for a while, then said, "Yes, I use my personal freedom to strive for my own good, but I believe that makes possible the good of all. If I don't hold myself to a higher standard, then what standard do I hold others to? Alexandre Dumas wrote a novel called The Three Musketeers. Their motto was 'All for one, and one for all.' Perhaps our Ways are not so different after all, Jung-Shan."

They fell quiet again, the only sound the waves breaking across the black-sand beach. Jed broke the silence.

"So, how did you end up working in your father's business?"

Jung-Shan's back stiffened. "I told you this already. My father decided I should go to graduate university in England. With the world paying all attention to China trade and diplomacy, he thought there was not much opportunity for a girl from Taiwan. Maybe there would be advantages for me to have a degree from one of the best business schools of England."

"How did that work out for you? No . . . wait. You came back. What did you plan to do after graduation?"

"England was very nice. I did not plan to come back. You already know why I did not stay."

"Yes. Interesting," said Jed. He was quiet, then said, "Why don't you head up to our room. I'm gonna call my office, then I'll be up."

They stood and Jed drew Jung-Shan to him. She put her arm around his neck and they looked into each other's eyes. They kissed briefly, then she pulled away and went inside. Jed stood, numb; he finally dug his phone out, inserted a new SIM card and dialed Gregg's mobile number. It was late here but early there; Gregg should be at the office.

The call connected. "Hey, Gregg, what's up," said Jed. Then he just listened. Then he said, "OK. We'll talk about it tomorrow. Afterwards." He clicked off and stood still. "Damn!" He popped out the SIM card, snapped it into pieces to resume its relationship with the sand below, and went inside.

Jung-Shan had finished in the bathroom. He brushed his teeth and washed his face, thinking all the while about what Gregg had told him, cursing like a sailor under his breath.

He slipped on the terry cloth robe and came out of the bathroom. She was already in bed, lying on her back, her long hair spread like latticework on her pillow. He could see no hump down the center of the bed. Man oh man, of all nights, he thought. He went to her bedside and sat down. Took her hand. Locked eyes with her. Waited to see what was going on.

"Jed," she said, "Will you tell me about being a soldier?" She cast her eyes down.

Jed was silent for a while, then said, "No."

Jung-Shan took her time responding. "You were injured. A bad injury. I feel sad for you being injured."

"But I'm fine now. Almost a perfect healing. No problem." He patted his right thigh.

"Jed," she said, looking up at him. "May I touch your injury?"

He took her eyes with his own, smiled, and said, "Sure," then guided her hand under his robe to his scar. He could feel her fingertips moving gently, exploring it. He could also feel something else and fought against it.

"So, this has . . . no . . . consequences for you . . . ?"

"At the time, of course it did. But now, no," he said. "We have a saying in the Army: what doesn't kill you makes you stronger."

"Hǎo!" she said. "Chinese have a saying like this too. They say strength is built on inner character and character is built on inner strength."

"Huh," said Jed. "Your saying is more about, um, values, morality. Kind of more spiritual. My saying is more . . . physical? More about life and . . . ?" He thought better of finishing the sentence.

Jung-Shan gave him a smile and settled back onto her pillow. Her face became serious. "Jed, we talk about consequences. My life has consequences too. As I told you, I met the Englishman and we were married." She frowned. "I thought, I am smart. I have done well at college, in the top of my class. After graduate school, I will be offered work in London. Perhaps as a consultant or in the business of trade or perhaps finance. I did not know my husband would oppose my working." She looked away from Jed. "He mostly say no to everything I wanted to do.

"My father at first opposed the marriage. He was happy when I left my husband. Not happy I am a divorced woman. Happy, angry, happy, angry. Make up the mind!" She burst out laughing to keep from crying. "He was of course happy I came back to Taiwan, so he gave me a job in Joyful. But he made me start in the simplest occupations. At first I worked in manufacturing for one whole year. Gau Tai-Ping was my boss."

"I've been meaning to ask you why your last name is Lai," said Jed. "It wasn't your husband's name . . . ?"

"No, is my mother's maiden name. I use it to respect Joyful business relations. Only a very few need to know I am daughter of Mr. Zheng."

"OK, yeah, I get that. But, um, how come your father opposed your marriage?"

"Traditional Chinese do not believe in marriage outside Chinese culture. We should keep our blood line pure, they think. Our families often consult a marriage counselor to make the best match for their son. Woman is not always allowed to choose her husband. Her family will seek the most auspicious marriage. I did not follow our custom. I picked the Englishman all by myself. My father, he was very angry with me at first. Even more angrier when I came home in shame from the failure of marriage. I did not tell him all, just that the Englishman was cruel to me, dominated me, made me very, very unhappy. That made my father angrier toward my former husband and nicer toward me." She laughed lightly again.

"That's really tough," said Jed. "Like being caught in a crossfire. I'm sorry."

"Do not be sorry. All of life works out for the best. This is my Way. My Buddhist way in life. Make mistakes, learn from them, keep the eyes looking ahead."

She turned to look toward the black, star-filled sky out the window and was silent. Jed looked at her face: her delicate ears, the strands of her long, shimmering coal-black hair, the way her lips met, how the corners of her mouth turned up. She turned back to look at him and said, "Want to know a secret?"

"Sure, if you want to tell me one."

She paused, then said: "The Englishman, he was very embarrassed about my reason for asking to divorce. He gave me one hundred thousand pounds to never tell anyone the real reason. Ha!"

Jed laughed. "That's very funny," he said, wishing he could ask for that reason but knowing better.

"You want to know the real reason?" she said.

"Only if you feel like telling me."

She pressed her lower lip into a tiny pout, gazed into his face, and slowly moved her head side to side as if her neck hurt. "After eight months, I asked him for an annulment of the marriage. He . . . he was not . . . a husband to me. He never told me why not. I could not live this way."

Jed was silent.

"You are the only person I have ever told," Jung-Shan said.

"Why? Why tell me?"

Jung-Shan pursed her lips. "Because. Because it is something . . . important you should know. About me."

Jung-Shan squeezed her eyes closed. Tears came. Her shoulders shook as she tried not to sob. Before Jed could say anything she said, "Can you please hold me tonight? I want to feel your body hold my body. Just hold me, please? All I want tonight, OK?"

He bent down and kissed her, this time for a long while, then he rose and went around to his side of the bed. He pulled off the robe and slipped under the comforter to find Jung-Shan's exquisite naked body waiting for him. He lay on his back and she pressed against him, shaking with sobs, her head on his chest. He stroked her hair over and over; gradually, her crying subsided. She turned on her side away from him, moving her body to signal him to spoon her.

"Um, maybe you should spoon me," he said.

MEANWHILE – STILL A GAKI

"Akiko, you are a novice espionage operative. You are a wagagama musumearei. A spoiled brat. In all ways, you are still a gaki," said the man wearing black glasses. They were back at Jianguo Hotel, sitting in the living room of the men's suite. People dressed like cartoon characters cavorted on the TV. With the sound muted, it looked ridiculous.

"Oh, shut your stupid mouth and send me home," Akiko shot back. "I never wanted to be part of your stupid operation in the first place."

"You will not go home, gaki, until I say so, or until you have satisfied your uncle's indebtedness to me," said black glasses. "And maybe not even then. I still cannot understand how you can bungle something as simple as a phone call."

"Give her a break," said the taller man. "We did not give her clear instructions for the words to speak."

"You shut your mouth! She spoke to the man in the Smithworks and did not ask him for speaking with this—Rick person. She just hung up, so now no one answers. We don't know if it is—aiii! We don't know anything!" He banged his fists again and again on the table. "Where are these bicycle people? Are they still in Taipei? Are they again in the United Hampshire States?"

"I think they are gone," said the other man. "I think they left the day we followed them to the airport. They took all their luggage and the bicycles. They checked in at the airline counter and went through security. China Airlines flight number 8 to Los Angeles left one hour and forty minutes later. So you see, none of this is Akiko's fault. It is my fault for not giving her clear instructions. But tonight, she and I will try to learn more, together." He cast the girl a knowing look. "We are going to break into their computer network using their mobile phone."

"Ah, you are both fools," said black glasses. "You cannot break into their computers with a phone. Besides, I think they are still hiding somewhere here in Taipei."

"Of course he can hack their computers with this mobile phone of Rick," said Akiko. "You are a stupid man, not to know this."

"Gaki!" Black glasses cried as he jumped to his feet and grabbed Akiko by the throat. He lifted her off the sofa. Her lungs gasped for air. Her eyes bulged.

"Stop! Stop now!" yelled the tall man. "We cannot win if we fight with each other. Let's go get a bowl of noodles and calm down."

Black glasses released Akiko, who fell to the floor wheezing. The tall man lifted her up and held her in his arms, petting her back and saying soothing words. Akiko looked over his shoulder at black glasses and mouthed a silent curse at him.

Black glasses mouthed "gaki" back at her.

The Bridge Across The Ocean

Jed awoke to the sound of the shower coming from the bathroom. He quickly slipped into his clothes and ran downstairs to David and Rick's room. "Guys, I talked to Gregg last night. The Smithworks computer system has been hacked."

"Oh, no! Our little espionage buddies again?" said David.

"I don't believe it," said Rick. "I just cannot believe this. Why? I just don't get it! Why are they coming after us again and again?"

Jed said, "You can believe it, but I'm not sure any of us can understand it, except they think we have something of value and they want to know what it is. And then they take it away from us." He sat down on the bed.

"This isn't right," said David. "Is it because of Angela? They're following her because she's an intellectual property attorney and then latching onto us?"

"Had to start there," said Rick. "But the phone calls . . ." He stopped, realizing his cellphone had caused that leak.

"You guys are trying to understand," said Jed. "Forget about the why. Focus on *what*. What do they want? They don't know. I tried to show them there was nothing of interest when they came sniffing around at the train station. Think about *how* we deal with them." He paused to let that sink it. "Counterespionage! We need to exploit their weak link and disarm them. Maybe the Japanese woman who was trying to get something out of Wei-Ting. Ah . . . hey, I just had an idea."

"What?" said David.

Jed was silent again. "Hmmm, not so much of an idea as an insight. Let me think about it a little, see if I can work it out. We'll talk later, OK?"

"Sure, Bossman," said Rick. "In the meantime, what about the hack back in Nashua?"

"Gregg's on it. He's called in a five-star cybersecurity company. Out of Virginia, he said. They're fixing the holes."

"Did we lose anything?"

"I've thought a lot about that. I don't think so. As you know, the Spinner data is only on my flash drive in Jung-Shan's office safe, and the backup is in our bank's safe deposit box. Nothing is stored on the server, for exactly this reason. The only other data—he wiggled his fingers—is the PowerPoint file on Rick's laptop, which isn't much, and that's locked up in Jung-Shan's office safe, too. Gregg pulled the plug on the Internet, so no way they can hack in again until the computers have been secured. The dude's a good GM."

"Is the hack going to disrupt our business?" said David.

"I wondered about that, too," said Jed. "Probably not if we aren't down for long. Now here's the thing, guys. Don't say anything about this to Jung-Shan. TII and Taiwan Micronics already got scared off by the information worms, but as far as anybody else knows they've left us alone since the night at the train station. Let's let 'em think that. Nobody needs to know about the hack. We need this meeting to happen. Now. We need to get things in gear, otherwise we're gonna be going home without a deal."

"Bossman," said Rick, "Maybe we ought to drop this whole thing. I mean, none of the bike companies back home wanted it, and now we've gotten ourselves in a real mess here. I don't think these espionage freaks are gonna leave us alone, ever."

"You forget, Rick, it wasn't that the American companies didn't *want* the Spinner. They wanted to *own* it. Their terms, not ours. And Joyful is the best partner we could hope for. They're building a new factory just to make NewBikes for worldwide sales. Twenty thousand NewBikes just for Taipei next year, and every one will have our Spinner drive! Who knows how big this could get? No, guys, we gotta take this as far as we can. We'll be millionaires. We can do a whole bunch of interesting stuff with our lives. Hell, we could retire if we wanted to."

"Is that what you want out of this, Jed? To be a millionaire?" said David. "After putting almost ten years into Smithworks, we're doing all right, aren't we? The Spinner has already cost us Luke's life. Now we're stalked by thieves. Is becoming millionaires worth all this—this grief?"

"No, no, Dave, you know it's not about the money for me. I don't want to sell Smithworks out and I could care less about becoming a millionaire. I'm just trying to make a point: Let's put the same energy and commitment into the Spinner that we put into Smithworks. Let's not be quitters when the going gets tough. That's not the way we raced, and it's not the way we've run either one of our bike companies. I mean, think how it would look to Joyful and Gregg and everybody else back home if we just tucked our tails between our legs and quit now because a couple dipshit assholes have been trying to scare us." He paused. "Think how Luke would feel if we quit now.

"These thieves are on a fishing expedition. They *think* we *might* have something, but they don't have a clue what it is. Am I right? Am I right?"

Rick looked down at his hands and said, "You just might be right."

David nodded. "You're probably right."

"Yes, I am right," said Jed.

"And," said Rick, "don't think for a minute we don't know you are crazy whacked-out, head-over-heels in love with Miss Jung-Shan Lai and don't want to lose face with her." A big grin spread across his face. "Hey, Bossman, I do believe you're blushing!"

"Lose *face*," said Jed. "You're an idiot, Rick, but I don't know how I'd ever get along without you."

"Just try not to," he said.

Jed stood up and grabbed David and Rick in a man-hug. "C'mon, let's have some breakfast and get out on those gorgeous bikes. This is what it's all about, guys. Riding our bikes. Right? I'm really lookin' forward to this three-island tour today."

They left Magong City, pedaling north on Highway 203. Jed noticed a small beach littered with detritus from the sea and the ships that sail it. They stopped, dismounted, to look at all the stuff that had washed up: rope, driftwood, leafy aquatic vines, bamboo poles, fishing nets, a variety of plastic and Styrofoam floats, large glass light bulbs, thousands of plastic water and tea bottles, single flip-flops, liquor bottles. An endless mass spread along the water's edge for hundreds of yards.

"That's really disgusting," said Jed.

David, eyeing a clot of flotsam, cried out, "Oh, my god!" The others rushed over. It was a human arm, pallid and partially eaten, ostensibly by fish.

"Time to get rollin," said Jed. They did.

Buffeted by the breeze off the water, they swiftly crossed the bridge from Baisha Island to Bei Hai Island. The wind changed direction, huffing into their faces. Jung-Shan dropped behind a bit as the wind grew stronger.

"Remember, everybody," Jed, now leading the ride, called back, "Mountains make you stronger, the wind gives you endurance." Jung-Shan downshifted, rose up on her pedals and stroked. Within a minute, she was riding beside Jed again. "*Tăo yàn*," she said to him.

"Huh?"

"You are a brat," she replied with a sweet smile.

They came to a fork in the highway; a sign on the right directed them to the Penghu Great Bridge, but Jung-Shan signaled them to turn off to the left instead. A short distance ahead was a temple-style city entrance arch, similar to the one in Fenggui; beyond they saw festive activities in the road. Cars and scooters were parked everywhere; music played, people dallied eating icees and snacks from carts, buying trinkets, burning joss sticks, crossing back and forth across the pavement from the tourist stands to tables on a large covered stone patio. "This is Tongliang. It is home of the Great Banyan."

"The tree, right?" said David. Jung-Shan nodded and pointed to the patio. "Oh, I get it," he said, seeing that the entire structure, made of stone posts and timbers crisscrossing from the patio over the roadway, was completely covered with root-like limbs and branches growing in every direction. "So that's all banyan trees?"

"All you see is *one* tree," she said. Here and there the former support system was visible: aged wooden posts and beams, painted in temple fashion and carved with the twelve creatures of the Chinese zodiac. A painted mural depicting the Tongliang banyan tree history spanned the patio wall.

"The Great Banyan is three hundred years old," said Jung-Shan. "One root. I will show you. This is the nature of the banyan. It becomes one with everything around it. That is why it makes people joyful." They parked their bikes and walked to the other end of the patio. "This is the Baoan Temple. Buddhist. You see the red ribbon over there? That is the Beginning root of the banyan."

"One tree. All from a single root. Quite incredible," said David.

"Huh," said Rick, "The original trunk." He walked toward it, touched the ribbon. "Seems like these people are partying more than praying."

"Buddhism celebrates happiness," said Jung-Shan. "The temple brings people together for joys. All good, all good. We should have a party too, have a prickly pear cactus icee." So they did.

Approaching the Penghu Great Bridge from Baisha, crossing to Xiyu, David called out, "Look! NewBikes!" Alongside the road, a bike rack held a dozen or more light-blue fat-tire bikes with red seats, a helmet dangling from every handlebar. They stopped to check them out.

"These are for tourism," said Jung-Shan, "free for people to ride across the Great Bridge. This is the longest bridge in all China, at least for the present." She grinned and spread her arms as if to encompass all they saw. "This is known as the only bridge to cross the ocean, even if only for a short distance. Tourists ride or walk across to hear the Roaring Gate waters below. The ocean makes very loud water sounds you will see . . . um, hear, for yourselves.

"Someday soon, perhaps these will truly be Joyful NewBikes with the Spinner drives," said Jung-Shan as she began pedaling.

"Woo-Hoo! I'm down with that!" said Rick.

They rolled through elegant stone arch onto the Penghu Great Bridge, past the two frolicking stone dolphins.

David said, "It seems like so much in Taiwanese?—Chinese?—culture has symbolic meaning. It's like some person or history or part of your culture is embedded into names. Like this bridge. Like the dolphins."

"Yes, David, you are correct," said Jung-Shan. "The dolphin is a treasured spirit animal to Chinese people. We are very proud of our long culture and everything that is part of it. It is our duty to honor it."

They hit the pedals, swooped through the arch and started across the bridge, now fighting a strong easterly crosswind. David and Jed rode together in front, Rick and Jung-Shan drafting.

"How long is this bridge?" Rick asked her. They pedaled past the concrete seawalls; big breakers swept from the sea under the bridge. The sound of the sea swells grew louder. "Wow, you were right, the waters *really* roar!"

Jung-Shan nodded. "It is about three-thousand meters long. The bridge across the ocean."

"Hmm. Almost two miles. This is the Taiwan Strait? The East China Sea, right?" Jung-Shan nodded. "It's beautiful, but the wind sure is strong."

They pedaled on, the roar receding. She raised her left hand and carved an arc in the air. "We ride—have ridden—in a big arc from Magong. North to Baisha, now south to Xiyu Island. The tip of Xiyu looks across the water at Magong. We are riding all this way, then we must go back the same way."

Rick grinned at her, but before he could say anything Jung-Shan hit the pedals and shot away from him. "Hey!" he shouted and took off after her. David and Jed joined the race and sooner than not they had reached the other side. More public-use bikes were parked at the Xiyu portal, but they had seen no other cyclists. The wind slacked off as they moved toward the center of Xiyu, and they rode more easily, passing tall Pacific spruce and silver willow trees and light blue utility boxes with fish painted on them.

"We will stop for lunch?" Jung-Shan called out, more of a command than a question; no one said no. A road bore off to the right and they hooked onto it, entering a small, seemingly deserted, village. Although they would never have recognized it as such, a restaurant stood at the junction of four narrow streets. "This is where we will eat," she said. "This is a respected restaurant. It is called in English 'Pure Heart.'"

"Pure heart or not," said Rick, "how do we secure our bikes?"

Jung-Shan pushed her bike over to an ancient barn behind the restaurant where an old man snoozed on a hay bale. She awoke him and handed him some money. "He will watch our bicycles. They will be safe."

"After yesterday, I sure hope so," muttered Rick as they rolled their bikes into the barn.

The restaurant walls were covered with photographs, many yellowed with age, each one of the owner with famous guests. Jung-Shan pointed to a commemorative plate, explaining that Chiang Kai-Shek's son had eaten here.

"Ah, fame, ah fortune," said David, "even passed on in the genes."

The menu was all seafood, exceedingly simple, everything a la carte. As they looked at the photographs of the dishes, the waitress made suggestions to Jung-Shan: they should have this, or they had to order two or more of that. Her manner was so imperious that Jung-Shan closed her menu and conceded the food order to the woman. The dishes came out and circulated around the table. It was good, and by the time the soup arrived, everyone was stuffed. The waitress returned and spoke tersely again to them; Jung-Shan turned to the guys and said the woman told her they should finish the soup, that it was good soup, that they would hurt the chef's feelings if they didn't.

After lunch, they toured Erkan village. "Houses in the village were built many long years ago of coral, then plastered over," said Jung-Shan. "This is the only place to see houses all made of coral."

They walked the narrow footpaths past row upon row of rather nondescript bunker-like houses. Chunks of coral, far from the pretty pinks and reds common to jewelry, were visible in places where the plaster had broken. "Coral beds under the sea are now protected as our national treasure," said Jung-Shan. "It is forbidden to harvest coral unless you possess government permits." Tourists milled about, taking pictures; villagers posed, smiling, and were tipped. Life-sized concrete statues of abstract cows dominated one villager's yard; beadwork and figures carved from wood and stone abounded in the tiny shops.

They hydrated, then swung their legs back over their top tubes and pedaled on to Neian, so reminiscent of a Mediterranean village. Jung-Shan said it was the wealthiest fishing town in all of Taiwan.

"So what Neian is telling us is that being a fisherman is very lucrative?" said Jed.

"That is so," said Jung-Shan. "The Penghu Islands are all about fishing. Yesterday you saw weirs. You have seen many fishing boats. Penghu is our name after the Portuguese word, *pescadore*. You recall the Pescadores buildings in Magong? Also Caffé Pescadore coffee shop? Pescadore is the word for fish. Fish, fish, all about fish!" She laughed her throaty, happy laugh.

They dismounted to visit the Taoist temple, then crossed the street to the piers where large, well-maintained fishing boats, festooned with those large light bulbs used to attract the fish, shared slips with luxurious yachts. They slugged down bottles of cool water and tossed the empties into a recycling barrel. Rick smiled at a girl passing by on her scooter, who smiled back before blasting off down the wharf.

"OK, if you are finished, Rick, can we go now?" said Jung-Shan.

"Where we going?" said Rick, feigning being dumbfounded.

Jung-Shan grinned, pointed up the road and said, "As I told you, now we ride back."

"Already?" said Rick, his eyes still following the girl on the scooter.

"Yes," she said, tightening the Velcro strap on her glove. "You have a problem with that?"

Jed cracked up, and David did, too.

So it was back on the bikes, up the winding street out of Neian to the top of the hill and onto the highway heading back. Jed looked at the road sign overhead; it said twenty-nine klicks back to Magong. About eighteen miles. Thirty, forty miles total today; not a bad ride. With a belly filled with fresh water, he was ready to ride. He stood on his pedals to climb the hill, Jung-Shan drafting tightly behind him all the way. Once on the straightaway, she pulled up beside him and stayed there. The klicks rolled by. Soon they were crossing the Great Bridge again. Jed said, "This bridge. It's called the bridge across the ocean, right?"

"Yes," said Jung-Shan.

"I was thinking it's like what we're doing. Smithworks and Joyful. We Americans and you Taiwanese. We're building a bridge across the ocean." They were both silent as they crossed the center of the bridge, where the crosswinds howled against them.

"One thing I'll never figure out as long as I ride is how the wind can blow in your face no matter which direction you're going."

She looked at him over her sunglasses, grinned, and said, "Luck."

They arrived at the inn mid-afternoon. Jung-Shan called her assistant to request the airplane while the guys got the bikes ready to go. Ashton and Min sent them off with a picnic basket lunch for the plane ride back. Jung-Shan retrieved her carry-on and handed them a round package shaped like a cheese or a cake. "This is forever tea from my family to yours," she said.

"Forever tea? Oh, Jung-Shan!" said Min.

"My family is forever indebted to you for your hospitality and kindness. We give you these forever teas forever."

"Ai! xiè xiè, Jung-Shan," said Ashton. "Please give our love and deepest regards to your father."

The Luxgen7 MPV taxi whisked them to the airport. "I am calling Mr. Zheng to tell him we are on our way back," Jung-Shan said as they waited for the bikes to be loaded. She wandered away while she made the call. Jed fidgeted, worried the meeting tomorrow would not happen, that TII and Taiwan Micronics might still be scared off by the agents of espionage. Jung-Shan returned, all smiles. "Now I am happy to tell you we are meeting with all partners tomorrow."

"That's great!" said Jed. "What happened to change their minds?"

"My father," she said, "is a very clever man. He likes to say, turn fear into ferocity. Like the tiger, right? Mr. Zheng has been talking to our possible partners. He told them he is convinced the NewBike will not be a success without the Spinner. Then he told them his secret, that Joyful is already a building new factory that will make only NewBikes. He said to them he has one hundred percent confidence in Smithworks as partner and in your Spinner technology. He says he thinks this is a golden opportunity to create stronger relationships between Taiwan and the United States.

"Mr. Zheng told them all these things, but they were still worried." Jung-Shan paused. "And this is where my father turned their fear into ferocity. My father told them the agents of espionage showing interest in the Spinner drive is proof that it is a valuable technology. But competitors cannot copy it. Not possible at all. He told them it can only be made if all four of our companies work together. Nobody can make the Spinner NewBike except us four, and our efforts will make us all rich! Smithworks knew this and so turned down the American bicycle companies because they lacked the foresight to see this great opportunity!

"The second clever way of my father was giving many, many compliments to Taiwan Micronics and TII. This is his way to say they would be very wise and farsighted to partner with Smithworks and Joyful. Now if they were to say they are not interested, they would lose face!" She was beaming with excitement and delight. "My father talked to them many, many times while we were gone. He turned their fear into ferocity! Now they are eager to have the meeting with you as soon as possible. So we meet tomorrow morning at 11AM."

"Wow, I'm not believing this," said Jed.

"Yes, you see, you can believe it." Jung-Shan couldn't take the smile from her face. "Mr. Zheng, he is a very clever businessman! Is it not so?"

"Oh, yeah, he certainly is," said Jed. "He most certainly is."

Threat Vector

The Thursday afternoon sun was setting on the tall, sleek T-shaped tail of the Joyful Bike Fokker 70 as it touched down at Taipei Songshan Airport and taxied to its private hangar. Inside, three cars awaited the passengers: the silver GMC Yukon SUV, the white Cadillac town car, and an older, nondescript Toyota Celica. Jung-Shan was first off and walked away dialing her iPhone. Jed and the guys trod down the airstairs and stood, stretching. She finished her call and came over to them. "I was speaking with Derek," she said. "He will arrive shortly. He looked for GPS tracking devices and bugs after we departed for Penghu and did not find anything. We will discuss his moving forward plan."

Derek arrived on a maintenance truck, dressed in coveralls. "Hey, great disguise," said Jed as they shook hands.

"Miss Lai," said Derek and bowed. "We are still in defensive mode here," Derek explained to the four. "It's quite possible they think you've departed the country, but nonetheless I suspect they're still here looking for you chaps." His eyes moved from Jed to Rick to David. "I have devised a plan to confirm these presumptions with as little risk as I can manage.

"Phase one of the plan begins now. Wei-Ting will load the bikes in the Jimmy and drive to the executive inn. He will park in the guest car park area, outside. If the worms are still surveilling there, they will no doubt see the vehicle."

"A red herring," said Jed.

"Certainly a more colorful term to describe a misdirection," said Derek, grinning. He went on to explain how Wei-Ting would stay the night, then drive the Jimmy to the car park beneath the Chiang Kai-Shek Memorial where it would remain all day Friday. Tomorrow night, he would drive back to Serenity Garden.

The second car, the limousine, would drop Jung-Shan at the Mingyao department store where she would lose herself in the crowds, eventually entering the Blue Line MRT entrance underneath. She would take the subway to the Shandao Temple station, then walk the subterranean pedestrian tunnel a block to the Joyful building elevator. When work hours ended, she would take a taxi to her apartment.

"Not least," said Derek, "I will drive you three in this Toyota to three different destinations. What they share in common is the MRT, by which you will be able to arrive undetected via the tunnels at the Crystal Palace hotel at differing times. But by all means, remain in the underground and follow the signage to the hotel lifts. You will perforce arrive in the lobby.

"When you do, rather than make you queue up at check-in, I have already obtained your room assignments and keycards." Derek handed out small envelopes with credit-card sized keycards tucked inside. "Once in the lobby, immediately board a lift designated for the guest floors. We are in executive suites on the 22nd floor. Miss Lai will not be staying in the hotel as before. However, I will be either nearby in my room or in communication with you at all times.

"I believe we can execute this plan and remain unnoticed by the information worms for as long as we wish." They all nodded.

"This is a good plan," said Jung-Shan, "but Derek has only explained the first stage. Here is what happens tonight after you are safely in your rooms and I have signaled my arrival at my apartment. After a few hours' time, Derek will drive the Toyota to the Crystal Palace car park entrance. He is already a registered guest, so he will let the valet park the car. He will leave and walk Linsen to the corner at Zhongxiao Road, turn left and pass Shandao Temple, then take the few steps to cross Shaoxing Street into Starbucks. It is just one city block from the hotel. If during this time you think something is not right, please leave a callback message for him at the hotel front desk. No text messages. Derek will order coffee and drink it slowly. He will walk to the hotel front desk several times. If no messages wait for him, it means the worms do not know where you are."

"What about you?" Jed asked Jung-Shan.

"I will send Derek a text when I am safely home," she said.

"I don't expect them to find you," said Derek. "My intention is to create a diversion that will leave them no alternative but to return to the Serenity Garden, where they will find the Jimmy parked in plain view. I want them to think you are in your inn rooms."

"Aha," said Rick.

Jung-Shan said, "Once he is certain we are secure, Derek will go back into the car park in order to take the MRT to the inn. Lucy will be on duty. She and Wei-Ting are informed about this phase of the plan. If the worms ask to enter, or if the woman housekeeper comes to the door, Lucy is to allow them to enter, but to call the police at once. Derek will be on watch within the hotel perimeter."

"It is at this place and time that I hope to catch the thieves in an unlawful act and have them arrested," said Derek.

"Speaking from my Army experience, this is a solid intelligence operative's plan," said Jed. "Bravo."

Derek grinned. "Perhaps the planning of an ex-MI6 intel operative?"

"So it's true!" said Jed. "I do have a question, one intel officer to another. What is your objective?"

"Twofold, Jed. Phase one is to determine if the threat vector is still present. To confirm that the agents are still operational," said Derek.

"And if they are?" said David.

"That informs a 'go' for phase two: Deploy either another misdirection or, more seriously, an operation to attempt an end to their pursuit, preferably with law enforcement ready to make arrests for the commission of a crime."

"A takedown," said Jed solemnly. Derek nodded. "Which do you anticipate happening at Serenity Garden?"

Derek nodded and said, "A trap which I believe is ready to be sprung. At no point do any of you take action. Agreed?"

"I agree, even though I wish we could take 'em down ourselves," said Jed.

"What he means is he wishes *he* could take them down," said Rick nodded. David nodded.

"Do I need to mention that you are Americans and that the information worms are Japanese? That both of you are, uh, outlanders on foreign soil?" said Derek. He looked around at the guys.

"I think it's a workable plan," said David.

"What do we do once we're in the Crystal Palace? Sit on our hands in our rooms?" said Rick with a silly grin.

"Just so. Please do not visit the lobby bar or restaurants," said Jung-Shan. "Order food or drink from room service."

"You could try on the new business casual clothes Jung-Shan bought you for tomorrow's meeting," Jed said.

"Wise ass," said Rick. "You said there's an underground route from the hotel to Joyful?"

"Yes, there is," said Jung-Shan. "Take the lift down to car park level two, then walk to Sector 2G. You will see an unmarked steel door. Access is by keypad only. Tap in 569385—that's JOYFUL—and press the pound key. The door opens into the lift. It will take you to the Joyful atrium only. You still need to check through security."

"Slick," said Rick. "Very slick."

"But you don't have a need to go there, at least just yet," said Jed to Rick. "OK, guys, let us hit the trail as you say in America," said Jung-Shan.

Jed grinned when she said "guys," pleased to hear she felt like she was one of them. "So you aren't staying with us?" Jed said to Jung-Shan. "I mean, at the hotel?"

She shook her head. "My apartment is within walking distance."

"Oh. Well . . . um, I need to talk with you and Derek about something," said Jed. "Can we talk at dinner?"

"Yes, of course," she smiled as she tossed her long hair away from her face. "A late dinner, if you please. That is phase three of the plan."

Phase one unfolded. Wei-Ting departed the hangar in the Jimmy for Serenity Garden. Jung-Shan left in the limo, ostensibly to go shopping. Derek, in the Toyota, zig-zagged the guys through Taipei traffic to their respective MRT stations. Everything went like clockwork, except when Rick arrived he didn't head up to his room; instead, he punched L1. The elevator door opened onto a brightly lit tunnel filled with shoppers, a mall indistinguishable from one above ground except not as expansive. Busy shops lined both sides, selling mostly women's clothing, shoes, jewelry. Rick gazed at the gorgeous women shopping all around him. The door closed, and he punched L2. This floor was a consumer electronics mall. To the left and right, the tunnel was a jam-packed personal technology marketplace: every imaginable cable, part, peripheral, laptop, software app and game. Shop after shop selling Taiwan Acer and Asus and MSI laptops.

"Wow," said Rick, awed. Not far away he saw a hub where tunnels branched off like spider legs. Derek had been right: he could get lost here quickly. Reluctantly, he made his way back to the hotel lift and used his keycard to access the twenty-second floor. There was the all-important afternoon meeting to prepare for tomorrow, and he had better not miss it.

Their rooms were five-star, with a floor-to-ceiling tinted-glass wall overlooking Taipei. Automatic sensors turned on the lights and air conditioning when Rick inserted his key card in the wall receptacle.

The huge flat-screen TV came on by itself and played a welcoming video. The bathroom was stunning: walls, floor and ceiling in rose marble. A glass-walled shower capacious enough for two, maybe even three. A Toto Washlet toilet. A beautiful flower-shaped sink poised atop a slab of marble, accented with a live orchid in a crystal vase. He showered, shaved, dressed and went to Jed's room. David was already there.

"Anybody have trouble getting here?" said Jed.

"No, but I'm sure getting tired of getting bumped into," said Rick. "These people don't want to walk on the right side, like Americans. Or the left side, for all it matters. Walkin' down the street is kinda like playing dodgeball."

David looked at Rick, wondering if he'd been out on the streets girl-watching, and shook his head. "Don't believe I've ever stayed in a hotel as elegant as this," he said, walking over to the window wall. "Wonder what that is?" He pointed at a complex below, which occupied an entire city block, maybe more. A portal with five arches opened onto a broad walkway toward a temple-like building at the other end. Twin staircases, separated by stone bas-relief, climbed to the tall doors of the magnificent white edifice with two blue roofs towering above. On each side of the walkway were classic Chinese buildings with red pillars all around and golden roofs atop, landscaped with elegant flower beds, manicured lawns, trees and gardens. The guys could see people—lots of people, the size of ants—strolling, climbing and descending the steps, taking pictures of each other.

"I sure wish Luke was here. He could tell us. Man, how I miss that guy!" Jed's face contorted with sadness. Rick and David suddenly looked like they were about to start bawling. Jed looked down at his phone. "Hey, guys," he said softly, "Let's get busy. We need to review the presentation."

"Wait," said David. "We need our stuff from Jung-Shan's office. Especially the computer, for the PowerPoint."

" She's coming over here. I'll text her," said Jed.

They talked about tomorrow's meeting strategy for the next hour or so. They expected it would be a mostly pleasant conversation, hopefully in English. "Joyful and us, we're like the computer software and hardware company," said David. "Micronics and TII are peripherals manufacturers. They make the ceramics and electronics to our specs, so in a way they aren't truly partners, they're suppliers. But we can't manufacture in quantity without them, so we have to treat them with the respect of partners. Most important, all four of us have to pay strict attention to their cultural protocols and business details. We don't want to be misunderstood. Our specs can't be subject to interpretation or substitution or cutting any corners."

There was a knock at the door. Rick answered; it was Jung-Shan with his laptop in its messenger bag. She quickly closed the door, passed it to him and said, "Derek has informed me there is possible identification of the targets at the executive inn. He saw two men with one woman walking in garden, near the car park. May be them. May be nothing. He will maintain surveillance at the inn and not come to the Crystal Palace now, but will try to join us at the restaurant where we are meeting for dinner."

"They already followed us to a restaurant once," said David.

"Tonight is very safe. We go to my uncle's hotel. It is a private restaurant in downtown Taipei. *Very* private. No worries about uninvited people."

"Are we gonna have to sneak around and hide all the time?" said Rick, clearly annoyed. "I'm sure gettin' sick of this." They had exited through the Zhongxiao underground shopping mall, emerging from an exit blocks away. Certain they weren't being followed, they hopped a taxi to the Long Du restaurant. The elderly uniformed elevator operator immediately recognized Jung-Shan and whisked them to the third floor, where Derek awaited them.

"Now Rick, try not to get your knickers in a twist," said Derek. "Remember, we are putting tradecraft into play."

"Tradecraft?"

"Sorry, I'm speaking in jargon. A plan. We've set up Wei-Ting and the Jimmy as a ploy to lure them. It may already be working. I'll keep you apprised."

Jed sat between Derek and Jung-Shan. While David and Rick conversed, he said, "I need to tell you both something: our computer network at Smithworks was hacked."

"*What?*" said Jung-Shan.

"When did this happen?" said Derek.

"While we were in the islands. No information was compromised, as best we can tell." He sipped his tea and continued. "They got in through a network trapdoor in the 3D printer, but Gregg says it self-wipes the files once it's finished printing and besides it's not connected to our local area network. So I don't know if it's a big deal or not, but I thought you ought to know."

"I would like to obtain a briefing from your security service and perhaps consult an expert of my acquaintance in Hong Kong," said Derek.

"Of course." Food began arriving. "I didn't realize your uncle owned this hotel, too," said Jed, anxious to change the subject.

'He also owns the Jianguo Hotel," she said.

While Rick and David fell into a protracted discussion with Derek about plan details, Jed thought about that. There was something he wasn't getting. He turned to Jung-Shan. "So . . . why was it that Angela recommended the Jianguo Hotel?"

"Hǎo. Angela is friends with my cousin, Tsai-Chi. Her father is my uncle. Angela is a good friend with Sun Xiaohui. You know this already, yes? We were all schoolmates with Lin Bao. We remain friends for all these times, long after high school and college. So you see, it is a small world."

Jed smiled. "Your uncle is your father's brother?" he said, glancing at the guys.

"No, this uncle is the brother of my mother."

"Your mother. You haven't mentioned her," said Jed.

"She is already gone to heaven," said Jung-Shan.

"Oh. I'm sorry."

"When I was six years old. A very young age to lose your only mother."

"I don't think there's ever a good time to lose your mother," said Jed. "Your father didn't remarry?"

"No. After that, he was in all ways devoted to raising his daughters. And to Joyful, of course."

"Of course. How did she, um, pass away, if I may ask?"

"In birth to my sister," said Jung-Shan.

Meanwhile – The Streets of Taipei

The small man with black glasses and his tall partner spent the better part of four days on the streets of Taipei, walking and taking taxis between the places they had last seen the Americans: the Grand Hotel, Serenity Garden inn, Taoyuan airport, the One Path massage spa across the street from the Jianguo Hotel, the train station, every klick of the MRT, and all the nearby restaurants they could find. They prowled all day and late into the night, searching for some sign of the Jimmy or their prey.

"Did you not plant the GPS tracking device on the truck?" asked black glasses of his partner.

"Of course, but only yesterday. The truck has not moved. Tracking device, it has a very limited range. I do not know . . . or perhaps they found it and deactivated it."

"Arrrgh," said black glasses.

Akiko, still working as a housekeeper at the inn, reported the Americans and their female Taiwanese associate had not returned to their rooms. Akiko had been unable to get Lucy or any of the staff to divulge names—or anything else, for that matter—about the guests, although she had not really tried very hard. The microphones remained active in the rooms, but of course had picked up nothing.

Their trail was, for all intents and purposes, dead.

It was the morning of the fifth day since the last sighting. The three were finishing another disappointing breakfast—cold fried eggs and spoiled fruit—in the hotel. Black glasses said, "This is all. They have left. I give up. We will fly home today." His tall partner mugged a disappointed look. Akiko silently cheered.

Half an hour later they were standing at the curb on Nanjing Road

East, about to step into a taxi that would take them to the airport, when Akiko cried out, "Hai! Look! It's their silver SUV!" She waved at Wei-Ting, who was heading for Taipei Songshan Airport to meet the guys, who would be returning from Penghu later in the day. Wei-Ting did not see her.

"I knew they were still here," said black glasses. "I am never wrong. We will follow," he said to his partner, pulling the taxi door open. "Akiko, take our luggage, go get our rooms back."

Agreement in Principle

They arrived on the eighth floor of the Joyful Bike building at 10:49 the following morning and were greeted by Jung-Shan and her father. "I am grateful you are a few minutes early," Zheng Ming-Chiang said, bowing. He escorted them into his private office, where they sat informally. "I have had many conversations with Mr. Huang of Taiwan Integrated Industry and Mr. Kueh of Taiwan Micronics while you were visiting Penghu," he began, entwining his fingers as he spoke. "Such a meeting as we are about to conduct, to discuss a joint venture between four companies, it is very rare in Taiwan. Perhaps anywhere, but especially since one company is American." Zheng locked his fingers together and continued, "I have emphasized to Huang and

Kueh that we must enter into business with you. We are four partners, each bringing most valuable business expertise together.

"I have told them I do not believe espionage agents would seek your business information if they did not think there was something of value to steal." He chuckled. Jed, David and Rick chuckled with him. Jung-Shan sat very still, expectant, hands in her lap, eyes on her father. "At first we think it is Shigerumaki after the Spinner. They are the world number one components maker, and we buy millions of gruppos from them each year. I asked, why would they risk losing our business this way? So I think it is not them.

"But then I think the agents are working for Guangdong Bicycle Works." Zheng said. "They are the number one Chinese bicycle maker and our number one competitor in mainland China market. Joyful has factories in Guangdong, too," he chuckled again, "but we are so confidential our companies could be on different planets!"

Zheng sipped his tea. He stopped and looked at the guys and his daughter. Jed raised his eyebrows. "Here is what I think," he went on. "The agents from Tokyo. They are scavengers. They follow your attorney friend Angela Xiao. They know nothing about you, but from you they learn about bicycles business. Then they tell Guangdong Bicycle that American bicycles people are meeting with Joyful to make a big business deal! They do not know this, of course, but it is how things look to the outside. And so they get money from Guangdong for their business espionage, to find out what the big business deal is. If they can find out what we are doing, they will get—what do you say in America, a finder fee?"

Jed nodded. "Sir, we are all agreed to stop them dead in their tracks, right now, before anything more can happen. We want these *worms* shut down, and we think Derek has put together a pretty good plan to get it done."

Jung-Shan said, "Phase one was implemented and carried out flawlessly by each of us. Nothing has changed since then. We'll see what happens when Wei-Ting returns in the Jimmy to the inn tonight."

Zheng nodded. "Jung-Shan and Derek have given me a briefing about the plan. I am in favor of it."

"Wait," said Jed. "Before we just sit on the sidelines observing what's going down tonight, just waiting for them to act, I think we need to stay flexible. Be prepared to change the game plan if necessary."

"We've tried to factor in as many contingencies to thwart them as possible," David explained.

"Xiè xiè, xiè xiè. I know this contingency planning to be your specialty, Mr. Bondsman. It would be very excellent to catch them tonight and have them arrested. Correct, daughter?"

"Yes, father." Jung-Shan smiled at Jed. It was the first time Zheng had acknowledged her as family. "We have discussed the most contingencies we can plan for. But we think we can stop them tonight, once and for all."

They chatted for a few minutes, then Mr. Zheng said, "We are all agreed on this? Yes? Now we will go to the meeting, striving to agree on the four-company business partnership."

"An agreement *in principle*," said Jed. "To see if we have the compatibility to work together."

"At the strategy level," said Rick.

"Yes, at the *strategy* level," said Jed. Apparently it was now his turn to approach the business deal with caution.

Mr. Zheng raised his eyebrows, but before he could speak, his daughter did.

"Today will be a conversation meeting, like our first meeting," said Jung-Shan. "We will take our time so everyone will get to know each other better. At the very high level. What you call strategy level. Jed, may be best for you to attend alone."

"I think it would be best for all of us to attend so the TII and Taiwan Micro teams get to know our team. We want everyone to want to work together. You, um, perhaps, should invite your two VPs again?"

Jung-Shan looked down, then at her father. "Of course," she said. "We also agree with forming consensus in business. It will be as it was before. My apologies."

"Mr. Smith is correct." said Mr. Zheng, standing to reach for his phone handset. *Make it so*, Jed said to himself. He smiled at Jung-Shan; she should not lose face. She smiled back, and the others shared the smile.

The meeting began at 11:00 o'clock sharp, everyone present and accounted for. Huang and Kueh immediately jumped protocol and began asking serious business questions: Clearly, they wanted to be Spinner partners. Everyone spoke English, but as before they often conferred with one another or with Mr. Zheng in Mandarin. Jed didn't mind; he understood how some things didn't translate well.

"We still have many details to work out to reach an agreement in principle," said Jed.

Everyone nodded, then David spoke: "Most important is how

to manage the manufacturing. No single company has all the technologies to do that. No single company should possess all the IP, for all the reasons you can think of. People, we are on the cutting edge of innovation and business partnership, so I suggest we implement the Drayton-Budinich hybrid value chain business model." He drew one on the whiteboard.

Huang and Kueh nodded with apparent enthusiasm.

Jed looked at Mr. Zheng, who nodded slightly and said, "Yes, of course, but I believe all parties will recognize it is in their best interests to work cooperatively with Smithworks, since without you we have nothing! Ha!"

Jung-Shan grinned, hiding it behind her fingertips.

It was a little past four o'clock; the meeting discussions were intense and had continued without a break for lunch, but now a tea service had begun. Servers brought in peeled shrimp, robin's eggs, caviar and toast, assorted fruits, a chocolate mousse and French éclairs. Everyone ate and drank with cheerfulness and gusto. Then, suddenly, they were saying good-byes, shaking hands, bowing. Mr. Zheng said to Jed, "They say they do not wish to offend your customs, but would it be possible to meet again tomorrow? It is Saturday, but they would like to talk more and take you on tour of their plants, too."

Jed smiled and said, "By all means, sir."

Rick said, "I can't remember the last time we *didn't* work on a Saturday. Or a Sunday, for that matter."

"Mr. Zheng, we appreciate all you've done to move things forward," said Jed. They were back in his private office. "Jung-Shan explained how you turned fear into ferocity. I'll remember that. Xiè xiè."

Zheng waved a hand dismissively. "It is in my interests, too," he said. "Joyful already committed to NewBike. You too have turned fear into ferocity today, Mr. Smith."

David said, "When we meet tomorrow, it might make sense to show them our PowerPoint."

Zheng spoke: "In my own honesty, David, I have seen your presentation and think we moved beyond it today. Perhaps show the artist's design? It is very appealing."

David nodded and smiled.

Mr. Zheng stood. "Tomorrow, I believe we will find we have become a very profitable and satisfying relationship. Do you agree, Jung-Shan?"

"Hǎo," she said, standing, then glancing quickly at Jed, "I agree very much."

Before dinner, Derek, Jed, Rick, David and Jung-Shan met with Wei-Ting where the Jimmy was parked, now in a dark remote corner of the hotel underground garage. The rotund little man smiled and bowed. "Your bikes inside," he said. "Want to go for a ride? I take you!"

"Not us, but we do want you to take someone for a ride," said Rick.

Wei-Ting looked confused.

Jed said, "Before you drove over here, you'd been parked at the executive inn since yesterday, right? Have you seen those people?"

Wei-Ting still looked confused, so Derek spoke to him in Mandarin. "Yes," he said. "They have been. I see them once walking outside last night."

"You were outside?" Derek said.

"Yes. Cleaning Jimmy. I already tell Derek."

"Yeah? Then what happened?" said Jed.

"They come back out. That is all."

"How long were they there?" said Derek.

"Not long," said Wei-Ting.

"Did they go inside?"

"No, did not go inside."

"Have you seen the Japanese woman?"

Wei-Ting lowered his head but did not speak.

Jung-Shan said something to Wei-Ting. He replied. "She was with the two men, the one with glasses and the tall man. Wei-Ting says he's followed our orders to the letter and did not try to speak with her."

"Good," said Jed and patted Wei-Ting on the shoulder. Wei-Ting raised his eyes and smiled. "Here is what I want you to do. Hang around the Jimmy like you've been doing. Be visible. Make sure they see you. After a while, go order something in the Dante coffee shop and take a seat. If we're lucky, the woman will come in looking for you."

Jung-Shan translated, just to make sure he understood.

"OK."

"Wei-Ting," said Derek, "You understand we are changing the orders now. We *want* the woman to see you. She will try to compromise you somehow, and you must let her."

"Com-promise? I do not know."

Jung-Shan explained.

"So," he said, his eyes lighting up, "she want to have drinks, I buy? She want to go to my room, is OK?"

"That's right," said Derek. "Now, this is important. Very important.

You let her compro—you let her know if she gives you some money, you will tell her all about the Americans and why they're here in Taiwan. Make her think you know something very important, something the Americans wouldn't want anyone to know. Get her alone. Ask her why she and the two men are interested. Get her to talk, but tell her nothing! You need to know what they want so you can say you'll get it for them. Do this well and she will promise you more and more money. And kisses. Tell her the bicycles are very special, very expensive." An idea struck him: "Say you can help her steal them."

"Tell her they are experimental prototypes," said Jed. "Each one has a different, extremely valuable technology, and you can show it to her."

"Very good idea, Jed," said Jung-Shan.

"It's unlikely she can make the deal and will have to go back to the men for approval. Tell her you will meet her at the Jimmy after dark. She'll call in the other two for the actual theft. Do you follow me so far?"

"Yes, yes," said Wei-Ting, clearly getting excited. "May be more than two. How much I say I sell for?"

Derek turned to Jung-Shan, who said, "These bicycles are our newest carbon fiber technology. They sell for more than 315,000 NT; in American dollars that is . . . I believe about ten thousand dollars?" So, you tell them you will sell all four for . . . ten thousand dollars US."

"But make sure you ask for *American* dollars," said Derek.

"Traceable. Slick thinking," said Rick.

"Trust me, it won't get that far," said Derek. "I'll be hiding in the shrubbery with my security team. Insist on the money first. They may or mayn't give it to you. Protest a bit. Go to the rear. Pretend you're too nervous to get it open. They must enter the SUV of their own accord. They'll unlock the hatch, climb in, begin lowering the bikes. Perhaps looking through the cartons we've left inside.

"I've already arranged a signal text to the police. We absolutely have to detain them for capture and arrest. Wei-Ting, once the hatch door opens, step back with the girl; just watch. I don't want you hurt or kidnapped. When the police come, run inside the hotel. Maybe we can get all of them at once."

Wei-Ting stood, listening, nodding.

"You think you can do this?"

"Oh, yes, I am certain I can do."

"Good for you, Wei-Ting," said Jed, and clapped him on the shoulder again.

"But will be very sorry about pretty lady from Japan."

MEANWHILE – GREED, FEAR, STUPIDITY

"Akiko, you probably think you have done an excellent job of getting this stupid driver to sell us the bicycles. I will now tell you all the things that make this a very bad situation," said black glasses.

Akiko looked at him, then at the other thief, then back at the leader. She opened her pretty little mouth to speak, but stopped when black glasses reached out and pinched her lips closed.

"Listen to me. You have learned nothing from the stupid driver except that he knows now for a certainty what we are doing and that he can profit by our espionage. You have given me nothing but concern that we are exposed. Now it will cost a great deal of money to learn whatever it is the Americans have."

"But . . . " said Akiko.

"But nothing except you are a stupid gaki, stupider even than the driver—what is his name? Wei Joon?"

"His name is Wei-Ting, and I think he's very cute."

"The problem is, Wei-Ting has no information. No knowledge. In a word, he has no chikara. *Power. He is like the taxi driver in Kowloon. Do you remember? The stupid man who thought he was a big shot agent of information because he listened to the two businessmen discussing a short sale in his taxi? Such a stupid man, and stupid on me for believing we could get in behind it and sell the information to a competing brokerage. You remember this?"*

"Ah so," said his partner, "I remember, that was a bad one. The man who was taking the bribe to short-sell was in truth the undercover police detective—"

"Hai, yes, enough, enough," said the man in black glasses, "I remember

all too well and I do not want to remember any more. Fortunately, we did not have any money in that little shippai." Fiasco. *"We were fortunate not to be identified as partners in the deal as well, something that little Akiko here did not think of and cannot protect us against if we are caught taking bicycles that do not belong to us from a car that is not our own. Is this not true, Akiko? What shall we do with stupid Wei-Ting once he lets us into the big truck? And how are we going to transport four bicycles from the inn to the Jianguo Hotel?"*

"Um, I see what you mean," she said, "but you are the experts in this— this kind of thing. I think I did a pretty good job of setting things up. I don't see why I should have to figure everything out for you."

"That is quite correct, Akiko. It is our job to use our chikara *to take this tiny morsel of information, perform our alchemy upon it, and turn it into a pot full of gold. Now go to your room. I must decide what to do with you when this is finished. Maybe I still decide to kill you, I don't know."*

"The best-laid schemes o' mice an' men"

"Think it'll work?" David said.

The five of them were dining on fried pork dumplings, cucumber salad, sesame pancakes, steamed rice, and spicy hot *ma po tofu,* which they had grown fond of, in a small restaurant without a name in some nameless alley behind Shandao Temple. The place had zero atmosphere, but the food was delicious.

After leaving the underground garage meeting, they had split up to elude potential surveillance. David and Rick spent an interesting hour traipsing through the consumer electronics stalls in the underground. Jed and Jung-Shan, acting like dutiful tourists, set out to fill designer-shop totes with stuff they really didn't need; merchants, upon seeing an exploitable American, quoted outrageous prices which Jung-Shan skillfully haggled back to something reasonable. Derek had killed time perusing security equipment, then went to Starbucks to check it out joining the others for dinner. Now they were feeling confident they were not being tailed.

"Yeah, Dave, I'm pretty sure it will go down as planned," said Jed, popping a dumpling into his mouth with his chopsticks.

"I just hope Wei-Ting doesn't screw it up," said Rick, putting words to what everyone was thinking.

"I just hope he will not be in danger," said Jung-Shan. "He is my responsibility."

"No covert op ever works to the letter of the plan," said Derek, leaning forward and speaking softly. "That said, these people are rank amateurs. We have the advantage."

"You mentioned that before. How can you tell?" said David.

"Primarily because they do not know if we have anything worth stealing. Second, because we've shaken their tail again and again. We've caught them at their game, as when they rummaged in the airplane carry-on compartment. Like catching them in the act whilst the Jimmy was parked at the train station. The clumsy search of your rooms at Serenity Garden. Seeing them enter One Path. Good grief!" Derek slapped the table and laughed out loud. "They should be utterly invisible until they decide to strike. And now, we're going to bait a hook and catch them flat-footed at their game."

He smirked and drank some tea. "Tonight's scheme—if in fact it occurs—will likely be, or lead to, the endgame. But for the next few hours, let us simply enjoy the evening."

They finished dinner and went for a walk, taking in the early-evening sights and scents of a progressive Asian city—but the sounds, not so much. The scooters buzzed around them incessantly, and not just on the street; every so often one came charging down the sidewalk, looking for a parking spot. People swarmed through street markets, buying fresh foods for dinner preparations. Lovely shop girls stood outside their stores, handing out advertising. Businessmen piloted their black BMWs and Audis and Mercedes' far too fast for traffic, weaving through foot traffic, bicycles, scooters and cars, whether driven and parked. Somehow, all coexisted and got people where they were going safely.

It grew increasingly dark, save for the brilliant light from street lamps. Traffic began to wane. They stopped at a bubble tea shop and ordered; Jed checked the time on his phone, excused himself, stepped outside and called Gregg. He finished the short call in the usual manner and rejoined the others. Derek gave him a quizzical look; Jed tossed Jung-Shan a smile. Jung-Shan caught it and tossed it back.

"Everything's cool again back at Smithworks," said Jed. He turned to Derek and said, "Gregg's getting a contact name and phone number at the security outfit for you to call." Jed looked at Jung-Shan again and said, "Sometimes your dad makes that same mischievous grin. Like when he talks about turning fear into ferocity."

"Jed!" Jung-Shan put her fingers over her smile.

"I really like your dad," said Rick. "He's way cool."

"And an elegant dresser," said David. "I couldn't get over those cufflinks he wore today."

"Yes, yin-yang are his favorite ones. My mother had them made for him." At the mention of her mother, Jung-Shan's eyes filled with tears. She dabbed them away with her napkin. Jed couldn't help it: he put his arm around her. She laid her head on his collarbone for a few moments, then sat up.

"Thank you. I am OK. I, I, still miss my mother very much."

David and Rick mumbled their apologies. They finished their bubble teas and went outside, where daylight was beginning to fade. "Is it safe to be walking around here at night?" said David.

"Very safe. There is hardly any crime in Taipei, believe it or not," said Jung-Shan. "Besides, you are big strong Americans. You can protect yourselves. You can protect me, too!" She laughed, and they joined in. She said, "But keep your phone and your money—how you call it?—yes, your bill folder—where you can touch to be sure they are safely with you. Front pockets of trousers is best. Do not let people bump into you."

"Don't let people bump into me? That's pretty tough to do," said Rick.

"Derek," said David, "why do we keep walking around? To see if those information worms are following us?"

Derek looked them over. "Sorry, chaps, I didn't propose our walk to bait a hook. I thought we might relax as we mark time before our phase two event which, by the way, we have no idea when might occur, if at all."

The guys looked at each other; at Jung-Shan. David said, "It was a nice thought, but speaking for myself, I'm just a bit too tense to enjoy this. The, uh, phase two event is pretty much all I'm thinking about."

Jed and Rick nodded.

Derek said, "That being the prevailing mood, perhaps we should return to the Crystal Palace, then I'll proceed by subway train to the inn." Jung-Shan looked around, nodded. It was agreed.

They stood in a crowd at a busy intersection, waiting for the walk signal. Scooters pulled into the white box painted on the street, ready to take off when the light turned green. It did, and they did. Pedestrians started across the street as cars and scooters nudged up to them, waiting for their right-hand turn to proceed. Derek, David and Jung-Shan were in front of Rick and Jed; a slight gap opened between them and a scooter jumped forward, trying to squirrel its way through. Rick let loose with a two-handed shove and yelled, "Why don't you wait your turn!" The scooter and driver went down. "What the hell's wrong with you people!"

Everyone stopped to gape. Rick looked at the driver, fist pulled back, ready to swing. Jed grabbed his arm and said, "Rick, stand down! It's a girl."

Rick looked aghast. He stepped over the scooter, which lay sputtering on its side, and reached out to the rider lying in the crosswalk. "I'm sorry, I'm sorry," he said, taking her arm and helping her to her feet. "I don't know . . . I just . . ." The girl pulled her arm back, bent down for her scooter, picked it up, hopped on and rode away without a word.

Jed gripped Rick's bicep and walked him away as quickly as possible. "Of all the dumb stunts," he said. "You're in a foreign country . . ."

"Yeah, sorry. I just lost it for a minute there," said Rick. "But man, did you get a look at her? Was she beautiful or what?"

"Time for you to keep a close watch on your feelings, man," said Jed, who by now was convinced Rick wasn't adapting well to life in Taipei.

Derek and Rick peeled off at the Jingfu Gate rotary and walked up Ren'ai Road to return to the hotel. Derek said it was time to begin surveillance; Rick said he was tired. Jung-Shan, Jed and David turned onto Ketagalan Boulevard, where she showed them the 228 Peace Memorial Park.

"This is perhaps the most important place in modern Taiwan history," said Jung-Shan.

"Why is it called 228?" said David.

"It is the honored date of the fighting, February 28, 1947," she said.

"Wait," said Jed, "I don't think I get it. Did the communists try to invade Taiwan? I thought . . ."

"Jed," Jung-Shan said, "I have told you this before. There is so much that is politics. Very complicated. Very complicated."

"And I understand I have no need to know," Jed replied.

They walked on, Jung-Shan in the lead, across Chongqing Road past the Presidential Office Building and down Baoqing Street, which turned into Chengdu Road. Suddenly they were immersed in throngs of young people. "This is called Ximending, or the Ximen District. It is a popular place for Taipei youth and tourists."

"Geez, I'll say," said David, looking around in wonder. "What are all these people doing here . . . oh, I get it. Friday night."

An entire street had been turned into a pedestrian promenade filled with color, light, scents of braised and steamed and fried finger foods, throbbing music: a very human celebration. Taiwanese girls wearing miniskirts, sporting long pink and green and red and honey-brown hair, hung on their boyfriends' arms. Crowds swarmed around a drummer at a full trap set in the middle of the intersection, pounding out a fantastic solo accompaniment to a hip-hop version of Hall and Oates' "Out of Touch" blasting from tall speaker stacks. Half a dozen costumed preteens jumped out of the crowd, prancing, swirling, dancing to cheers and applause. The intersection was surrounded by towering buildings upon which enormous color LCD screens displayed commercials, cartoon characters, music videos, movie clips. McDonald's. Starbucks. KFC. Subway. The *bzzzzz* and *braaaat* of scooters was now and again drowned out by the growl of motorcycles. Three young men jumped into the intersection juggling colored volleyballs, whispering things that made people laugh. Carts of delicious, fresh-cooked street food, everything the Taiwanese loved to eat. Hair salons. Designer clothing shops. Night clubs with names like Playground and Go-Go Club. Cute little animal cartoon characters grinning on flashing neon signs. A Friday night, all-night, street party, the best way to keep from thinking about what might be going down at the Serenity Garden Executive Inn.

"Crazy," said David.

They walked and watched a while longer, then went back the way they'd come. David bid them good-night and headed for the hotel. Jung-Shan and Jed passed through the iron gates of the Shandao Temple and sat on the stone steps. "This is a Buddhist temple," said Jung-Shan.

"Yes, I remember you are Buddhist," said Jed. "Do you go to church or temple or something? Like Christians go to church on Sunday?"

"Some temples have Sunday meetings, but no, I do not go to these. I love Buddhism because it says we are part of everything and everything in the world is part of us. We are all one with everything, and so I try to practice my Buddhism all day, every day. There is no need to go to one place at one time to love Buddha." She paused, smiled at him. "Do you go to the church of your family?"

"No, not any more. I did when I was a kid, but after spending time in the Army it just didn't make sense to me. I guess there's a god or something, but I don't think it's guiding the humanity of earth. Christians often say what happens is God's will. I'm more into, like, what you personally believe. I like to quote Jean-Luc Picard, the *Star Trek* captain: 'Make it so.' When stuff happens, it's up to each individual to decide what it means to them, then make it so."

"So, as you have said, we can be captain of our own fate?" said Jung-Shan. Jed nodded. "But you do not believe stuff we do not control is meant to happen to each of us? That we are at the hands of karma?"

Jed shook his head. "Karma happens, but it is not fate. Karma is what we create for ourselves. Fate happens whether we want a thing to happen or not. Doesn't matter. It's the opposite of karma." As he said this, Luke's accident flashed through his mind: *was that fate or karma?*

Jung-Shan said, "So in karma, you think if you live life with pureness in your heart and try always to do good things, you will have good results in the next life? And perhaps in this life, too?" She looked at Jed, her eyebrows raised.

"I don't believe we have an afterlife," said Jed. "What happens here shapes me and guides me now. Do the right thing, always. Live for today. This is it."

"Sometimes I think that too." Jung-Shan took Jed's hand and sandwiched it between her palms. "You are a good man, Jed. I think you are one of the best. You do not make fun of other people. You always try to be fair. Your life is setting the example for others to follow. This is the best Way. But if you do not go to your church, how you stay this kind of person?"

Jed took Jung-Shan's hand as she had taken his. "I guess I don't think about it much. It's just what I am because of what has happened to me. I want to be free. I want to be all I can be, and so I want the same thing for others." He paused. "Some of that philosophy, if that's what you'd call it, I guess I'd have to say comes from bicycling. Your dad knows this. He said it when he described his philosophy of cycling, 'Love the ride, love life'. Boy, he really caught me by surprise when he asked what mine was.

"Look at these kids all around us, having the time of their lives tonight. Isn't that freedom? Don't all human beings want freedom, however they define it for themselves? If you believe in freedom for yourself, you have to believe in freedom for everyone. Sometimes you teach that in lessons, but I think mostly you have to teach it through being an example. My dad taught me a lot, and I respect him more than anyone. He never forced his ideas on me, but he was always there when I needed him."

"I think you are Confucian," she said. "You embrace the same ethic and moral Confucius taught. You are always a student, learning from wise teachers. Like Confucius. He taught us the Way. We all seek the Way, even if we do not know we are seeking it. To be one with nature and live life to our best. It is very simple. You found your Way riding your bike."

Jed rose to his feet, excited. "Oh, yeah, absolutely. Everything is clear or becomes clear to me when I ride. I work stuff out. Not intentionally; it just happens. I see clearly what needs to be done or get fixed or whatever. Finding my Way, huh?"

"Yes, Jed. It is your Way and your way to the Way. Both. All together. It is so good for us to have the inside and the outside in harmony, like this."

Jed paused, wondering if Jung-Shan was talking about humans in general or about the two of them in particular. *Was she saying we're close? That we have a . . . relationship?* "I don't know what I'd do if I couldn't ride," he said. "I was scared after the bomb shrapnel hit me that I wouldn't be able to. But I knew I wouldn't give up. I'd use everything I had to heal. And I did. So I guess that's a good example of the inside-outside harmony, huh?"

"Very good," she said. "Very good chi flowing through and around you."

Jed sat again, took Jung-Shan's hand in his, suddenly determined to gain clarity in the words they were saying to each other. "I often think about the energy I feel when I'm with you," he began; then, unceremoniously, his phone vibrated. He pulled it out of his pocket. "Wow, do you realize it's almost 11:30?" He read the text message. "It's Derek. He and Wei-Ting are on their way to the Crystal Palace."

"Derek?" said Jung-Shan. "Why is he with Wei-Ting? Perhaps something is not so good. Let us go."

They walked quickly around the corner to the hotel car park and were passed in. The Jimmy was parked beneath bright lights near the elevators. Derek was standing at the open passenger door. Wei-Ting sat on the seat, a white gauze bandage wrapped around his head.

"What has happened?" said Jung-Shan, rushing to attend to him. Blood had left a red spot on the gauze.

"I am sorry, Miss Lai," he started, then his head drooped. "So sorry. I make big mistake. I think I am fooling Akiko, but she way in front of me."

Jung-Shan looked at Derek. He gave her a wry smile, but said nothing.

"Akiko is the Japanese woman?" said Jed.

Wei-Ting nodded to Jed and said, "I try to do as you say, Mr. Jed. I see Akiko work as housekeeper in the afternoon. Tell her come back to my room after dark. We kiss and kiss again. Ohhh, nice kisses! Then she say she hungry, want me to take her to dinner. I take Akiko outside to my Jimmy. She want to drive it to restaurant.

"We stop beside driver door like Derek tell me to do so I can kiss her some mores. She want to get inside so I take keys out of my pocket. I open door so she can climb up big step. She wears tight dress, very hard to step up, so I am helping her. Then I feel big hurt in head and see stars. Wake up on ground. All doors of Jimmy open but nobody is here. Doors all open. Bikes and everything gone. Sorry, sorry, sorry, Miss Lai!" He began to cry.

Jung-Shan turn to Derek and spoke in stern Mandarin.

"I was in my room," said Derek, "waiting for Wei-Ting's text message. It happened so fast. I'm sorry Wei-Ting was injured, but this may be for the best. Now they know we have no secrets. Just nice bikes for our American friends. And it's all been captured by the inn's surveillance cameras."

"You may be right," said Jed. "The more I think about it, the better this sounds. Now they will—I hope—think they have no reason to stalk us."

"Yes, I believe we are in control," said Derek. "We can report this to the police. Once they're found, we can choose to prosecute for assault, breaking and entering, grand theft. Or no."

"But first we must find them," said Jung-Shan.

"Not that difficult," said Derek. "Facial recognition from the security tapes. Match them up right smart from their passports when they came through customs and immigration. Perhaps from their lodging as well. My guess is they are at the Jianguo Hotel. In point of fact, I think they've been there all along. I think we have enough information to find them and go after them with the full force of the law on our side."

"Yes!" said Jed, pounding a fist in the air.

"But it may not come to that," said Jung-Shan. "Not if they think we have nothing to hide."

"Except, of course, we do," said Jed.

Jung-Shan locked eyes with Jed. "So, is this fate or is this Karma?"

Meanwhile – Room 288, Serenity Garden Inn

"Quickly!" said the man wearing black glasses, pushing a red and a blue Joyful Dragon Fire CF with each hand toward the patio entrance to Serenity Garden. "Move! Move quickly!" he barked at his tall partner trailing behind with the other two bikes, one white, the other black, who replied, "I am moving as quickly as you!" Akiko came running, carrying the box of Joyful Bike brochures and handouts, passing the two men as she reached the door. She unlocked it and held it open for them. They rolled the bikes into the laundry room, where they got on the utility elevator and rode up to the second floor. A minute later, both thieves and bikes were behind the closed door of Room 288.

"Now we shall find out just what these Americans have been trying so hard to hide from us," said black glasses. "Akiko! You have left the tools in this room?"

"Hai, in the closet."

"Well, what are you waiting for? Bring them to me!"

"The box of tools is very heavy," she said. "Do it yourself."

"I'll get it," said the taller one. Soon the two men were surrounded by wrenches, hammers and screwdrivers as they began stripping parts. Each picked up an electric cutoff tool and began sawing the frames into pieces.

"Stop! Wait until morning," said Akiko. "You will wake every person staying in the inn with that noise."

They passed a fitful night: the man in black glasses took the bed, making the tall man and Akiko sleep on the living room floor. She was the first to awaken. Quietly stepping into the bathroom, Akiko changed into her

housekeeper's uniform and quietly slipped out of the room.

When the man in black glasses awoke, he kicked the taller man a few times. "Get up! Get up!" he shouted. "Let's get started."

"Where is Akiko?" said the taller man.

"I assume she is getting us breakfast food. Come on! Get up!"

They began looking inside the severed pieces of carbon fiber tubing for information: papers, flash drives, data cards, whatever form they imagined the information might take. They were so absorbed in their work they did not notice Akiko had not yet returned.

"Madame! Madame!" said Akiko when she found the head of housekeeping. "There is loud noise coming from Room 288. I do not like the sound. Please come see what it is!" The woman, accompanied by the inn security officer, entered the second floor hallway. The noise was deafening. The officer inserted his keycard in the lock, drew his pistol and pushed the door open.

The two men were sitting on the floor, backs to the door, surrounded by lengths of carbon fiber bike frame tubing and handlebars, cables, brakes, gears, shredded seats, cut-up tires and inner tubes, wheels with the hubs ripped off. They shrieked like Bruce Lee as they cut the tubing into pieces, carbon fiber dust floating in the air, its fine white powder covering everything. The security officer bellowed something at them. Startled, they switched off their cutters and turned to look.

The police were called; from the hallway, Akiko told them she had seen the bikes a few days earlier in a very large silver American SUV in the inn parking lot. She did not know who the men were, she did not know from whom the bikes were stolen, and she did not know why they were in this room, cutting the bicycles into little pieces. "No matter," said the detective, "we can obtain much of this information from surveillance tapes."

"Ohhhh," said Akiko. "The robbery is recorded on security camera?"

"Hai," said the inn security officer in Japanese. "We have surveillance in car park, outside building doors, lobby, hotel staff laundry, cafeteria, maintenance areas. We have camera everywhere."

As the interrogation proceeded, Akiko slipped away, never to be seen again.

Don't Half-Step

"I know how old you are, Jung-Shan," said Jed. It was 8:30 the following morning, Saturday, half an hour before the second meeting between the four companies. They sat in the executive lounge area on the eighth floor, sipping freshly brewed coffee.

While Jed and Jung-Shan were awaiting Messrs. Kueh and Huang the Japanese information worms, handcuffed, were being led out the service entrance of the Serenity Garden Executive Inn, a first the inn management was far from happy about.

Mr. Zheng was in his office, his door closed.

"Who told you?" she said. "Suzie?"

"Nobody. I figured it out all by myself." He withdrew a piece of paper from his portfolio and unfolded it, turning it around so she could see it was a paper placemat from the cafe where they'd dined the night before. Bright red, with advertisements bordering a Chinese zodiac mandala, images of the twelve animals and descriptions in Chinese and English. "If you're a sheep, you're twenty."

"Very nice work, but not correct," she said, her face all smiles.

"Huh?" he said.

"Xiè xiè. Very nice compliment, Jed." She grinned.

He took out his pen and began scribbling on the back of the placemat. "OK, I think I got it. You're thirty-two."

"That is correct. I wish I were still twenty." She pretended to sigh.

"Well, I think you look twenty," he said, and laughed softly. "I think I figured out what I am. A rabbit! How cool is that?"

Jung-Shan gazed at the ceiling for a few moments, then said, "So, you are thirty-six." They held each other's eyes. All her shyness about eye contact had left. It occurred to Jed that he was now able to see her face without its blurring, and likely had for some time. *Since Penghu, for sure. Wow, how could I have missed that?* He looked into her deep, warm brown eyes, the dainty eyeliner surrounding them, the delicate touch of green on her eyelids, her slender eyebrows arcing on her un-furrowed forehead, the way her thick, silky black hair drew away from her temples, flowed behind her ears and gathered at the nape of her neck, the silver-and-jade earrings depending from her earlobes, her rose-tinted cheeks, the shiny red lipstick that animated her smile, the smooth line her jaw drew around her face like a sensual aura.

Trying to take all of her in was taking his breath away. Perhaps better to change the subject.

"Um, uh, so, how's Wei-Ting?"

"You know Derek took him to the hospital last night," she said. "He is still there. They say he has a very little concussion." She pinched her thumb and forefinger together. "I think he is more frightened than hurt!" She smiled a weak, wan smile.

They looked up to see her father approaching. "Ni Hǎo. Good morning," said Mr. Zheng. They stood; he greeted Jed with a slight bow. "Wei-Ting is, ah, how you say, recovering?"

Jung-Shan smiled and nodded. He began speaking rapidly in Mandarin to her. She replied in kind, then briskly walked away to her office.

She returned with a stack of paper printouts. "My father asks us to read your translated PowerPoint for correctness. Also meeting agenda," she said, giving Jed three copies of each document.

"Great," he said. "So, today we talk business?"

"Yes," said Zheng. "We pound the brass tacks today, as you say in America. I am filled with American sayings this morning!" He laughed, then looked around. "Where is Mr. Saundersson and Mr. Bondsman?"

"They got up a little late. They're eating breakfast at McDonald's. They'll be here in a few minutes."

"I see. We will go over the agenda as soon as they arrive." He turned to Jung-Shan and crossed back to his office.

Jung-Shan whispered, "Jed! Contact David and Rick to come at once! To be late for this meeting is to show lack of respect!"

Jed dug his phone out and texted them.

"Good," she said. "Now we read."

Zheng reappeared as Jed finished. "This looks good," said Jed. "I assume you've been in limited partnerships before, like doing the OEM business?"

Zheng nodded.

"Then it seems to me you should be in charge of management," Jed said.

"Joyful speaks through the head of business development," he said, making a slight bow toward his daughter. "I depend on her judgment and we follow her decisions, but we must strive always for consensus between all partners. Please remember, Mr. Smith, without your technology we have no partnership, no business. We need your total attention to every one of the smallest details."

Jed thought about that. He knew it, of course, but had he considered every single micro-detail? *How could I, with all this IP espionage on top of everything else? The business details are so detailed, and getting more so. Can I run two businesses at once?* He was going to have to read the document over and over to scrape all these infernal details out of it.

The agenda listed "issues of consequence." Jed wasn't sure what they might entail, but this was probably one of them. He nodded to Mr. Zheng and cast a look toward Jung-Shan, who signaled him back. *She's so beautiful, and so smart,* he thought. *She wants me to make the decision.*

"OK, I'll manage the partnership," he said, "with Jung . . . er, Ms. Lai." Zheng nodded. Jung-Shan smiled and nodded.

Rick and David hurriedly walked in, wearing suits and ties. Everyone moved to the conference room and briefly reviewed the agenda, then the phone intercom beeped. "The others have arrived, on time," Jung-Shan said pointedly, and stood to greet them.

The meeting concluded around mid-afternoon, but not before David projected the Spinner image from the PowerPoint deck on the room screen. The men murmured to one another, nodded their approval, then slurped down the last of their lattes. Meeting adjourned, they stood, shook hands all around, bowed, and left the Joyful building. The guys headed down to street level and walked the short distance to the Crystal Palace, just to stretch their legs.

When they regrouped back in his room, Jed was trying to think more deeply about the issues of consequence. His thoughts butted against one another: preparation for their next meeting: the urgency imposed by getting to market quickly; securing the Spinner on the bike; insuring competitive advantage; neutralizing the worms. He wondered if they had been stopped by the arrest. Were they incarcerated? Back out on the streets already? *Gotta get in touch with Derek, see what's up.*

Jed thought about how they were departing in two days, after ten great days here in Taipei and on the Penghu Islands with Jung-Shan. What was it going to be like to go back to Nashua, New Hampshire? Such a bright future on the horizon if they could keep this partnership together. *Have to call Gregg tonight, give him the good news. We should talk to Suzie about starting on a Spinner logo design, too. A sticker we can put on the NewBikes.* Managing the partnership was already exhausting him.

Suzie? Wait! Didn't she already fly back to the States? "Hey, all," he said, "Anyone know if Suzie's gone back?"

"No, I don't," said David.

Rick shook his head. "Last time we heard from her was when we left for Penghu."

Where in the heck was she? Why hadn't they heard from her? Jed's thoughts raced. *Could she have been . . . kidnapped?*

"She is with her family, of course," said Jung-Shan. "We talk every day. You want to speak with her, Jed?"

"Yeah, yeah, I do," he said, remembering he was using a disposable phone with a new SIM card every time he made a call. Of course Suzie couldn't call him! He fished in his coat pocket for the burner. "Do you have her number?" Jung-Shan nodded and took her iPhone from her purse. "Does she know we're flying back Monday?" Jung-Shan nodded again as she tapped her phone's screen. Dreaded thoughts about what had happened at Narita in the Sakura Lounge flooded Jed's mind. How would they deal with that? Jung-Shan handed her iPhone to Jed. "Hello, Suzie?"

"Ni hǎo, Jed! How are you and Rick and Davey? Did you have a nice time in Penghu?"

"Yes, we had a terrific time. How are you? Good, good, glad to know you're OK. I'm sorry, I sort of lost track of you. Thought you already flew back, ha ha. Forgot about the disposable phone thing, but Jung-Shan says you two have been in touch. Do you have any news about

Luke's funeral?"

"No," said Suzie. "Family Lin still waits for feng-shui master to choose best day."

"You have no idea? Like is it going to be in a week? A month? Six months?"

"Yes, it is true, I have no idea," said Suzie. "What news do you have about the information worms?"

"I need to call Derek, you know, the security guy, about that. We just got out of a partnership meeting. Hey, did you know we fly back Monday? Did you know . . . ?" The questions started to tumble out, then abruptly stopped. Jed thought, *How could I have been so neglectful of Suzie?*

"Yes, I know," she said. "I will be ready."

"Good. We have a lot of work to do on . . . the Spinner."

"Jed?"

"Yeah?"

"I have for you some news of my own."

"What's up?" said Jed.

"I am going to be married."

Fate

"**N**ǐ hǎo! Good morning, Jed," said Jung-Shan when he answered his room phone.

"Hey, Nǐ hǎo ma?" he replied, feeling groggy, now remembering the night before. He looked at the clock. It was Sunday, 8:15. "What's up?"

"I would like to spend the day with you."

Jed sat straight up in his bed. "Ah, sure. I'll tell the guys. What have you got planned for us?"

"Only you. No guys today. I will arrange for Derek to take the guys on a tour of their choosing. OK?"

Jed's heart began pounding. "Uh, sure. Great! OK! Sounds great!"

"OK to pick you up in front of the Crystal Palace? Ten o'clock?"

"Sure."

Derek had been waiting for Jed, David and Rick in the hotel lobby when they returned the day before, bearing the news of the information worms' capture and arrest. They found a secluded, comfortable sitting area in the lounge and ordered drinks. Exuberance bubbled like a Beitou Hot Springs geyser. Liquor and laughter splashed all over the lounge, but quieted down somewhat upon the arrival of Jung-Shan and her father. Derek found himself telling the story over and over, even after everyone had already heard it. All that pent-up stress had to be dissipated, and it was. They partied until midnight.

Jed stepped out the hotel at exactly ten o'clock to find Jung-Shan standing beside a white Audi TT convertible wearing a jade-green pantsuit with a mandarin collar. Her long hair, loose today, fell all around her shoulders. *My god, she looks fantastic*, thought Jed. Ever since stepping into the shower, he'd been rehearsing what he wanted to say to her. He'd made up his mind: Today was the day.

As he approached, she reached out her hand. Jed took it and pulled her into a brief embrace. She gave him a quick kiss on the cheek. "I hope this is not too early for you," she said.

"Oh, no, I'm usually at Smithworks by seven," he said. "Funny, I thought the jet lag would mess me up pretty bad, but it hasn't."

"Not as much as the number of drinks you had last night?" she replied, bright eyes and a wicked smile dancing on her face. "Jet lag will be much worse going east tomorrow," she said. "You fly through two days in one."

"Well," he said. "So, what are we doing today?"

"No business. I want only to show you my country, eat some good food. Talk. You like to hike, maybe? Go to the ocean?"

"It all sounds good. Let's go."

The hotel valet bowed and opened the door for Jung-Shan. Jed climbed in; the interior was immaculate. She pressed a button on the console; the top folded down. She pressed another button and the engine sprang to life. Wiggling the shift lever into first gear, she touched the gas, the exhaust roared, and the TT sprinted into traffic on Zhongxiao East Road.

"Nice ride," said Jed, smiling at her.

Jung-Shan glanced over at him, a sweet grin on her beautiful, happy face. "I love my little TT car," she said, her hair flying free. They stopped at the light on the corner of Zhongxiao East Road and Zhongshan South Road; she flipped on her left turn signal, reached up and swiftly pulled her hair into a ponytail. "My father gave it to me for my thirtieth birthday, but I never have enough time to drive it. I work too much!" she said in an explosive laugh.

South on Zhongshan, they reached the familiar Jingfu Gate roundabout, where she made two complete high-speed circles around the gatehouse, then sped north on Zhongshan through sleepy traffic across Taipei, the Grand Hotel coming into view, then on into the countryside. They passed through villages and crossed a small river—Jung-Shan said it was the Shuangxi Stream, reminding him they had cycled across it as they returned from Beitou—and continued north through rural areas given over to rice paddies and farmlands until they reached a small town and the intersection with Route 2, where she turned east.

"That is the East China Sea," she said, pointing through the windshield. "We are at the northern tip of Taiwan."

"Really," said Jed, "so close."

"Taiwan is a small island," she replied, "oceans all around, North China, East China, South China."

They drove west a few klicks before Jung-Shan slowed and parked the car. "See the beach?" As they drew closer, Jed saw an outdoor café with tables sheltered by colorful canvas umbrellas on a large deck. The sun was bright, the air slightly cooled by the ocean breeze. Some people strolled; others sat together on the café deck enjoying food and drink and the excellent day. "Let's go!" she cried as she jumped out of the TT and began running across the beach, waving her arms, sending gulls into the air, turning around and running back to him, reaching for his hand, seeming to dare him to be free.

Jed thought, I *haven't seen enough of this spirited side of her*. He could feel her spirit. He loved her. *Yes, there it is, I've said it and it's how I really feel. I love her. I love Jung-Shan and I have to tell her today.* He caught her hand, pulled her into his arms, lifted her face to his and kissed her.

They sat at a table on the restaurant's sea-bleached deck, drinking tea, as large oceangoing vessels moved slowly from west to east amid dozens of small fishing boats. They watched two fishermen wielding long poles from atop a concrete sea wall, pulling in fish, dropping their lines to a woman on the beach below who unhooked the fish and put them in a plastic bucket. They watched each other, wondering who would speak first, what would happen next.

The talk turned to Suzie and how she was now betrothed. "I was so surprised when she told me. I really didn't know what to say," said Jed. "I mean, I said 'Congratulations,' but . . ."

Jung-Shan said, "It is customary of Chinese marriage," she said, "for parents to choose the mate for the children, often when they are only in primary school."

"Why?" said Jed. "Why were they, you know, matched up?"

"Another old custom. Parents choose children's mates for auspicious reasons, perhaps best known only to themselves. Often parents know each other and feel harmony in joining children together. They do not need to be good friends, as long as they know about the family's character and social position, of course. But ideal mates should also be of the right age difference, and in *Shēngxiào*. That means compatible in astrology signs. All factors are carefully thought about for making the best marriage."

"But Suzie was engaged to Luke, and, and now, so soon . . ."

"No, I am sorry to tell you they were not engaged. Sun Xiaohui, she is a good girl who does not wish to live in shame with a man not married to, so she tells all of you they are engaged. This, they knew, is accepted in American culture. But they only lived together to share the rental cost."

"Huh! Well, we all thought they were a good couple," said Jed, "and we thought they were engaged, even though Suzie didn't wear an engagement ring."

"I will tell you what I think," said Jung-Shan. "I think she and Lin Shieh-Seng, they were very, very fond of one another, for they had known each other all of their lives. Not quite in love, maybe, but in time, possibly yes. If they had stayed in America, definitely yes. Shieh-Seng—Luke—he, I think, was very proud to have her by his side and so he agreed to go along with what she wanted you to think. Maybe he thought it would lead to real love, an engagement and marriage. Maybe that is what he wanted, and he hoped it was what she would want too, after some time has passed."

"But then there's the accident, so she comes back here . . ."

Jung-Shan explained that both Suzie and Dejan, the boy she'd left behind, had more or less forgotten they were promised to one another even before Suzie left to attend RISD. Her return to Taipei had brought him to the Lin home to express his condolences, and seeing her again was pretty much all it took for both of them.

"Well, I'm sure I don't know how other people's relationships work, but from what you say, it sure sounds like it could have happened that way."

"Yes, of course it is the way it happened. It is exactly what Sun Xiaohui told me."

Jed laughed and so did she. "Ah, Jung-Shan," he began, then hesitated. "Are we—I mean, you and I—are we, uh, harmonious? With the, you know, Shēngxiào and all?"

She turned her gaze toward the sea and watched an old fishing trawler pass by. Dozens and dozens of seagulls circled above it, as if waiting for a meal to begin. As if cued by the birds the waiter appeared with menus, so they decided to have wǔcān. Jung-Shan ordered all fresh fish dishes.

The waiter left. Still, she did not reply to Jed's question. Jed waited. He looked out to sea and thought about commerce, how oceangoing ships crossed the wide waters that separated, yet brought together, great countries. It was what Smithworks was doing with these three Taiwanese companies. Could their partnership bring these two countries closer? And what of Jed and Jung-Shan? Surely they were more than ships in the night.

Jed remembered their first kiss inside the Dragon Pagoda, how she had pressed her lips to his without drawing back. The time they had spent together compelled him to love her beyond rational thought. He understood her propriety at the Villa Italia; actually, he respected her for it. But she had opened up to him in so many ways; why would she do that if she didn't feel love or at least a growing affection for him? And now today: she had asked him to spend the day with her. Was something important going to happen? Jed hoped it would . . . well, he would just hold onto the undefined hope in his heart. Better not to let his expectations run wild.

Their meal arrived: steamed mussels and crab, fried squid, shark fin soup, boiled shrimp with the heads still attached, grilled tuna chopped into large chunks. As they began to eat, she held up a bite with her chopsticks and said, "Fresh. Very, *very* fresh!"

Jed said, "Yeah, there's so much taste. Delicious. Very, *very* delicious!"

They finished lunch and continued their drive along the coastal highway, the East China Sea to their left and ahead, the stubby, steep mountains to the right, their green gowns sweeping down to the sea. Jung-Shan rested her hand atop the gearshift lever as they cruised. Jed reached over and put his hand on top of hers. She entwined her fingers with his and held tight.

They reached the outskirts of a large city. Jung-Shan said, "This is Keelung City. The most rain of any city in Taiwan. This is very large port for Taiwan."

She swung the wheel of the TT toward the Maritime Plaza. Jed pointed: an enormous, inflated yellow animal floated on the water near a cruise ship. They drew closer. "Wait," he said, "isn't that the Sesame Street rubber duckie?" Jung-Shan grinned.

Storefronts lined Xiaosan Road, one fish market or restaurant after another, stall upon stall butted up against the next. They parked and walked around for a bit. Jed pointed up; the sky on the horizon was turning from blue to gray. "Rain?" he said. She nodded. They headed back to the TT, put the top up and left the docks of Keelung City.

Jung-Shan headed southeast past the sheltered inlets and small harbors where a few fishing boats were anchored, awaiting their next voyage. They turned inland where short stretches of tiny houses and rows of shops clustered. An occasional shed was lit up with flashing neon lights and blinking signs resembling traffic lights. Seductively clad young women stood outside, beckoning. "What's that all about?" said Jed.

"Betel nut shop," said Jung-Shan. "Workers chew the betel nut so they can forget how hard they work."

"So it's a kind of drug?"

"Yes, but it is legal here. Unfortunately, chewing betel causes black teeth. And cancer in the mouth."

"But the workers chew it anyway?"

"It is the same as tobacco, isn't it?" she said.

Approaching an intersection with a 7-Eleven, Jung-Shan pulled over and said, "Would you like to drive?"

"Oh, sweet," said Jed.

She smiled; they leaned toward each other for a little kiss. "Turn to Yangjin Road, here," she said.

Jed did in fact love driving the little TT over the hilly, curving road toward Taipei. "We are passing through Yangmingshan National Park," she said. "Remember?"

He nodded, smiled and said, "it would be awesome to bike these roads."

Often, the densely forested mountaintops were shrouded in mist. He let the car run fast and sure through the curves, leaving Yangjin Road in favor of a narrow road down the mountainside into a small village.

"This is Beitou District. Do you remember?"

"Of course I do," said Jed. "The hot springs place. We wanted to spend more time here."

"Yes, and now we have returned from the other direction. Some say Peitou, some say Beitou. Both are the same. See the steam?"

Jed followed her fingertip and saw large clouds of steam rising from somewhere just out of sight.

"There is the Beitou mineral baths area," she said, "You did not see this last time, but today you will. Let us park and visit."

Jed parked in a nearby underground car park and, hand in hand, they toured the museum. "My people must have a history museum for everything!" she said. Outside again, they walked the path to the Beitou Thermal Valley, where they could look down upon the inviting hot mineral springs. People sat on rocks beside the healing waters, soothing their feet and their souls.

They walked into the familiar downtown area. "It is tea time, Jed," said Jung-Shan, stopping. "Shall we go to this lovely Japanese tea room?" They entered the lobby of the Lotus Blossom Hotel. A waterfall, illuminated with thousands of tiny lights, shimmered down a stone wall from a second-floor balcony into a sinuous stone-lined channel flowing throughout the lobby. Jed stopped to look; large, colorful koi swam back and forth. He followed her into the tea lounge.

"To our wonderful day," said Jung-Shan, touching her porcelain teacup to his. The china was so fine Jed could see the level of his tea through it.

"To you, for making it possible," he said. "Xiè xiè, Jung-Shan. Hey, that sounds like a rhyme in a poem!" She smiled. "You are a poem, Jung-Shan, as lovely and interesting and beautiful as poetry."

She looked down into her teacup. "Xiè xiè," she said.

"I need to tell you something," said Jed, pausing to gather his courage. "We haven't known each other very long. And it's been a long time since my divorce and, well . . ." He stopped, searching for words. "Well, I haven't, you know, dated much. Because I just haven't been interested in anybody, but—"

"I have fallen in love with you too, Jed," Jung-Shan interrupted. Her eyes glistened with emerging tears.

He set his cup down before he dropped it. "Oh, Jung-Shan, I—I— really have fallen in love with you, too."

"I know. This is why I asked you to spend this last day together, before you have to go back . . . home. I wanted to be all alone with you today for this reason. I want us to be together all day and all night, if that is all right with you."

Jed nodded, unable to speak.

"But I must tell you this. Very important. Please understand." Jed leaned toward her. "I have reserved a room for us in this hotel," she waved her hand in the air, "a very special room with the mineral springs flowing into the bath. We will share one bed."

Jed thought his heart had stopped.

She took his hands in hers. "But Jed, I must ask for us to honor same sleeping terms as on Penghu Islands. No towel in the middle, but please have the respect for me."

"But, if we love each other . . . " he said.

"Is a promise I have made to myself." Her eyes implored him to understand her words. "I have never made love with a man in all my life. After my marriage, I have never slept in same bed with any man. Until you." She stopped speaking. Jed looked at her, trying to fathom the depth of her emotional wounds. "I am afraid what . . . um, to make love . . . means now, because my husband did not want to be with me. My promise to myself is, I will make love only with my much loved husband."

"OK, I understand that," said Jed, all the complications of a relationship really sinking in. Each of them had known life in different marriages, different cultures, different lands separated by eight thousand miles. And a lot of heartache. Jed recalled the words to a Linda Ronstadt song about the heart being like a wheel: once bent, it cannot be mended. He hoped that wasn't true.

"One more thing, also very important," she said. "When I married that Englishman, my father became very angry with me. He did not want me to marry him. He wanted me to marry one of my own kind, a Taiwanese man, the son of his friend. I told him love does not see the difference in race, but still he was very angry with me."

She sat back and Jed saw tears welling up in her eyes again. "My father would not speak to me for a long, long time. I knew he is the father and must always be obeyed. Still I did not obey. I wanted to be right, but when I came home it was from a failed marriage. I was wrong. It took a long, long time to earn the love and respect of my father again."

Now tears poured down her cheeks. Jed reached out to brush them away, but she shook her head. He looked into her face. Her tears shimmered like diamonds; she raised her napkin to dab them away. *She's even more beautiful in sadness*, Jed thought, and wondered why that should be.

"So what we know?" Jung-Shan continued, "What Jung-Shan and Jed know. We know we love each other. This I know is true. You know is true. But my father will never approve my marriage to another man who is not of Chinese. I cannot hurt him this way a second time. And I cannot give myself to you because you are not the man I am obliged by my old culture Way to marry. But I love you, Jed. I will love you best way my heart knows how, always. I will never marry another man. Can you love me in this simple way?"

Again, tears streamed down her cheeks in testament to the overwhelming sadness of thousands of years of culture and tradition she had held inside for so long. She bowed her head and raised the napkin to hide her shame, but her shoulders quivered and shook. Jed felt sobs welling up in his own breast and fought to stuff them back down. He flashed back to their discussion of Suzie and Luke. Marriage, family customs, really were different in each culture. But were the expectations of love so very different?

"I don't know," he said, his voice hoarse with pain. "I don't know if I can . . . accept that. I really don't. I'm being as honest as I can." He leaned forward and raised her chin. Her face was a mess of tears and conflicted emotion. He held her eyes with his own for a long time, then once again felt tears on his own face.

Very softly, she said, "*Mingyùn*. It is our fate."

After a long moment he took her hands in his and said, "I think we've had a beautiful day. I think we ought to continue our day and evening and night as beautifully as we can. Because right now, all we have is today. We'll have to deal with our tomorrows as they happen. So let's just be together and—and in love—for this day, OK?"

Jung-Shan sniffed. A crinkly little smile crossed her lips, then another. "OK," she said.

Lugubrious

EVA Air Flight BR2198 became airborne the next day at 1500 hours, circling slightly to the west as it turned northward toward Tokyo. Jed looked out his window seat in business class—Joyful had upgraded all four of them—and wondered if Jung-Shan was still at the Taoyuan International Airport, looking up into the sky to catch one last glimpse of his aircraft as it left. They had shaken hands, then exchanged a *beso-beso*, a little kiss on each cheek.

As if the night before had never happened, he thought.

Jed leaned his head against the window and closed his eyes. Of course it had happened. Of course she would be businesslike today, in front of Suzie and David and Rick and Wei-Ting and Derek, in a public place like an airport. But last night. He couldn't get last night out of his head. He had no idea two people could be so intimate, so loving, so sensual with one another, without . . . . *And I just shook her hand and let her walk out of my life.*

The Airbus 330 reached cruising altitude and the flight attendants entered the cabin to take drink orders. Jed ordered a Scotch on the rocks. When the attendant arrived with his drink, he thought *This is stupid. Why am I drinking hard liquor? I never do this. Why do I think I need a drink?* He waved it away and asked for an iced tea. He climbed over the snoozing Rick beside him and crossed the aisle to David and Suzie.

"Hey, Jed," she said. "Are we going to do it?"

"Yes indeed we are," he said. "You talked to Angela, right?"

"Yes, and she will be in the lounge, as before. She is certain she will be followed. As before."

"I hope so. But I wonder if it will be the same two worms."

David said, "Don't you think they're still in jail in Taipei?"

"Possibly," said Jed. "I hope so."

"Angela told me she's been followed by different ones at several times," said Suzie.

"Hmmm. Maybe it doesn't matter. Maybe they're all in the same gang, so to speak. Well, it's a good plan. Let's see if Rick can pull it off."

David grinned. "Oh, he'll pull it off all right."

The attendant approached again. Jed drank some tea, fidgeting with the glass, but didn't return to his seat. The young woman stood looking at him with a patient gaze until they stopped talking. Then she asked if he wanted anything else. Jed shook his head.

David reached out, touched Jed's arm. "You OK, man?"

"Yeah, yeah, I'm OK," said Jed. "Just a little edgy."

"Because of what we're going to do at Narita?"

"Well, of course because of what we're going to do at Narita!" Jed snapped. "Sorry, Dave." Under his breath he said, "I think I need a cold shower. Again."

"What?" said David.

"Nothin'. You guys have a good time with Derek yesterday?"

"Yeah, we did. We went back to that awesome massage place, One Path, then he took us to the Taipei 101 Tower. Very impressive architecture. Designed to look like bamboo. It was the tallest skyscraper in the world for a few years, then a taller one went up in Dubai."

"How tall is it?"

"Uh, doh, a hundred and one floors? Just pulling your chain. About fifteen hundred feet. You should see it when we go back."

Jed nodded. *When we go back.*

"We had an outstanding dinner in a seafood place," said Rick. "All the shellfish were hanging out in a stone tide pool the restaurant built in the lobby. You got to pick your own, like we do with apples and blueberries back home. Enormous crabs! Lobsters, too!" He did the fisherman-measurement gestures with his hands. "Then we went bar-hopping. I think we got a little drunk. I know Wei-Ting did," he chortled.

"Did you get in touch with Gregg?" Jed smiled, trying to act nonchalant.

"Sure. He's keeping everything going, but he wants his Girl Friday, as he calls Suzie, back to help him."

"I talked to Gregg too," said Suzie. "He told me what he wants me to do. We are all set. I will try to get a good sleep on airplane and I can be busy first thing when we are back in our Smithworks office."

"Did you tell Gregg about, your, ah, plans?"

"No," she said. "Very busy conversation about work. I will tell him in the face when I see him."

"He'll be happy for you, I'm sure," said Jed, although he was in fact not so sure. "You have a good time with your family?"

"Yes, very good time, thank you. Nice to be home."

David said, "Your fiancé. De-jan . . . ?

"OK to call him Johnny," said Suzie.

"Yeah, so Johnny's OK with you coming back to the states?"

"Yes. He knows is not forever. He has already waited for me quite a long time, don't you think?" She laughed, and Dave and Jed laughed with her.

"Taiwan's a very nice country," said Jed, thinking about the Sunday drive with Jung-Shan, his heart seizing up in his chest.

"We are all going back for Luke's funeral?" said Suzie.

"I don't know, Suzie. I hope so. We'll have to go back to work on the contracts for the new business, but will that coincide with Luke's funeral? I just don't know." Jed gave her a hangdog look, eyes and mouth drooping. "The airfare's so expensive. How can Smithworks justify making two separate trips? Seems like a long shot . . . " His let his sentence dwindle away.

"Yes, Jed, quite so, to make two auspicious times into one is quite a long shot," she said, but in her mind she was already reading between Jed's sentences.

Angela was waiting at the Sakura Lounge welcome counter for them and the plan went right into action. She stepped quickly to Suzie and shook her hand, then turned to Rick and put her arms around his neck, giving him a long, sweet hug. Rick, acting a little off-guard, wrapped his arms around her waist as she lifted one foot behind her, tilting into him. It was a good show. Angela put her lips to his ear and said, "They've followed me here."

They went down the steps to the lounge, much as they had before, except for the show Rick and Angela were putting on. They fussed with each other, fed each other food, clinked drink glasses, touching and laughing all the while. Rick was clearly enjoying every bit of it.

They were driving Jed crazy with longing for Jung-Shan.

Beside them rested Rick's nice new tan leather briefcase. Angela withdrew papers from her own and handed them to Rick. He looked them over, said a few words to her, then stuffed them into his. She pulled him over and nuzzled him with her nose, whispering about the two who were watching their every movement. They were not the same two, of course, but they were dressed similarly in jeans, T-shirts sporting big Kanji characters, and Converse high-top sneakers. They stared sullenly at Angela and Rick's antics from across the room. There was no shotgun microphone in evidence.

In a voice a little louder than necessary, Rick stood up said, "I really should clean up. I must smell awful." Angela pretended to protest, but Rick shook his head and left, taking the briefcase.

As he waited for the elevator, he saw a man wearing a suit and tie descend the curved staircase past his floor. The two worms remained at their table, now grinning, seemingly nonchalant, although one was holding a finger to his ear. Rick glanced back at the man in the suit; he had a finger to an ear as well.

Rick entered the men's shower and massage facility and was greeted by a JAL attendant who gave him a keycard for room number four. The man on the staircase entered and immediately spoke to the attendant in Japanese in a typically strident and harsh tone of voice.

Rick walked to his shower room. He closed the door, leaving it just off-latch, and set the briefcase on the birchwood bench. He turned on the shower and stood over the sink so the large wall mirror reflected the door he'd left slightly ajar.

He took out the new HTC smartphone, thumbed in a text message, but did not send it. Then he heard a click and saw the suited man in his mirror. He punched Send; the text message went to Narita Airport Security. The man glanced quickly around the room, snatched Rick's briefcase and slipped out.

According to plan Rick had to wait a few minutes, which felt like hours. Then he strode quickly to the front counter where a police officer was speaking to the thief. Rick's briefcase rested between the man's feet. An airport security officer stood behind him. Two officers approached with the street-grunge worms from the lounge.

"This is your briefcase, sir?" said the police officer.

"Why yes, it is," said Rick. "It wasn't where I left it in my shower room, so I came looking for it. Why does this man have it? Who are these men?"

"*Osu osu,*" said the officer. "We will take care of this. You must come to the security office to give us a statement before your departure." He bowed and handed Rick a business card.

"Of course," Rick said, "just give me a few minutes?" He grinned at the three crooks as he opened the briefcase, threw the sheets of paper

Angela had given him into the trashcan, and removed his toothbrush and toothpaste.

Back at the table, Jed gave Rick a high-five. "Thanks, Angela, for spotting that guy in the suit," said Jed.

"Of course," she said. "I know him. He's surveilled me before. Several times. One develops an instinct for this sort of thing."

"Well, we got our revenge."

"Actually, we didn't," said Rick.

'What?" said Jed.

"They arrested the suit for theft, but not the two bangers. They claimed they didn't know the suit and he said the same. I told the police I saw them talking to each other with some kind of headset, but they didn't have any surveillance gear on them. I don't know how or where they ditched it. The cops had to let them go."

"Aw, shit!" said Jed. "Sorry." Angela smiled.

"Geez, I hope they don't follow us back to New Hampshire," said David.

"I wouldn't worry about that," said Rick. "They were escorted off Narita by the airport police and told if they ever returned they would be arrested for trespassing."

"Yes, that's good, but none of this will end the surveillance of me," Angela said. "There will always be one more, two more . . . another and another and another. I must always watch for them, and you should, too."

Rick leaned toward Angela, a sympathetic look on his face. "I'm really sorry about that. Do you have any idea who they are? Who they work for?"

"No, not really," she said, patting Rick's hand. "They could be anybody, working for anybody or nobody. They are scavengers. They work in underground networks with only one thing in mind: Steal to sell for personal gain. They have learned it is easy to steal and sell business IP. They do not know or even care how they hurt people." Angela touched her lapel: "They do not care that they hurt *my life*. But they are . . . usually. . . . very careful not to break the law. I think you were quite fortunate to catch these ones. This one. But still, it may never be proved that they were business intelligence thieves on some company's payroll. A smart lawyer—like me—could have such a case dismissed easily."

Suzie leaned forward and said, "That is so sad. No way to live a life."

"I'm sorry too, Angela," said Jed. "We all are. I'm most sorry you—we—have to conduct business as if it was war."

David said, "I guess it was predicted a long time ago—about two thousand years ago, if I remember correctly—by a Chinese general named Sun Tzu."

"*The Art of War*," said Angela. "We read it in my MBA business strategy course and I have read it again and again. He said you must know your enemy and know yourself in order to win battles. Today, the wars of the past between sovereign states are now fought in business."

"Yes, that's true," said David. It's too dangerous to the world order to fight out-and-out wars between countries, so they're fought by proxy: Vietnam, the two Koreas, even Syria."

"Don't forget Afghanistan," said Jed.

"More to the point, the real wars are being fought over intellectual property: Dow's titanium dioxide, Microsoft Windows, DoD, Monsanto's seeds, pharma, credit card data—it goes on and on," said Angela.

"Sun Tzu say the best fighter subdues the enemy without fighting, so you are the best, Rick!" said Suzie, and they all laughed.

Nashua seemed dull, almost lifeless, after their time in Taipei. The traffic was all cars, plodding along in orderly lanes, stopping at red lights. Not a scooter or bicycle to be seen. If commerce was underway in the storefronts and shopping centers, it was invisible behind tinted glass.

Lugubrious, thought Jed as he pedaled the streets to Smithworks. *Life seems lugubrious here, like people are just going through the motions. The guys and I live to ride. We work to build bikes and ride them, and to give the joy of riding to others. But once we deliver a bike to a customer, we rarely hear from them again. We don't often know if we have given them joy. So we fall back on our personal cycling to fill up on joy. I guess I should be happy for what I have, and never mind what I don't. Like I'm feeling about Jung-Shan. Be Joyful—ha! —of the fact that we'll be working together, so at least I'll get to see her once in a while. Be content to accept that we love each other, but that it's never going any further than where it is right now.* Never. *Can I live with that?*

Jed rolled into the Smithworks factory parking lot and around back to the loading dock. He hefted his bike onto a shoulder, pulled open the old steel door, walked across the old plank floor to the old grated door of the old freight elevator. *Jed Lugubrious and his old, old life.*

He thought about how, for nearly ten years, he had fueled his life with this company: the bikes, the business processes, the business of running a business. He worked each day with the same three or four people, the same people with whom he rode and ate and drank beer and played. He had stanched the bleeding from little Jed's death. It had taken five years but he'd healed, as best he knew how, from losing his son and then his wife. *I just simply moved on from thinking about that stuff. Up until now. Now it's all opened up again. I feel this sickening feeling in my guts, like I just got shot. That "Oh my god, I'm dead," feeling. I thought I'd conquered that by making great days from the everyday with work, new ideas, cycling, my three best buddies in the world. But Luke's dead, and now I've gone and fallen in long-distance love. But my love for Jung-Shan is going to be . . . what's that word? Unrequited. So now the same-old, same-old just isn't going to cut it.*

Jung-Shan had broken through the crust of the everyday he had created to protect himself, and like an erupting volcano she had given him new life. Real life. The promise of love between a woman and a man. Yin and yang. And no sooner had he felt the new life-force well up inside again, it had been snuffed out.

By real life.

He loved her. She loved him. But it would never go further. They would never be truly together, married. He was here, in Nashua, New Hampshire, USA. She was in Taipei, Taiwan, ROC. Eight thousand miles separating them.

How can I ever reconcile the distance . . . no, not between these two places, but between these other obstacles that keep our hearts apart?

The elevator stopped at the third floor. Jed opened the grate and parked his bike in the employee bike stand. The slot reserved for him, the one Gregg had painted the BOSSMAN plaque for. He looked at his phone: 7:17. He climbed the remaining flight as fast as he could, unlocked the fourth-floor door and stumbled into his office, dialing as he did. There was a long pause, then another, then the strange international ringtone.

"Wei?" the voice said as he dropped into his chair. "Wei?"

"Jung-Shan."

"Jed."

Going Home

"Welcome back, son. Good to see yah," said John Jedediah Smith *pere*, clapping Jed on the back and push-pulling him onto the back porch. A week had passed, and with it most but not all of the jet lag. Jung-Shan had been right, it was harder going west to east.

Jed, Rick, David and Suzie had been busier than they thought possible. Suzie, bless her heart, had not missed Jed's not-so-subtle comment about two return trips to Taiwan. As soon as they were back in the office, she set her administrative acumen and people-skills to work arranging the business meeting and the funeral on an overlapping schedule. Now, with everyone settled back into their routines, Jed knew it was time to visit his parents at Cherry Hill Farm.

"Let's hear all about that trip to Formosa," said his father as they sat down in white wicker lounge chairs on either side of a matching table, upon which John had already set a bottle of Maker's Mark. "Bought this here bottle just for you and me, to celebrate your big business deal!"

"Dad, we were in Taiwan," said Jed. Out of courtesy to his father, he clinked glasses and took a small sip, even though it was only mid-afternoon.

"Formosa's what your granddaddy called it," his father replied. "Lotta our boys got fancy silk jackets over there. Red dragons and gold tigers stitched on 'em. Or was it gold dragons and red tigers? Oh, hell, maybe that weren't Formosa even; maybe it was Okinawa. But never mind. How'd it go? You boys get your deal for that bike gear thing all sorted out?"

"Not quite," said Jed, and explained the meetings. "I think it'll happen, but not as quickly or simply as we'd thought. Taiwanese businessmen insist on making sure there's a solid personal relationship before making the business deal itself."

"Sounds like just the opposite of how we do things here, heh, heh." John tipped his glass up and poured so much bourbon into his mouth that the ice cubes clinked against his teeth.

"Yeah, you're right. I was kind of surprised. Jung-Shan told me this and I think it's true: business done quickly is business done badly. It was one reason we were there for so long . . ."

John grinned.

"Hello, darling," said Helen Smith, coming up the porch steps with a basket filled with tomatoes, Swiss chard and summer squash. Jed stood and kissed his mother on the cheek. "I'm sorry I didn't hear you arrive, but as you can see, I've been in the garden. John, why are you making Jedediah drink that awful firewater of yours? Let me get you a glass of iced tea, dear," she said and opened the screen door.

"Thanks, Mom," said Jed. "Yeah, so as I was saying, first we had to just sit around and talk about ourselves and life and all sorts of pleasantries before we could talk about business. Oh yeah, and no business discussions over meals. The Joyful Bike business development director was our hostess and guide. She was great. Really smart. She kept teaching us how to behave. She'd say, 'It is customary' to, like, give a gift when you meet someone, or leave a bite of food on your plate, or . . ." and as he spoke, Jung-Shan filled Jed's thoughts once again. His thoughts and his heart.

Helen, standing behind him, giggled. "So you've fallen for this Chinese lady, hmmm??" She put his glass of iced tea on the table.

"Taiwanese, mom," said Jed.

His father chuckled.

"Wait! What makes you say that? Did one of the guys . . ."

"Jed, you're our son," said his dad. "We can read you like a book!"

Jed took a big swig of iced tea and smiled. "Yeah, I fell for her all right."

"What's her name?" said Helen.

"Jung-Shan Lai. I mean Zheng," said Jed. "Except they say their last name first, so she's Lai Jung-Shan. Her father is the founder of Joyful Bike. She uses her mother's maiden name, Lai, for business. Her mother passed when she was six."

"What's she look like?" said John.

"Long, long black hair. Incredible green-brown eyes, like agates." Jed leaned back. "She's just beautiful."

"It's nice you've found somebody after all these years alone," said his mother.

"Wait, you two. Hold on. It's probably not going anywhere," said Jed. "We would have to make a whole lot of things work out that probably won't."

"I imagine their customs are very different from ours," Helen said matter-of-factly.

"It'll all work out if *you* want it to, son," said his father. "That's the spirit that made America the greatest country on earth." He picked up Jed's bourbon and handed it to him, then lifted his own. "It's the man's job to chase the woman until she catches him!" he said, and howled with laughter at his own joke. They clinked glasses. This time, Jed drank with his father.

"Do you have any pictures of your new romantic interest?" said Helen.

"Mom, please," said Jed.

"Well, do you?"

Jed, his thoughts drifting once again toward Jung-Shan, said, "Ah, yeah. Yeah, I got some pictures. On my phone." He dug it out of his pocket.

Two drinks later, the iced tea set aside, a somewhat inebriated Jed had told his parents all about Jung-Shan, but now his mother had gone inside to wash her vegetables and start dinner. "I don't know what else I can do, Dad. She loves me. She told me so . . . in just about . . . every way possible. But she won't go against her father's wishes again. She thinks it would dishonor him, and respect for elders is a real big deal with the Chinese."

John Smith splashed more bourbon in their glasses, tipped his back for a contemplative sip. "Well, there's only one thing you can do, Jed."

His son turned toward him, his eyes lighting up. "What's that?"

"Talk to her father."

Jed flopped back in the chaise and raised his eyes to the late afternoon sky.

"Boys!" said Helen through the screen door. "Dinner is served!"

Between bites, Jed said, "Dad, what's up with the investigation up in Lincoln? The guy who murdered Luke?"

His father shook his head morosely. "I don't have one damned thing to report," he said. "That sonofabitch police chief Lemieux won't investigate. Says it was an accident. I think you'll recall I twisted Colonel Hooper's arm because legally the accident occurred on a state highway, but he says Lemieux and his clodhopper cops contaminated the site and there's no useful evidence. They didn't take photos, they left a bunch of broken bicycle parts on the roadway that got runned over by other traffic—"

"What about the truck? I saw bike paint and scratches on the truck."

"Gone. We know who was drivin' it, but that truck has been cleaned up so good you'd never know anything happened to it."

"Well, geez, isn't that evidence enough?" said Jed.

"You don't understand. I mean it got detailed so good you can't even tell it got detailed."

Jed set his fork and knife down, closed his eyes. He was silent a long time, then said, "Are you telling me this guy is gonna get away with killing Luke, one of my three best friends in my whole life?"

John gave him a dour look. "That could be just what happens, son."

"That will not happen, Dad. Count on it. I will *not* let that happen." Jed rose from his chair and began pacing the dining room.

"You're a chip off the old block if I say so myself," said his father. "But you gotta know when to hold 'em and when to fold 'em. I've given this my best shot and nothin' is happening. Accidents *do* happen, son."

"Sure they do, Dad," said Jed, stopping in front of his mother's china cabinet to turn and stare at his father. "It's just that this isn't one. No way. I saw it happen with my own eyes, in real time. I can't let it go that easily."

"Jed," said Alice pointing, "Oh! Jed, there, right beside you. I saved those newspapers for you. They're articles about the accident."

"*Not* an accident," said Jed and picked up the two papers. One was *The North Country Gazette*, a weekly, the other the *Concord Press-Intelligencer*.

"There's something you should know," Jed said. "Three agents of business espionage stalked us in the Tokyo airport and then followed us all over Taipei."

John Smith leaned forward, elbows on the glass tabletop. "What? I don't believe it. Why? What the hell was that all about?"

Jed explained.

"For the love of God," said his father, shaking his head.

"It's the way the world does business now. I got to know the security chief at Joyful Bike and we talked a lot about it. He says everybody steals from their competitors. It's how they get ahead. Stealing is cheaper than spending your own money on R&D. Steal it, get it to market faster, beat the competition.

"If these agents of espionage, as they're called, were hired by one of the bike makers here in the States and were following us, it just confirms for me that the so-called accident with Luke was no accident at all. Unfortunately for Luke, it was a stupid and clumsy attempt. The driver was probably somebody they hired. Maybe he was only supposed to veer into one of us, not actually hurt or kill anybody. Maybe his aim wasn't so good. I'll bet they didn't even care which of us got hurt, so long as they got a bike. But they didn't."

"Dear Lord," said Alice, "who would agree to run over someone on a bicycle?"

"Certainly nobody I know. A New Hampshire boy would never do something like that," said John.

"Right, Dad, at least nobody we know would hire on for that. Anyway, the Japanese espionage thieves followed us all over Taipei for days. I didn't tell you, but Joyful gave us these awesome carbon fiber bikes. Ten-thousand-dollar bikes. These bungling espionage worms stole 'em, right out of our SUV. But we worked with Joyful's head of security and caught them red-handed! But by then the worms had literally destroyed our bikes.

"And then I'm talking to Gregg and he tells me somebody hacked into our computers. Even though we caught two of the espionage agents in Taipei, well, there were three of them, but one of them, a girl, got away. Then at Narita we caught one of their partners trying to steal Rick's briefcase. They're all over. They could still be after us, just hanging around until we show up again. No way to know for sure if they are or aren't. But I think somebody knew, or thought they knew, we had some kind of technology they wanted to steal. Maybe it started when we were trying to make a deal with one of the American bike companies. Or maybe it didn't have anything to do with that. Maybe it just kind of happened because they were following Angela and targeted us. I don't know. They broke into our hotel rooms and stole all of Rick's phone info. Then they saw us with Jung-Shan—"

"Son, you're not making any sense and besides, you're giving me a headache. Look, it's getting late, so let's call it a day and get a good night's sleep. This'll keep until coffee in the morning."

Seasons of Change

"OK, let's get started," said Jed. All the Smithworks employees were assembled in the third-floor open space. A sideboard luncheon had been mostly devoured, and the sated employees were sipping Starbucks iced coffees or Cokes and eating cookies.

Jed stood with David, Gregg, Rick, and Suzie and smiled at his people. "I want to tell you about some changes in the company, but let me start by saying your jobs are totally secure and nothing will change for you—not even your salaries." There were snickers around the room. "And Smithworks will continue to make the world's most excellent and innovative custom bikes for our customers.

"What *is* going to change is who's doing what upstairs," said Jed, pointing a finger at the fourth floor. A few more snickers and guffaws.

"Most of you know we've been developing a new cycling product, and I'm pleased to say it works and will be a great success. We're calling it 'The Spinner.'

"We—Luke, really—saw a new market emerging for cycling: the business commuter and urban shoppers. People who didn't ride for passion but for convenience, and for some folks because gas had gotten too expensive to drive to work every day.

"Europeans, and in particular the Dutch, have been avid commuter cyclists for generations. They built sturdy bikes, the kind with, you know, with a basket on the handlebars?" More snickers from the employees. "Yes, the ones we Americans made fun of, right?" Jed continued. "But US cities were starting to think about this same kind of commuter bike, one people could rent to ride to work or between shopping errands. Short trips, like going to the dentist." Much laughter. "That new market is beginning to emerge as each city—in typical American style, of course—develops its own business model for providing short-term rental bikes. But I can tell you it's gonna be a big deal.

"Now, during this same time frame, Luke and I were working on the problem. As we saw it, that problem was, and remains, that city folk don't want to shift gears and they don't like riding up inclines. How could we solve that problem? The Spinner was the solution. It would be like a fixie bike, but it would store energy from pedaling and release it when the rider needed it, like to speed up or climb a hill.

"We knew right from the start that we'd need to partner on building the Spinner because there are four distinct technologies involved"—Jed ticked them off on his fingers—"the software, a microchip controller, and the technology that took the place of a heavy, bulky battery. Oh, and a bike. We didn't know companies in all of these industries, but

Luke did. In Taiwan.

"When we had a prototype ready, we went out to the three big bike makers. Remember, I wanted to keep this all-American. None of them wanted to partner. They just wanted to buy the Spinner and our intellectual property, like it was a McDonald's hamburger, and then do whatever they wanted with it. I might add they weren't offering much for it, either. Rightly or wrongly, the four of us agreed that we had put too much of ourselves into this idea to sell it outright. We wanted to stay with it all the way down the line.

"But then, thanks to Luke," Jed paused and lowered his head. All heads in the room bowed for a silent moment. Jed spoke again. "Thanks to Luke, we began talks with a Taiwanese bike company, Joyful, the biggest bike maker in the world, and they were interested in partnering with us. Not only that, they suggested we work with two other Taiwanese companies. Luke knew a lot about them. They could help make the device.

"You all know that David, Rick, Suzie and I were in Taiwan earlier this month. The meetings went well, very well." Jed paused; no, no reason to go into more detail. "We are on our way to a contract and an amazing bike, the Joyful NewBike, fitted with The Spinner!"

The employees burst into spontaneous applause and whooping. "Thank you, thank you, people," said Jed.

"Anyway, here's what's gonna happen. In order to, ah, preserve and defend Smithworks, we have been advised by our attorneys to form a new company. I'm naming it Spinnerworks. You all will continue doing exactly what you've been doing. No changes. Smithworks and Spinnerworks are two separate businesses. Period.

"I'll be heading Spinnerworks, so we'll have a change of management at Smithworks. Moving forward, you will have a new CEO and COO. I'm proud to announce that David Bondsman is now your new CEO. Rick Saundersson remains the CFO and Gregg Colarusso is now our COO. I see these trusted business partners and friends as a tricorn management team, working together to manage Smithworks and also coordinating and collaborating with me in my new role. I'm not going anywhere; I'll still be right up there!" He pointed at the ceiling again. *Probably not true but who knows*, he thought. "So, let's give it up for our new management team!"

The assemblage applauded and hooted and stamped their feet in affirmation. Jed grinned and threw his arms around David, Rick and Gregg.

"One more thing. Dave, Rick, Gregg, Suzie and I will be heading for Taiwan again shortly, for two purposes. One, of course, to close the deal with our soon-to-be partners, and two, to attend Luke's funeral services. I know you all will join us there in spirit." Once again the room fell silent.

"Actually, there's a third bit of news. Sun Xiaohui, better known to us as Suzie, will not be returning from our next trip. She is marrying her childhood sweetheart and remaining in Taipei. Congratulations, Suzie!"

Voices rose in a roar. People rushed to give Suzie a hug, a handshake, their well wishes. A party atmosphere ensued. Jed watched, a thin smile on his lips, then he walked over to the window wall. Outside, signs of a premature September were becoming evident: leaves were turning from green to gold, yellow and bronze, falling and floating by on the Nashua River, which reflected the slanting sunlight from bank to bank.

His thoughts drifted back to riding alongside the rivers in Taipei:

the Tamsui, the Keelung. The Penghus. Over the crashing waves on the bridge across the ocean with Jung-Shan. Inwardly, he sighed as he thought of the approaching New England fall and how much he would like her to be here with him, right now, looking out the window at this autumn scene. *Maybe if I could get her over here for a week or so I could convince her to . . . be with me. Maybe convince her to go against her father's wishes again, like she did in England. Maybe we could be together here and run the Spinnerworks business side-by-side. Well, Jed, that's a lot of maybes.*

He glanced at his iPhone: almost 1:30. That made it 1:30 in the morning in Taipei. He couldn't call her now. He'd have to wait until later in the evening. He hoped he could hold out that long. He wanted to hear what she said when he told her all the good news.

"OK, gang, anybody have questions?" he called out. They did, and Jed and Rick and David answered them. Afterwards, Jed said, "Let's continue the celebration. Take the rest of the day off, with pay. A company bike ride for anybody who wants to join me. Let's do the Smithworks Classic. Otherwise, just enjoy this beautiful day any way you want to."

They all knew the Smithworks Classic route, and nearly everyone went on the ride. Jed was riding toward the rear of the peloton, watching his fellow workers as they pedaled the hills and valleys of southern New Hampshire and northern Massachusetts, talking to each other, laughing, sprint-racing in occasional breakaways. *Everybody's having a good time,* he thought. *This was the right way to end the meeting. But it's also, in a large way, the end of my running Smithworks. I want to be with Jung-Shan and lead the Spinnerworks company to success. That probably means relocating to Taipei. I know that's the path of greatest risk, maybe not because of the business aspect, but because I don't know if I can live with the decision Jung-Shan and I have made. I don't want to live in a world without love.*

Jed, back from the ride, stowed his bike and climbed the stairs to his office. He was flat-out crazy about the bicycle design Joyful had come up with for the NewBike. Although inspired by the 1950s Schwinn cruiser, it bore 21st-century aerodynamic flair: everything about it said light, crisp, lithe, fun, even sexy. Both men and women were going to love this bike. Neither would have any hesitation in riding it around town, even with its step-through frame and a basket on the handlebars. And once they experienced the Spinner, well . . .

Suzie knocked at his door. He looked up. "Can I do anything for you, Jed?"

"Yes, as a matter of fact you can," he said. "Would you please get on the phone with our travel agent and make our reservations to Taipei?"

"All done, Bossman."

"All done?" said Jed.

"Weeks ago. I arrange funeral and business meeting in the same trip for us."

Jed smiled and said, "Well done, Susie. I knew if anyone could pull them together, it would be you."

"Thanks, Bossman." She giggled and they both laughed.

"Luke's funeral is all set?" She nodded.

"What do we need to do for it?"

"Nothing. We all go to funeral. Business meeting, you decide."

"How soon?"

"In twelve days' time."

Jed relaxed. "Xie xie, Suzie."

"Yes, I am so glad the Lin family finally have made the auspicious date for Luke. Funeral is very simple. You guys wear dark suits. No red color tie. Wear white armbands; Jung-Shan will get them for us in Taipei. I will order flowers on behalf of Smithworks.

"Ceremony is very simple. People will chant. Much incense will be burned. You will receive a white envelope with candy inside. Put the candy on your tongue; it is to make loss of friend less bitter. Maybe you are asked to stand and speak to people about Luke, but I do not know yet. Maybe read a poem. Most of the people will not speak English, so please keep that in mind. Also keep in mind, no saying good-bye.

"After the funeral, Lin family will host one big dinner for everyone at a restaurant. Oh, forty-nine days after funeral, go to Buddhist temple and say prayers for Luke."

Jed was silent, looking at Suzie, then said, "Do you miss him?"

Suzie crumpled. Tears poured down her cheeks. Her lower lip quivered as she nodded rapidly up and down, not lifting her eyes from her hands. "I must go now," she said.

Jung-Shan picked up her ringing iPhone. "Wei."

"Ni hǎo, Jung-Shan," said Jed.

"*Ni hǎo ma*, Jed?" What's up?

"I miss you. I miss you every day. All day. All night, too."

"Jed, it is business time. We cannot talk this way. I am very busy."

"All right. How is the NewBike bike coming along?"

"The design department is hard at work on change orders," she said.

"I think we will fabricate the final iteration within the next few days."

"Great. We just made our reservations for . . . uh, coming back. For Luke's funeral," he said. "And the business summit," he added.

"I know. That is good. Sun Xiaohui has provided all the details. We are preparing here."

"Of course. Will you be at the airport to meet me?"

"I don't know. Please have Sun Xiaohui fax your itinerary. I really must go now, Jed. Good-bye."

Taking Care of Business

"It is good to see you again, Mr. Smith," said Mr. Zheng, bowing. "It is good to be back, Zheng Ming-Cheng," Jed said, bowing back, glancing at Jung-Shan, who also bowed. "I have brought you gifts from New Hampshire," he said, handing each of them a small box tied with a ribbon.

Father and daughter sat down on the sofa and Jed dropped into a chair opposite. They opened their gifts, filigree silver earrings with a small diamond in the center for Jung-Shan, cufflinks made of Afghan lapis lazuli for her father, handcrafted by artisans from the League of New Hampshire Craftsmen. She gave him the sweetest smile he had ever seen in his life. *It's a good thing I'm sitting because my knees were about to buckle and I'd be sprawled on the floor*, he thought. Wei-Ting had picked them up at the airport, alone, but here she was, waiting to see him.

Her face was not a blur. Her beautiful dark brown eyes did not move from his own; her lips, painted a soft red, were slightly parted, but nonetheless, he could feel nothing emanating from her.

They discussed the business deal and what remained to be worked out in the meeting that afternoon. Zheng said it would be the first of many meetings. He excused himself from lunch; Jung-Shan and Jed walked to her office. He closed the door and took her in his arms. She let him, but when he tried to kiss her, she turned her face to the side.

"Jed, please," she said, wrapping her arms around his waist and hugging him, her head pressed against his chest. "Please, no. It is too hard. It cannot go forward. We must stop here. Please. It is too hard, too hard."

He let go of her, feeling hopelessness and love in equal measure. The confluence, then the schism, of the two began driving him back inside the old shell he'd created after he and Marty split. *Women! Nothing but pain! I'm done with this shit!* he said to himself, knowing it was a lie. He moved away from her.

She said, "Jed, we must focus on business. We have so much important work to do, so let us give all the attention to our business at hand." He nodded, saying he had already made preparations for the meeting.

"But Jed, there is still time for wŭcān. We should eat a meal before the meeting. Gather strength. Then we can work on the final strategy for bringing all parties together."

"I don't think we need to have wŭcān to discuss it. I need to go back to the hotel. I'll discuss it once more with Dave, but I think we're all set. See you at the conference room at two." He held her gaze until she dropped her eyes. He could see the disappointment on her countenance. *Sorry, but you can't have it both ways*, he thought.

The following day Luke's funeral was held at a small rural Buddhist temple in the hills above the Tamsui District, not far from where they had bicycled. An urn containing his ashes rested atop the beautiful wooden casket. Vases four feet tall filled with massive arrays of flowers encircled the room, which was completely filled with people swaying and moaning to the sad, traditional Chinese music. Jed, David and Rick sat in the front row with Luke's family.

Luke's father rose and spoke for perhaps fifteen minutes about his son. Lin Bao, Luke's sister, accompanied by Suzie, came to the podium and read a poem she had written for her lost older brother, breaking into tears several times. Several uncles and cousins spoke next, then Jung-Shan gave Jed a nudge and said, "Go." All spoke in Mandarin.

Jed walked to the podium and set his notes down on it. He felt very awkward and out of place, unsure why he was standing in front of sixty or seventy people who probably wouldn't understand a word he said. When he looked up to face them, he saw Jung-Shan standing beside him. "Speak slowly, so I can keep up with translation for you," she said.

Although the words came haltingly at first, Jed soon forgot his inhibitions and spoke freely of how he felt about his fallen friend. "We were friends for half our lives. We were cyclists and students and business partners, but most important we were always friends. True friends. Sometimes we laughed and played, sometimes we solved problems. But one thing that never, ever concerned us was coming from different cultures and countries and heritages. We never judged.

We were just . . . two guys who enjoyed being together.

"Lin Shieh-Seng discovered in college that he had an ability called *deep learning*. He could think things through, solve very complex problems, using algorithms at a very high level of abstraction, and it came as naturally to him as . . . I don't know what. He was always thinking way ahead of everyone else, like a chess player."

Jung-Shan halted several times, apparently trying to convey these complex ideas.

"Luke saw all kinds of applications for our bicycle drive concept," Jed continued. "He saw ways to integrate different technologies, like electronics and ceramics, that nobody had ever thought possible. He was even thinking about ways to use cold fusion.

"I believed in him. I loved him and I miss him more than I can say. I'm bitter to have lost my friend in such a violent, absurd, disrespectful way. That is unfinished business and I promise to the Lin family it will be properly finished.

"But for today, I can only tell you of my respect and love for Lin Shieh-Seng, one of the best friends to walk this earth. No one can ever take the place of Lin Shieh-Seng in my heart. Or in my life. I know Rick Saundersson feels exactly the same." He looked at Rick, who was silently weeping. David could not raise his head. Suzie's sobbing could be heard throughout the room. Johnny held her hand, helpless to do anything more to comfort her.

As Jung-Shan finished translating, people began crying out loud, bowing again and again, keening, sharing Jed's grief, his anger, his loss. Tears poured down Jed's face until he could speak no more. Jung-Shan guided him back to his chair and held him to her heart. Once he was himself again, they held hands until the end. *Finally, in sorrow, we are close again, but I wonder if it will last once this is over.*

Equity

J ed should have known it, should have expected it, but just hadn't thought it through. Here he was, two days after Luke's funeral, back in the air on his way home. Rick had flown back right after the funeral to attend to Smithworks business. Over the past week or so, Jed and David had taken care of every last specification from TII and Taiwan Micronics. David and Tai-Ping Gau had worked out the new composite aluminum and carbon fiber crankset fabrication. Zheng had called a subsequent meeting to agree upon the configuration changes and sign the partnership agreement. The legal document joining the four companies created a stack of paper nearly an inch high. It was a masterpiece. That's what Smithworks's attorney, who of course had written it, called it: a masterpiece. Even if it was in fact a masterpiece, the lawyers for the three Taiwanese

315

signatories were the world's best masterpiece detectives, for they found seventeen issues and errors in need of examination, determination, clarification, revision, and fixing. Jed suggested they could annotate and initial the changes, but no, they asked (politely) for a new, clean document. That was a level of detail Jed hadn't anticipated, but now realized he should have.

So Joyful had graciously bought him a four-thousand-dollar first-class plane ticket for a nonstop JAL flight back to Boston. It felt a little odd, since David was elbow-to-knee in coach, but it was just what Jed needed: near-silence, food and drink on call, and a private pod in which to rest and think. Still, it bothered him to think of his CEO crammed in the back, so he asked Hikari, his flight attendant, to move him to the one of the empty pods in first class. Not a problem, she said, smiling. No charge.

He drafted an email covering all the issues to resolve for Spinnerworks LLC, and yet another as a to-do list for related matters Rick had to attend to at Smithworks. He let thoughts of Jung-Shan drift in and out of his consciousness as he worked on these documents. When he thought about their conversations, the word that recurred over and over was *business*. She skillfully kept anything personal or intimate completely out of their interactions. *Business, business, business. Was that all she could think about?* No, of course not. He knew she was doing it with an iron will, to keep distance between them. She was stronger than he; it seemed she could keep her love for him from asserting itself. What a dirty trick that first husband had played on her, taking away her essential pride of womanhood. Then her father: how she had lost him, then recovered him, and now could not risk losing him again. She had taken her love for Jed as far as she could, but now would not let it go any further.

Jed threw his head back and closed his eyes as he recalled again their last night together in Beitou, the intense intimacy they shared. *She takes my breath away, with every touch, every look. With every tiny detail of her being she has captured me, hook, line, sinker, dock and pier. Now I am hers forever. No, not forever, but nevermore. Ahrgh!*

The pain, the frustration, the loss twisted inside him like a disease, a living death worse than death itself.

How can she not be feeling this, too?

But of course it's entirely possible she is.

Jed thought about Marty, how it had seemed easy for her to walk out. How a couple of other women he'd been serious about had broken up with him seemingly without experiencing any pain. *Women must be able to let go of love more easily than men.* Or maybe they've simply mastered not showing it. *Oh, well. Men aren't supposed to understand women, just love them. And I do. Oh, man, how I love Jung-Shan, to the bursting point of my heart, to the depths of my soul.*

My soul?

I am not the captain of my soul anymore.

She is.

Jed forced his thoughts away from her, and they fell into the other abyss: Luke's death. The funeral. All those people mourning a young life snuffed out without cause or reason. The last time he'd cried like that was at another funeral. Little Jed's. He really didn't want to go there, but got stuck in it anyway. He knew he'd never get over either loss. The law had meted out what it considered sufficient punishment to the guy who took little Jed's life. Some, but not nearly enough. But at least it was better than no punishment at all, which was where Luke's accident seemed to be heading.

Jed's resolve grew stronger: Whoever ran Luke down had to pay for it, and he was going to make sure they did. One way or the other. The more he thought about it, the angrier it made him. That sonofabitch killed his friend and thought nothing of it. No longer did it matter if he was an agent of espionage or just a construction worker, he was a stone cold killer, and he was going to pay for it.

Jed realized that his anger was a source of strength: he'd become upset at the business meeting over the others being so nit-picky. Everybody in American business understood there are changes, and that most of them can be endorsed by hand. Yet here he was, flying back to New Hampshire on a pricey flight to get a perfectly typed document with no scribbles or initials on it. This drove his resolve to solve the contract's remaining problems and issues quickly and effectively.

Now it occurred to him that he could do the same with Luke's murder. Not to have done so earlier had simply been a matter of having too many irons in the fire at once. He hadn't given Luke the time, or the respect, he deserved. Well, he would now. He was a trained intelligence—*and counterintelligence*—officer. He could do this.

Jed put on the Panasonic noise-canceling headphones, plugged in his iPad, and scrolled to The Eagles' "Long Road Out of Eden." He thought about everything he knew and what he didn't know, how to answer those questions and turn them into a solution.

Finally, weary of thinking, Jed drifted off to sleep. Jung-Shan appeared in his mind's eye as the Eagles sang "What Do I Do With My Heart," but that was a question he just couldn't answer right now.

Rough Justice

It was after dinner at Cherry Hill Farm. The guys were sitting on the porch as Jed talked to his dad. "I've examined what's left of Luke's bike frame, and it has white paint on it. There are a couple of stripes of it on the top tube and some of the left handlebar grip. No doubt this is paint from the truck."

"Son, how you gonna prove anythin' with white paint? White is white is white."

"You remember when I was here a few weeks ago? Before I went back to Taiwan?"

His dad nodded. Helen came out of the house with a plate of cookies she had just baked. Everybody grabbed one.

"Remember when Mom asked me if I had a picture of Jung-Shan? Well, guess what. Until that moment, I'd forgotten I took pictures of New England Energy Cooperative truck number L-213. Dad, I have a photo of the right side of L-213 with scratches of from Luke's bike. There's white paint on Luke's bike. There's red paint on the truck."

"Circumstantial evidence," said his father. "It may look good, but you'll hafta make it stand up in court."

"A lab comparison would—*would have*—given us proof. Evidence. We have to have evidence. I understand, and that's why I need your help tomorrow. Can you get Colonel Hooper and bring him to Lincoln about five o'clock?"

"He's a busy man, but I 'spect I can try," said John Smith.

"Great. Park in the Lincoln Mills Marketplace parking lot. Near the police station, but not right in front where Lemieux could see you."

"And then what?"

"Wait for my call."

Rick and Jed walked into Ski Bum's Tavern about half an hour after the NEEC crew had arrived. Jed wanted to be sure his target had a few beers in him before they got there. Jed slid into a booth near the door; David followed a minute later.

Rick sauntered down the bar, took a stool near the five NEEC workmen and ordered a draft beer. The bartender brought it; he lifted the mug, drained it, and banged it down on the bar. "Son of a BITCH!" he said, loud enough to startle the others. "SONOFABITCH!"

"Wadder you hollereen' about?" said François, the burly, black-haired man they called Frenchy.

Rick turned to him and stared, his facial expression strained and angry. "Fuckin' guy on a bicycle. I just about killed the dumb son of a bitch."

The NEEC workers chuckled.

"I'm comin' up here from Woodstock, right? And he's in front of me, right? I'm bein' careful, I see him on the right side there, I look at the cars comin' at me, I look back—it wasn't even a second—and the dumb sumbitch is crossing in front of me, cuttin' across the road into Lambert's Country Store. I'm grabbin' brakes, the cars comin' the other way are grabbin' their brakes, you know? A second slower hittin' the pedal, that jerkoff asshole woulda been road kill."

Now all of them were listening, chuckling, nodding. Jed had gotten up and was walking along the bar toward them, ostensibly heading for the men's room.

"Hell, you oughta hear Frenchy's story," said one of the men, pointing at the black-haired man. "He's got a better one than that!" The men guffawed.

"Yeah, *c'est vrai*," said François. "I freaking hate *cyclistes*. They think they can do anything they want. Like the road is theirs and not mine." He stared at Rick, his eyes narrowing to tiny black BBs. "I showed this *cycliste*. I run over the fucker. He was riding *a quartre*. I wish I could have runned over all four of them."

"Yeah?" said Rick. "Good thing you didn't, Frenchy, 'cuz then I wouldn't be here to pound you into dust."

François didn't miss a beat: he swiftly turned on his stool and swung a fist at Rick, but Jed, furious after what the man had just said, was right behind him. He grabbed Frenchy's wrist and pulled it down, hard, arcing it up behind the man's fat back. Rick punched him square in the nose, which began bleeding profusely. François lowered his head and Jed delivered a karate chop to the back of his neck.

The big man sagged. Jed, still holding the man's hand, shoved it up his back, lifting the arm to pull him upright. François screamed and clambered to his feet as fast as he could, trying to avoid the wrenching pain. Jed threw a hard punch into his gut; François hurled his beer bottle. Rick bent his knees slightly and delivered an uppercut to François's jaw. Jed let go of Frenchy's arm and slugged him in the face, first with his right fist, then his left. The big man went down again. He was about to grab him, pull him back to his feet for another pounding, when David caught his arm and said, "Enough, Jed. Enough."

François lay on the floor in a puddle of beer, vomit and blood while the other men sat on their stools, stunned. Jed and Rick faced them, along with David. "Anybody else?" said Jed, his lips drawn taut against his teeth, fists clenched, rage emanating from his eyes. He really wanted someone else to stand up and fight him. The workers sensed this at a primal level and remained on their stools. The only sounds in the bar were Jed's stentorian breathing and Taylor Swift singing "Should've Said No" on the jukebox.

"Frenchy?" Jed nudged him with his sneaker. "Hey, FRENCHY! *Comment allez-vous?* Wanna take a ride to the police station?" The big man didn't move.

Rick stepped over him and fastened a plastic quick-cuff around his wrists, then yanked it to pull him, yowling in pain, to his feet. "You boys stay right here," he said to the others. "Don't follow us if you know what's good for you." Rick propelled Frenchy out the door and sat him down on the steps while Jed called his father.

Four minutes later, Colonel Hooper and John Smith pulled up in a brown-and-green State Police Ford Expedition SUV. Rick and David pulled François to his feet. "Here's your hit-and-run killer, Colonel Hooper," said Jed.

"I din't do nothin', I dint do nothin'," François slobbered. "*Les hommes* beat me for no reason and *j'accuse* them of *assaillir.*"

"Oh yeah?" said Rick and removed his iPhone from his shirt pocket. He tapped a few buttons and the conversation recorded in the bar could be heard:

"Hell, you oughta hear Frenchy's story. He's got a better one than that!"

They listened to Frenchy confess, then Rick clicked off.

"Well?" said Sam Hooper.

"I din't run over him on purpose!" said François. "I told *la grande fable*. I just want to be the beeg man in front of others. *Ce était un accident simple!*"

"No, you meant to hit him," said Jed. "I know because I saw you. David saw you. Rick saw you. We're the guys riding the other bikes you wanted to hit. We're eyeball witnesses and now we have your confession on tape. You're going to jail for murder, François Goncourt."

"Lemieux told me to be quiet!" he said. "I did not mean it, but it happened. *Assay-dent!* I went to him after you came to our shop. I knew I would be caught. I knew it was wrong. *Mon frère* said I would bring bad news to NEEC and I would be deported. They made me be quiet!"

"I think it's time to have a little talk with Chief Lemieux," said Hooper, and that was pretty much that.

The NewBike

J ed was telling Jung-Shan the Frenchy Goncourt story as they had drinks in the lobby lounge of the Crystal Palace Taipei. "Hooper smelled a cover-up and ordered Chief Lemieux to stand down, then sent a trooper to NEEC head Albert Goncourt's house and placed him under house arrest. Oh, yeah Albert was head of the local NEEC office. I heard the charge was concealing evidence, but it might go all the way to being an accessory to manslaughter, like his brother Francois was charged with.

"In the end Albert was fired, and since he was a Canadian citizen deported but ordered to return to stand trial. Lemieux was allowed to resign, and of course chose to leave the country on his own."

"No charges were brought against Lemieux?"

"Nope. Cops always protect their brothers in uniform, no matter what."

"And François, ah, Frenchy?"

"He's in the Grafton County jail, awaiting trial for vehicular manslaughter. It's a lesser charge than murder for some reason. Probably because the driver can always say it was an *assay-dent*. Whether it was or wasn't isn't relevant. What is *very* relevant is there were other witnesses besides us who saw it. Definitely hit-and-run, and that's François's Achilles heel."

"He will go to prison?"

"He'll get two years, maybe more. I hope more. If he'd been drunk, or even if he'd had a couple of beers, the sentence would've been harsher. Up to ten years. But we'll never know that, because of his buddies and his brother and Lemieux covering up for him. Our testimony is pretty important because we saw it. We gave statements. I might have to testify at the trial."

"What of the theft of Rick's briefcase you told me about? At Narita? Did you say one man did not get arrested?" said Jung-Shan.

"I'm not really sure. As far as I know the briefcase thief is still out there. There were the two others. Who and how many there's no way to know. Some could still be trying to find us. They might still be following Angela. I just don't know."

"And what about them following us?" said Jung-Shan, taking a sip of wine.

"The two who were in Taipei are in custody for theft of our bikes. You know that. They destroyed over fifty thousand US dollars' worth of property! They'll be tried and convicted and get some pretty stiff sentences, unless I'm sadly mistaken," said Jed.

"The girl, Akiko," he swilled some Taiwan Beer and continued, "You know she escaped when the police raided the hotel room. The police have her picture and name from customs, but as far as they know, she hasn't tried to leave the country. She probably has no money and besides, knows she'd be arrested at customs."

"Probably living in the underground economy," said Jung-Shan. "Very easy for people to live on outside edge of Taiwan society. Maybe she gets work in a restaurant, or another hotel, or sell foods on sidewalks. She would be left alone, I think."

"I kinda feel bad for her," said Jed. "She might have gotten dragged into this thing, but I get the feeling she helped get those two caught and arrested. Now she's trapped in Taiwan and can't go home."

"Fate or Karma?" said Jung-Shan.

Jed had no answer for that. He just tipped his head back, took another swig from his beer bottle, and stared at the ceiling.

The waitress stopped at their divan, smiled, bowed, and asked if they would like another beer or glass of wine. They smiled, shook their heads. After she had bowed and walked away, Jung-Shan said, "I hope other IP thieves learn from this that there are consequences if they are caught. And maybe stay away from Taiwan."

"I'm afraid that may never be possible," he said. "Rick, Dave and I talked about this. IP theft is underreported and is mostly considered a cost of doing business. That's unfortunate, but Dave thinks there is diminishing interest, in part based on the increased risk. If by some chance word gets back to the agents in Tokyo, it would be that nothing of value was found. They may not learn the agents were arrested, in part because your father and many other businessmen don't want the world to know what happened.

"But in any event, we're going to have a lot more risk, or exposure, once the Spinners go on NewBikes. Can't do much about bike theft, but is the Spinner easy to copy? Reverse engineer? Nope, I don't think so. Steal off the bike? Maybe, but it would automatically self-destruct. Regardless, I don't think we can act like there's no threat. Thomas Jefferson was our President many years ago. He was a very intelligent man who said, 'The price of freedom is eternal vigilance.' IP threats are everywhere: hacked cellphones, surveillance gear in hotel rooms, blabbing taxi drivers, cyberattacks on our networks and computers. As much as I hate to say it, or even think about it, we have to be constantly on guard against business espionage."

Jung-Shan was quiet, her legs curled up under her on the divan, a tiny pout on her face.

"Hey, here's some very good news," said Jed, and she perked up. "I don't think I told you this. Worldwide, when a cyclist is killed, a white bike is placed at the scene. They're called ghost bikes. I've seen them several times riding around New England. We chained one to a road sign for Luke, but there's a foundation Smithworks supports, so together we're creating a permanent ghost bike memorial statue to Luke where he was struck down. So anybody, whether they're cycling or driving, will hopefully pay more attention and be more alert for cyclists."

"Yes. That is very good news. You have told Luke's family?"

"Geez, I just got here! I'll see them in the next few days and tell them about it. And you might be interested to know we're funding the foundation's efforts to raise bicycle-safety consciousness, and creating ten memorial scholarships in Luke's name."

Jung-Shan raised her eyebrows and smiled. "This is wonderful news. The scholarship is at MIT?"

"Two, actually. One at MIT and one at National Taiwan University."

"Joyful will make the same contribution as Smithworks at both universities," said Jung-Shan.

Jed smiled, said "Xie xie," and shook her hand, rather formally, she thought. "I have a lot of work to do, Jung-Shan. I have to get everybody and their attorneys together to review the partnership agreements—*again*—and get them signed. And I need to—"

"Yes, I know all these things, and I have prepared a project management worksheet and have scheduled all of these meetings and appointments for us."

"Us?"

"Yes, you and me. We will be the business team leaders of NewBike. You will remember my father gave me this job."

"Well," said Jed, waving a la-di-da hand in the air, "I guess it makes *business* sense."

"Yes, good business sense," either missing or ignoring Jed's gesture. "We are a good team, Jed. We will get this going. I already have five people of marketing and sales prepared to begin working with Rick."

"Rick won't be working with us," said Jed. "I made him the CFO of Smithworks. He's helping Suzie short-term with the initial business and financial details for Spinnerworks, but that's all. We'll be working with her.

"I decided not to bring Rick on this trip because he got stressed out a lot here. You know, complaining about people bumping into him, the scooter incident. Dave and I think he's, ah, too high-strung for, ah, big-city life, and besides, I need him at Smithworks."

"Who will take Rick's place?"

"I just told you. Suzie."

"OK," she said. "I have good news, too."

"Yeah? What?" said Jed.

"Gau Tai-Ping has prepared two NewBikes for us to test ride. They are in our Jimmy, waiting for us."

"That's great," said Jed, noting her use of plural pronouns. "Which reminds me, how is Wei-Ting?"

"He is fine. His head injury was not too serious. But he told me he would like other work, not to drive cars anymore!" She laughed her deep-throated laugh.

"Not a bad idea. Well, it's late and I need some sleep," he said, stretching, yawning.

Jung-Shan, comfortably curled up on the divan, almost looked disappointed for a moment. "Yes, good time for us to sleep. We will be very busy tomorrow and for some time to come. Please look at the project management dashboard and task list for you and for me. We can discuss it, make changes if necessary, over breakfast."

Jed paused, then said, "I'll probably just order some coffee from room service. I'll meet you at the office at, what, eight o'clock?" They held each other's gaze for a moment, then Jed got up and said, "Good-night."

"Jed!" Jung-Shan almost shouted his name. He turned.

"What?"

"Um . . . I have one more question." She paused. "François. Frenchy. Did he tell why he hit Luke?"

"Yeah, he did," said Jed, his face in a deep frown. "He was trying to get a cigarette and his pack of smokes fell off the seat. He was bending over, trying to pick it up, and the truck veered to the right. So in the end, it really was what Lemieux called it. And what Frenchy himself said: an *assay-dent*. If he'd stopped and admitted that, he probably would have walked away a free man."

The two Spinner NewBikes Tai-Ping had sent were awesome. His was silver, hers was red; otherwise, they were identical. They spent several hours riding the Tamsui and Keelung Riverways and agreed the NewBike was ready for full-scale production.

By late October, agreements had been signed and all four companies were working ten-hour days on the NewBike project.

In November, NewBike manufacturing began in Tai-Ping's new building. The sales and marketing staff, using a computer-generated graphic image of the NewBike, had received twenty-two thousand advance orders, mostly from New Taipei City, but several more large orders from cities in the United States and Germany.

In December, contracts for distribution channels were initiated and Spinner installations began. Jed was amazed at how quickly everything ramped up, so much faster than in the States. Marketing decided it wanted Jed as its spokesperson. On the strength of his and Joyful's names, worldwide NewBike orders quickly rose to three hundred thousand.

In late January, a minor glitch occurred: The Chinese company manufacturing the bicycle wheels said it couldn't deliver because of "prior commitments."

"This is to be expected," said Mr. Zheng. "This is the way Chinese companies sometimes use to 'negotiate.'" He got on his plane and headed for Jinan. When he returned, he not only had wheels on their way but an order for half a million OEM Spinner NewBikes from the company for exclusive sale and distribution in China.

Deliveries to Taipei's NewBike program began in late February, followed by the first container ship scheduled to steam out of the Port of Kaohsiung, destination Long Beach, California. In April, a champagne celebration was held at the factory with the first Spinner NewBike on display. It was followed by an hours-long banquet dinner, with dish after dish and toast after toast. Afterwards, Tai-Ping drove Jung-Shan and Jed to the Zuoying THSR station for a late-night train back to Taipei.

They were still tipsy, Jung-Shan uncharacteristically so, when they settled into the familiar adjacent first-class seats. Jed leaned back and closed his eyes. He could feel Jung-Shan wriggling around, as if trying to get comfortable. "Jed," she said. When he didn't respond she gave his arm a little poke. "Jed!"

"Please, I'm tired," he said.

"Jed," she said again, taking his arm and shaking him until he looked at her. "I have question. We have been at hard work together for five months and three weeks. Every day we work together. We see each other all day long. But you never look at me. And you do not wish me a Happy Valentine's Day."

Jed turned his head toward her. "What do you mean I don't look at you? I look at you all the time," he replied tactfully but anguished that he had to resist mention of Valentine's Day.

"Not the same way as in the beginning," she said. "You remember once you said when you look at me I am not of focus. You could not see into my eyes. Remember?"

"Yes."

"Now it is the same with you!" She raised her voice ever so slightly.

"I look at you but I do not feel you there. Like you are somewhere very far away."

Jed turned his gaze back to the front. "I suppose I am. I've been thinking a lot about this business and my business back in Nashua. I miss my partners, of course. But since I've been here, I've begun to miss myself."

"How do you do that, miss yourself?"

"I mean I don't know who I am. Back home, I had an identity I was comfortable with. Here, in this completely strange country where only a few people seem to speak my language, I . . . this is hard to explain, but I've seriously started to wonder who I am. I want to know myself. All my life I've defined myself by what I *do*, not what I *am*.

"There was a good reason for that: I didn't really take the time to know myself. I defined myself at MIT with materials science. I defined myself as an officer in the United States Army. I defined myself with bicycle racing. I defined myself with Jet Bike and then Smithworks. I even defined myself as husband to Marty and father to our son. Now I don't have any of those things to define with any more.

"I've tried defining myself with the Spinnerworks and NewBike, but it's just not there. Doesn't work anymore. And I still haven't found what I'm looking for inside myself. Who the real Jed Smith is, deep inside."

Jung-Shan said, "Chinese have a saying: to know the Tao one must find that which has no name. It is the origin for everything."

"Oh, I know that one," said Jed. "We have a poet who wrote about going away from a place, and when you come back you know it for the first time. Same idea. This is, um, smaller, because it's just about me. Inside. It's deep in my most guarded, secret place where I don't let anybody in."

"Your place of pain and loss. The place we hurt the most." She reached out and gently placed her hand on his.

"It was that. It's not any more. Now it's the place where I want to let go of pain and find the real me, from scratch. So, as soon as you and I have the business running smoothly, I'll be leaving." He casually removed his hand from hers and tucked both hands behind his head.

"What?" Jung-Shan almost cried out. "You are going where?"

"I can't say for sure. Maybe not just one place. I have a friend who has an old stone country house in France. He'll rent it to me for as long as I want."

Jung-Shan slumped back into her seat, angrily crossing her arms over her chest.

Jed turned toward the window, looking at her out of the corner of his eye. "There was a time when I thought I had found myself with you," he said, softly, "but as you said, we weren't meant to be really together. I used to think we—not just you and me but all people—were meant to have a mate. Your yin and my yang. But it's awfully hard to find and then keep the right one. You've made it clear you'd been hurt too badly by your first husband to give yourself again. You said you made a mistake going against your father's wishes and you wouldn't do it again. So there is no future for Jung-Shan and Jed. So now I wonder . . . I wonder if my path isn't to be alone, a yang without a yin. I'm trying to accept that."

"You are not being fair to me," she said. "Not fair to just walk away after all we have done. Not fair to our business and not fair after all my father has done for you."

He turned to look at her. "Yes, that's right, it *was* business. Just a business relationship. Weren't you the one who said that first? Well, the business is established now. I don't need to stay here to run the business day in and day out. You can do that just fine without me."

"Jed, you know it is not just about business. Spinner and NewBike are the same as Jed and Jung-Shan. This . . . you and I have always known. I—we—"

"Americans have a saying, 'you can't have your cake and eat it, too.'"

"I do not know anything about eating cake but not eating cake," she grumbled, "but this is not what we agreed." Jung-Shan turned away to stare out the window into the dark night.

In the days that followed, Jung-Shan avoided Jed and he avoided her. He rarely came up to the eighth floor, and when he did it was to see Mr. Zheng. If she saw him crossing the sitting area to her father's office, she would get up and close her door. Jed's meetings with her father were often lengthy, and she struggled to quell her desire to know what they were discussing.

A week passed, then another. On a Friday afternoon, Jung-Shan heard a knock on her door. It was Jed. "We have a situation at the factory," he said.

"What? What is happening?"

"I'll tell you on the way, but we need to get down there right away. Your father has approved our taking the helicopter. Here," he said, handing her Joyful factory coveralls, "put this on and meet me on the roof in twenty minutes."

In the air, she asked again what the problem was at the factory. "It may be a production line halt or it may be nothing. At this point, Tai-Ping is on top of it, but like a good soldier he called me with the alert and I said we'd get right down there."

They sat side-by-side in the Airbus Eurocopter's caramel-colored leather seats, so close their thighs touched, watching the scenery below pass by at one hundred fifty miles per hour. When the 'copter touched down on the Joyful pad less than two hours later, the pilot didn't cut the engine. "Wait here a minute," Jed said and jumped out, ducking under the rotating blades and running into the NewBike factory office. Two workers came out pushing NewBikes, one red, one silver. Jung-Shan watched as they locked them into the skids' bike racks and tossed two backpacks into the passenger compartment. Jed came running back and jumped inside. "Let's go," he said to the pilot, who nodded and pulled the pitch lever. The chopper rose. Jed said nothing, and neither did Jung-Shan.

They flew west and were soon over the waters of the Taiwan Strait. Nose slightly tipped down, the chopper banked to starboard and picked up speed, bouncing and wriggling as it crossed the ocean swells below. The view was incredible.

Jed withdrew some papers from his messenger bag, turned to Jung-Shan and handed them to her.

"What is this?" she asked.

"It's a *business* agreement," he said. "An agreement between you and me to enter into arbitration. I'll give you a very brief summary. It says you agree to go to the Penghu Islands with me of your own free will. Ditto for me. We agree to think about and discuss our relationship in my chosen location until we reach a mutually agreed-upon decision about where it's going into the future. Read it."

"Decision? About our . . . *relationship?*" She stared at him, trying to catch her breath.

"Yes. I do think we have a relationship, but the nature and definition of it is unclear." Jed fought to say nothing more.

Jung-Shan said, "Do you have a pen?"

Yin and Yang

Fifty-five minutes later, the chopper thumped down gently at Penghu Airport. The pilot cut the engine; its blades slowed and dipped, whispering into silence. Jed and Jung-Shan stepped out of the cabin and were greeted by a taxi driver named Deng, who loaded their bags and bikes into his Luxgen mini-van, then headed toward Magong City.

The two looked at each other, smiling a little, remembering their time spent here not so long ago. Deng turned north before Magong, following their cycling route on 203 until reaching the North Sea Visitor Center once again.

It was now early March, 2012, and not particularly warm as they stood on the dock waiting for the ferry. It arrived, then promptly departed. Fifteen minutes later it docked at Jibei, where everyone disembarked. Jung-Shan and Jed pushed their bikes across the dock and, mysteriously for Jung-Shan, they boarded a small fishing boat.

"Another boat?" she said. "We are not visiting Jibeiyu?"

"Follow me," was all Jed would say.

The fishing boat chugged north along the east side of Jibei, reached its tip, then headed west into the rolling swells of the Taiwan Strait. It wasn't a comfortable crossing, so they were glad when they saw a white lighthouse at the southern end of a tiny island. The captain glided to a stubby old wooden dock where a fishing boat was tied up. Not a soul was in sight. "Here we are," said Jed and paid the captain.

"Where?" she said. "Where are we? I do not know this island."

"It's called Kanyuan Island. The closest Penghu island to China."

"Kanyuan. That means to see far. The lighthouse."

"You got it. Let's go," said Jed, shouldering his backpack.

They mounted their bikes and took to the trail, really more of a wide path through tall sawgrass, and pedaled straight up the middle of the island. As elsewhere, the path was sand and crushed seashells, brilliantly white in the sunlight. After twenty minutes of riding, Jung-Shan spied the distinctive roof lines of a temple. Just ahead a narrow footpath turned toward it. They dismounted and walked their bikes to a wide basalt stone terrace.

Before them stood a simple, handsome two-story wooden temple with a bright red and gold roof, dragons guarding from its intricately painted corner eaves. Four basalt steps led up to two very tall red wooden doors, guarded on either side by stone dragon and tiger statues. Long dormitory buildings with many doors flanked the temple.

"Why do we stop here?" said Jung-Shan.

"It's a Confucius temple. And monastery."

"You think I do not know this?" Jung-Shan stood over her bike, glaring at him.

"This is where we're staying." Jed smiled just a little.

Jung-Shan swung her leg off her bike and made as if to turn around. "It's in the arbitration agreement you signed," he said. "Maybe you didn't read that." She glared at him. "I believe we need to remove ourselves from the everyday world in order to understand our place in the universe. Our place here on earth as individuals. And in relationship with each other—beyond being business associates—if that's at all possible." He spoke softly, without derision or irony in his voice.

Jung-Shan's heart sank. Now embarrassed, she lowered her gaze.

"So I found this isolated monastery and made arrangements. We can stay as long as we want. As long as it takes. We'll wear the robes of monks. Or you can wear your coveralls if you prefer." He grinned. "We have our own rooms for sleep and meditation. OK?" He looked at her; she raised her face and looked back at him, stronger now.

"Yes, OK, Jed."

"For the first forty-eight hours we'll fast. Water or tea only, to purge our bodies of toxins and stimulants. Believe me when I say this will be harder for me than for you. We can spend an hour or two together at midday and again at sunset. We can go for walks and bike rides. After the first two days, we can take meals with the monks if we want to.

"We both signed the arbitration agreement. I'm committed and I hope you are, too. Whatever it takes to cut through all the noise and distractions of our lives, to get rid of our egos and prejudices and resentments. To become as clean and pure in our thoughts and feelings as we will be in our bodies. That's what I want. I was gonna go away and do this alone. Because I know I need it. Then I thought, maybe we both need it. Maybe we discover our own definition of yin and yang."

Jed took a small red silk bag embroidered with gold filigree from his pocket. He pulled its gold drawstrings open and withdrew two silver disks the size of a Taiwan fifty NT coin, enameled with the black-and-white yin-yang symbol. He handed one to her. She held it and turned it in her fingers. "See, it has your name on the back. Mine too."

Jung-Shan opened her mouth to speak, but Jed said, "This isn't a game. I just want each of us to decide for ourselves what we want from each other without any outside influences or distractions. *None.* Really *really* think, and feel, it through. If you decide you don't want to be together, just keep your coin and tell me you're ready to go back to Taipei. I'll do the same." He held her eyes tight with his own. "But if you decide you want us to be together, give me your coin when you're sure. In every way. In your heart. Your spirit. Your body."

She nodded. Jed couldn't tell if she was happy or sad.

The temple doors opened; a tiny monk in a simple yellow robe stood on the stone veranda. He smiled, put his hands together and bowed. Jed said, "I believe this is our *daoshi.* Oh yeah, the monks meditate once in the morning and once in the afternoon. Either of us can join them whenever we want. Or we can just stay in our cells and meditate alone. Who knows what we might discover?" Jed said, smiling.

"Yes, I think perhaps this is all good things for me," said Jung-Shan. "And for you. And for both of us." She smiled brightly. "I am happy to be here with you."

Jed smiled back at her, his heart wishing desperately to leap from his breast to hers. He fought the feeling back and reached into his backpack. "Here," he said, handing her a small leatherbound book with a gold tassel hanging from its pages. It was Lao Tzu's *Tao Teh Ching*.

"Xiè xiè, Jed. I know Lao Tzu's teachings, but I have never read this book. I will read. I will learn. I will treasure. Xiè xiè, xiè xiè." She bowed to him, then stood on tiptoe and kissed him quickly on the lips.

The daoshi, whose name was Wu Ling, showed them to their cells. Jed's was in the Wen Miao compound on the right side of the temple. Jung-Shan's was in the Guo Xue chambers on the left side. Their cells were utterly bare, save for a straw mattress covered in sailcloth. A thin blanket. An earth-colored habit and leather sandals. A handful of monks lived in the dormitories and did not socialize much; they were there to practice *wu wei*, action through inaction. Trying not to try.

Over the next few days, a routine emerged: Jung-Shan and Jed would join the monks at dawn for prayers to the rising sun on the east-facing veranda, sip morning tea, then return to their private cells until the morning hour of meditation with the other monks in the temple or the courtyard. All joined together on the sunny side of the temple for a hot vegetarian noon meal, sitting lotus-style around a low round table. Afterward, they performed their designated chores—the monks took fish from the weirs and cultivated their own vegetable garden—before returning to their cells for rest and private meditation. There were late afternoon prayers, honoring the sunset; Jed and Jung-Shan would spend a few moments together afterwards. Dinner was a meal commonly ignored, but the monks often gathered in the temple after dark to pray, light joss sticks, and chant together.

Jung-Shan and Jed did not speak to each other of their meditation;

somehow it felt right to keep their thoughts and words to themselves. Yet Jed increasingly found meditation difficult and turned to Master Wu Ling for guidance. Language was a barrier, but he did not want to discuss his failings with Jung-Shan. As he and Wu sat facing one another, Jed struggled to convey to the old monk that he hardly knew how to start. Yet Master Wu understood without words; he pressed both hands to his heart, turned toward the sea and pointed. Then he brought his hands together, one atop the other and pushed them away from himself into a shoo-shoo motion toward the horizon. The horizon. Eventually Jed figured out that Master Wu was teaching him, and began practicing it in earnest.

He thought about wu-wei and just sat quietly, being in no-being. A morning mist still clung to the earth, making the line of the horizon separating sea and sky nearly indistinguishable. Sometimes the master would stare to the west for hours, so Jed stared too, but the more he did, the more the sea and sky looked like one and the same: no horizon. Were not the clouds moving? Did not the sea stir and pulse? Perhaps a view of the horizon was inhibited by the grass waving lightly back and forth, back and forth. But maybe not. Maybe it was there but not there.

Even as he grew more uncertain what he was looking at, Jed's stare did not waver. Suddenly he saw and understood: He could not tell whether it came from within or without, but he felt a growing awareness that he was not supposed to see the line of the horizon. He was just supposed to see the uninterrupted flow of nature; that the grasses, the ocean, the sky and clouds, were a oneness. Since he saw each, yet also saw them all as an indistinguishable whole, he realized he was part of it as well. The whole world was so alive, eagerly waiting to be discovered, and so was he. The oneness of earth, sea and sky could not exist unless he was there to experience it. It took Jed's breath away.

Wu wei.

That evening he told Jung-Shan what he had seen, what he had learned. She smiled and touched his hand. "I have difficult times learning, too," she said. "We must learn we cannot have things on our terms, but must allow them to become part of us on their terms. This is a very difficult lesson I always have to remind myself about. We must learn this truth over and over again."

"To let things happen in their own Way. It's not what we American kids were taught," said Jed. "We were taught to differentiate and define everything in our own terms. Then you knew what was yours and could figure out how to take what was not."

Jung-Shan gave him a wry smile. "Very funny! There are no auspicious moments for the Western man?"

"Hmmm. I guess I don't understand what an auspicious moment would be."

"It means you must wait until everything is right, then be wholly present so you can be part of it. Otherwise you play the game of life like luck."

"Luke's family waiting for the auspicious moment for his funeral."

"Yes."

Wu wei.

Jed fell silent. He realized that he had been trying to possess Jung-Shan, as if she were something to buy in a store: *You can have whatever you want, just take it.* That was the former bicycle-racing, enterprising American Jed. Now, he was developing an Eastern sensibility. He wondered if they had an auspicious moment awaiting them, here, together. But being *here* was not it; the auspiciousness was in the process, the enlightenment, not the destination. He felt incredibly inept.

Jung-Shan touched his hand again; Jed realized he'd closed his eyes. Staring into some otherness. "You have been reading the *Tao Teh Ching*?" He nodded. "Master Lao-Tzu says awareness is what man seeks," she said. "It is attained by the man who has humility, understanding, and patience. These are the three treasures. They bring man into harmony with nature. That is awareness. That is the highest goal."

Slowly, steadily, Jed saw how meditation was peeling layers upon layers of beliefs, attitudes, and prejudices away. All the ingrained stuff his years of living had saddled him with were becoming points of self-contention: *Where did that come from? What does it mean to me? Is it worth keeping? Does it need to change? Should it be modified or replaced with something else?*

At first this dialogue with himself was a jumble, but in time he began to sort it out as if it was a business problem, a process, except now it was based on spiritual values. He realized he had to toss out anything and everything he had assumed to be true or useful, because they were things almost always founded on ego. He was learning he could not trust habits or preconceived assumptions, because he could not determine where or how he had acquired them.

Over time, he realized his mind was capable of being either trustworthy or not, independent of what he thought he was thinking. *I think something, and I either believe it or not based on what my thoughts tell me. It's a closed loop. No way to verify the truth of what I'm thinking. Maybe that's why mankind invented religion, to turn critical decisions over to a higher power. But still, I don't think that's the Way.*

Incredible. He began to understand what the *Tao Teh Ching* meant when he read that if the world said something was true or beautiful, it was probably just the opposite.

Thought. Word. Action. Self. All these things he was flushing away to create a true sense of himself. Jed spent hours and hours mired in shame, embarrassment, remorse, regret for things he had thought, said, and done in his life. He cried for each person he had ever harmed or insulted or betrayed. He even cried for François, a pitiable creature whose self-understanding was practically nonexistent. Even thinking that, Jed had to accept the core truth: he had no right to judge another person or their thoughts, words, or actions.

He wondered how Jung-Shan's meditating was going. Whenever he saw her, the question almost left his lips, but each time he held it back.

One day they walked in silence along the cliffs overlooking the fish-trap weirs in the surf below. Sometimes they would see villagers and monks wading in the water, harvesting the fish. The wind, never absent, grew stronger, chillier, billowing the monks' robes, making Jung-Shan's hair whip around her lovely, serene face. There was something growing purer in their silent communication. As he thought about it, he realized he was letting go of his desire to own and possess her. He no longer wished for the outcome he had come here for. That outcome had come from ego. He realized they were here together in the purity and silence of just being.

They rode their bikes often, down to the lighthouse and back, sometimes on the narrow footpaths along the cliffs, loving the bicycle they had created together, marveling at the elegant performance of the Spinner drive, exhilarating in the freedom to ride without ever seeing a car or scooter. The days at the monastery passed; neither could recall how many. The winds grew calmer, the sun warmer.

As they rode one day, Jed mused on the "it" questions he had come to realize were the basis for understanding the world for most of his life. What was "it"? Why was "it"? How was "it"? Where did "it" come from? "It" was an utter abstraction. Every answer to an "it" was based upon some material perception. But how would "it" be explained by the Tao?

There was no meaning for "it" as a way of knowing oneself and life. The line of the horizon was presumed to be an *it*, but was that so? Sky, water, earth, all existed without it. A wave of understanding, greater than anything he'd ever felt, swept through him.

Jed looked ahead at Jung-Shan, pedaling away, committed to the ride. For all their time here, she had not once withdrawn. Not once, not in any way. But neither had she given him her coin. He knew he had changed, had now learned how to let go of *it* questions and practice a non-discriminating, non-judgmental non-analytical Way of thought. And he knew, not with his mind but with his heart, that she had been growing and changing, too.

A welling up of his connection with her took his breath away in a half-sob. His bike wobbled and he braked to a stop. He coughed against the emotion pouring out, then tears were streaming from his eyes. A loud cry emerged unbidden from his lips, a cry that expunged a clot of emotion like nothing he'd ever felt in his life. *Where had that come from?* Then he knew: it came from the dark place inside where he'd stuffed all his life's pain and suffering, all the emotions he'd never let himself feel when they were happening: the deaths and injuries to soldiers he had commanded, the moment when the IED exploded, the loss of his son and then his wife, the struggles starting a business, Luke's death, Jung-Shan's rejection. Myriad events, big and small, all pain he did not know how to let go of. The *its*.

Until now.

Up ahead, Jung-Shan heard him sobbing. She glanced back over her shoulder, stopped, turned and rode back, rolling to a stop beside him. They stood over their bikes looking at one other. Nothing was said. Jung-Shan put her arms around Jed's waist and pressed herself to him. He wrapped his arms around her shoulders. They held each other tightly, as if they would fall into some kind of abyss if they didn't. Jed rested his cheek on top of her head. Jung-Shan clung to him tighter and tighter. They trembled from the intensity of the emotions flowing between them.

Finally they let go of one another. She looked up at him and he at her. Jed brushed her cheek with his fingers. Kissed her on the forehead.

"Look," she said, pointing behind him. The sun was peeking through the clouds clustered between the earth and the sky, illuminating the tips of the tall grass. "The day grows long at the horizon."

Jed smiled. "How do you know?"

"Know what?" she said.

"That there is a line at the horizon."

"Because I see it. Look. It is there for us."

He looked, and it was.

Jed was about to say something when Jung-Shan pressed her hand into his. He felt something in his palm. In an instant, he knew it was her yin-yang coin. He dug his coin out of his pocket and put it beside hers, between their palms.

Jung-Shan gave him a little smile as her chin began to quiver. Her eyes became tiny clouds pouring rain down her cheeks. Jed felt his own tears coming too. They kissed for a long, long time.

That evening, they sat across from each other at the monk's table, enjoying the celebratory meal the monks had prepared for them: rice with chunks of fish and tofu in small bowls. Every time he tried to pick up a cube of tofu, he ended up chopping it in half. She put a bite of tofu in his mouth, then one into her own. She repeated with bites of fish, and rice, a holy act of communion.

"Jed."

"Yes, my darling?"

"Happy May Day," said Jung-Shan.

"Today? It's the first of May?"

I think so. It is spring, of that I am certain."

Well, that makes it special, for sure," said Jed.

"I love you."

"And I love you, with all my heart."

"I want to be with you, always," she said, her eyes reflecting the candlelight.

"And I want to be with you always, for each and every day of our lives."

"But we have forgotten something."

"What?"

"My father. All these days, I have never once thought of him. I have only been thinking of life without you and I know that cannot be. So all I think about these days is how to make life be right for us. I have forgotten the matter of my father. I am sad, for I know he will not approve of our marriage."

"Oh, yeah," said Jed, "I forgot about something too," and handed her a handwritten note on Zheng Ming-Chiang's stationery. It read:

My Children, Jung-Shan and Jedediah

I bless you both in your new life together.

Your Father, Ming-Chiang

Jung-Shan's face softened as she read, then turned as bright as a star. "Oh, Jed."

"Remember all those private talks I had in your dad's office?"

"Oh, Jed," she said again and nodded. Jed nodded. They could not take their eyes from each other's or stop smiling.

"I have something else for you," he said, and handed her a small red velvet box.

∞

"There is no good in anything until it is finished."

— *Genghis Khan*

Acknowledgements

Bridge Across the Ocean began its life with the title *Shift* in 2012, written because of the murder of Alexander Motsenigos. It became *White Bike* in 2015, by which time hit-and-run cycling deaths were, in Neil Young's words, like "soldiers cutting us down." Both versions were revenge stories, but with the passage of time and life-experiences in general, and my travels to Taiwan in particular, it morphed into the novel you're reading today.

I'm grateful for the support and encouragement of many people during the years I've written and revised *Bridge*—again and again and again. Each revision was indeed pleasurable and made it, IMO, a better story. Many thanks to the following individuals who graciously read all or portions of the manuscript during its development and who offered editorial comments:

Luke Bencie, Managing Director at Security Management International, LLC, and author of *Among Enemies: Counter-Espionage for the Business Traveler* for his expertise in intellectual property espionage. *Bridge* could not have been written without Luke's knowledge.

David Bond, with whom I've spent hundreds of hours on a bike saddle and who taught me how to ride like a Tour de France cyclist.

Dory Fiamingo, an ardent supporter of my writing who gave me one of the most thoroughgoing reviews/edits in the life of this book. For that, and for being a superb writer and excellent human being, I thank you from my heart.

Ruby Fink, who has produced three of my novels as audiobooks and is a fine novelist herself, for reading *Bridge* and suggesting it would make a great motion picture—then taking it upon herself to write a treatment, which she is sharing with film developers and producers.

Daniel J. Finn III, a practitioner of the law and friend of rare insight and intelligence who guided me through the intricacies of the legal details of today's business contracts environment—and not a few points of history.

John Gantz, my brother from another mother, co-author extraordinaire on two previous works of nonfiction, and fellow wheelman who rides the Pan-Mass Challenge every year. John's review and ongoing interest and encouragement were deeply meaningful.

My publicity team, Kourtney Jason and Casie Vogel of Pacific & Court in Brooklyn. I've known and worked with Casie for over ten years on various editorial projects, so when she teamed up with Kourtney to combine their expertise, I knew I had to hire them. I did not make a mistake in doing so.

Shiao Yu Lee, a dear friend who introduced me to the wonderful bikeways of Taipei. Shiao Yu, I'm looking forward to that next tour you promised.

My brother Gregg, for allowing me to personify him as Gregg Colarusso, Joyful's bike-painter extraordinaire. The real Gregg Rochester does indeed create and paint custom designs on bicycles: http://greggrochesterart.homestead.com/bicycles.html

Reiko Miyagawa, my neighbor, who read all the "Meanwhile" segments and gave me the correct translations of Japanese phrases—and slang.

Acknowledgements

Andrew Peat, video documentary writer/director/producer of *Scotch: A Golden Dream* (Amazon Prime Video), who, with his wife, Maria, owns the nonfictional Villa Romana Bed & Breakfast in Magong City, Penghu Islands. He was supportive in more ways than I can enumerate.

Michael Mavilia Rochester, my nephew and the Editor of The Fictional Café, an astute reader who so generously gave me an in-depth analysis of this book on more levels than I could have imagined—right down to the characters' slang and colloquialisms.

Jonathan Shih, Taipei artist and culture maven, who helped me keep the Taiwanese and Chinese aspects of my story factual.

Tung-sun Tung, for his sturdy high-tech comments about my completely fictional Spinner technology, as well as certain cultural facets of life in Taiwan.

Not everyone has read *Bridge* yet (which strikes me as a good thing) but these folk have been avid fans and supporters of my writing this novel and the earlier Nathaniel Hawthorne Flowers trilogy.

My stepsons, Industrial Designer Daniel Chu for the conceptual illustration of the Spinner, and Oliver Chu, a super-tech guy who works at Samsung, for his help and advice with the presentation you can see on the website.

Paul Lai, my brother-in-law, a civil engineer in Taipei. Paul designed and built the dragon-shaped Shilin MRT Station described in Chapter 6, "Escape." Nice job, Paul.

Chia Wen Lee, who researched the Taipei "YouBike" on behalf of the book and provided wise and informed counsel on international business law and lawyers, inasmuch as she is one herself.

Chris Li and Eric Diig, owners of The Bikeway Source, a five-star bike shop at the end of the Minuteman Bikeway in Bedford, Massachusetts.

I bought "Black Beauty," my Giant TCR carbon fiber road bike from them . . . and a few more bikes for my family and myself. It was Chris who helped arrange my tour of the Giant factory during one of my trips to Taiwan. These guys have never failed to ask me how *Bridge* is coming along. I'm grateful for their friendship and their five-star customer service.

Caitlin Park and the Baristas at Fictional Café, where excerpts from *Bridge* appeared. I co-founded "FC" with Caitlin in 2013 and at the time of this writing, it has grown to nearly a thousand Coffee Club members in 67 countries. Caitlin's editorial sensibilities are quite refined and I always follow her advice and suggestions.

My son and his wife, Josh and Jamie Rivers, who have steadfastly and wisely, I think, refused to read drafts over the past near-decade. Josh says they're holding out for the Audible version, but may relent when the eBook is available.

My most sincere thanks to my production professionals. Having worked in publishing for as long as I have, I understand just how complex and difficult are the tasks and skills required to get all the gears meshing:

Sophie Hanks, for her handsome interior design and endless patience making corrections.;

Melanie Marston of Marston Creative for her graphic design work on the cover and interior art, including those smart-looking chapter heads using the beautiful Hed three-spoke bike wheel. Melanie is also my webmaster. Hed Cycling is another of my favorite innovators.

A shoutout to Michael Piekny of HubEdits for his copy-edit and proofreadings (both of them). Sometimes it seems like catching a bird on the wing would be easier than catching the myriad little typos in a manuscript.

Acknowledgements

Tim Knickerbocker and Marie Bott at Books International for transforming my words into real books in their state-of-the-art printing plant. BI is on the cutting edge of innovation for authors and indie publishers.

John Woods of CWL Publications for producing an early version of *Bridge*, when it was still 120,000 words in length.

Last but far from least: My gratitude to Victoria "Tori" Merkle, Associate Editor at Joshua Tree Interactive. Tori joined JTI while still in college, and since has created a successful business offering her diverse and well-honed editorial skills to authors and small presses coast to coast. Among her many accomplishments for me, Tori did what I could not: edit *Bridge* down to 86,000 from almost 120,000 words, thus making it publishable. The story is so much better for her editorial acumen. Her advice and nurture for the manuscript have proven wise and spot on again and again. Thank you, Tori. You have been a great partner these past three years, and I cannot say *Xie xie* enough to you.

I feel similarly fortunate to have spent my life in the writing and publishing business. It's certainly changed over the years, especially in one very positive way: the communities. When I got my start, writers were pretty much isolated from other writers; today, in large part thanks to the internet, we can choose to be members of groups of all kinds, from a local reading group to one on Facebook or Instagram or LinkedIn. In between are myriad special-interest groups, such as the two closest to me: my own author site, JackBoston.com, where I publish two blogs for my subscribers, and FictionalCafe, where writers and artists from all nations and interests share their creative work with the entire world. Thank you, everybody. It doesn't get any better than this.